DANGEROUS
GROUND

Peril in the Park Series

Book one: Avalanche

Book two: Dangerous Ground

Dangerous Ground

Book Two of Peril in the Park

By
Gayla K. Hiss

Dangerous Ground
Published by Mountain Brook Ink
White Salmon, WA U.S.A.

The website addresses recommended throughout this book are offered as a resource. These websites are not intended in any way to be or imply an endorsement on the part of Mountain Brook Ink, nor do we vouch for their content.

This story is a work of fiction. All characters and events are the product of the author's imagination. References to real locations, places, or organizations are used in a fictional context. Any resemblance to any person, living or dead, is coincidental.

Scripture quotations are taken from the Holy Bible, New International Version®, NIV® Copyright ©1973, 1978, 1984, 2011 by Biblica, Inc.® Used by permission. All rights reserved worldwide.

ISBN 978-1943959-31-0
© 2017 Gayla K. Hiss

The Team: Miralee Ferrell, Nikki Wright, Jenny Mertes, Cindy Jackson
Cover Design: Indie Cover Design, Lynnette Bonner Designer

Mountain Brook Ink is an inspirational publisher offering fiction you can believe in.

Printed in the U.S.A. 2017

In loving memory of my grandparents,
Rufus and Artie Robertson

Acknowledgments

After the extensive research required for the first book in this series, *Avalanche*, I anticipated less would be needed for *Dangerous Ground*. As the story evolved, however, it soon became apparent that I would need crash courses in archery, bow hunting, horseback riding, emergency medicine, plus much, much more. Thankfully, I had a great team of people who generously shared their knowledge with me and helped give this story a strong foundation. Special thanks to: Kevin Dodson, Gretta Emery, Christina McConnell, Jeff Hiss, Jenny Mertes, and Don for their significant help with my research for this book.

Many thanks also to my readers and supporters. I couldn't do this without your encouragement and prayers. And to my hardworking, multi-talented publisher, Miralee Ferrell, for mentoring me and helping me grow as a writer.

And to God, who inspired me with this story and continually reminds me that in Christ we are never alone.

A father to the fatherless,
a defender of widows,
is God in His holy dwelling.
God sets the lonely in families,
He leads forth the prisoners with singing;
but the rebellious live in a sun-scorched land.

Psalm 68:5-6

CHAPTER ONE

KATE PHILLIPS CAREFULLY NAVIGATED HER MIATA through the torrential downpour as she approached Great Smoky Mountains National Park. It had been a long, difficult drive from Nashville in the storm. What was she thinking, coming here on a night like this? If not for the mysterious business card with the newspaper clipping about the investigation into her uncle's recent death, she'd be safe at home right now.

She didn't even know her uncle. Had never met him. But a month ago, out of the blue, he sent her a letter to apologize for not being there when she'd needed him. He said he wanted to make it up to her. She'd never replied. Why should she? The man hadn't shown one iota of concern for her or her mother—not even when her mother passed away fourteen years ago. Then suddenly he has a change of heart?

Still, Owen Bentley was her mother's only brother and the last link to her mother's family. That alone had persuaded Kate to come in search of answers about his death, and make the impromptu trip that Sunday afternoon. Mack, her supervisor with the Marshals Service, had been urging her to take time off anyway. When she'd called him at home yesterday, right after she'd discovered the business card and clipping in her mail, he approved her two-week vacation request over the phone. But with church, packing, and making last-minute arrangements, she'd left later today than she had wanted. Now it was after dark and the storm had become more threatening.

She peered ahead into the gloom, not wanting to miss her turn. Lightning flashed, exposing a hooded man in the road. Images of his bandaged face and hand and his wild eyes instantly burned into Kate's memory like a scene from a horror movie. She jerked the steering wheel to avoid him and lost control. Her car skidded across the wet pavement, careening down a slope toward the woods. A large tree loomed ahead but she was going too fast to stop. Turning the steering wheel and stomping the brakes, she made a frantic attempt to avert disaster. The crash of metal and glass was the last thing she heard before the airbag punched her in the face and chest.

The tapping of rain roused her to her senses. Where was she? The collision had scrambled her brain. She raised her head and pushed the deployed airbag away. Battered and sore, she gingerly touched her face, tracing the liquid on her cheek—was it blood?

After flipping on the dome light, she touched her cheek again. Moisture, not blood—*Whew!* Kate glimpsed something big and dark to her right. Turning to see, she gasped at the massive tree occupying the space next to her. The sudden need for air compelled her to touch the button on her left. The window wouldn't open. She tried the door. Jammed. *Lord, if this is a nightmare, please wake me up.*

A bright beam appeared in the distance—a man holding a flashlight. When he reached her car, he shouted through the glass. "Are you okay?"

She nodded.

"I'll be right back," he said, then disappeared.

Alone in her confusion, Kate relied on her instincts. Shifting toward her door, she attempted to shove it open, but the ache in her left shoulder forced her to stop.

The light returned. When she saw the man carrying a crowbar, she exhaled with relief.

"I'll pry it open," he shouted.

While he inserted the crowbar into the crack and pressed against it, using his body for leverage, she pushed from inside. The door gave way, and Kate lurched to the left. Her seatbelt prevented her from falling out, but aggravated her shoulder injury.

Slowly, she righted herself and spotted the man bent over, fumbling through the wet autumn leaves. She stared at him as she massaged the top of her left arm. "What are you doing?"

"I dropped my flashlight." He scooped it up and wiped his muddy palm on his soaked jeans as he came toward her, illuminating the car.

"How far away is the Cades Cove Campground?" she asked.

"Camping tonight, in this rain?" He frowned at the dark, stormy sky. "You'd be better off staying at the motel in Tyler's Glen. It's only four miles from here."

He reached for her hand, and she jerked away.

"It's all right." His voice was calm and reassuring. "I'm an EMT. I only want to check your pulse."

"Oh." Allowing him to proceed, she watched with a wary eye as he placed two fingers on her wrist, not sure if she should thank him or draw her gun from her backpack— where was her backpack anyway? She turned stiffly and looked over her shoulder. It lay pressed between the tree and the console.

"Your pulse is fine." When he'd released her hand, he pointed to the passenger side of her Miata. "I wish I could say the same for your car. You're lucky to be alive."

Reaching for her pack, she groaned in pain.

He shined the flashlight toward her. "Don't worry about your stuff right now. Look at me."

She squinted into the light.

"Your pupils aren't dilated. That's a good sign."

"But now I'm blind," she replied in a dry tone.

"Only temporarily."

She released her seatbelt and started to get out.

"Whoa." The man held up his hand, blocking her path. "Sit still for a minute while I call for a paramedic."

As he made the call, Kate turned and yanked her backpack free. She set it on her lap and opened a pocket to feel inside. Her gun was still there. She retrieved her phone and waited until he'd finished talking to the dispatcher. "What did they say?"

He slipped his cellphone in his pocket. "Unfortunately, all the paramedics are out on other calls. It's a busy night with the storm. We're under a tornado watch too. It could be at least an hour before an ambulance arrives."

"I can't wait that long." Lifting her pack, she struggled to her feet, but the sharp pain in her shoulder seized her.

His brows pinched together as he gently coaxed her back to her seat. "Hey, now, take it easy. Where's the pain coming from?"

Setting her pack on the console, she considered his question, then touched her left shoulder. "Right here." Next, she pointed to her collar bone. "And here . . . It's a little sensitive around my eyes and nose too."

He carefully examined her face, shoulder, and clavicle area. "Nothing feels broken. You're probably bruised from the impact of the seatbelt and airbag. Are you experiencing any numbness in your feet or hands, or any neck or back pain?"

His close attention spurred her heart to racing. She was glad he'd already checked her pulse. "No, mostly my shoulder."

"That's good. However, I'd still like you to wait for the paramedics."

"Thanks, but it's already dark, and I need to pitch my tent. Once I'm at the campground, I'll be fine." She used her phone to find her destination on a map.

A gust of wind whistled in the trees as the rain morphed into sleet-like pellets.

When she glanced up, the lines deepened on the man's forehead. "I can give you a lift," he said, "provided you agree to see a doctor in the morning."

He seemed exceptionally accommodating, but she didn't want to take any chances with a stranger. Her job as a deputy marshal, in addition to having lived on the streets, had taught her to be extra cautious around people she didn't know. "Look, I appreciate your help, but I don't even know your name. I'll call for a park ranger or someone from the sheriff's department to take me."

"With this storm, they'll all be busy with emergencies. It could be hours before someone comes." He retrieved his wallet from his back pocket, then shined the light on his EMT identification card so she could see. "My name is David Jennings. I'm a volunteer firefighter. Sorry I didn't introduce myself earlier." Raindrops dribbled down his forehead into his eyes, making him grimace. "Now let's get out of here before the storm gets worse."

Lightning pierced the sky, followed by a loud boom. The noise triggered a flashback of the car accident. Kate shuddered at the memory.

"Hey, it's okay." He spoke in a soft Southern accent. "You know what they say about lightning—it never strikes the same place twice."

"Then this should be the safest place on earth."

A lightning bolt struck a tree nearby, sending sparks flying in the air. Kate winced as the deafening roar of thunder pounded her ears.

David stared at the tree in amazement. "Then again, I never believed that old saying." He focused on her again. "Are you able to walk?"

"Yes." She rose to her feet, defying her shoulder pain and eager to get out of the weather.

"My truck is at the top of the embankment. Let's go."

She went with him and climbed the slippery slope as rain

mixed with hail pummeled the ground. When she stumbled, he placed his arm around her and protectively ushered her toward the road.

She yelled over the wind and rain. "I'm fine. I don't need any help."

"We're under a tornado watch. We don't have time to argue."

The hail morphed into chunks that clattered as it hit the earth.

Kate quickly capitulated and let him assist her as they climbed the rest of the way. Wet and cold from the storm, she grudgingly appreciated the warmth and strength of his body next to hers, which calmed her and made her feel safer.

When they'd reached his pickup, he released her so he could open the passenger door. Then he helped her step onto the running board. Once she was seated inside, he handed her his keys. "Start the engine and warm it up while I go get your things."

After he'd disappeared in the storm, she stuck the key in the ignition and started it. As soon as she'd flipped on the headlights and heater, she realized he'd put complete trust in her, a total stranger, with his truck. She could easily climb over the console and drive away. But how would she get her luggage and gear?

Her gun! It was still in her backpack. She had to get it.

David returned with his hands full. He opened the door to the driver's seat, and she twisted around, inciting her shoulder ache. "Where's my backpack?"

"Right here." When he lifted it so she could see, she snatched it from his hands. "You're welcome." Light sarcasm laced his voice.

While he stowed her camping gear and small luggage in the rear seat of his extended cab, Kate set her pack in her lap. She confirmed her personal Glock was still inside, along with her wallet and the mysterious business card and newspaper clipping that had led her there.

Having loaded all of her things, David climbed into the driver's seat.

When he called to cancel the paramedics, Kate touched the gun in her backpack and scanned the dark forest bordering the road—the part she could see in the beam of the headlights. The hail and lightning had subsided, but a steady downpour continued to tap the windshield as a country song played on the radio, filling the awkward silence while they waited for the foggy windows to clear.

She studied the man from the shadows. He appeared about her age—in his late twenties, maybe a little older. His dark dripping hair curled at the ends around his handsome face, reminding her of a boy who had been playing too long in the sprinklers. His rain-soaked T-shirt and jeans, however, revealed broad shoulders, strong muscles and a lean physique.

He sneezed.

"Bless you." She hoped he wasn't catching a cold. Guilt needled her for being harsh with him earlier. "I'm sorry, I didn't mean to sound like I was ordering you around, especially after everything you've done for me."

The corner of his mouth ticked up. "It's understandable considering what you've been through tonight." Reaching for the door handle, he glanced her way. "I'll be back in a sec."

"Wait! Where are you going?" Still shaken from the accident, she didn't want to be alone. But he had already left.

Within a minute, he'd returned. "Here." He handed her a wool blanket and a bottle of water as he got in. "You're shivering."

A sigh escaped her lips as she took the items. "Thanks." She tugged the blanket around her shoulders and drew it close. "What about you? You must be freezing in those wet clothes."

He shrugged it off. "I'm okay."

"Where did you get the water and the blanket?"

"I carry an emergency kit in the bed of my truck."

She smiled, impressed. "You must have been a Boy Scout."

"Eagle."

"For real?"

"Scout's honor." He gave her the three-finger scout salute. After a moment, he cast her a sideways look. "Now that the worst of the storm has passed, when are you going to tell me how your Miata got wrapped around a tree in the Smoky Mountains?"

She rubbed her temple, recalling the disturbing details. "A hooded man crossed the road right in front of me, and I swerved to avoid him."

David frowned with a slight headshake. "Not the best night for a walk in the park. At least you didn't hit him."

"No, I'm thankful for that, but it was so strange."

"What?"

"How he came out of nowhere, and he had a bandage on the right side of his face. His hand was wrapped too."

David's eyes sparked with interest. "Sounds like a zombie. What else do you remember about him?"

"That's it, really, except for his terrified expression when he saw my car headed toward him." She sighed deeply. "I shouldn't have come here. If I had stayed home, my car wouldn't be wrecked."

"Look, I know you have reservations at the campground, but I think you'll regret not staying in a warm, dry motel tonight."

She knew he was right. After everything that had happened, the last thing she felt like doing was pitching a tent in the rain. "Is the motel in Tyler's Glen nice?"

"It's nothing fancy, but it is clean."

"Works for me. As long as it has a hot shower and a warm bed, I'll be happy." She was already looking forward to it.

"So you're from Nashville?"

His casual remark caught her off guard, and she clenched the gun in her backpack. "How did you know that?"

"I saw your license plate when I went to get your luggage. It said Davidson County."

"Oh." She relaxed her grip on her Glock and watched the lightning show in the clouds overhead, not inclined to talk about herself or why she'd come.

Having checked his mirrors, David put the truck in gear and made a U-turn on the highway. "Maybe it's none of my business, but what's a girl from Nashville—driving a red convertible—doing way out here on a night like this?"

She pretended to be indignant. "You have something against red convertibles?"

His heart-stopping smile revealed straight, white teeth. An amused gleam twinkled in his eyes. "No, but I do wonder how you packed so much into such a tiny car."

"It wasn't easy," she replied with a slight grin. "What about you? When you're not rescuing city girls out in the boonies, what do you do?"

"I'm in agriculture," he replied with a business-like flair.

"As in farming? Isn't that the main business around here?"

"Farming and funerals, unless you work at the new chemical plant—but we have a world-class farmer's market and a couple of RV parks. Plus, you can't beat the scenery."

His reply amused her.

"The lady *can* smile."

"My teeth are the only part of me that doesn't hurt."

He reached across to open the glove compartment and took out a small bottle. "Here."

She squinted at the label on the over-the-counter painkillers. "You *are* an Eagle Scout, aren't you?"

"You didn't believe me?"

She swallowed a couple of pills and chased them with a

sip of water. "I do now." After setting the water bottle and pills in the console between them, she turned in his direction. "Seriously, I appreciate that you stopped to help me. I don't know what I would have done if you hadn't."

His eyes shifted in her direction. "I never could resist a red Miata convertible in distress. Hopefully, you'll be able to enjoy the rest of your camping trip."

Until the mystery behind her uncle's death was solved, it would be hard for her to enjoy a vacation anywhere.

They passed a reduced speed limit sign. The next one read Welcome to Tyler's Glen, Population 2047.

A couple of minutes later, David turned onto what she assumed, in the dark and pouring rain, was Main Street. She caught sight of a sign that confirmed it and remembered the Main Street address on the business card. Maybe David could help answer a few of her nagging questions without her having to divulge too much about herself and the reason she'd come. "So this is Tyler's Glen . . . I just read an article about a man dying in a house fire here recently."

Shadows obscured David's features as he glanced in her direction. "It was a propane tank explosion."

"That's horrible. Did you know him?"

He blew out a long breath. "Owen Bentley. He lived down the road from me."

Interesting. David and Owen were neighbors. She turned her attention to the road when David slowed the truck. They were approaching a large neon sign with the words Tyler's Glen Motor Inn in bright, garish letters.

"Here we are." He drove into the parking lot and passed the long, one-story building with a string of efficiency units, stopping in front of the office.

Kate looked at the nearly full parking lot. "I sure hope they still have vacancies. It is tourist season in the Smokies."

David turned off the engine. "This isn't exactly the Opryland Hotel, and it's a Sunday night. You should be able to find a room. If not, Gina at the front desk will refer you to the bed and breakfast in town. It's only a block away. I can wait and take you there, if you'd like."

She smiled, appreciating his offer. "You've done more than enough for me tonight. I can take it from here."

When he got out, Kate set the blanket aside and zipped the pocket of her backpack.

He opened the door to the backseat and reached for her belongings, peering at her over the console. "By the way, the local sheriff's department has a website with a number you can call to report the accident."

"Thanks." She turned to her door and studied the dark sky and falling rain through her window as she prepared to make a dash for the motel.

"Hold on," he said. "Don't forget the water and ibuprofen. You're going to need them in the morning."

She stowed the items in her backpack before she jumped out in the rain.

He joined her under the awning outside the motel office, hauling her bags and camping gear. "You should stop by Doc Granger's first thing tomorrow and get checked out."

"Is he on Main Street too?"

"No, he needed a larger building and moved to First."

She grinned. "So there is another business in town besides farming, funerals, and chemicals."

"I'm not sure a growing medical clinic is anything to brag about." A touch of irony resonated in his voice. "You know, I'd feel better if you'd let me take you to the doctor's house tonight to be on the safe side."

After everything he'd done, she didn't want to impose again. He must have better things to do than chauffer her around town. Besides, other than being bruised and sore, she felt fine. "I'm all right. All I need is a nice hot shower and a good night's sleep." The light from the motel office revealed his masculine feature and the hint of disappointment flickering in his clear blue eyes. "Hey, if not for you, I'd probably be wandering around in the pouring rain like that guy I almost hit."

"At least you had a car."

"True, though I'm glad I didn't have to sleep in it tonight." She extended her hand to him in gratitude. "Goodnight, David. And thanks again for everything."

He received her handshake with a humble smile. "Take care of yourself, and stay out of trouble, okay?"

After the young woman entered the motel office, David waited outside long enough to make sure Gina had a room for her. He didn't want her to walk to the B&B in the rain. Through the large lobby window, he could see the attractive blonde with shoulder-length hair checking in. He'd been so consumed with helping her, he hadn't thought to ask for her name and number. Now he wished he had.

She saw him and waved, giving him a nod to confirm she had a room. Satisfied, David returned to his truck. The temperature had dropped, making it feel colder than normal for mid-October, especially since he was completely soaked.

Or maybe it was her mention of Owen's death that had triggered his sudden chill. With Owen gone, he wondered what would happen to his property. Guilt pricked him for thinking such thoughts. He remembered that Owen had started coming to church recently and even tried to talk to him a few times in passing, but after the way the old man had tricked his father, David couldn't bring himself to trust him.

By the time David pulled out of the motel parking lot, the rain had slacked off. Stopping at an intersection, he recalled the woman's description of the man she'd almost hit. He sounded more phantom than human, except for the bandages. Somewhere out there was an injured man who was lucky to be alive.

Kate emerged from the small bathroom dressed in her pajamas, feeling refreshed after her long, hot shower. The mirror over the sink had revealed bruises forming on her face, shoulder, and chest. Fighting exhaustion and pain, she sat on the bed and carefully reclined until she rested against the sheets.

It was good she had called the sheriff's office and her insurance company immediately after she'd checked in, before it got any later. The sheriff's deputy she'd spoken to had given her the number of a local car mechanic who worked long hours in town. She had called him next and asked him to tow her car to his shop. Her Miata was probably totaled, but she'd see what the mechanic had to say in the morning.

It had been one of the worst nights of her life, and yet she felt thankful to be alive—and grateful for David's help.

As she rested on the bed, relishing the comfort of being warm and dry again, she hoped David was faring as well right now. Her Good Samaritan had been a real godsend, getting her out of that jam. When she first saw the blinding beam of his flashlight, she wondered if she had died and gone to heaven. His wet, wavy locks and tall, strong build gave the striking man an almost angelic appearance.

She smiled, picturing him standing outside the motel office with his riveting blue eyes glittering under the awning. He might have an angelic side, but the warmth in his lingering gaze as he had said goodbye was more like flesh and blood.

Reaching for her phone on the nightstand, she groaned

from her aching muscles. She opened a photo of a smiling, middle-aged couple, and caressed the screen with her finger. Seeing Jim and Rose Tucker brought back happy memories of the times they'd shared together, and also a painful sense of loss.

Jim, her father figure and a deputy marshal like herself, had been killed four years earlier in the line of duty, and Jim's wife, Rose, had recently died from cancer. Though Kate was an adolescent when they took her in fourteen years ago, she thought of them as her parents.

With Rose and Jim gone, Chase and Jenny Matthews were her closest family now, though they weren't related by blood. Once her mentor with the U.S. Marshals Service, Chase had always been like a big brother to her. Now he and Jenny lived in Washington State, where he worked for a county sheriff's department. Kate couldn't have made it this far without Chase and Jenny's love and support. They had encouraged her to come and stay with them after Rose's funeral, but with Jenny now expecting her first baby, Kate didn't want to intrude.

She missed them terribly. She hadn't felt this lonely since she was a teen, living on the streets. The pain from her grief and sorrow hurt more than her bruises. *Lord, if I have any family left,* she prayed, *help me to find them.* She kept her head bowed for another moment until a sense of peace washed over her.

Releasing a heavy sigh, she set her phone on the nightstand by her bed and grabbed her wallet next to it. She removed the business card that had led her to Tyler's Glen. After re-reading Lester Crane's name and law office address on the front, she turned it over to see again the anonymous printed note glued to the back—

Contact Lester Crane in Tyler's Glen, TN. Tell him your mother was Owen Bentley's sister.

CHAPTER TWO

THE FOLLOWING MORNING, KATE GROANED AS she got out of bed. The ibuprofen had helped her sleep, but had worn off. Not only her shoulder, but every muscle in her body ached like she'd been run over by a stampede of horses.

When she looked in the bathroom mirror, the bruises under her eyes had formed dark circles. After covering them with makeup and taking a couple more ibuprofen, she dressed in her new jeans and a teal blouse, hoping to meet with the lawyer. The first thing on her to-do list, however, was to find the mechanic and see if he could fix her car.

Despite her sore muscles, the beautiful autumn day and fresh mountain air energized her as she walked down Main Street with her backpack slung over her shoulder. Exploring the sleepy mountain village, she couldn't help thinking about her mom.

Never one to talk much about her childhood, her mother seemed to have severed all ties with her family before Kate was born. Without knowing the reason why, Kate assumed there must have been a falling out.

Learning of Owen's death had only added to Kate's sense of loss and loneliness. He obviously hadn't cared enough to take her in after her mother had died or he wouldn't have given consent for her foster parents to raise her—or maybe Child Protective Services had deemed him unfit to take her in. Whatever the case, she still couldn't help being curious about him and wondering if he had any children. She'd always wanted brothers and sisters, but cousins would be nice too—and perhaps they could shed light on the reason behind her mother's mysterious estrangement from her family.

Stopping at the drugstore to buy a paper, Kate noticed a poster on a stand outside. It was promoting the harvest festival later that week. If she had someone to go with, she might be interested, but since she didn't, she moved on and went inside the store.

When she found the newspaper stand, the headline on the front page of the Tyler's Glen Gazette immediately caught her attention. Removing the top copy from the stack, she quickly scanned it. The article stated that the sheriff's department suspected arson in connection with her uncle's death, but didn't provide any more details.

After paying the cashier for the paper, she put the nine dollars in change in the pocket of her jeans and tucked the paper under her arm before she exited the store. Walking down the block, she came to an old brick building with the words Rick's Auto Repair and the business hours painted on the door. Glad to see they opened at eight, she checked the time on her cellphone. Five after.

Fumes of motor oil, gasoline, and rubber immediately clogged her nose upon entering the garage. Looking around the old converted warehouse, she saw three cars in various states of repair. She called over the country music playing on the radio. "Hello?"

A head popped up from behind the raised hood of a Chevy sedan. "Hey."

She side-stepped the tools, rags and jugs of automotive products. "Are you the mechanic?"

The young man came out where she could see him, wiping his hands on a rag. He was tall, clad in greasy coveralls, and wore an old University of Tennessee ball cap over his short blond hair. He looked younger than she'd expected from the professional, competent voice on the phone. His gangly build gave him the appearance of an overgrown teenager.

"I'm Rick Travis. What can I do for you?"

Rick? He couldn't be the shop owner, could he? "I'm Kate Phillips. I contacted you last night about towing my car."

"Oh, yeah. I brought it in this morning. It's pretty messed up. From the look of things, it's a wonder anyone survived."

She didn't want to think about that. "A volunteer firefighter stopped to help me. David Jennings."

Rick nodded with a chuckle. "That sounds like David, all right—always there when you need him. He's gotten me out of a few jams too."

"You know him well?"

"In a town this small, you pretty much know everyone, whether you want to or not. Are you a tourist or something?"

"Kind of. I live in Nashville."

"I figured that from the license plate. I'll take you to what's left of your car. It's in the backlot. This way." He gestured for her to follow as he strode toward the open garage door at the rear of the building.

Kate gasped when she saw the mangled remains of her Miata parked outside. "Can you fix it?"

Examining the car, he rubbed his chin. "I can, but the insurance company will say it's totaled. You're better off buying a new car than paying me to fix this one."

She sighed. "Great. Where can I rent a car around here for a couple of weeks without paying a fortune?"

He lifted his ball cap to scratch his head. "There aren't any car rental places in town, but I think I can help you."

Encouraged, she perked up. "Yes?"

He gestured for her to follow him to the storage building adjacent to the lot. After he entered a security code, the garage door lifted, revealing an old Ford pickup inside. "There she is," he announced with pride.

Kate's hopes deflated. "Do you have anything a little

newer?" *And sportier.*

He eyed her indignantly. "Are you kidding? This is a 1965 Ford F-100. They don't make 'em like this anymore." He waved her toward the cab. "Come here, I'll show you."

She followed him to the driver's side and listened while he gave her an overview of all its unique features. Well, half-listened. Mostly she was thinking, *How am I going to get out of this gracefully?*

After he'd finished, she pressed her palms together and touched her fingertips to her lips. "Obviously, this truck is very special to you. I wouldn't want to risk damaging it."

"After what happened to your Miata, I think you're safe for a while. You know what they say about lightning . . ."

She cringed, remembering the tree being struck when David had said the same thing. "After last night, I have my doubts about that. Anyway, I can't drive a standard transmission."

"It's a Ford-o-matic." He patted the hood of the truck like a cherished pet. "Even if I had something else, it wouldn't be as reliable as this baby. It's a classic."

The truck did have a shiny new coat of baby blue paint and appeared well cared for. "It's in excellent condition. Did you restore it yourself?"

"Not that one. A friend did. He paid me to keep it here and look after it."

"Then it's not yours."

"It is now. He transferred the title to me a couple of weeks ago."

"That was generous of him."

"Yeah. I tried to talk him out of it, but he insisted. Said he was getting up in age and needed to get his affairs in order. He wanted to give it to someone who would appreciate it." The subject had dampened Rick's youthful enthusiasm.

Judging from his somber face, Kate guessed that his

friend had met an unhappy ending. She felt bad about bringing the young man down. "Still, I wouldn't feel right." She said it as gently as she could.

"You'd be doing me a big favor. It needs to be driven."

She was running out of excuses—not that she was in a position to be too particular. As long as it had four wheels and an engine, she should be happy. "All right then. What's the rental charge?"

He stared at the truck as he thought it over. "Tell you what, I'll contact your insurance company. If they tell me which salvage yard they use, I'll buy the Miata from them, and we'll call it good. It'll take a while to find the parts, but I think I can rebuild your car, and then resell it for a nice profit."

"What if the salvage yard is in Nashville?"

"It's only four hours away. I can drive there with my truck and tow it back." Amusement glimmered in his eyes. "My mom will probably go with me. She loves Nashville."

Kate was encouraged by his generous offer. "You've got yourself a deal."

He handed her a slip of paper. "Here's the insurance estimate. My website address is there too. Feel free to call me if you have any questions."

So he *was* the owner of the garage. Impressed with his thoroughness, she scanned his detailed report. This guy could have a future on Wall Street. "Thanks. At least my Miata was paid off and not brand new."

"I'll get the keys for the truck."

While he went into the main building, Kate inspected the old pickup, trying to imagine herself driving it. It wasn't exactly her style, but it was only for a few days.

Rick returned, dangling the keys. "Can't wait to try her out, huh?"

"I've never driven a truck before."

"Once you get used to it, you'll never go back to that

little sports car. Just try not to run into any trees." His wary glint as he handed her the keys made it clear he was only half-joking.

"I'll do my best. Hey, you didn't happen to know Owen Bentley, did you?"

A mixture of surprise and sadness emanated from his face. "Yeah, I knew him. His funeral was only a couple of days ago."

Sensing the young man had a personal connection with her mother's brother, she hesitated a moment. "Does he have any other living relatives around here?"

"Not that I know of. He was a loner for the most part, but we both liked to restore classic cars. People thought he was a stingy, cantankerous old man, but I knew him better than anyone, and he had a good side too." Rick turned away with a pained look. "I gotta get back to work."

"Okay. Sorry for keeping you so long. Thanks again." She tucked the paper into her backpack.

As Rick headed to the garage, he glanced over his shoulder at her. "By the way, that pickup—it was Owen's."

At five of nine, Kate had parked the F-100 in front of Lester Crane's office. After confirming the address was the same as the one on the business card, she got out and quickly inspected her parking job. She missed her tiny Miata. Still, she was grateful to have any wheels at all, though it felt strange driving a vehicle that had belonged to her deceased uncle.

After grabbing her backpack from the bench seat, she locked the pickup and went to the door of the lawyer's office. A distinguished-looking gentleman with graying hair answered her knock with a cordial grin. "Hello, may I help you?"

"Are you Lester Crane?"

"Yes," he replied.

"I'm Kate Phillips. I came all the way from Nashville, hoping to speak to you. Do you have time today?"

He stared at her a moment with a raised brow, then stepped aside. "Actually, I don't have any appointments until this afternoon. Please come in."

Entering the spacious office, Kate noticed the impressive law library lining the walls and the beautiful painting of the Smokies behind the large desk in the center of the room. The top of the desk was covered with campaign posters bearing the lawyer's picture.

"Excuse the clutter," Lester said. "You see, I'm running for mayor, and the printer delivered these posters this morning." He collected the sheets, rolled them up, then stashed them on a shelf behind his desk. Turning around, he gestured to the empty chair in front of him. "Please, have a seat and make yourself comfortable." His soothing genteel accent could easily lull her to sleep if she wasn't on a hunt for answers about her uncle.

"Now what can I help you with, Kate?" he asked, sitting across from her at his desk.

"It's about Owen Bentley."

Glancing down, he hesitated in responding. "I take it you've heard about his death."

"Yes." She'd driven four hours in the storm and wrecked her car for this meeting, so she might as well get to the point. "This may come as a shock, but I'm his niece."

His eyes bulged for an instant. "But that's impossible. Owen doesn't have any family."

The lawyer's words instantly dashed Kate's hopes of finding any other relatives.

"Are you all right?" he asked in a concerned voice.

Kate brushed off her disappointment. "My mother was Mary Bentley. She grew up here in Tyler's Glen."

Something had registered in Lester's face when she'd mentioned her mother's name. "But Owen told me Mary had passed away."

Kate nodded. "Fourteen years ago. She didn't talk much about her family, but did tell me she had an older brother named Owen. I'm here because of this." She took the business card from her backpack and handed it to him. "It came with a newspaper clipping about the investigation into my uncle's death."

Lester gave it a glance. "I don't understand. It's my business card."

"Look at the back."

He flipped it over and read the note. "Who sent this to you?"

"I was hoping it was you. It was sent anonymously, but from someone who knows I'm Mary Bentley's daughter."

Lester released a long breath as he studied the card. "If this is true, it certainly changes things regarding the settlement of Owen's estate. Unfortunately, he didn't have a will. I kept telling him to make one, but he never got around to it. Stubborn old soul."

The mention of a will turned Kate's thoughts to her mother's last words before she died. Near the end of her life, she occasionally rambled incoherently, but this time she seemed more lucid and struggled to tell Kate something about a will and her father, though she didn't use her father's name. By then he had deserted them, and as far as Kate knew, her mother didn't have a will—not that she had much of anything to leave her anyway.

"Now that Owen's gone, I wish I'd been more persistent about it," Lester continued, refocusing Kate's attention. He was looking at her earnestly, his hands clasped together on his desk.

"An article in the Gazette today said that arson may have caused the propane explosion that set his house on fire."

Lester shook his head, his friendly features hardening. "If it was arson, you can rest assured I'll do everything in my power to catch the perpetrator and bring him to justice."

"But the election isn't until November. I hope whoever did it will be arrested before then. Who's the mayor right now?"

"I am, actually. I'm the deputy mayor pro tem. The previous mayor resigned."

"Resigned? Why?"

"He didn't get along with the town council. They were angry because of his support for the chemical plant moving to town."

Must be the chemical plant David had mentioned. "Sounds like a tough crowd. Sure you want to be mayor?"

He chuckled and shrugged. "It's a thankless job, but somebody's got to do it."

Kate took a piece of paper from her backpack. "This is my birth certificate. See, it has Mary's name on it."

After carefully inspecting the document, Lester appeared convinced. "Well, I'll be! I knew your mother, and your father, Norman. We went to the same school. He and I used to hunt together when we were boys. What's old Norm up to now?"

The mention of her father's name took her back to her childhood. For as long as Kate could remember, her parents didn't get along. Though it had never been clear why, Kate sensed it had something to do with her.

Lester was looking at her expectantly. "I wouldn't know," she replied. "I haven't seen him in years." It suddenly occurred to her that her father might have returned to Tyler's Glen when he left her and her mother. Since becoming a Christian, Kate had finally come to terms with his abandonment. When she thought about her father now, it only elicited a slight tug on her heart and a sense of pity—for him, not her. Even so, she didn't care to run into him.

"I see." Lester returned the birth certificate and business card to her. "My, this is quite unexpected. Without an heir, Owen's property would have been auctioned off, but this changes everything. If what you say is true, that makes you the sole heir of Owen Bentley's estate."

She stared at him in disbelief. "*Sole heir?*"

He confirmed with a slow nod. "When the town hears about it, there will be some mighty disappointed people. The ownership of your uncle's land has been hotly contested for years. I'm afraid this will only add fuel to the fire."

"Hotly contested by whom?"

The man leaned back in his chair. "Owen's neighbor, David Jennings."

Lester's words echoed in Kate's mind as she walked down the block to see the deputy sheriff she'd spoken with the night before. *Owen Bentley's sole heir.* What would she do with property in Tyler's Glen? It should have gone to her mother, not her. She didn't know a soul in this town. No, that wasn't exactly true. She knew David and Rick, and now Lester. Of course, once David learned that she would inherit Owen's property, he probably wouldn't want anything to do with her.

Before their meeting had ended, Kate had asked Lester to keep it confidential that she was Owen's niece and had made an appointment to see him again on Thursday morning to discuss next steps regarding her uncle's estate. After Rose's recent passing, dealing with another death in the family was the last thing she needed.

Finding the sheriff's humble substation next door to the post office, Kate noticed how tiny it was compared to the marshal building in Nashville. Going inside, however, she saw it had the same Spartan décor, with walls painted in government-beige to match the drab carpet and furniture. Law enforcement budget constraints appeared to be a problem everywhere.

A burly officer came out of a doorway in the back and saw her standing there in the main office. "May I help you?"

"I'm looking for Deputy Harlan Travis."

"You've found him," he replied, a friendly smile stretching across his round face. "You must be Kate Phillips." He strode up and gave her a firm handshake. "Nice to meet you in person. Did Rick tow your car to his shop this morning?"

"Yes, I stopped by there earlier." Remembering his last name was also Travis, she rubbed her earlobe, wondering if there was a connection. "Are you two related?"

The man nodded. "He's my son."

"No kidding." She never would have guessed, since Rick didn't resemble his father much at all. "He's been a big help."

"Good. Rick knows his stuff when it comes to cars." The deputy turned and motioned for her to follow. "Come with me and I'll get you a copy of the accident report for your insurance."

They passed a coffee maker emitting a stale java odor almost as strong as the fumes in Rick's garage. The deputy paused and gestured to it. "Can I get you a cup of coffee?"

"Uh—no, thank you," she replied politely, the thought turning her stomach.

He stopped and moved behind a desk with a computer monitor. A dark-stained University of Tennessee mug was sitting next to the keyboard and mouse. The deputy reached for a sheet of paper and handed it to her. "Here's a copy of the report. Did Rick think he could fix your Miata?"

"Probably, but as far as the insurance is concerned, it's totaled. He's letting me rent his Ford F-100 in exchange for what's left of my car."

"Owen Bentley's classic?" Harlan's face twisted with a

bemused expression. "That old geezer wouldn't give a red cent to a blind man, yet he gave my boy that old truck and helped him start his business. I'm still scratching my head over it."

She flinched at the man's offhanded remark, though he couldn't know she was Owen's niece.

"I guess I shouldn't talk that way about a dead man," he said in a softer tone, "but I'm married to a Holbrook, and the Holbrooks and the Bentleys have been feuding since the Civil War. Unless you're a Holbrook, there's no point in me trying to explain it. Sometimes I don't understand it myself."

Neither did she, but she was a stranger in town and didn't care to get into the middle of an ancient dispute. She wondered how the deputy would react if he knew she was a Bentley. "Maybe that was his way of trying to bury the hatchet."

"I suppose anything is possible," he replied, sounding unconvinced. "Owen was a hard one to figure out. Shame he died the way he did though."

"I understand your office is investigating his murder."

His eyebrow shot up. "You aren't a reporter, are you?"

"No, but I am interested in the case. Have you made any arrests yet?"

"Not yet."

"Do you have any leads?"

"We're still working on it." He slanted his head in her direction. "Why do I get the feeling there's something you're not telling me?"

She hesitated for a moment, then took a deep breath. "Owen Bentley was my uncle, on my mother's side."

He blinked as it registered and dropped into his chair across from her. A hint of ruefulness softened his demeanor. "About what I said earlier regarding Owen and the ..."

"It's okay," she told him, whisking her hand. "We weren't close. In fact, I've never met him." She reached for her backpack and retrieved the newspaper clipping and business card. "The day before yesterday, I received these in the mail. That's why I came here. I'm hoping you might have answers to what happened and why."

He looked over the two items. "Who sent these?"

She took a seat in the chair across from his desk and leaned in his direction. "That's what I've been trying to find out. I spoke with Lester Crane earlier this morning. I thought he might have sent them, but he says he didn't. Until yesterday, I had never set foot in Tyler's Glen, and I didn't know a soul in this town before then."

He returned the articles to her, then leaned against his chair in amazement. "You're really Owen's niece?"

She affirmed the ironic truth with a nod. "By the way, I'm also a deputy marshal."

He snorted, then shook his head. "I knew it. You're too nosy to be a civilian."

"I'll take that as a compliment, but I'd appreciate it if you'd keep what I've told you between us for now. You know how people talk."

"That I do, especially in a small town like this."

She looked down at the accident report in her hand. "I may have wrecked my car, but I'm glad I didn't hit the man who crossed in front of me. He looked in pretty bad shape already."

The officer's eyes narrowed. "What do you mean?"

She told him about the young man's bandaged face and hand, giving as many details as she could remember.

"That's very interesting. Someone called in a report late yesterday afternoon and said they'd spotted a hooded man with a bandaged face prowling around their farm. Might have been the same man you saw wandering around in the storm last night."

"Maybe his car broke down."

"It's possible, but we've had several reports of a prowler

in the area recently. If the man you saw is our prowler, at least now we have a better description of him."

Kate's pulse accelerated. "Has anything been stolen?"

"Not that I know of. He's probably a drifter passing through. We get plenty of those around here."

"You have my phone number. I'd appreciate you letting me know if you hear anything more about him."

"Why? You think he might be a fugitive?"

"I don't know, but when someone mysteriously shows up and unusual things start to happen, it makes me suspicious."

The deputy sheriff rubbed his chin. "You and me both."

Kate glanced at the clock on the wall. Ten-thirty already. She still needed to check out of the motel and hopefully see the doctor before lunch. "Thanks for the accident report. I should be going."

After leaving the sheriff's substation, Kate kept thinking about the hooded man. Could he be the prowler? And what had caused his injuries? She remembered David joking that he might be a zombie. Zombies and ghosts didn't bother her, but fugitives—that was a different story.

CHAPTER THREE

ON HIS WAY TO THE TOWN council meeting at eleven-thirty that morning, David thought about the beautiful woman with the greenish-blue eyes he'd helped last night. He regretted the way he'd left her alone at the motel, without wheels. However, he had the distinct impression she was more than capable of taking care of herself. When he'd assisted her to his truck in the storm, it had surprised him to discover how strong she was. Beneath that delicate-looking, feminine exterior was no helpless waif. Her rock-solid muscles and fierce independence seemed more characteristic of an athlete.

As he walked down Main Street, David spied Joe Campbell stepping out of Lester Crane's office and coming toward him. The two men acknowledged each other with cool stares.

Joe stopped in front of him with a sly look. "I thought you should know there's been a new development concerning Owen Bentley's estate. The plans to auction off his property have been cancelled."

Given the source, David was skeptical. "Where did you hear that?"

"Lester just told me, but he wouldn't give me any details."

As Joe swaggered away, David sneezed. He hoped he wasn't getting sick. His thoughts returned to last night and the chill he got in the rain, and the mysterious woman—

Then he saw her, heading his way.

At first, he thought his eyes might be playing tricks on him. But she was real, and walking right up to him with a radiant smile.

"Hi, David. I was hoping I might run into you today. You'll be happy to know that other than a few bruises Dr. Granger gave me a clean bill of health."

"That's great." Pleased she'd taken his advice, he couldn't help gazing into her teal eyes. Last night, they appeared greener. They seemed to change with whatever she was wearing. "How about your car?"

She sighed. "Not so good. It's totaled." Then she pointed to the old blue pickup parked in front of Lester's law office, down the street. "Rick Travis rented me his truck."

"You're driving that?"

She laughed at his reaction. "I'm still trying to get the hang of it. It's not like driving my Miata, but I found plenty of room for all of my luggage and camping gear when I checked out of the motel."

He smiled at the irony of the gorgeous woman behind the wheel of the relic. "I'm surprised Rick let you drive his Ford. It's a real classic."

"I think he felt sorry for me when he saw my wrecked car, or maybe he simply wanted what was left of my Miata."

David chuckled. "Knowing Rick, it was probably the latter. By the way, you didn't tell me your name last night."

"Oh," she said with an embarrassed look. "I'm Kate. Kate Phillips. By the way, you were right about staying at the motel. I'm pretty sore today, but at least I had a nice shower and a good night's sleep. Now that I'm rested up, I'm looking forward to seeing the Smokies in daylight."

He glanced at the blue sky over the famous mountains in the distance. "You should have ideal camping weather for the next few days. You picked a great location too. I like to ride my horses on a trail near Cades Cove."

A spark gleamed in her eye. "You have horses?"

"A couple. Do you like to ride?"

"Yes, but I haven't done it in years."

"I can take you if you'd like. There are trails in the park."

"When?" she eagerly replied.

Her enthusiasm sent his heartrate into a gallop. "How about tomorrow?"

Kate's face beamed. "Perfect. I can't wait."

Neither could he. His chance encounter with her had been fortuitous. Not only did he know her name, but he'd get to see her again tomorrow.

They took out their cellphones and quickly exchanged phone numbers. When they had finished, Kate inclined her head with an appealing look. "Do you know a good place to eat in town? The motel didn't serve breakfast, and I'm starving."

"Bubba's Diner. It's nothing fancy, but the food is great. It's on my way. Come on, I'll walk with you."

She glanced at him as he accompanied her down the street. "Care to join me? My treat."

"I would—unfortunately, I have a town council meeting." Her invitation made him wish he could skip it, but he couldn't let the other council members down.

"You're a volunteer firefighter, an EMT, and also on the town council?"

"One of the council members dropped out."

"And you volunteered." An amused inflection sounded in her voice. "With all your volunteer work, how do you ever find time to make a living?"

He returned a humble shrug. "I manage somehow."

They strolled together down Main Street, passing the drug and hardware stores. When they came to a small restaurant, David stopped and gestured to the sign on the window. "This is it. Like I said, no frills." He waited as Kate peered through the glass at the tables and booths with checkered tablecloths.

Her gaze shifted in his direction. "Sure you don't want to ditch your meeting and join me?"

"Don't tempt me, or I might."

"No, you wouldn't. You're an Eagle Scout, remember?" Her eyes glittered at him like aqua gems as her hair shimmered in the sunlight. "What's on the agenda today for your meeting?"

"A prowler is supposedly lurking around town, and people are getting a little spooked."

Her expression became more serious. "Deputy Travis mentioned the same thing when I picked up my accident report this morning. Any idea who it might be?"

He shook his head. "Some guy in a hoody, roaming the countryside at night. Without more details, it could be almost anyone."

Kate's brow arched at his remark. "Yes, anyone, including the man I almost hit."

Kate sat in a booth, her elbows resting on the checked tablecloth as she studied the menu. It had been a busy morning, but she'd gotten her business out of the way so she could enjoy the rest of the afternoon. Her thoughts wandered to her previous encounter with David. If not for his unmistakable blue eyes and heart-swooning smile, she might not have recognized him all clean and dry. His dark hair appeared straighter and a shade or two lighter in the sun compared to last night in the rain. But wet or dry, he was certifiably gorgeous.

Too bad he couldn't join her for lunch and chat with her longer. At least she'd see him tomorrow. Maybe by then he'd be able to tell her more about the mysterious prowler haunting the locals.

It was hard to imagine such a decent, level-headed guy like David squabbling over a piece of property. Still, until she knew him better, it was probably best to keep her kinship with Owen to herself.

A cute waitress wearing tight-fitting rhinestone jeans and a hot pink T-shirt came to her table. "Hi, what can I get for you?"

"I'll have the house salad, please, and iced tea." The aroma of hamburgers grilling and potatoes frying tempted Kate to change her mind.

The young woman stared at Kate, her eyes twinkling as if something about Kate's order was amusing. "You're not from around here, are ya?" A country twang accented her voice.

"No, I'm from Nashville."

The woman placed her hands on her hips, revealing hot pink fingernails that matched her shirt and the fading streaks in her teased black hair. "No kidding? What brings you to Tyler's Glen?"

Kate's gaze traveled across the room to the cook, an overweight man with a crewcut and tattoo-covered arms. He stepped over to the register, frowning impatiently at the waitress. "Who's the man behind the register?" Kate asked. "He doesn't look happy."

The woman glanced his way. "Oh, that's just Bubba. He can wait. It's not every day that I get to talk to someone from Nashville."

Reading the woman's name tag, Kate didn't want to be rude, but after the long morning, she needed something to eat. "Nadine, I'd like to chat, but I'm pretty hungry. How long do you think it'll be before I get my salad?"

Nadine pressed a hand to her chest. "Oh, I'm sorry." The embarrassed blush on her face nearly matched her fingernails, shirt, and streaks in her hair. "You must think I'm such a country hick for going on so. I'll take care of your order right away."

She brought the iced tea almost immediately, and Kate

sipped it while she checked her text messages and did a search for Owen's address on her phone. Ten minutes later, Nadine brought Kate's salad.

While she ate, Kate felt eyes watching her. She looked around at the other patrons chatting and laughing in the casual café, oblivious to her. Then she spotted Nadine and Bubba observing her from the kitchen. She chalked it up to curiosity about the new girl in town and ignored them.

A few minutes later, Nadine returned to her booth with a pitcher of iced tea and refilled her glass. "How is everything?"

"Good, thanks." Kate started to take another bite of her salad, but noticed Nadine still standing there, hovering. "Yes?"

Nadine set the pitcher down on the table and leaned forward, her face beaming with excitement. "I'm on my break right now, and I thought since you're alone, maybe you'd like company. I'd love to hear all about Nashville. It's my dream to make it big there one day."

A few bites of the salad had helped to satisfy Kate's stomach and the health-conscious side of her, though her taste buds would have preferred the fried food. Feeling more accommodating now, she gestured to the empty bench across from her. "Have a seat."

Nadine grabbed an unused glass from another table and poured herself some tea, then eagerly slid into Kate's booth.

"By the way, my name is Kate Phillips."

"I'm Nadine Rogers." Despite her girlish effervescence, the waitress was probably only a few years younger than Kate. "Do you know any country music stars? I'm pretty good with a guitar, and I've written a few songs. All I need is an agent."

Kate dabbed at a bit of salad dressing on her chin with her napkin. "I wish I could help you, but that's not my line of work."

The corner of Nadine's mouth twitched with disappointment. "Then what do you do there?"

"I'm in law enforcement."

"Like a cop?"

"Sort of. Actually, the U.S. Marshals Service."

"Oh." Nadine's earlier enthusiasm plummeted. "Are you here for work?"

Kate detected the nervous inflection in the waitress's voice. The prospect of her being in town on official marshal business obviously made Nadine uncomfortable, but why? Was she hiding something? "No," Kate replied. "I'm camping in the park."

The woman's face brightened, and she relaxed. "I'd give anything to live in Nashville."

Kate gathered from the wistfulness in Nadine's tone that it was something she'd probably dreamed about all her life. "Tyler's Glen seems like a nice enough town."

Nadine sighed. "It's okay, but it's not all cherries and gumdrops. The people here—they might seem friendly and all, but underneath their smiles and waves, they're full of gossip and venom."

"Really?" Nadine's candid remark mildly shocked Kate. "Everyone I've met so far has been nice."

"You're new in town. You don't have any baggage—at least none the town is aware of yet." The shift in topic had suddenly changed the girlish waitress sitting across from Kate into a hardened, jaded woman. "But watch out, because if you do, and word gets out, they'll turn on you in a heartbeat and never let you live it down."

The bell chimed at the door. A moment later, the heavy clomp of a man's footsteps approached Kate's table, then halted right behind her.

"Hel-lo, Na-dine." The deep Southern drawl coated in molasses caused Kate to turn her head. A bearded man wearing cowboy boots and a hat studied her with an impertinent stare. "I'm Joe Campbell." He lifted his hat, uncovering a head full of curly brown hair. "I don't believe we've met."

Nadine rose abruptly. "I better get back to work."

Kate watched the waitress disappear into the kitchen. She suspected Joe's arrival had something to do with her quick departure. Though he was too brash and eager for Kate's taste, the thirtyish cowboy-wannabe seemed relatively harmless. If he had something to hide, he probably wouldn't make such a big production of introducing himself in a public place. "I'm Kate Phillips."

He reached to shake her hand. "You must be new in town. I have a memory for pretty faces."

Kate stifled a groan. Joe was pouring it on thick, but if she wanted answers to what had happened to her uncle, the forward man might be a good resource. "You're right. I am new in town. I thought I'd grab lunch before doing a little sightseeing."

"If you're looking for a tour guide, I'd be more than happy to oblige."

"That's very generous, but I'm sure you have more important things to do."

"For you, I'll make an exception . . . And if you're looking for adventure, I know a few hidden gems you won't find in any travel guide."

"Yes, I'm sure you do." She sent him a sly look. "However, I've had enough adventure after that violent storm last night—speaking of violence, wasn't there a man killed in a propane tank explosion somewhere around here? I read about it in today's paper."

Joe muted his eagerness. "It's a crying shame what happened to him. Makes you wonder what kind of sick person would do something like that, but with strangers prowling the countryside these days, I guess nobody's safe."

The man with the bandages flashed in her memory.

Focusing her thoughts, she continued probing Joe about Owen. "Did you know the victim well?"

"We weren't best buddies or anything, but Owen used to go bow hunting with Lester and me occasionally—Lester's the lawyer in town. He's running for mayor."

"Bow hunting?"

"You know . . ." He demonstrated shooting an invisible arrow at a target. "Bullseye!"

His antics didn't amuse her. "What do you hunt?"

"Mostly deer and turkey. Hey, I could teach you. I have a shooting range on my farm."

"Thanks, but I'm not into hunting—at least, not animals." His macho manner made it hard to resist ribbing him a little. "Do you use real arrows or imaginary ones?"

He grinned, revealing yellowed teeth, probably from chewing too much tobacco. "The real thing. You should try it. It's a lot of fun."

"It sounds dangerous. Imaginary arrows would be safer."

Snorting derisively, he glanced away.

Nadine passed their table and he snatched the pen from her apron pocket. She stopped and placed a hand on her hip, glaring at him as he jotted something on a napkin.

"Thanks, Na-dine," he said as he raised the pen to her without looking up.

Nadine rolled her eyes and grabbed it, then marched away.

Joe moved to get up. "It was nice to meet you, Kate. If you change your mind about bow-hunting or need a tour guide, you can reach me at this number. Enjoy your trip, and watch out for the bears."

Bears. After he swaggered away, Kate stared at the number on the napkin. The mention of bears in the park gave her a slight chill, but she'd rather take her chances with them than a wolf like Joe Campbell.

After lunch, Kate drove out of town toward the park. Shadowed by the Smoky Mountains, the scenic country road hugged riverbanks, peaceful valley cornfields, and meadows dotted with cattle and horses. Despite Nadine's warning, Kate found this place to be beautiful and charming. Probably because of her family roots, she felt a strong connection here. But with her uncle gone and no other living relatives, she was the last of the Bentley clan. That made her a little sad. "Looks like it's just You and me, God," she said aloud.

I will never leave you or forsake you.

She gazed at the sky. "I know."

Headed toward the national park, Kate braked at the four-way stop that intersected with Maple Creek Road. From her online search, she knew Owen had lived on that road. Why not check out his place while she was in the neighborhood? Maybe she would discover something that would help explain what happened to him. After taking a left and driving a couple of miles farther, she noticed an impressive house on a hill across the road. The contemporary residence with large picture windows facing the mountains looked like something from a home and garden show.

A quarter of a mile from the nice house, Kate came to an overgrown lot with the name Bentley on the mailbox. As she decelerated, she spotted a sign nailed to a tree nearby. Printed in bold black letters were the words Posted: No Trespassing. She turned left into the drive anyway and parked in front of a burned-up rubble heap that was cordoned off with bright yellow tape. The remaining concrete foundation and scorched chimney told her this must be what was left of her uncle's house. Taking her backpack with her, she jumped out of the truck to look around.

The storm had washed away most of the soot and ashes, but she caught a whiff of the burnt wood and smoke now and then as she walked across the weeds and surveyed the charred remains. The thought of her uncle's torturous death gripped her heart. She now regretted not responding to his voice message when he had wanted to apologize for the past. If she had, maybe things would have gone differently, or at least she could have known more about him. *Forgive me, Lord.*

Her mind returned to puzzling over who had mailed Lester's business card with the clipping. Someone who seemed to know things about her and her family that she didn't know herself.

Kate stepped away from the ashes and walked the perimeter of the overgrown jungle that was once a front lawn. Either her uncle hadn't been into landscaping, or he was disabled and couldn't mow the grass. She remembered Rick and Harlan's remarks about him being stingy. Too stingy to pay for someone to cut the yard maybe, and yet generous enough to give Rick his classic truck.

She recalled finding an old family photo years ago. It was taken when her mother was a teenager. Standing next to her was a solemn-looking young man. When Kate asked her mother about him, she said he was her older brother, Owen. Kate kept asking questions, but her mother didn't want to talk about him. The subject seemed to make her sad. Not long after that, she suffered a stroke after a routine surgery. She took a turn for the worse and passed quickly, so Kate never got to ask her about Owen again. Now she wished she knew more about him.

Traipsing through the muddy yard, Kate headed toward the large red barn, a good distance away from the remains of the house. A fall breeze swept her hair across her face and sent orange and gold leaves floating down from the trees bordering the yard. She noticed a small orchard near the barn with neglected apples hanging from the branches. A few had fallen on the ground to rot. She wished she had a basket handy to pick them.

The weathered barn looked structurally sound, but the busted lock on the door made Kate suspicious. Someone had broken it. Was it before or after Owen had died? She unzipped the pocket of her backpack and withdrew her Glock. Holding it in the ready position, she slid the large door open and stepped inside. To her left, she found a light switch and flipped it on.

Lingering odors of horses, leather, and engine grease permeated the stale air. Instead of livestock, a small green tractor and three old cars in various states of restoration filled the central area on the ground floor, with an empty hayloft overhead. The right corner of the barn had been converted into a workshop. Satisfied that she was alone, she returned her gun to her backpack and headed in that direction.

The place was a mess with tools and car parts scattered across the ground. Had Owen left things this way, or was it the aftermath of the deputy sheriff's investigation? Noticing the cluttered workbench with an odd assortment of tools and hardware, she stopped to check it out.

Spying a huge spider resting on the surface, she jumped away. From a distance, she watched for signs of life. It didn't move. After a few moments, she grabbed a pitchfork leaning against a support beam and poked the creature with the handle to confirm it wasn't alive. *A fake.* And not even a spider, but something else. *Very funny, Owen.* Relieved, she focused on the other items.

Among the odd assortment of tools and clutter on the work surface was a digital meter sitting near several small, empty vials. What was it for? It looked like a type of thermometer or testing device. She lifted her gaze to the shiny things dangling from a large peg board behind the bench on the wall. Fishing lures—dozens of them. And five fishing rods leaning in the far corner on the other side of the workbench. Apparently, Owen was into fishing, big time. She reached for a lure that resembled a type of fly, admiring its craftsmanship. Stepping away from the bench to hold it to the light, she thought the eye-catching ornament would make a cool Halloween earring, or a prank. Then she noticed the others that resembled insects similar to the one on the workbench.

A gust of wind howled in the rafters. It startled Kate and caused her to drop the lure. When she stooped to pick it up, she noticed the variety of parts and components in the trash can. *Owen had made the lures.* She couldn't help being impressed.

Her eyes roamed the collection of paint cans, tool boxes and stacks of automotive repair manuals on the bottom shelf of the workbench. She spotted the manual for the classic Ford F-100 she was driving and picked it up. Flipping through it, she found an envelope with University of Tennessee Department of Agriculture printed on the return address.

She took it out and saw that it had already been opened. After removing the letter inside, she unfolded it and began to read the handwritten note addressed to Owen, dated a little over two weeks ago.

It was good to see you the other day. About that matter we discussed, I'll see what I can do and get back to you.
Sincerely, Roy

She folded the letter and returned it to the envelope before placing it in her backpack. Too bad Roy hadn't included his last name, but he must work for U.T. She wondered if *the matter* he had discussed with Owen had something to do with farming, given that he worked for the

Department of Agriculture, or was it something personal?

Turning around, Kate spotted a bullseye posted on the far wall. Nearby hung a conventional recurve bow and a more intricate compound bow for hunting, along with a quiver of arrows for each bow. She remembered that Joe had said he went bow hunting with Owen and Lester. It had been quite a while since Kate shot an arrow, but she couldn't resist trying out her uncle's equipment.

She set her backpack on the ground and went to remove the recurve bow and quiver. After depositing the quiver beside her backpack, she took an arrow with green and red fletching for feathers and positioned herself in front of the target. As she raised the bow shoulder level with her left arm, her shoulder seized in pain. Cringing, she lowered the bow and decided to stop before her shoulder completely froze up. Besides, it didn't feel right using her uncle's things so soon after his death.

With a wistful sigh, she returned the bow and quiver to their place on the wall. On a small table was red and green fletching material and glue with a couple of carbon arrow shafts. Not only did Owen make his own lures, restore old cars, but he fletched his own arrows. A man of many talents.

She'd spent enough time in the stuffy barn. It was a beautiful day and she wanted to be outside. Heading for the door, she grabbed her backpack, then flicked off the light and slid the barn door closed.

In the fresh air once again, she decided to do a little more exploring and went around to the back of the building. She discovered a muddy trail and followed it along a babbling creek, through a field of cornstalks. She stopped and broke off an ear of corn. Removing its husk, she noticed it was ripe. But who would harvest it now?

A flock of crows flew into a tree nearby. Watching them, she observed the position of the sun in the sky. It was early afternoon, and she wanted to set up camp before dark.

Taking the ear of corn with her, she turned and headed toward the pickup.

After she'd passed the barn, a loud bang went off and a bullet ripped the ear of corn from her hand.

She ducked and ran for cover behind the truck. Another shot rang through the air as she hunkered down. It buzzed over her head.

Crouching low beside the driver side door, she unzipped her backpack and withdrew her gun and her badge. "U.S. Marshal!" she yelled. "Hold your fire and put your weapon down."

Another bullet struck the rear tire, deflating it with a loud pop. Either her shooter was a bad shot, or he was only trying to scare her away. Regardless, she couldn't take any chances. Quickly, she assessed her options. Her best defense would be to peer around the truck engine and return fire.

As she started to move, the window above was hit, shattering glass over her. Keeping her head down, she shook off the shards and scurried toward the front of the pickup.

Another bullet struck the windshield.

Staying low, she released the safety on her Glock, her heart pounding. On the count of three, she peered around the headlight, aimed, and pressed the trigger. *Boom!*

The incoming fire stopped. After a brief pause, she wondered if she'd hit her assailant. The clamor of breaking twigs and branches in the distance told her he was still alive and fleeing. Her weapon ready, she peered around again. Spying movement in the woods, she traced it with her gun, resisting the impulse to shoot without a good visual.

When the sound in the woods faded, she pulled her cellphone from her pocket. Keeping her weapon handy, she called 911 and reported the incident. Then she waited for what seemed an eternity for the sirens.

Deputy Travis came in response to Kate's call. After she told him what had happened, he checked the premises and inspected the damage to Owen's truck. Seeing the blown-out windows, windshield, and tire, the deputy called his son Rick to come tow the pickup to his garage. Kate unloaded her belongings from the truck and waited with Harlan for Rick to arrive.

When the mechanic pulled up and got out, she handed him the keys. "I'm so sorry about your truck. I'll pay for the damages."

He waved it off. "Dad told me it's mostly broken glass and a flat tire. At least the bodywork was spared."

After Rick had been so generous and trusting with his prized possession, she felt like she'd let him down. And yet it wasn't her fault. "Still, I insist on paying for it."

"Thanks, but first I have to find replacements for them. Then I'll see how much they cost. It may not be that big of a deal."

It was to her. Classics like that weren't like those apples in Owen's orchard. They didn't grow on trees.

After Rick had left with Owen's pickup, Harlan gave her a lift to the sheriff's substation to make her report.

Seated across from the deputy's desk for the second time that day, Kate wondered if she'd ever make it to the campground.

Harlan had a shrewd look in his eye when he'd finished entering her report on the computer. "Since Owen's property is posted, I'm wondering if the shooter thought you were a trespasser."

It struck her that the deputy didn't seem too surprised by the incident. Then the light dawned. "You know who it is, don't you?"

He picked up a pencil and leaned back in his chair. "Sounds like Virgil Crane."

"Lester Crane's father?"

"His uncle."

"Well, I hope you're going to arrest him for aggravated assault."

He silently twirled the pencil between his fingers.

She came out of her seat. "Don't tell me you aren't going to do anything because he's related to Lester."

The deputy stopped fiddling and put the pencil down. "Virgil lives across the road from the Bentley place and hunts there sometimes. He and Owen go way back, and they had an understanding that he could hunt on Owen's land."

"But it's not his property."

"True, but Virgil is practically deaf. He probably didn't hear your voice. If he'd wanted to kill you, he wouldn't have missed. But I'll go see him and tell him not to hunt there anymore." Then he smirked a little. "Once Virgil finds out you're a marshal, I doubt he'll bother you again."

She wasn't the least bit happy about it, but this wasn't her jurisdiction and she didn't want to alienate the deputy who was in charge of the investigation into her uncle's death. "By the way, the lock on Owen's barn door is busted. Was it like that before?"

The deputy frowned. "No . . . When we came to investigate the fire, I found Owen's original lock had been tampered with. After we finished searching the barn, I installed a new one. Did anything else strike you as odd?"

"You mean, besides looking like a tornado went through there?"

Harlan snorted with a slight twinkle in his eye. "Tidiness was never Owen's strong suit. I'll check out the lock and take another sweep around the barn later today." His serious expression became apologetic. "This is actually a very peaceful place. It's a shame your visit here has gotten off to such a bad start."

"Especially when it comes to cars and trucks."

He chuckled. "Maybe you'd have better luck with horses."

She thought of David and his offer to take her riding. Maybe he would give her a lift to the campground. "By the way, I did find something interesting in Owen's barn." She retrieved the envelope from her backpack and handed it to him. "The person who wrote the letter inside is named Roy, but there's no last name. Do you know who it might be?"

Harlan rubbed his chin as he read the note. "Probably Roy Timmons. He grew up in Tyler's Glen and moved to Knoxville, but he still comes here to hunt from time to time."

"Do you have any idea what matter Owen would want to discuss with him?"

The deputy's lips shifted to the side. "Could be anything from farming to hunting. It's not much of a lead if that's what you're thinking." He returned the letter to her.

"You're probably right," she said, feeling disappointed. "When you investigated the barn, did you notice that meter on the workbench next to the small vials?"

His growing impatience was evident in his long exhale. "Look, Kate, I know Owen was your uncle and you're a deputy marshal, but you need to trust us to do our job. We'll get to the bottom of what happened, I promise. Right now, our top priority is to find the weapon used to kill him."

"You mean the source of the explosion that caused the fire?"

"No. The fire didn't kill him, Kate. The coroner's report says he was stabbed to death."

CHAPTER FOUR

HARLAN HAD TOLD KATE TO KEEP the fact that her uncle was stabbed under wraps for now, until they uncovered the murder weapon. The town was already in an uproar over the explosion, and he didn't want to add fuel to the fire. The question still remained—who had killed Owen and why?

Before she left the deputy sheriff's office, she called David and asked if he could give her a ride to the park. While she waited outside with her luggage and camping gear, she took a seat on a nearby bench and used her cellphone to find a number for the U.T. Department of Agriculture.

A woman answered, asking how she could direct her call.

"Dr. Roy Timmons, please."

"He's not in today. If you'd like, you can leave him a message."

Disappointed that she couldn't talk to him, Kate persisted. "It's very important that I speak to him today. Do you have his home or cell number?"

"I'm sorry. I'm not allowed to give that out."

Kate had to settle for leaving him a voice message with her name and number, asking him to call her as soon as possible. If she told him what it was about on the recorded message, it might scare him away, so she wanted to be discreet.

David pulled his truck next to the curb in front of her.

Stashing her phone in her pocket, Kate quickly rose and came to the passenger door to speak to him through the open window. "Thanks for coming to my rescue again, especially on short notice."

He got out and went around to help her load her things.

"Your timing was perfect. My council meeting had just ended, and I was about to leave." An inquisitive gleam flickered in his eyes.

"What?" she asked.

He slanted his head. "What happened to the Ford classic? Other than saying you had problems with it, you didn't tell me the whole story over the phone."

How could she explain what had happened at Owen's place without also revealing she was his next of kin? Rick was already aware of the shooting incident because he had towed the F-100 away. Despite the mechanic's curious glances, he hadn't probed while his father was there on the case. She hoped that being the deputy's son would deter him from telling anyone else. Right now, the only ones who knew she was Owen's niece were Harlan and Lester. Since they were both government officials, she was counting on them to keep it confidential. Nadine's warning about the town's penchant for gossip had already convinced her that the fewer people who knew the truth, the better.

"It's a long story," she finally replied to David. "If you don't mind, I'd rather talk about something else. I'm just happy you were available to take me to the campground."

His gaze lingered on her for a moment before he changed the subject. "You know, I could take you to Knoxville to rent a car. It's not that far away."

"The way things are going, my car insurance may drop me before the day is done." She widened her eyes in a humorous gesture. "Besides, no rental car company will match the sweet deal Rick is giving me to rent his truck. I'm sure he'll have it fixed in no time, and I don't want to make things more complicated than they already are." She handed David her sleeping bag.

He stowed it in the backseat. "It's a nice afternoon. We *could* take our ride today instead of tomorrow—if you're game. My friend, Pete Logan, works in the park. I can ask him if he'll give me a lift home when we're done, and I'll return with my truck and trailer to bring the horses back."

She paused as she lifted her luggage for him to load. "You don't mind?"

His face scrunched in irony. "Let's see, riding horses or working on a day like this, which would you choose?"

"When you put it like that, I don't feel so guilty." She smiled as she passed him the bag containing her tent. "By the way, how did your meeting go?"

"First, it was a prowler. Now everyone's afraid we have an arsonist lurking around."

"They must have read the article in the *Gazette* about the arson investigation." She reached for her backpack and took out the newspaper. "See, it's the front-page story."

David's jaw tensed as he glanced at the headline. He closed the door to the backseat. "Now you're starting to sound like the people on the town council."

A short while later, Kate had turned her attention to the beautiful scenery outside her window as David drove them to his farm. When he turned right, onto Maple Creek Road, she remembered that he and Owen had been neighbors. As they approached her uncle's farm from the opposite direction she'd come earlier, Kate noticed a small country church with stained glass windows and an old cemetery behind it. "Nice church."

"Thanks—that reminds me, the grass in the cemetery is getting too high. I need to cut it this week."

She turned to look at him. "You attend there?"

"Along with half the town. What about you—do you have a church in Nashville?"

"Yes, but it's not quite the same since my foster mother passed away a couple of months ago. I always sat with her. I've been feeling a little at loose ends lately. I'm hoping this trip will help me to figure things out."

He glanced at her, compassion flickering in his eyes.

"You came to the right place. Whenever I need to get away from it all, I head to the mountains."

Another half mile down the road, an impressive blue Victorian house with white trim came into view. The charming home looked more like a country inn than a farmhouse.

"That's Grace Holbrook's farm," David said as they crossed a bridge over a creek, probably the same stream that ran behind Owen's barn and through his cornfield.

Kate recalled the deputy mentioning the feud between the Holbrooks and Bentleys and noted the stark contrast between the stately farm and her recollection of Owen's old barn and the ash heap remains of where he had lived.

Beyond the Holbrook house was an empty fenced-in meadow with a large white barn behind it. "Looks like Grace has taken Clementine for a ride," David casually remarked.

"Clementine?"

"That's her palomino. Grace Holbrook is quite a horsewoman."

They traveled a little farther, and Kate pointed to the rundown shack across the road up ahead. "Whose place is that?"

"Virgil Crane's."

Still steaming about the shooting incident, a part of her wanted to stop and give Mr. Crane a piece of her mind.

"It ought to be condemned, if you ask me," David continued, "but Virgil's been living there all his life."

David slowed his truck as they approached it, and Kate stared at the place. "Why doesn't he fix it up?"

"Lack of funds, I imagine. He lives off the land, hunting and fishing. Our acting mayor, Lester Crane, is his nephew."

"Wouldn't the mayor want to help his uncle out?" she asked, remembering that David didn't know about her business with Lester concerning Owen's estate.

David's eyes shifted to her for a moment. "They aren't

that close. Frankly, I think Lester is a little ashamed of him."

"Why—because he's poor?"

"That, and Virgil is sort of a hillbilly. You see, Lester is running for mayor in the election next month, which requires him to hobnob with the upper crust campaign donors."

"Tyler's Glen has an upper crust?" She didn't mean to sound so surprised.

He turned his head slightly. "If you count the handful of executives who work at the chemical plant in town—and Joe Campbell." His prickly tone conveyed his disregard for the town's elite, especially Joe.

They passed Virgil's house, and David pointed out Owen's farm on the other side of the road. "The man you asked me about yesterday whose place burned down. That's where he lived."

Kate turned to look out her window, not letting on that she'd been there earlier. She was glad Rick had already towed her uncle's pickup away. That would have been a dead giveaway. "Were you friends with him?"

David reacted to the question as if he'd tasted sour milk. "Not exactly. His land used to be owned by my family. Eleven years ago, when we fell on hard times, my father went to Owen to borrow money."

"Did he loan it to him?"

"Owen told him he'd buy his land, with the understanding that when my father could afford to repay him with interest, he'd sell it back to him." David released a prolonged breath. "A few months later, my dad inherited money and land from his aunt, but when he went to Owen to buy the property back, he refused to sell it to him. I was hoping to bid on it at Owen's estate auction, but now that doesn't look like it's going to happen."

Kate remained silent, feeling conflicted. This was obviously not the time to tell him she was the reason for the auction being cancelled. And as much as she sympathized with David, she couldn't let her feelings affect her decisions regarding her uncle's estate. She came to get answers about what had happened to her uncle, not get sidetracked with someone else's problems.

An eighteen-wheeler with Rydeklan Chemicals written on the side blew past them from the opposite direction.

"Those truckers think they own the road," David muttered. "This town hasn't been the same since the chemical plant moved in."

He turned into the next driveway on the right and drove up a hill. At the top stood the mountain home that Kate had admired earlier. David parked his truck in the driveway in front of the two-car garage.

"This is where you live?" she asked, surprised.

He turned off the engine and rested his forearms on the steering wheel, gazing at the custom home. "Welcome to my man-cave. What do you think?"

"It looks more like a man-*villa* to me."

The corner of his mouth turned up modestly. "Come on, I'll give you a tour."

When Kate opened her door, a lively gray dog jumped up to greet her.

"Smokey, get down!" David firmly told him.

The dog reluctantly obeyed.

Kate laughed and petted the border collie mix. "It's nice to meet you, Smokey."

David strode to her side of the pickup and whistled the dog away so she could get out. "Please excuse Smokey. He gets excited when we have company."

Taking her backpack and slinging it over her shoulder, Kate went with David to the front yard where tall maple trees dressed in orange, gold, and red shaded the well-groomed lawn. While David called his friend Pete about giving him a ride home from the park, she admired the natural wood exterior of the house and its large picture windows, imagining their spectacular view of the mountains and valley.

"It's all set," he said when he ended the call.

"Great. Thanks for doing that. It seems like a lot of trouble."

"Not when it's the perfect day for a ride."

Perfect, all right. She caught herself gazing too long at his face and redirected her attention to his home. "One day when I buy a house, I want one like this."

His sideways glint conveyed curiosity. "When will that be?"

"Not for a while. I can barely afford my little condo and Miata." The thought of her wrecked car elicited a wistful sigh.

"I know the feeling. That's why I had to build it myself in my spare time, but it took forever. I only finished it last year."

"You mean—when you weren't farming, or at town council meetings, or fighting fires or being a Good Samaritan—you built this? No wonder it took you so long to finish it." She sent him a teasing glance. "Do you think you could find the time to build me one too?"

He chuckled softly. "Maybe, if you built it here. Nashville's too long of a haul."

His appealing tone and the playful spark in his gaze almost convinced her to do it, but the idea of moving to Tyler's Glen was not part of her plan. *Stay focused, Kate.* "I was wondering, if Owen bought your family's property, where did you get this land to build on?"

"It was my aunt's."

"This is part of the property she left to your father?"

He answered with a nod. "It's not nearly as much land as we lost to Owen, but it's enough for me to make a living." He peered at the afternoon sky. "If we're going to make it to the campground tonight, the tour of the inside will have to wait. Let's head to the barn."

The rich scent of fresh-cut grass and garden herbs spiced the air when they came to the spacious yard behind the house. The generous deck off the back was fully outfitted with an oversized grill and patio furniture. Kate looked around, noticing the brown barn and cornfields beyond. She pointed to the orange mounds in the garden on the opposite side of the lawn. "Are those pumpkins? They're huge."

He gestured for her to follow. "Come on. I'll show you."

When she caught up to him, he opened a small gate for her to enter the sizable garden. She stared at the giant pumpkins. "How did you grow them so big?"

"My father taught me. It's something we did together."

After David finished showing her around the garden, he stopped at a shed and picked up two halters with lead ropes and escorted Kate to a fenced-in meadow near the barn where two horses grazed. "Come on, I'll introduce you to Samson and Delilah."

She walked with him to the fence.

When he called to the horses, a magnificent chestnut whinnied and galloped toward them. A gray mare followed closely behind. David spoke to each of them like children, petting their necks and patting their faces. They returned his affection with low, contented nickers.

"Feel free to pet them," he told her. "They're friendly."

She gently let Delilah sniff her hand. The horse then allowed Kate to stroke her face.

"Looks like Delilah has taken a liking to you."

Kate smiled, drawn to the docile creature. "She's beautiful." Samson nudged her with his nose, not wanting to be left out. "I see how Samson got his name, but Delilah for the mare? It doesn't exactly fit her sweet personality."

David rubbed Samson's face, then slipped on the halter. "I'm not the one who named them. I bought them from Ruby Henderson after her father passed away." He opened the fence and gestured for Kate to go with him inside. "We'd better saddle them up before it gets any later."

She followed as David led Samson and Delilah to the barn. Inside, she helped him groom the horses with curry combs, and she watched as he skillfully cleaned their hooves and fastened their bridles and saddles. The animals towered over his tall frame. They looked so huge now, Kate wondered why she had ever decided to do this.

"When was the last time you rode?" he asked.

"In high school. A friend of mine let me ride hers sometimes, but they were more like ponies—not nearly as large as Samson and Delilah." She reached for her backpack to secure it over her shoulders.

"Let me help you with that." David moved behind her and lifted her pack for her to slip her arms through the straps, then he eased it over her shoulders. She tossed him an appreciative smile. Suddenly aware of his closeness, warmth coursed through her, flooding her cheeks. As she slowly faced him, his brilliant smile and the glimmer in his gaze made it impossible to focus on anything else, much less horseback riding.

He stepped away and commenced giving Kate a quick refresher on how to ride. Afterward, he handed her Delilah's reins. "It'll be safer if we wait until we cross the road to ride the horses." Then he proceeded to lead Samson out of the barn and corral with Kate behind him, leading the mare.

When they came around the house to the driveway where David had parked his truck, Kate called out to him. "What about my luggage and camping gear?"

He stopped and looked over his shoulder. "I'll drop them off to you tonight when I return for the horses in my truck."

They continued leading the horses to the edge of the road, where David stopped with Samson. Kate hung back with Delilah a few feet behind them until he confirmed the coast was clear. After looking both ways and listening for a moment, he clicked his tongue, signaling Samson to cross with him. Before they could take another step, a loud horn bellowed from an eighteen-wheeler careening around the curve.

Ears pinned, Samson reared on his hind legs and squealed.

"Whoa!" David cried, holding firm to his horse's reins to restrain him.

Kate gripped Delilah's reins as the truck zipped past. The mare snorted and backed farther away from the road, but refrained from bolting. Relieved, Kate rewarded her with an affirming rub on the neck. "Good girl."

"It's okay, Samson," David said, coaxing his horse with a calming voice. "Take it easy."

"That truck came out of nowhere." Kate's heart was still thumping in her chest.

"No, I know where it came from."

From the slight edge in his voice, she made an educated guess. "The chemical plant?"

He nodded, his jovial mood subdued by the incident. Once they'd crossed the road, however, his pleasant nature had returned, and he addressed her with an eager grin. "Ready?"

She gave a confident nod, not letting on that she had a few butterflies. But was that due to the horse, or him standing so close? She turned to Delilah and stuck her left foot in the stirrup, reaching for the saddle horn. When David's strong hands circled her waist to boost her, she hesitated. As a marshal, she took pride in being able to hold her own. She looked over her shoulder to protest, but his guileless face changed her mind.

"There you go," he said, gently hoisting her until she could swing her leg over and settle into the saddle. She had strained her shoulder a bit as she mounted, but David's easygoing, accommodating manner relaxed her, and she found herself appreciating the special attention of her attractive tutor.

Her shoulder injury and the reckless trucker soon faded from Kate's thoughts as they traveled along the trail toward the park. The rocking rhythm of her horse's gait and the scenic, tranquil countryside in the shadow of the ancient, blue-gray mountains soothed and delighted her. The leisurely ride and stimulating banter with David provided a refreshing diversion from the disturbing recent developments weighing on her mind.

They crossed a wooden bridge over a creek and turned right at the fork, heading toward the brilliant foliage of the park. Soon after entering the forest, the trail became more rugged as they continued traveling the southeastern route.

As the horses stepped over scattered branches from the storm the previous night, the car accident resurfaced in Kate's memory. But her peaceful surroundings and the lovely day lessened its emotional impact.

They had reached a wider stretch of the trail and David slowed Samson so Kate could ride beside him. He casually ran his fingers along a low-hanging fir branch as they rode together. "What is it you do in Nashville, Kate?"

The question unsettled her. If she told him she was a deputy marshal, he might put two and two together. With his past history with Owen, she couldn't let down her guard. Not until she knew who had killed her uncle. "I try to make it a practice not to talk about work while I'm on vacation," she breezily replied.

His brow furrowed for a moment. "Not a bad rule, I guess. Is the subject of camping off limits too?"

"No, but I've only been once, four years ago in the Cascade Mountains."

"That's it?"

She shrugged and nodded. "A mother bear attacked our

camp, and I had to be rescued from a botched river crossing. Other than that, I had a great time." Her dry tone drew a chuckle from him. "I've been wanting to give it another shot to see what camping is like without the drama."

David turned his head slightly. "At least you survived."

"Yeah, thanks to Buck pulling me out of the river." She caught the curious look on David's face. "He's a colleague— I mean, ex-boyfriend." She didn't want to rehash the subject of work again.

"Oh." David was silent for a moment. "When did you two break up?"

"A few months ago, but it should have been much earlier. I knew for a long time there wasn't a future for us, but he was a good friend, and I didn't want to lose that."

The birds singing in the trees and the clopping of Samson and Delilah's hooves filled the pensive silence after her disclosure about Buck. She realized it was the first time she'd thought about him since she'd left Nashville. They came to a wooded lot with an old barn and rustic cabins. Kate and David dismounted their horses near the entrance.

"What is this place?" she asked.

"It's a church camp. I thought you might enjoy a short hike to the falls."

"Absolutely!" And her injured shoulder could use a break from holding the reins so long. She followed with Delilah as David led Samson to a sturdy-looking fence rail to tether the horses. Kate looked around at the boarded-up buildings. "This looks like a nice place. Why is it closed?"

"It needs repairs. I've been volunteering my time, helping when I can. The owner is a friend and has had a hard time making ends meet. He's thinking about selling it. I hope it doesn't come to that."

"Maybe you can buy it one day and fix it up?" she said in a cheerful tone.

He returned a wistful grin. "I wish I could, but I don't

have that kind of money."

"What's it like when the camp is open?"

"We take the kids fishing and hiking, coach basketball, teach Bible studies, things like that."

"Sounds like fun." The scenic, peaceful retreat was a far cry from her life on the streets in her youth. "I wish I could have come to a camp like this when I was younger."

David led her to a foot trail behind the barn. They hiked through the forest until they reached a viewpoint that overlooked a deep canyon with a waterfall on the other side. The cascading waters tumbled down the cliff wall into a pool far below, forming a translucent rainbow from the watery mist. If the Garden of Eden had been set in the Smokies, Kate imagined it would look something like this beautiful, secluded place.

She spoke to David while admiring the falls. "It's so peaceful, like you can hear God speaking in the water's roar."

David leaned against the rail, staring at the picturesque scene. "Coming here always helps me clear my head and think things through. This is where I found the Lord—or I should say, where He found me. When my father died, this place made me feel closer to God, and somehow I knew things would work out eventually."

His spiritual disclosure caused her to contemplate her own plight. Suddenly, she became aware of the piney scent in the breeze and the birds singing. A squirrel came looking for a handout. She shrugged apologetically, wishing she had brought one of her granola bars as he scampered off. Being in nature like this raised the question that had been plaguing her soul lately. *What is Your plan for my life now, Lord?* She longed to hear His answer in the rumble of the falls.

Crossing her arms, she breathed in the refreshing air. "I've been feeling kind of lost since my foster mom passed away."

He lowered his head and nodded in understanding.

After staring at the pool of water below the falls, he lifted his gaze to her. "What happened to your birth parents?"

She unfolded her arms and moved next to the rail for a better view of the canyon. "My mother died of complications from a stroke, following surgery . . . I was fourteen. Before she died, my father left for work one morning and never came home."

David faced her with an incredulous look. "You mean he abandoned you and your mother?"

The painful memory seemed like a lifetime ago. So much had changed since then, and Jim and Rose had been so good to her she couldn't feel sorry for herself. "I think he was looking for an excuse to leave. Still, it wasn't easy. After he was gone, we had no money to pay the rent or buy food. When my mother passed away, I became homeless and lived on the streets. The brother of someone I knew offered me a job, and I jumped at the opportunity, no questions asked. It started out okay. Running errands, delivering packages and things like that. Then I became a lookout . . ."

David frowned uneasily and cleared his throat. "What sort of a lookout?"

Finding it hard to meet his searching gaze, she focused on the falls instead. It had been years ago, but it was still difficult to talk about. "I warned the drug dealers and prostitutes when police were in the area."

After a brief silence, David shifted his stance as if he wanted to comfort her. She stepped away, longing for the solace of his embrace, but not his pity. And with her uncle's death hanging over her, she didn't want anything to hinder her purpose in coming.

He paused and addressed her in a quiet voice. "What happened?"

She released a muffled groan from the agonizing memory. "One day, I got very sick and was late to my post on the corner. I didn't find out until later that there had been a sting operation going on. Several top people in the gang were arrested. Eventually they arrested the kingpin, Ralph Tourreni too." Her former gang leader never forgot when he thought someone had betrayed him. After he was sent away to prison, the ruthless thug had sent her notes via his flunkies, warning that he would kill her when he got out. It had been five years since she'd last heard from him. She didn't know if that was good or bad, but at least the threatening notes had stopped.

"Did you get arrested?"

She shook her head. "But I knew it was only a matter of time before Raptor—that was Ralph's street name—would take his revenge on me. Eventually, I took refuge in a local shelter downtown. That's where I met Jim and Rose Tucker. They brought me home and kept me safe."

"Your foster parents sound like great people."

Thinking about them filled her with profound sadness, but also gratitude for their love and support. "I don't know why I'm telling you all this," she said, wiping away a tear. "I try not to think about my past too much, and what I had to do to survive."

"I'm sure losing your foster mom is bringing back a lot of memories."

Acknowledging the truth in what he'd said brought her peace about her recent struggle to move on after Rose's death. "If it hadn't been for the Tuckers, I wouldn't have known about God's love and grace." David's eyes reflected compassion as if he understood the pain of loss she was going through. "What about you?" she asked. "Do you have any family left?"

"Both of my parents are gone too."

"No siblings?"

David's jaw tightened and he looked away. "A brother, but I haven't seen him in years."

"Oh." From his reaction, she decided not to probe

further, but she wondered how a man as responsible and caring as David could become estranged from his own brother.

"It's getting late, and we've got one more stop on our tour."

Her spirits lifted with anticipation. "What's left?"

"Cades Cove."

When they returned to the church camp, Kate was curious about the old barn. "What's in there?"

David gestured for her to follow. "I'll show you." They stopped at the door, and he entered the combination for the security lock. "Unfortunately, we've had a few problems with theft and vandals. The lower windows kept getting broken so I boarded them up, along with the other entrances. Rick Travis helped me install a stronger, more secure door and this new combination lock."

"Rick volunteers here too?" she asked.

"When he can spare the time. He's our fishing coach."

Once they went inside, David flipped on the lights.

The loft had been removed and the main area had been converted into a good-sized recreation center. Though the lower windows and doors were boarded, a row of windows had been installed high above, close to the crossbeams and rafters, illuminating the place with natural light.

A variety of basketballs, soccer balls, and footballs were stored in bins on the worn wooden floor. The rest of the space was filled with well-used gym mats, basketball goals, and other athletic gear.

"As you can see, we could use new equipment. We also need a new roof before summer, but right now funds are pretty scarce." David opened a tall cabinet. It contained a collection of archery bows and arrows, badminton rackets, fishing rods and tackle, rope, and croquet sets.

Seeing the archery equipment piqued Kate's interest. "Are you an archer?"

"Basketball is more my speed."

"I actually competed in high school and college. Jim encouraged me. It was something we did together, like you and your dad with the pumpkins."

"That must have been fun. Bow hunting is big around here, but I prefer farming to hunting, I guess."

David secured the building before they left, then they remounted their horses and headed into the park. He led her past the campground where she had reservations to the eastern edge of the picturesque valley known as Cades Cove. It was already six p.m. and the crowd of people visiting the popular tourist destination had dwindled as dinner time approached, leaving the deer to graze freely in the lush, grassy meadow.

David halted Samson and waited for Kate to ride up beside him.

She gazed at the canopy of colorful trees along the trail and the misty mountains surrounding the valley. "It's so beautiful here."

He stared at the pastoral view with a wistful look. "Believe it or not, this was once a thriving farm settlement in the 1800s. My great-great-great grandparents came to Tyler's Glen from North Carolina around the time Cades Cove was settled."

"You feel a special connection to this place, don't you?"

"I guess it's in my blood." He glanced at his watch. "It's getting late. We'll have to save the eleven-mile Cades Cove loop for another day."

She liked the prospect of another outing with him in the park. It must be nice to come from a family with such deep roots. No wonder Owen's land meant so much to David. It had been in his family for generations. She couldn't blame him for wanting it back—and now, with her uncle gone, she was the only person left who stood in his way.

CHAPTER FIVE

KATE RODE BACK WITH DAVID ALMOST a mile beyond her campground and past the picnic area to Anthony Creek Horse Camp, where he could hitch his horses until he returned for them with his truck and trailer. Then he would drop her off at her campsite on his way home.

The small wooded horse camp consisted of three primitive sites and a vault toilet. Only one other horse occupied the open hitching stalls when they arrived—a beautiful palomino.

"That looks like Grace's horse, Clementine," David said as he dismounted.

Kate slid off Delilah with her backpack and gave him the reins. While he tethered the horses in the stalls, the aroma of steak grilling stirred Kate's appetite after the long ride. She traced the scent to a fire pit near a tent pitched on one of the sites.

A silver-haired woman, dressed in blue jeans and a plaid shirt, emerged from the tent. She looked at them and waved. "Hi, there." Her gaze traveled from Kate to David. "I didn't expect to see you here today, David."

He walked to Kate's side. "I thought that was Clementine in the stall."

"Yes, I decided to take her for a ride while the weather is still nice." The woman's eyes sparkled at Kate. "I see you've brought a friend with you."

Kate went with David to Grace's site. He stopped to gather a few fallen branches in their path and laid them next to the small stack of wood by the fire pit. "Kate, this is my neighbor, Grace Holbrook."

"Nice to meet you, Katherine," Grace said in a hospitable Southern voice.

"Actually, I go by Kate," she gently corrected.

Grace chuckled and shook her head. "You remind me of my grandson. His name is Frederick, a perfectly good name, but he insists on being called Rick." Then she took a moment to study Kate more closely. "You look very familiar. Do I know you?"

Kate was doubtful. "I don't think so. I'm not from Tyler's Glen."

"She's planning to stay at Cades Cove Campground," David said. "I found her in the middle of the storm last night—"

Grace raised her hands in the air. "Oh my, wasn't that something? My power went off and didn't come on again until early this morning."

"I hit a tree on my way to the park," Kate told her.

The older woman frowned with concern. "I'm sorry to hear that. Are you all right?"

"I will be. Mostly, I'm sore from the seatbelt and airbag. Under my makeup, I have raccoon eyes."

"It sounds like the Good Lord was looking out for you."

Kate acknowledged Grace's comment with a respectful nod. Despite everything that had happened so far, at least she hadn't been seriously hurt. She tried to focus on that and being thankful instead of letting the accident and the shooter get to her.

Grace addressed David. "What happened at the town council meeting today? I wanted to go, but had an appointment with Doc Granger."

"You didn't miss much—only more speculation and rumors about what happened to Owen."

"So tragic. Of course, people are upset. Owen wasn't my favorite person, but no one should die like that."

Kate remembered Deputy Travis's comment about the

feud between the Holbrooks and Bentleys. At least Grace didn't want Owen dead. Harlan's disclosure that her uncle was stabbed before the fire made Kate suspect the explosion had been a ruse to cover up the murder. Until the mystery behind who did it was solved, the speculation would continue and make it more uncomfortable for her when the town learned she was Owen's relative and sole heir.

David stepped closer to the steaks and foil-covered potatoes roasting in the coals, and took a deep, appreciative sniff. "Are you planning to feed an army, Grace?"

She glanced at the grill and laughed. "I invited Rick and Harlan to join me, but they both called after I put the meat on the grill and said they couldn't make it."

"You don't mean Rick and Harlan Travis?" Kate asked.

"Why, yes. Harlan is my son-in-law and Rick is my grandson. Do you know them?"

She kept forgetting how small Tyler's Glen was compared to a big city like Nashville, and how often people's paths crossed. She could appreciate the advantages of a close-knit community, but as Nadine had pointed out, there was also a downside when you wanted a fresh start. "Deputy Travis took my accident report, and Rick towed my car into his shop."

"He also loaned her Owen's old pickup," David added.

Grace's mouth fell open. "*The classic?* What did he want in return?"

"He's going to buy what's left of my Miata from the salvage yard and rebuild it." Kate missed her little sports car. Maybe she should buy it back from Rick after his overhaul project. "I think I got the better end of the deal—though the truck is in his shop for repairs, and I'm without wheels again."

David tilted his head toward Kate. "You never told me what happened to it."

She hesitated, still not ready to divulge her relationship

with Owen to David or Grace. The woman was a Holbrook after all and Kate was technically a Bentley. She didn't want to get in the middle of a family feud tonight after everything that had happened at Owen's place earlier. "Oh, a blown-out tire, and a few other things were busted on it." While that was true, Kate was afraid she hadn't been very convincing.

The older woman paused for a moment and exchanged doubtful looks with David. "That's surprising, with all the time Owen and Rick spent restoring it."

David's discerning gaze lingered on Kate as he spoke to Grace. "What about Julianna? Couldn't she come?"

Kate was glad he had changed the subject, but from the curious flicker in his eyes, she suspected he still had questions about her story.

"Oh, she's never been much of a horsewoman or a camper. She might break a nail." Grace rolled her eyes, and her exaggerated expression made Kate giggle. The woman raised her index finger toward her. "Now you, on the other hand, look like a natural-born equestrian to me."

"Hardly," Kate replied, "but I am getting the hang of it."

Grace gestured toward the grill. "Since you're both here, why don't you join me for dinner? As you can see, I have plenty."

Kate exchanged eager looks with David. "Sounds better than the canned stew I packed in my luggage. But what about your friend who's coming to pick you up, David?"

"Thanks for reminding me." He checked the time on his watch. "I need to meet Pete Logan at the picnic area in a few minutes." He turned to Grace to explain. "Pete's giving me a lift home. I'm afraid I'll have to pass on dinner, but you two enjoy yourselves. I'll be back for my horses in a bit. Kate, I'll help you pitch your tent since it'll be dark when I return."

Kate suppressed a sigh as he walked away, wishing he could stay. Grace's voice drew her attention.

"Pull up a log and have a seat. I didn't have room for my

camp chairs on Clementine." The woman took out two plastic plates and utensils from her bag to serve the steaks and potatoes. She shook her head at Kate. "I should say, it's better than canned stew." She reached in her bag again and retrieved a bottle of water for each of them.

Kate sat on the log. She already felt comfortable with Grace. The woman's bright eyes, combined with her zest and youthful appearance, belied her golden years. "I've seen your house from the road. It's very nice."

"Thank you. I hope you'll come visit me." Grace stared at Kate for a moment, causing her to wonder if the bruises from the car accident were that obvious. "You're very pretty, you know. Young men must be swarming to you like bees to honey."

The woman's bluntness amused her. "Not exactly."

"How long will you be camping?"

"I took a couple of weeks off from work."

"Two weeks in a tent?" Grace scrunched her face. "You should come stay with me. I have plenty of room."

Touched by her offer, Kate smiled politely. "Thanks, but I couldn't."

"Why not? I'd enjoy the company, not to mention it would be much more comfortable than staying in a tent."

The heat from the glowing coals warmed Kate as the temperature began to drop with the setting sun. "It's very nice of you to offer, but I don't mind camping, Mrs. Holbrook. Besides, I already made reservations at the campground."

"Should you change your mind, you can always cancel them for a nominal fee."

Shortly after they had finished dinner, David backed his trailer into the camp to load his horses.

Kate was helping Grace clean up and took her flashlight from her backpack to meet him as he exited his truck. "Too bad you couldn't stay. You missed a delicious meal."

"Sure. Rub it in." He flashed her a teasing grin.

She realized it had been a long time since she'd had such a good time. "Hey, thanks again for letting me borrow Delilah and riding here with me today."

"Anytime you want to go riding, give me a call. I'm always looking for a good excuse."

"I'll keep that in mind, but hopefully Rick will have the truck fixed soon."

Grace strode up, interrupting them. "I thought of something. Why don't you camp here on my site with me, Kate? I'm allowed up to six people."

Kate considered the kind offer. She would prefer to stay here with Grace overnight, but she had a reservation at the other campground.

A brilliant smile lit up David's face. "That's a great idea. I can stop by the campground office on my way out and let them know to cancel your other reservation so you can get a refund."

He won Kate over with his enthusiasm. She lifted her shoulders. "Why not?"

"Excellent!" Grace's eyes glittered in the sun's last rays. "With that settled, I'll leave you two alone while I put a couple more logs on the fire."

David unloaded the camping gear from his truck and helped Kate pitch her tent. They stowed her luggage inside it. When they had finished setting up her camp, he stared at the twilight sky. "It's getting late. I should be going." But the intensity of his gaze told her he wanted to stay.

She strolled with him to the horses in the nearby stalls.

Stopping to untether the mare, he turned to Kate. "I could leave Delilah here overnight so you can ride her in the morning,"

Kate reached to pet the horse's face, and Delilah nickered at her. "No, I think she's better off with you. You know how to care for her."

He gazed at Kate in the dusky shadows as the hooting of an owl reverberated through the cool night air. "I'm glad you're staying with Grace. You two can keep each other company tonight."

Though she was used to being alone, his concern was endearing. "You don't need to worry about me. I'm tougher than I look."

"In that case," he said, handing her Delilah's reins, "maybe you can give me a hand installing a new roof on the barn at the church camp."

Kate shook her head at his suggestion as a smile tugged at her lips. "Nice try. I may be tough, but I'm still on vacation."

His shoulders dropped in mock disappointment. "Just my luck."

They led the gelding and mare to the horse trailer. Before loading Samson, David opened his saddlebag and pulled out a park brochure. "Here's a trail map so you don't get lost. I'll text you the number for my friend Pete, who's a park ranger."

"Thanks," she replied. His concern for her well-being warmed her heart like those coals in the fire pit had warmed her body.

"Oh, by the way, make sure you stow all your trash in the bear-proof garbage cans. This place is notorious for bears."

Another warning about the bears. Ever since her adventure in the North Cascades, the thought of bears and river rapids always made her a little uneasy. "Thanks for reminding me."

After David left with the horses, Kate joined Grace by the campfire and sat beside her. "I'm surprised we're the only ones here tonight."

"This place is usually packed every weekend in the fall," Grace said. "But a lot of campers leave by Monday to go back to work. That's why I came today. I was hoping it would be quiet like this." She gazed at the stars. "Beautiful clear night. Perfect for stargazing—and for roasting marshmallows." Pointing to the small duffle bag between her and Kate, Grace beamed with an enticing look. "You'll find all you need in there, graham crackers and chocolate too." She took a sip from her camp mug. "I also made some tea that helps me sleep. You're welcome to try it."

"Great, thanks." Kate began searching for the s'mores ingredients in the bag. "Too bad Rick and Deputy Travis couldn't come."

Grace took a stick and poked the coals. "They're both very busy these days. So is my daughter, Julianna." She reached over and patted Kate's hand. "But I'm glad you're here. It's nice to have company tonight. I wish David could have stayed too."

So did Kate. Her ride with him that afternoon had cheered her up after the disturbing shooting incident at Owen's place.

"One day, that young man will make some lucky young woman a fine husband," Grace continued, in a less-than-subtle tone.

Kate pierced her marshmallow on a skewer while Grace extolled David's virtues. "Speaking of David, he told me about his family's land dispute with Owen Bentley."

"Oh, yes. David's never gotten over his father selling their farm to him. I think he blames himself for it."

"Why would he blame himself?"

"Well, it all started about twelve years ago, when David was in college."

Kate held her marshmallow over the coals. "I didn't know he went to college."

"Yes, he had a scholarship to Vanderbilt. I still remember his father, Noah, boasting that his boy was going to be a doctor someday. Unfortunately, those were lean years for farming. Noah had an especially hard time of it with

David away at college. Then his younger son Danny got into trouble with the law . . . Noah spent every last dime he had paying for Danny's legal defense. When his son was convicted and sent to prison, it hit Noah hard. Not long after, he got sick with pneumonia. David left college and came home to help him and take care of things on the farm, but Noah was too far gone by then. He died shortly after David returned."

The thought of David giving up his dream of becoming a doctor to look after his father made Kate want to cry. She thought of her own mother and how difficult it had been taking care of her by herself. "Did David ever return to college?"

"No. His father's death devastated him. After that, he lost interest. I think he always felt responsible for what happened because he was away at school instead of at home helping his father with the farm and the legal bills. Of course, it wasn't his fault. Now that Owen's gone, I'm sure David will try to buy the land back."

The fact that David still didn't know she was Owen's niece hovered over Kate like a dark cloud. It was only a matter of time before the whole town found out. But how would he take the news? "Is David's brother still in prison?"

"Word is he was released a couple of months ago. After all the trouble he caused his family, I don't expect he'll ever come around here again." Grace pointed to Kate's skewer. "Your marshmallow is burning."

Kate looked at the gooey, charred blob at the end of her stick. "Uh-oh." She pulled it from the flames and gingerly slid it off the tip of her skewer onto her chocolate-laden Graham cracker.

While she carefully picked the black parts off, Grace continued talking. "Noah sold a small tract of land to Joe Campbell's father too."

Surprised, Kate glanced at Grace. "Joe? I met him

today."

Grace's eyes flickered with interest. "Where?"

Kate licked her fingers after sandwiching the marshmallow between the crackers. "At Bubba's Diner. I was having lunch, and he came over and introduced himself."

"Humph. I bet he did."

Having met Joe, Kate could understand Grace's strong reaction. "I take it you don't like him very much."

Grace rolled her eyes. "Let me give you a little friendly advice about Joe. He goes after every pretty face he sees. As a result, he has a string of ex-girlfriends angrier than a bunch of wild boars in a porcupine den. I wouldn't want you to become one of them."

"Thanks for the heads up. I recently broke up with a guy who had a similar problem, and I don't want a repeat. You were saying he also owns land that used to belong to David's family?"

The glow of the coals seemed to make the lines in Grace's face appear deeper. "Arnold Campbell left the land to Joe with his estate when he died five years ago. Needless to say, there's no love lost between Joe and David because of it either. It's a shame too, because they were best friends when they were kids."

Kate pictured how David might react if she sold Owen's property to Joe. He'd probably never speak to her again—and who could blame him? "I take it Joe won't sell the property to David."

"No, he's building an empire. Some of his property borders the back side of the Bentley farm and mine, next to the old Henderson place. Willis Henderson passed away a year ago and left his house and property to his daughter, Ruby, who lives in Florida now."

Kate recalled the name. "The woman David got Samson and Delilah from?"

"That's right. Anyway, Ruby asked Joe to look after the property for her. In exchange, he hunts there from time to time. He owns more property than anyone else in the county, most of it purchased through bank foreclosures. He's pretty unpopular around here because of it, but it's made him rich. We're all still angry about him selling a good tract of farm land to that awful chemical company instead of another farmer." Grace's harsh tone matched the disgusted look on her face.

Kate savored a bite of her s'more, then decided she'd better change the subject before Grace had a stroke. "I'm curious about David. Since he's such a great guy, why is he still single?"

Switching the conversation to David again seemed to have worked. Grace appeared more relaxed now, and her voice softened when she spoke. "I think it's because he needs a wife who's interested in more than farming and canning tomatoes—not that there's anything wrong with those things, but there aren't many women around here who are interested in anything outside of Tyler's Glen. And if they were, they probably wouldn't be content to stay here. They would rather live someplace more exciting—like Nashville."

Finishing the last morsel of her treat, Kate thought of Nadine and her big dreams of going to Nashville and writing country music.

Grace yawned. "My, it's getting late. I think it's time for me to turn in. Aren't you sleepy yet?"

"I want to enjoy this warm fire a little longer, but you go ahead."

The older woman slowly rose to her feet. "Well, goodnight. If you need anything, give me a holler. I'm right next door."

After Grace disappeared inside her tent, Kate went to her own and found her mug. When she'd returned, she poured herself a cup of Grace's tea and sat next to the fire ring to savor the remaining warmth of the coals.

Staring at the dying embers, she thought about everything the woman had told her about Joe, David, and David's brother, Danny. She would never have guessed her Good Samaritan had such a troubled past. It made her sad. She wanted to believe that somewhere out there a normal family existed without the pain and heartache both she and David had experienced. Maybe that was too much to hope for, even in Tyler's Glen. Beneath the pleasant facade, the town appeared to be smoldering with conflict and tension, ready to explode.

Kate awoke in the middle of the night, certain that she had heard a strange noise. She rubbed her eyes, fighting grogginess, and started to wonder if the noise had been real or a dream. *What had Grace put in that tea?*

A moonlit shadow fell across her tent. Remembering David's warning about bears, Kate reached for her backpack to get her gun. Then the shadow morphed into a silhouette of a large buck with enormous antlers. She breathed a sigh of relief and released her pack.

Snuggled in her sleeping bag, she laughed at herself for overreacting. At least the deer had interrupted her vivid dream about a prowler invading her tent. She shuddered at the hazy vision of the man going through her things. The disturbing image prompted her to click on her flashlight to do a cursory scan of her belongings. Satisfied that all of her luggage and camping gear were there and undisturbed, she rolled over and closed her eyes, hoping the nightmare would not return.

CHAPTER SIX

THE SOUND OF BIRDS WOKE KATE much earlier than she had planned or wanted. She checked her cellphone. Six-thirty in the morning.

After unzipping her tent and popping her head through the flap, she detected faint hints of sunrise coloring the eastern sky. She quickly ducked back inside and slipped on a pair of hiking pants and a sweatshirt. Remembering the nine dollars change in the pocket of her jeans from when she'd bought the paper yesterday, she transferred the money from her folded jeans to her hiking pants, and went outside.

Grace was already tending a frying pan over the fire. "Good morning," she said in a chipper voice. "Breakfast is ready."

The aroma of bacon and fried eggs immediately fueled Kate's appetite as she took her seat on the log by the fire.

"What are your plans for today?" Grace asked as she filled Kate's plate and handed it to her.

Kate gazed at the clear blue sky above the trees. "I think I'll hike to Spence Field. The park brochure David gave me says it has a great view of the Smokies in North Carolina."

Grace nodded. "Perfect day for it."

"What about you?"

"My daughter, Julianna, is taking me shopping in Knoxville later today, so I need to head home right after breakfast."

"That sounds like fun."

The woman turned up her nose slightly. "I'm not much of a shopper myself, but Julianna loves it."

Since Grace had to leave early, they quickly finished their

breakfast, and Kate helped her take down her tent and pack Clementine for the ride home.

"Are you sure you're okay camping by yourself?" Grace asked, holding her horse's reins.

"I'll be fine."

"Well, you have an open invitation to stay with me if you change your mind." Grace mounted her horse and waved.

After the woman rode away, Kate checked the time on her cellphone. Eight. Still early enough to beat the tourists. Since she didn't have a vehicle to secure her belongings in, she decided to leave her tent and things as-is, with the exception of her wallet and backpack, which contained her gun, water bottle and a snack. She'd return for everything else after her hike. Then she'd deal with how to transport it all to the other campground later.

With her pack strapped over her shoulders, she headed toward the Anthony Creek Trail on foot. As she approached the trailhead, she spotted a majestic-looking buck before he leaped into the woods. Perhaps, the one shadowing her tent last night? It reminded her of the deer grazing in Cades Cove near sunset last evening, and thoughts of her ride there with David filled her with joy and anticipation. When would she see him again?

Five miles later, hiking at a good clip, she reached Spence Field at the Appalachian Trail junction. Stopping to rest from her vigorous hike, she shed her pack to retrieve her water bottle and a granola bar to eat while she enjoyed the spectacular view. From her grassy alpine meadow, Kate could see the rolling mountaintops far into the distance. The clear fall morning provided excellent visibility of the peaks splattered in a spectacle of color.

Kate took a seat on a fallen log and made herself at home, sipping water from her bottle while admiring the scenery. She lost track of time, thinking about everything Grace had told her last night, especially as it pertained to

David, as well as mulling over Owen's estate and what she would do with it.

"You've found my favorite spot."

She turned her head in the direction of the friendly male voice. The sight of David standing at the far end of her log bench quickened her pulse. "David? What are you doing here at this hour?"

"Sorry, I didn't mean to startle you. I thought you might need help moving to your new campsite, but since you weren't there, I decided to take a hike and get a jump on the tourists."

"Where's Samson?"

"At home with Delilah. I drove in." After a brief pause to look at the view, he focused on her. "May I join you?"

She gestured toward the unused portion of the tree trunk. "As Grace says, pull up a log."

Once he'd settled next to her, his eyes shifted in her direction. "You looked so serious a minute ago. What were you thinking about?"

She lifted a leaf from the ground, crumbling it in her hands. "If you could live anywhere, David, where would you go?"

He scratched his shoulder. "I haven't really given it much thought. But this is my home. It's where I belong. What about you?"

"That's the problem. I don't know where I belong anymore. Now that Rose is gone, I don't feel like I have much keeping me in Nashville anymore, except my job."

"What about here?"

"In Tyler's Glen?" She erupted in laughter.

His eyes glittered in the sunlight as he watched her. "What's so funny?"

She wondered why he couldn't see the irony himself. "For one thing, I'm not a farmer or an undertaker."

"Or a chemist?"

"Right. Besides which, bears and I don't get along," she said lightly.

"Bears?"

She scrunched her face with a silly look. "Last night, I thought I heard one. Then I saw the shadow of this huge buck, right next to my tent."

"At least he didn't snag it with his antlers. That would have been a real mess." David had a deadpan look on his face. "You know, I've lived here my whole life and have never once been attacked by a bear." He gestured toward the scenic peaks in the distance. "And when I look at those mountains, I can't imagine living anywhere else."

"It is beautiful here, and Tyler's Glen is a nice town. Maybe if I'd lived in a town like that when I was younger, I wouldn't have ended up on the streets."

His tone became wistful. "I wish I could say that everyone in Tyler's Glen has a roof over their head and food in their belly, but we have people struggling to get by too, even a few that are homeless. The lucky ones stay in the campground when they can, and the churches pay their camp fees. The town has plans to build a community outreach center to help them. Phase one is to establish a food bank."

That captured Kate's interest. "Wow, that's great."

"We also want to start a job training program to help people get on their feet, and maybe one day we'll add a shelter. Right now, we need a building and someone to organize and run the food bank—Interested?"

She knew he was only kidding, but the idea did intrigue her. "Thanks, but it would be a very long commute from Nashville. What about you?"

"I don't have the time right now. Plus, it would be better to have a person in charge who's been homeless and benefitted from a shelter and food bank, someone who understands how to meet those needs."

She clasped her hands together and inhaled the

mountain air. "I'm sure the right person will come along. Have you advertised it?"

"Not yet. We need to get a building first."

"You have one in mind?"

He nodded. "There's an old feed warehouse that hasn't been used in years. It's in the perfect location in town. There's only one problem—Joe Campbell owns it. His father left it to him when he passed away several years ago. The town has offered to buy it from him, but he's holding onto it, probably to sell to some rich developer."

Based on her first impression of Joe and her conversation with Grace about him, that didn't surprise her. But she didn't want to dwell on Joe right now. "You came all this way to make me a job offer?" She sent David a winsome look. "Grace told you I would be here, didn't she?"

He raised his finger as if to deny it, but then brought it to his chin. "Well, I might have run into her as I was leaving my house." He suddenly appeared a tad bashful. "I wanted to see you—I mean, to see how you're doing. Camping, that is."

The slip of his tongue amused her and gave her a slight thrill, but the nagging voice in the back of her mind poured ice water over her excitement. *Would he be spending so much time with her if he knew she was Owen's heir?*

A slight rustling in the bushes launched her to her feet. She clutched her backpack, ready to unzip the pocket with her gun. "What's that—a bear?"

Jingling came from the same direction.

David remained seated and calm. "Bears don't jingle."

A little dog with a cute terrier face and shaggy brown fur appeared from the bushes and loped toward Kate.

She set her pack on the ground and reached to pet him. "Hi, there, little guy."

His tail wagged a little, jingling his license tag.

"Hey, that's Owen's old dog, Buster." David rose to his feet. "Virgil's been looking for him."

Kate stared at the stray. "Look how thin he is. He's starving, poor little thing."

"He looks sickly too. We ought to take him to the vet."

"You think Buster has been living in the park all this time?"

He crouched down and extended his hand for the dog to sniff, then scratched him behind the ears. "Could be."

"Will anyone want to take him in?"

"Virgil might, but he can barely feed himself. I'd take him, but Smokey will probably get jealous."

Kate wistfully looked at Buster. "I've always wanted a dog."

"He seems pretty fond of you. Why don't you take him? But first, we'd better get him down to the campground before any rangers or bears see him. No dogs are allowed on the trails in the park. Bears and dogs are a dangerous combination."

"Oh, I didn't know." She stood and patted her thighs, coaxing the dog. "Come on, Buster, let's get out of here before a bear finds you."

The dog followed as Kate went with David down the trail. When they'd reached the junction with the Anthony Creek Trail, they turned left. They'd gone about a mile and a half along the path when Buster sniffed the ground and moseyed off into the woods.

"What's he doing?" Kate asked.

"He must smell something."

The dog approached them again and whined, urging them to follow, then loped away toward the laurel bushes.

"Buster!" Kate caught up to him a good distance from the trail, at the base of a tree where he was digging. "What's down there, huh?"

She bent to get a better look while Buster rooted deeper into the ground. He uncovered something red, and she crouched down and grabbed a stick to help him dig it up.

"What's going on?" David asked when he joined them.

"Buster's found something."

The persistent terrier had exposed a dirt-crusted material.

David stared at the discovery. "What is it?"

"I don't know, but I'm going to find out." Kate slipped off her backpack and unzipped a pocket. She removed a pair of rubber gloves she kept for emergencies and the paper bag filled with her lunch. She dumped the food in her pack. After tugging her gloves on, she bent to clear the rest of the dirt and leaves from what looked like a matted, stained towel. She carefully lifted the top layer—and gasped.

In the towel was a knife. And the dark red traces on the light fabric appeared to be blood.

"Is that what I think it is?" David's voice was low and ominous.

After the initial shock, Kate remembered that Owen had been stabbed to death, and the deputy sheriff was still looking for the weapon. *Did this knife kill her uncle?* It would explain why Buster had stayed in the park and led them here.

Something flew above and struck the tree directly overhead. Kate hit the ground, then peered up. It was an arrow lodged in the trunk.

David had ducked next to her, hidden by the laurel and rhododendron bushes. Another arrow pierced the tree where he'd been standing.

She turned and shouted. "U.S. Marshal! Drop your weapons and come out with your hands up!"

David shot her a confused stare. "Kate, what are you doing? Quit horsing around and let's get out of here."

"Shh, David. I've got this." Shedding her pack, she unzipped the pocket where she kept her Glock. Plunging her hand deep inside, she rummaged through the compartment. *Empty?* She peered into the vacant space. "My gun! It's missing."

"Your what?" David cried, his voice rising.

"Stay down. I'll explain later." The silence in the distance alarmed her. She shifted away right as an arrow flew past, striking another tree behind her.

Buster gave a low growl.

"U.S. Marshal! Stop shooting!" she yelled. Dodging again, she evaded a fourth dart that landed in the leaves a few feet away.

She quickly stuffed the towel with the knife in the open compartment of her backpack, then slung the pack over her shoulder. "Let's go." Staying low, she motioned to David to head toward the large boulder a short distance away.

He nodded in agreement.

After a mad dash, they took cover behind it.

Buster had followed them, and Kate grabbed him and pulled him close.

Cautiously, she peered around the rock in the direction of the shooter. They were in a hollow with brush too dense to see anything. Their assailant must have been shooting from a higher vantage point.

"What happened back there?" David whispered.

She took a deep breath to steady her pounding heart. "I think somebody is trying to kill us."

Another arrow struck the exposed part of her pack, barely missing her arm. She let go of Buster to yank it out. The red and green fletching at the end of the carbon shaft matched the ones in Owen's barn.

The dog roamed ahead of them.

"Buster!" Kate sprang from behind the rock and slipped her backpack over her shoulder, following the terrier.

David ran with her deeper into the woods.

A rustling sound halted her. To her right, she spotted a bear wandering through the forest, no more than twenty feet away. Her heart jolted with adrenaline as she pointed it out to David.

"Slowly back away and do what I do." He waved his hands and talked in low tones.

Kate mimicked his moves. Remembering David's warning about bears and dogs, she anxiously scanned the woods for Buster, but didn't see him. That was probably for the best right now. A few moments later, the bear lost interest and lumbered away.

An arrow zipped by and struck the tree next to Kate and David.

She ducked and glanced over her shoulder, searching for their attacker. A distant figure disappeared behind a tree, but she couldn't see a face.

David grabbed her hand. "Come on!"

As they bushwhacked through the forest farther down the mountain, Kate looked back and spotted the dog trotting behind. She stopped and called to him. "Hurry, Buster!" The little dog couldn't keep up.

"Kate!" David called as she lunged for the dog. He brushed past her and gently scooped Buster up, cradling him in his arms.

A rustling in the bushes urged her to flee. "Keep moving!" she warned David.

They slipped through the woods toward the sound of flowing water, dodging sinister-looking vines that dangled from tall trees above like a ghostly game of hide-and-seek. Having finally reached a trail by the creek, Kate heard the thud of a hiker's shoes approaching from the opposite direction. She and David crouched behind a thick bush and remained hidden until they could see who it was.

When a man in a park ranger uniform appeared, David rose and called out to him. "Pete! Man, am I glad to see you."

Pete Logan, David's park ranger friend, had escorted Kate and David down the rest of the trail to David's truck. From there, Pete drove Kate to the Cades Cove ranger station, while David took Buster to the vet in Tyler's Glen to get checked out.

As Pete drove, Kate searched her backpack and discovered that not only was her Glock missing, but so was her wallet that contained her credit and ATM cards, along with her money. All she had left was the nine dollars in her pants pocket. Now she was sure the foggy vision of the prowler in her tent had been more than a bad dream. It was as real as those arrows shot at her.

She couldn't get over the fact that someone had tried to kill her twice since she'd arrived in Tyler's Glen. Well, the shooter yesterday hadn't tried very hard. The archer, on the other hand, had clearly meant business and started launching arrows right after she'd found the knife in the blood-stained towel.

At the ranger station, when Kate reported the incident and turned over the knife wrapped in the dirty towel, Vicki Bates, the law enforcement ranger at the front desk, stared at her in disbelief. "You're sure they were real arrows and not toy ones?"

"Look, I'm a deputy marshal." Kate removed her badge from her backpack and showed it to her. At least the thief hadn't stolen that too. "I also have some experience with archery, and I know a real arrow when I see one." She took out the arrow that had pierced her pack. "Here's one of them." She handed it to Vicki, then rested her bag on the counter and pointed to the hole in the canvas. "Toy arrows don't pierce trees and backpacks."

Vicki inspected the arrow, taking a greater interest. "That's very odd because hunting isn't allowed in the park."

"Well, whoever shot this one didn't get the memo, and he certainly wasn't aiming for a deer. Look, I know it sounds incredible, but there's another witness who will corroborate my story."

"What's his name?" Vicki asked, poised to enter it into the computer.

"David Jennings."

The ranger stopped typing. "David—from Tyler's Glen—Jennings?"

"That's the one."

She peered at Kate from the corner of her eye as she typed his name. "And how is David these days?"

The inquisitive gleam in the ranger's eye alerted Kate to the fact that Vicki had more than a passing interest. "He's fine."

"Tell him to give me a call sometime. I haven't seen him in ages."

Annoyed by the woman's personal request, Kate played it cool. "I think he's busy with his farm and volunteer work."

Vicki rolled her eyes. "Some things never change." Returning to the business at hand, she focused on her computer screen to finish the report. "Do you have any idea why someone would want to target you in the park?"

"It may have something to do with the knife I found. However, it's the second time in two days I've been shot at, first with bullets and now with arrows." She told Vicki about the shooting incident on Owen's property and referred her to Deputy Travis for the official report. "By the way, do you know when forensics will have the blood on the knife and towel processed and matched?"

"Probably by the end of the week."

"I'd appreciate you giving me a call when you have the results."

"I'll make a note of that." Vicki stopped typing and addressed her in a courteous tone. "I'm sorry you've had all this trouble on your vacation. Is there anything else we can do for you, Deputy Marshal?"

Kate realized she also needed to report her stolen wallet and gun. At least it was her personal Glock and not her service weapon, which she'd left secured at home.

Having finished her report, Kate stepped outside the building while Pete spoke with Vicki about the incident. Seeing that she had no cell service, Kate mulled over how she could get to town and call her bank and credit card companies to report her stolen cards. She also needed to move her things to the other campground. And she was hungry. She'd need another transportation plan soon. Being without a car was becoming a real pain. Having a target on her back wasn't so great either.

CHAPTER SEVEN

WHEN KATE HAD EXPLAINED TO PETE that she needed a ride to Tyler's Glen to make some calls, he volunteered to take her. As he drove out of the national park into cell service range, Kate immediately called her credit card company and the bank to report the theft. She requested her new credit cards be shipped to Rick's garage since she thought he wouldn't mind, and she didn't have a mailing address since she was staying in the park. Unfortunately, it would take a few days for them to arrive.

Next, she called Rick to let him know about the pending credit cards and to see when the Ford truck would be ready.

"I ordered a new windshield and windows," he said, "but they probably won't arrive until next week."

"Next week? I can't make it that long without a car. Any idea where I can get another one?"

"Not a car, but you can borrow my mom's bike until the truck is fixed. You're both about the same height so it should work."

She pulled the phone from her ear for a minute. "I'm sorry. Did you say *bike?*" Not wanting to impose on Rick's mother, a woman she hadn't even met, Kate politely declined his offer.

This was ridiculous. If not for the discovery of the knife today, she'd be tempted to pack up and go home. But she wasn't going to give up that easy, not when her uncle's death still remained a mystery.

She called David next to check on Buster.

When he answered, David told her that he'd left the vet clinic and was finishing up an emergency call. He couldn't talk long, but said he'd meet her at Bubba's after he finished. She hoped he would give her a ride back to the campground.

Pete dropped Kate off at the diner so she could get something to eat while she waited for David. When she walked in, business appeared slow and she didn't have any trouble finding an empty table. She sat in a chair facing the door so she could watch for David.

By now, it was afternoon and she was starving. She scanned the menu to find the least expensive items since she only had the nine dollars left. Without money or credit cards for a hotel, Grace's offer to stay at her place was Kate's best option, and it wouldn't be far out of the way for David to take her there since it was close to where he lived.

Nadine waved to her. "Hey, Kate. I was hoping I'd see you again. What have you been up to?"

"Oh, you know, camping and hiking." She tried to act casual, preferring to keep the shooting incidents to herself. "How is the songwriting going?"

The smile on Nadine's face vanished, and she dismissively flicked her wrist. "That was just a silly dream. I don't have time to do that with work and everything."

This was not the same effervescent woman who couldn't wait to talk about her music. Her eyes looked puffy and tired. Something must be bothering her. "Is everything okay?"

The waitress had a faraway look.

"Nadine?"

"Huh? Oh. I—I'm a little overwhelmed right now, that's all. Bubba needs to hire more help." When she'd finished taking Kate's order, she grabbed the menu and disappeared into the kitchen.

The bell chimed as someone came into the diner. Kate turned her eyes toward the door, her spirits lifting. But it was Joe, not David.

He'd already spotted her and was swaggering to her table. "Well, what do you know?"

His annoying habit of popping up unexpectedly began to make her suspicious that it might not be by accident. "What a coincidence seeing you here again, Joe." She coated her words with touch of sarcasm.

He took the empty chair across the table from her. "I'm glad I ran into you. I hate to eat alone."

"Hey, I'm expecting someone!"

"That's okay. I'll keep the seat warm."

Nadine returned with a glass of iced tea for Kate. She stopped and scowled at Joe.

"Hello, Na-dine," he said in his syrupy Southern drawl. "Please bring me my usual. And make sure you put our checks together, sugar. This one's on me."

Ignoring him, Nadine looked directly at Kate.

"Separate checks, please." She might not have much money on her, but she'd gladly spend every last cent rather than be obligated to Joe.

"Gotcha." Nadine made a point of frowning at Joe before she left.

As the waitress walked away, Kate wondered if she was one of Joe's many ex-girlfriends that Grace had alluded to.

Joe shook his head at Kate's refusal of a free meal. "I was only being friendly, you know."

"Sure you were."

He rested an elbow on the table and pulled at his beard. "I hear we're going to be neighbors."

She narrowed her eyes at him. "Where did you hear that?"

After glancing around, he lowered his voice. "When Lester Crane told me that Owen Bentley's estate wouldn't be auctioned off, I had my lawyers in Knoxville do a little digging. I have to say, it sure threw me for a loop to learn that old Owen had a niece, especially one so pretty."

She rolled her eyes. "Give it a rest, Joe. Surely your lawyers must have also told you I'm a deputy marshal."

He cleared his throat and straightened up a little. "They did happen to mention that fact."

"Now that you know who you're dealing with, why don't you get lost?"

He dropped his smooth façade. "I will, as soon as you tell me what a city gal from Nashville is going to do with a farm in Tyler's Glen?"

"That's none of your business."

"Well, if you decide to sell, come see me first. I'll give you a good price for it, even though some say it's cursed."

Since he was so nosy, she decided to turn the tables on him. "What do you need with more land, Joe? I've heard you already own most of the county."

His eyes popped for a moment, then his lips stretched into a crooked grin. "Not quite, but I'm working on it. Since Owen's property borders mine, it would give me more privacy from my annoying neighbors."

"Have you considered a fence?"

"Funny *and* feisty—I like that in a woman."

Another chime at the door. This time it *was* David. Kate waved to him, anxious to hear about Buster.

He started to raise his hand, but when he caught sight of Joe peering at him from her table, he froze. Instead of joining them, he took a seat at a small table next to a window, and near the door.

Joe twisted back around to face Kate. "Speaking of annoying neighbors . . ."

She eyed him sharply. "Go find yourself another table, Joe."

He didn't budge, but leaned closer with a sinister look. "Be careful about letting David cozy up to you. He only wants Owen's property. He might seem like a white knight, but he'll do anything to get his family's land back. *Anything.* Trust me, I know."

Kate didn't want to get in the middle of Joe and David's

feud. She especially didn't appreciate Joe's insinuation that David's only interest in her was because of Owen's property. David didn't even know she was Owen's niece. *At least, she assumed he didn't.* Now she began to wonder if he might, or was Joe trying to yank her chain?

Nadine emerged from the kitchen with their food. "Here you go. One salad and one cheeseburger with fries." She set their lunches and drinks in front of them, not making eye contact with Joe. "Is there anything else I can get you, Kate?"

"No, I'm fine."

"Change of plans, Na-dine," Joe told her. "Now I'd like mine to go."

She rolled her eyes. "Whatever." After snatching his plate, she disappeared into the kitchen. Moments later, she promptly returned with a bag and stiffly handed it to him.

When Nadine left to wait on other tables, Joe rose from his seat and grinned at Kate. "I enjoyed our little chat. That's the good thing about living in a small town, we're bound to keep running into each other."

She didn't bother looking at him. "Bye, Joe." *And good riddance.*

As he headed for the door, she turned her attention to David. He and Nadine were talking. She couldn't hear what they were saying, but from their serious expressions she could tell it wasn't about the weather. David said something to her, and she snatched the menu out of his hand and rushed into the kitchen, clearly upset. He rose to follow her, but seeing Kate, he paused and dropped into his chair. Staring out the window, he tapped his knuckles together.

Kate rose from her seat and went to the restroom. The door was ajar. Thinking it was unoccupied, she entered the small room and found Nadine sobbing in front of the mirror.

After locking the door so they wouldn't be disturbed, Kate placed a sisterly arm around Nadine's shoulder. "What's wrong?"

Nadine dabbed her mascara-stained face with a tissue. "I'll be all right." She glanced at Kate in the mirror. "Have you ever been in love? I mean really in love?"

Remembering her misguided infatuation with Buck, she spoke compassionately. "I thought so once."

"Why does it always have to break your heart?"

Nadine's mournful look filled Kate with indignation. "What did David say that upset you?"

She shook her head. "It's not his fault."

Someone knocked on the door. "Is anybody in there?" It was a woman's voice on the other side.

"We'll be out in a minute," Kate shouted, annoyed by the intrusion.

"Please hurry," the woman pleaded.

Nadine straightened and sniffed, pulling herself together. "Would you please tell Bubba I had to leave?" Before Kate could answer, the waitress swiftly unlocked the door and slipped out.

When Kate followed her, she nearly collided with a woman and a little boy who was obviously in potty training. "I'm sorry we took so long," she said to the woman.

Catching a glimpse of Nadine as she exited through the front door, Kate noticed David standing at his table, looking dejected and torn as if he wanted to go after her.

Distressed by Nadine's emotional meltdown, Kate spun around and marched toward the kitchen to find Bubba and give him Nadine's message. Once she'd delivered it, the overweight cook shook his head and muttered something unintelligible.

Returning to her table, Kate's gaze wandered back to David. He looked her way at the same time, and they stared across the diner at each other. Despite Nadine telling her it wasn't David's fault, something he'd said had clearly upset her.

David rose from his chair and joined Kate before she sat

down. "Can we talk?"

She reminded herself of his dust-up with the pretty waitress and Joe's warning. What had Nadine meant when she'd said it wasn't his fault—not only that, she'd asked if Kate had ever been in love—could David be an old boyfriend who'd broken her heart? Regardless, she still wanted to know the state of Owen's dog.

She gestured to the chair Joe had vacated. "Have a seat. How is Buster?"

As he settled across from her, he pushed away Joe's drink. "He'll be fine, but the vet said he's suffering from malnutrition and an infection. He's giving him a round of antibiotics and nutrients, so he needs to stay at the clinic at least overnight. It may take a few days before Buster is well enough to go home."

The tension in her body relaxed with gratitude that he'd taken the dog to the vet, and she decided to give him the benefit of the doubt. "How did your emergency call go?"

"It was only a kitchen fire. Fortunately, no one was hurt and the damage was minimal." His brows pinched together. "What did they say when you reported that crazy archer to park officials?"

"I don't think the ranger who took my report believed me until I showed her my marshal badge, but I have a feeling you'll have more sway with Ranger Vicki than I do."

"Vicki Bates?"

"Mm-hmm. By the way, she said to tell you hello and to give her a call sometime."

A tinge of red colored his face. "We've known each other since grade school."

"Well, she's definitely not in grade school anymore."

He grinned uncomfortably and scratched the back of his neck. Then he turned the tables and put her in the hot seat. "Did you find your *missing gun* yet?"

"Oh," She bit her lip. "About that . . . I guess I owe you

an explanation."

"No, you don't."

"Huh?"

"I get it. You came here to get away from a stressful job, and you're still grieving for your foster mom. Now I know why you didn't want to talk about work."

There was truth in what he'd said. Mack, her boss, had been wanting her to take time off ever since Rose had died. But she didn't know what she would do or where she would go—until she'd received the anonymous note on the back of Lester Crane's business card. That was another mystery she still needed to solve. "Really? You're okay with it?"

"Why shouldn't I be? But from now on, I'll be on my best behavior."

Relieved by his positive reaction, she relaxed. "I'm actually a deputy marshal, and you don't have anything to worry about—unless you're a fugitive in disguise," she said with a smile.

"Do you enjoy what you do?"

"Most of the time. But lately I've been thinking I'd like to reach people and help them before they resort to a life of crime, you know? Like what my foster parents did for me."

He nodded. "That's what we want to do with the outreach center."

It was nice that he understood how she felt. "About the gun," she said. "It's my personal one. In my line of work, you can never be too careful. That's why I like to have it with me, even on vacation—which reminds me, remember when I told you I thought I heard a bear last night?"

"Yeah?"

"Well, I also dreamed that a prowler entered my tent—only it wasn't a dream. He stole my gun and took my wallet. I told the park rangers about it today when I reported the arrow shooting incident."

Creases formed on his brow. "You think somebody is

targeting you."

She sighed at the thought. "After the arrow attack this morning, it certainly appears that way." The memory of the shooter at her uncle's place also crossed her mind, but she couldn't mention that to David without telling him she was Owen's niece. From his serious expression, he already had enough to deal with for one day.

"After what happened this morning, Kate, I don't think you should stay at the campground tonight."

She lowered her gaze, acknowledging his concern with a slight nod. "As much as I don't want to change my plans and cancel my reservations, I've come to the same conclusion. Grace offered to let me stay with her, and I'm thinking of taking her up on it."

"That's a great idea. I know she'd enjoy your company."

"Do you have her number? I'd like to call and talk to her about it."

After he'd shared the number with her, his voice sounded less certain as he broached a new subject. "I was surprised to see you here with Joe. I didn't think you two knew each other."

"Oh, he introduced himself to me yesterday when I had lunch here. And I wasn't *with him*. He came to my table uninvited."

The tension in David's expression eased. "What were you two discussing when I came in?"

"He was just being a pest. I thought he'd never leave." She sipped her iced tea, hoping he would drop the subject of Joe. "Did you notice how upset Nadine was earlier? She was in tears."

He glanced down, lightly rapping his knuckles on the table. "She's going through a rough time right now."

And a broken heart. The question was, who had broken it?

When he gazed at her again, his mood seemed more upbeat. "It's too bad you live so far away. We could sure use your help with the outreach center. Hey, I have an idea—the harvest festival is this week. Why don't you come with me this Friday, and you could meet the members of the outreach center committee? Maybe you could share a few ideas for how to get started."

Though it sounded more like a business meeting than a date, his invitation to go with him excited her. But then she remembered Nadine's tear-stained face and Joe's warning. As much as she wanted to go, she reminded herself that she wasn't looking for romance. She came to get answers about her uncle's murder. "It sounds like fun, but I don't think so."

The hopeful spark in his eyes dimmed. "Are you sure? I think you'd enjoy it."

His disappointed look prompted her to gently touch his hand. "It's nothing personal."

He stared at her hand on his. "Is it because of your ex-boyfriend? If it makes any difference, we don't have to go together. I'd rather you enjoy the festival without me than not at all."

She smiled at his concession. "I'll think about it. There is something you could help me with though."

"What's that?"

"I need to get my tent and luggage from the campground to Grace's."

"You got it."

Kate called Grace before they left Bubba's, and she sounded delighted that Kate wanted to stay with her, even insisted on it, which immediately put Kate's mind at ease. Then David drove her to the park to fetch her belongings. On the way to the horse camp, they stopped at the campground office so Kate could cancel her reservation. The woman helping her also gave her a reprieve until five to remove her things from the horse camp without incurring an additional charge.

After David pulled into the horse camp and parked,

Kate jumped out and approached her tent. Something felt wrong. Glancing at the ground, she spotted part of a foil granola bar wrapper.

"What is it?" David asked.

"Someone's been here today." She bent to unzip the door and look inside. Her clothes and things were scattered across her sleeping bag and the floor of the tent. She crawled in and searched her luggage.

David popped his head inside the door flap. "Wow! What a mess."

"And all of my food is missing."

"Raccoons?"

She looked around but didn't see any holes in the tent. Whoever had stolen her food was adept at using zippers. "More likely, a scavenger of the two-footed variety."

After Kate and David had loaded her luggage and camping gear in the backseat of his truck, he drove out of the horse camp and turned in the opposite direction of town.

"Aren't we going to Grace's?" Kate asked.

He regarded her with a mischievous glint. "I promised you a tour of Cades Cove yesterday, remember?"

"Yes, but it's getting late, and I've already taken so much of your time already."

"I always keep my promises." The levity in his declaration made her smile. "It would be a shame for you to come all this way and not actually see Cades Cove. That is, unless you'd rather not." He glanced at her for confirmation.

"Actually, that would be nice." She looked forward to a relaxing drive through the scenic valley after the crazy day she'd had.

It was late afternoon when David slowly drove them

along the eleven-mile one-way loop through peaceful grassy meadows, surrounded by the Smokies. Marveling at the beauty and serenity of the historic farming community, Kate felt the tension and stress in her muscles melt away.

David pulled into a parking area and turned off the engine. "Let's take a walk and stretch our legs."

He escorted her to the preserved mountain village comprised of three old churches and seven cabins. They started their tour with the Elijah Oliver cabin, built in the early 1800's. After they'd climbed the wooden steps to the porch, David moved aside to let Kate enter first.

She marveled at the stark, one-room dwelling with stone fireplace that had once housed an entire family. "It must have been hard for the settlers to leave everything behind and start a new life in these mountains."

"Probably," David replied, "but they liked it well enough to stay and make a home here. And they weren't alone. At its peak, Cades Cove had about 685 residents."

Their tour continued with visits to the rest of the cabins, the churches, as well as the sorghum mill and blacksmith shop. The last stop on the loop was the Carter Shields Cabin. David parked his pickup near a large maple in full fall splendor. Kate picked up a leaf with a long stem from the ground, twirling it as he escorted her along the picturesque path to the plain log house cloaked in brilliant foliage.

Exploring the empty cabin with the stone fireplace made Kate a little nostalgic for simpler times. "What were the names of your ancestors who settled in Tyler's Glen, David?"

He had been studying the log construction of a wall and moved to the opposite side of the hearth from her. "Jacob and Eliza Jennings."

Kate pictured the young, newly-married couple, beginning their life together so proud and grateful for their humble dwelling. "I bet they'd be proud of you."

He shrugged modestly. "I don't know. Maybe they'd be

disappointed that the land they worked so hard for is no longer in the family."

The reminder of land dispute made her sad. "I think they'd want you to be happy regardless of the land."

"Maybe . . . I guess we'll never know."

As they walked toward David's pickup, Kate noticed something lodged in the vibrant tree that wasn't there earlier. Her stomach curdled when she saw it was an arrow with red and green fletching. A small piece of paper was pinned to the trunk. She strode ahead and pulled the arrow out.

David joined her by the tree. "What does it say?"

After warily scanning the peaceful-looking surroundings, she read the printed note. *Today was target practice. Next time I won't miss!*

CHAPTER EIGHT

ON THEIR WAY OUT OF THE park, Kate and David stopped by the Cades Cove ranger station to let Pete know about the threatening note and the food stolen from Kate's tent. Pete said he'd notify Vicki, and they'd look into it. Kate wished that more could be done to catch whoever was behind the incidents that had plagued her today. She was thankful, however, that she had a safe place to stay in the meantime.

As David drove her to Grace's, Kate noticed his demeanor had changed since they found the arrow with the note. He seemed preoccupied and serious. The note had obviously troubled him. Not that she took it lightly, but it wasn't the first time she'd been threatened. She recalled Raptor's threats from the past and hoped he wasn't behind this one. The knife discovery must have rattled someone's cage, which made her all the more determined to keep digging until she got answers.

By the time they pulled into Grace's drive, it was already six. Exiting David's truck, Kate inhaled the clean air and resolved not to let the disturbing events of the past twenty-four hours spoil her evening.

The stately two-story home with intricate white trim framing its grand front porch and bay window could easily have been the subject of an artist's painting. To the left of the house, Clementine grazed peacefully in a fenced-in pasture near the barn, while chickens roamed freely in the yard.

Kate had a feeling the quiet, country atmosphere was exactly what she needed right now and was glad she'd taken Grace up on her offer. With her backpack slung over one shoulder, she opened the rear door to the cab of the truck and began unloading her things as David did the same from the other side.

"If Grace's home is as nice inside as it looks outside, I might move in permanently," she said to him from across the backseat.

He returned a smile that would melt butter. "Sounds good to me. With a marshal next door, I won't need to lock my doors."

Each carrying articles of her belongings, they walked together to the front porch. She cast him a sideways glance. "After what happened this morning, you might be safer if I had stayed in the park."

A glimmer of irony danced in his eyes. "Before you arrived, this was a nice, peaceful community."

"Right—you only had prowlers, arsonists, and propane explosions to deal with."

After they climbed the steps to the door, Kate admired the Victorian-style bay window to her right as she knocked.

It didn't take long for Grace to answer. Her eyes sparkled when she saw them both on her porch. "You're just in time for dinner."

David politely excused himself. "I only came to deliver Kate's luggage."

"Please stay and eat something. I have more than enough food."

He glanced at Kate for her vote.

"Fine with me," she replied with a casual shrug.

"Good, it's settled," Grace said with a clap of finality. "Now come on in and make yourselves at home."

David let Kate precede him through the door as they followed Grace into a long hallway. Kate marveled at the majestic staircase in the entrance, feeling as if she'd crossed over a threshold in time. The mint-condition, solid-oak floors beneath her feet gave off a distinctive woodsy smell, laced with a slight musty odor that permeated the historic home. But despite its age, the place felt warm and inviting. She loved its character and imagined it must have been quite a showplace in its heyday.

"Your house is amazing," she said to Grace, her voice echoing off the high ceilings.

"Why, thank you. My husband Wade took great pride in keeping it up. I'm afraid I haven't done as good a job since he passed away. It was built by his great grandfather in the late 1800s. Four generations of Holbrooks were raised here." She turned toward the grand staircase. "Come upstairs, Kate, and I'll take you to your room."

Carrying her luggage, Kate tried to keep up with the spry woman as David followed them. When they'd reached the top, Kate looked around the spacious second floor landing that was illuminated by an exquisite floral stained-glass window adorning the front-facing wall.

"Your bedroom and bathroom are over there," Grace said, gesturing to the two doors on the right. "My bedroom is across the hall from yours." She led Kate into the second room on the right.

The old brass bed, covered with a wedding ring-pattern quilt, and the other antique furnishings instantly made Kate feel at home. She set her luggage and backpack down and went to the large window and peered out. Facing east, she had an impressive view of the mountains across the road. "I can see the Smokies."

"It's the best view in the house. My daughter Julianna spent many an hour looking out that window when she was young."

Kate loved the window seat and imagined herself sitting there, reading or daydreaming out the window as a girl. She turned to Grace and smiled. "It's a lovely room. I appreciate you letting me stay here."

"The pleasure is mine," Grace replied with a warm smile.

"Now I'll see to my cooking. Come downstairs to the kitchen after you've settled in."

After Grace left, David stood at the door with Kate's camping gear. "Where would you like these?"

She pointed to an empty corner. "Over there for now. Thanks."

While he deposited her things, Kate turned to the graduation pictures of the young woman and man on the nightstand. "Are these Grace's children?"

David moved beside her and looked them over. "Yes, that's Julianna."

"Rick's mother and Deputy Travis's wife, right?"

He nodded, then gestured to the other picture. "That must be Grace's son, Frederick. I was too young to remember him. He died fighting overseas."

As Kate looked at the sandy-haired young man with the carefree grin and bright eyes, sadness touched her heart for his ultimate sacrifice. "I think Rick favors him. Do you think he's named for his uncle?"

"Probably." David took a closer look at the picture. "My father was good friends with Frederick. Dad told me funny stories from when they were kids, like the time they fell into one of the local caves and had to stumble around in the dark until they found a way out." He paused with a sad look. "Too bad he died so young."

His words caused Kate to wonder if Frederick Holbrook had known Owen and her mother. They would have been close to the same age.

The aroma of Grace's cooking alerted Kate's stomach that it was time to eat, so they headed downstairs to the French doors off the hall that opened into the living room. Kate was immediately drawn to the charming red Victorian-era loveseat and matching chairs around the fireplace, across from the bay window she'd seen on the front porch. She ran her hand over the fabric, marveling at its richness. "Look at all these wonderful antiques."

"If it wasn't a home, it could be a museum. I'm kind of afraid to sit on anything," David said.

After admiring the writing desk and curios, Kate went to the fireplace against the far wall. A pair of brass candlesticks and more family photographs rested on each end of the mantel, with an old clock between them. Drawn to the pictures, Kate examined the faded photo of a young couple more closely. She instantly recognized the woman with the youthful sparkle as Grace. The man beside her must have been her husband, Wade. Beside their picture was another one of Frederick, this time dressed in his Army uniform. He appeared quite dashing with the stars and stripes behind him.

"There you are." Grace came into the living room, wiping her hands on a dish towel. "Dinner is ready."

Kate picked up the photo of the couple. "This is you with your husband, isn't it?"

Grace joined her by the mantel and took the picture. "Yes, that's my Wade, God bless him." She set the picture back in its place and tenderly brushed her finger over it. "Happiest years of my life were spent with that man." She paused a moment, then turned to Kate and David. "Our dinner is going to get cold while we're in here reminiscing."

Kate sniffed the air as they followed Grace through the comfortable den filled with more antiques, including a roll-top desk, a comfortable-looking couch, and bookcases filled with old classics.

Grace stopped and took them on a quick detour to show Kate the roomy enclosed back porch off the den, with a two-person swing, an antique trunk, and a view of the garden and barn. Grace pointed out the storage closet, and the back entrance to the hall with the staircase, both accessible from the porch.

The tempting odors coming from the kitchen reminded Kate that she'd only had a small salad earlier—at Bubba's when Nadine had left in tears. She still wondered what on earth David could have said that would have upset her like that.

Grace glanced over her shoulder at Kate and David as she led them through the den. "I hope you like chicken and dumplings."

Exchanging raised brows with David, Kate shrugged. "I've never had it, but if it tastes as good as it smells, I can't wait."

Entering the generous kitchen, Kate stopped to admire the antique sideboard against the wall with a matching oak table in the center of the room. A china hutch stuffed with lovely glassware graced the corner. The old with the new provided a comfortable, homey atmosphere for cooking or gathering around the table to talk.

Kate and David helped Grace finish setting the food on the table.

"You take Wade's seat at the head, David," Grace said.

He hesitated but didn't argue as he politely waited until Kate and Grace had taken their places across from each other before he sat between them.

Grace addressed him again. "Would you do us the honor of saying the blessing, David?"

He bowed his head and began. "Dear Lord, thank you for this food we are about to eat, and for bringing Kate safely here . . ."

Moved that he'd included her in his prayer, she added a silent thank-you for bringing David into her life and giving her a place to stay at Grace's.

After he'd finished, Grace passed the homemade chicken and dumplings to Kate, along with garden-fresh greens and yellow squash. It all looked so delicious, Kate filled her bowl and plate with more food than she could possibly eat. *There goes my health-food regimen, but I am on vacation.*

"David, how's the seed corn harvest going?" Grace asked.

"It's mostly done. I plan to finish up your field this week. I was thinking that Owen's fields need harvesting too. The corn will rot before long if nobody takes care of it. According to Joe, the plans for Owen's estate auction have been cancelled. It could be a long time before anyone takes possession of that land."

Grace's eyes widened. "Did Joe say why the plans were cancelled?"

"Nothing specific, only something about new developments."

"I hope it's something good, and not bad."

"Maybe a relative has come forward," he said.

Kate stared at her bowl of dumplings, wondering if she should say something.

"What will you do if you can't buy your family's land back?" Grace asked him.

He stopped chewing his food and swallowed with a gulp. "Once I finish harvesting the corn, I'll see what I can find out, assuming Joe doesn't beat me to the punch. He's probably already working a deal with someone to buy the land and counting the money he'll make selling it to another big corporation like Rydeklan Chemicals."

"Heaven forbid." Grace pressed her palm to her chest.

Alarmed by the older woman's distress, Kate put her spoon down. "Grace, are you okay?"

David's face constricted with a mix of worry and regret. "I shouldn't have gone on like that. I didn't mean to upset you."

"I'm fine," Grace whisked her hand in the air. "I guess the thought of Owen's land being developed next door left me a bit speechless. I think we should change the subject to something more pleasant." Her expression brightened. "How is your garden doing, David?"

Her hunger returning after Grace's rally, Kate dipped her spoon in her dumplings and took a tasty bite of the plump doughy noodles, waiting for David's reply.

"Good. I'm planning to enter my pumpkins in the festival again this year."

"No doubt you'll win again too." Grace turned to Kate. "David has won the prize for the biggest pumpkin for the past five years in a row."

"After seeing his pumpkin patch, I'm not surprised." Relief buoyed Kate at being able to talk about something else. It wasn't that she wanted to deceive them, especially after they had been so kind to her. But if Grace was upset by what David had said about Joe developing Owen's property, how would she handle learning another Bentley would soon inherit the land next to hers? It might send her over the edge.

David's voice interrupted her thoughts. "Speaking of pumpkins, Grace, are you donating your famous pumpkin pie this year for the raffle?"

"Of course. Pecan too."

He leaned toward Kate as if he were leaking a government secret. "Grace's pumpkin and pecan pies are the best in the county."

Kate laughed, then spoke to Grace. "I love pumpkin pie. When my new credit and ATM cards come in and I can get some cash, I'd like to buy a few tickets."

"That's not necessary, dear. I'll make one especially for you. But what happened to your credit cards?"

Kate told Grace about them being stolen from her tent.

"Goodness." Grace's brows rose.

"My gun was stolen too."

A surprised look crossed the woman's face. "Your *gun?*"

"Kate's a deputy marshal." David regarded Kate with admiration.

Intrigue glimmered in Grace's eyes as she smiled. "How interesting, especially for a young woman. Good for you, Kate. My son, Rick, wanted to go into law enforcement when he finished his tour of duty . . . unfortunately, he died when his convoy was ambushed, two days before his leave to come home for a visit."

Kate glanced down, her heart swelling with sympathy for the kind woman.

Grace dabbed at her eyes with her napkin, and her cheerful disposition returned. "So, David, what's this I hear about you entering Samson in the horse show?"

Curious, Kate looked at David and saw a spirited grin on his face.

"You heard right, Grace. I hope Clementine is ready for some stiff competition."

"Oh, she'll be ready." Grace's tone was confident.

Kate enjoyed their sparring as she finished her meal. A part of her wanted to be there, if only to see the two of them compete. Going with David would be icing on the cake.

After finishing her vegetables, Grace peered at him. "How is Samson coming along with his training?"

"Pretty well, but he still has trouble with the square maneuver. I've been working with him on that, but as you know, he's pretty excitable. I'm bringing him to the stable tomorrow morning for the preliminary rounds of judging. I can come by with my horse trailer and pick up Clementine too."

"That would be wonderful." Grace's eyes darted to Kate. "David, you should ask Kate to go with you to the festival."

His gaze shifted in Kate's direction. "I already did, but she turned me down."

"Oh." Grace's lips tightened.

Kate shrank from their disappointed looks. "It wasn't anything personal."

"Maybe *you* can convince her." David smiled at Grace, his eyes twinkling.

The woman tilted her head at him. "Didn't you tell her about all the delicious food, the rides, the horse show, and the archery competition?"

Kate piped up. "Did you say *archery*?"

David and Grace stared at her and nodded.

Kate raised her hands. "Okay, okay. I'll go to the festival on one condition—we all go together."

Though he wanted to stay longer, David went home right after dinner. He knew Kate needed time to rest and relax. Finding the knife in the park was bad enough, but to be hunted down with arrows like an animal was appalling. To make matters worse, she had witnessed the awkward scene between Nadine and himself at Bubba's.

He wanted to tell her why Nadine was so upset, but it wasn't his place. It didn't seem like the right time either. Sitting at his desk, he took a pencil and snapped it in two. If Nadine had only listened to him and taken his advice, she could have been spared the emotional turmoil she was going through now.

Staring at his computer screen, he tried to focus on his harvest schedule, but Smokey came up beside him and pawed at his leg. He petted the dog and thought about Buster, still at the vet's. Strange that after his disappearance following Owen's death, the dog would suddenly show up in the park and lead them to the knife. But dogs did peculiar things when their owners died.

The morbid thoughts haunted him like that archer who had chased Kate and him down the mountain. At least the authorities had the knife now and were investigating it. But it brought home the danger that came with Kate's profession. What if the incident had nothing to do with the knife? As a member of law enforcement, she probably had her share of enemies. Had one of them followed her to Tyler's Glen to settle a score?

His muscles clenched at the idea of someone wanting to

harm her. Yet, as much as he wanted to keep her safe, he knew she could take care of herself. And he liked that about her. It made her all the more fascinating. He was glad she had finally agreed to come to the festival, even if she wanted Grace along to avoid being alone with him. But given the short time she would be here on vacation, he had to prepare himself that a relationship beyond friendship might never develop between them.

Glancing at the clock, he realized it was late, and he had a busy day tomorrow. "Smokey, it's past your bedtime."

The dog barked and cocked his head.

As David rose from his chair, he saw a distant light coming from Grace's place. He might sleep better tonight knowing Kate was staying nearby, but he wouldn't rest easy until they got answers about her missing gun, the knife in the blood-stained towel, and the flying arrows.

Late that night, Kate lay in bed thinking about her uncle and the prospect of inheriting his land. What would happen when David and Grace learned the truth about her? Would they believe her story about the anonymous note on the business card leading her here? Whoever sent that note had to be from Tyler's Glen. If they knew her mother's relationship to Owen, did they also know who killed him?

With someone targeting and threatening her, Kate decided it was best for Grace and David not to know about her relationship with Owen, at least for now. Especially, if it might put them in danger.

An old King James Bible lay by her bedside. Perhaps Julianna's? She picked it up and thumbed to the book of Psalms. After the distressing day, she located Psalm 23 and began to read it to remind herself of God's love and protection. A few minutes later, when she felt more relaxed, she placed the Bible on the night stand and yawned. She fluffed her pillow and rested her head against it, uttering a prayer of thanks to God for keeping her safe as she drifted off to sleep.

A loud bang outside jolted her. "*What?*"

Another gunshot immediately followed.

Kate jumped from her bed and ran to the window. Darkness obstructed her view. Throwing on her robe, she rushed across the hall to Grace's room and called through the door. "Grace, did you hear that?"

A few moments later, the woman emerged in her nightgown with a perturbed expression. "It's that old buzzard, Virgil Crane. He's hunting on Owen's property again."

"Can't you call the sheriff and stop him?"

Grace shook her head and sighed. "Honey, it wouldn't do a bit of good. He can't hear worth a lick."

Kate frowned, confused by Grace's inaction. "That's no excuse."

"Don't worry. He's just an old mountain man with a notion that nobody should own the land."

"But it's still trespassing."

"Owen gave him permission. And as much as it aggravates me, it's kind of sad to think of him not being able to hunt there anymore." Grace patted her on the shoulder. "Why don't you go back to bed, hon? He's probably finished hunting by now."

Back in her room, Kate sat up, wide awake. The shooting had stopped, but she doubted she'd get much sleep. Chasing fugitives seemed relatively innocuous compared to dodging arrows in the park and encountering trigger-happy trespassers. So much for a peaceful vacation in the mountains.

CHAPTER NINE

KATE AWOKE WEDNESDAY MORNING TO the aroma of bacon cooking. She glanced at the clock on the nightstand by her bed. Already eight a.m. Ten minutes later, she entered the kitchen, dressed in a plaid flannel shirt over jeans, feeling refreshed and less achy after a good night's sleep.

"There you are," Grace said in a chipper voice. She stood by the stove, using tongs to remove the bacon strips from the skillet and placing them on a serving dish. "You saved me from having to go upstairs. The coffee pot is on the counter, cups are in the cabinet. Help yourself."

After Kate had filled her mug and taken a sip, she joined Grace by the stove. "It smells yummy. Is there anything I can do to help?"

"Why thank you, but it's all taken care of." She served an omelet from another skillet and handed the plate to Kate.

"You're spoiling me, you know," Kate said as she took her plate to the table and sat down. "I'll be fat as a cow if I keep eating like this."

Grace put a hand on her hip, giving her a sidelong look. "Nonsense. You could do with a little more meat on your bones. Besides, you're still recuperating from your accident."

After they'd prayed together, Grace whisked a napkin over her lap and took a piece of toast from the stack in the center of the table. She slathered it with butter, using quick, efficient knife strokes. "I'm happy you decided to stay here last night. I would have been worried about you camping all alone. I'm sure your parents wouldn't like it much either."

Kate reached for a piece of toast. "My parents are gone."

Grace had brought the toast to her mouth, but stopped

and slowly returned it to her plate. She wiped her hands on her napkin. "I'm sorry to hear that. What about grandparents?"

"Nope. It's only me."

"Bless your heart." Grace's voice was soft and compassionate. "That must be hard at your age."

"I've been on my own before, when I was much younger, but God has always watched over me. I couldn't have survived otherwise." Kate told Grace about her life on the streets, and Jim and Rose taking her in and their influence in leading her to the Lord.

Grace's eyes glistened with tears. "When I learned my son Frederick had died fighting overseas, I didn't think I could go on. I clung to my faith like a life preserver. That's what got me through."

Kate nodded, recalling all the times that had been true for her as well. "With Rose gone, I'm still feeling a little adrift right now, but I know I'll eventually reach the shore."

Grace gave her an encouraging smile. "I'm sure you will, honey. Give it time. The mountains are a good place to get away and figure things out."

"That's what David told me." *Of course, she hadn't had much of a respite with people shooting at her and stealing her gun.*

"Speaking of David, he came by early this morning to take Clementine to the festival stables. I'll be going later today for the preliminary judging of the horse show. You're welcome to come with me."

"Thanks, but I think I'll hang out here if you don't mind."

Grace took a sip of her coffee and slowly set the cup on the table. "You know, you won't hurt my feelings if you and David want to go to the festival without me tagging along. I don't mind going solo."

Kate shook her head in protest. "No, I want you to come with us."

Grace eyed her perceptively. "Why don't you want to be alone with David?"

Should she tell her about Nadine? She hadn't known Grace very long, but already sensed she could trust her. The fact that David was so fond of the woman confirmed her own initial impressions. Maybe if she confided in her, Grace could give her advice or insight about David and Nadine's relationship. "Yesterday, while I was eating lunch at Bubba's, David said something to Nadine that upset her so much she left in tears."

Grace's brow lifted. "Ah, I see. Do you know what he said?"

Kate shook her head. "But I spoke to Nadine briefly, and she said it wasn't his fault."

"Then you should take her word for it," Grace said matter-of-factly. After a brief pause, she used a more tender tone. "Something else is bothering you about David, isn't it? Whatever it is, you can tell me."

Knowing Grace and David were old friends, Kate hesitated to say anything that would tarnish her good opinion of him. Yet there was another side to him that she couldn't reconcile. Until she understood more about David's fixation with her uncle's property she'd never fully trust his motives. "It's his obsession with Owen Bentley's land."

Grace quietly leaned back in her chair with a thoughtful expression. "You know, when Wade first asked me to the social at the local grange, I turned him down too, not because I didn't want to go with him, mind you, but because he was a Holbrook, and I didn't want any part of the Holbrook–Bentley feud."

"What changed your mind?"

"He persisted in asking me out until I finally told him the truth. Then he laughed and told me if that was the only thing standing in the way of me going out with him, he'd pay a visit to Wallace Bentley himself and make a peace offering."

At the mention of her grandfather's name, Kate had to know more. "What happened?"

"That hateful bully chased him off his property with his shotgun."

It didn't surprise her that the man who had somehow alienated his own daughter should refuse a genuine olive branch, but it still made her sad. "You married Wade anyway?"

She smiled wistfully. "I figured if he loved me enough to try to end an ancient feud, he'd probably be willing to do whatever it took to make a good marriage. Our marriage wasn't perfect, not by a long shot. We had a few feuds of our own that had to get sorted out from time to time, but we loved each other enough to put aside our differences and forgive one another, and that made all the difference."

"Well, I don't see David ever giving up his dream of owning that land again."

"Instead of presuming what he will or won't do, why not be honest with him about your concerns and hear what he has to say? He might surprise you."

After yesterday, she didn't need any more surprises, especially bad ones. As long as David wanted the land she would inherit, no amount of sage advice could predict how he would react when he learned the truth about her. But Grace was right about needing to be honest with him—and she would—as soon as she tracked down her uncle's killer.

Having cleared the breakfast dishes, Kate called the U.T. Department of Agriculture a second time to see if she could reach Roy Timmons. She still wanted to ask him about the letter he had sent to Owen shortly before his death. But again, he wasn't answering his phone. Kate left a voice message for the receptionist to return her call, hoping there might be another way to contact him.

Afterward, Kate went outside to help Grace harvest the squash, Brussels sprouts, greens, and herbs in the garden. Kate didn't expect the weeding and picking the ripened vegetables to be so absorbing. Of course, a big part of it had to do with Grace's hands-on instruction about gardening and farming that sparked her interest. She couldn't remember ever working so hard and liking it this much.

"If I'm becoming a nuisance following you around, please let me know," Kate said as she walked with Grace to the henhouse. "Your life here is so different from mine at home. I'm fascinated by it."

"It's good to see you enjoying yourself," Grace replied. She stopped in front of the chicken coop and pivoted suddenly in Kate's direction as if she had something important on her mind. "Kate, I don't know you all that well, and it's none of my business, but I don't think the real reason you came all the way from Nashville to Tyler's Glen was to go camping."

Kate scratched the back of her head, weighing how much she should tell her. She had wanted to protect Grace in case learning her full identity might somehow put her in danger. Yet Kate disliked pretense, and from the determined look in the woman's eye, she wouldn't settle for anything less than the whole truth. "You're right," she finally admitted. "I didn't want to tell you at first because of the feud between the Holbrooks and the Bentleys, and because I didn't want to upset you."

Setting her egg basket down to listen, Grace waited expectantly.

"You see, I'm Owen Bentley's niece."

Grace covered her mouth with her hand. "*You're* Mary Bentley's daughter?"

Kate affirmed it with a nod.

The woman slowly removed her hand, studying her in fascination. "No wonder you look so familiar."

A kernel of hope lifted Kate's heart. "You knew my mother?"

"Why, yes. She went to high school with my son, Frederick. But you said your parents were gone."

"My mother and foster parents are. My father left us years ago, and to be honest, I don't know what happened to him."

"What happened to Mary?"

Kate shared how her mother had died when she was young.

"I'm so sorry. I had no idea."

Observing the chickens pecking nearby, Kate went on. "My mother wasn't close to her family. I don't know much of anything about her life before I was born. Whenever I asked her, she didn't want to talk about it." She lifted her eyes to Grace. "I wouldn't have known about Owen's death except for an anonymous tip I received before I came here. I still don't know who sent it or why."

"How odd."

"That's not all. Strange things have been happening to me ever since I came to town. It's as if someone doesn't want me here."

"What kind of things?"

Kate hesitated, but Grace's motherly concern and compassion opened the floodgates and compelled her to tell the woman about the shooting incident at Owen's, the discovery of the knife, the arrow attack in the park, and the threatening note pinned to the tree.

"Good heavens!" Grace's hand went to her heart.

Now Kate wondered if she should have told her. "I didn't want to upset you or put you in danger, but since I'm staying here, you have a right to know the truth."

"Come here," Grace said, giving Kate a big hug,

reminding her a little of Rose, who always had a listening ear and a warm embrace when she needed it. "I'm glad you told me," Grace said as she released her. "And don't worry about upsetting me. I'm as tough as they come, and I don't scare easy. I know how to deal with snakes in the henhouse."

Kate couldn't help smiling at the image of Grace, the snake slayer. After confiding to the sympathetic woman, she felt a huge weight had been lifted off of her. "Deputy Travis thinks the shooter at Owen's was Virgil."

"No wonder you were so upset about him hunting last night."

"By the way, we found Owen's dog in the park yesterday. He was in pretty bad shape. If we hadn't found him, he probably would have starved. He's at the vet's right now recovering."

"Poor Buster," Grace said in a somber tone.

Kate gave Grace a moment to let all she had told her sink in, and prepared herself for the worst. "Now that you know I'm a Bentley, do you still want me to stay here?"

"Of course!" Grace looked squarely at Kate. "I married a Holbrook, that's true, but I never held Owen responsible for what his ancestors did. In a way, I pitied him. He led such a solitary life and was too tightfisted and self-centered to share it with anyone."

"Except Rick and Virgil," Kate reminded her.

She acknowledged that with a gleam in her eye. "Rick was quite fond of your uncle. They shared a love of restoring old cars. Owen was good to him and gave him the money to start his own car repair business."

"Why would someone want to kill him?" Kate asked.

"I don't know. The whole thing is tragic. I'll never forget the sound of those fire truck sirens in the middle of the night. When I looked out my window, flames had completely engulfed his house."

"Do you know where he's buried?"

Grace nodded solemnly. "In the cemetery behind the church I attend. I plan to go this Sunday. Why don't you come with me?"

Maybe she could learn more about her uncle and her family at the cemetery too. "I'd like that."

"As for being a Bentley, I don't care if you're related to Attila the Hun—you're staying here, and that's that."

Grace's kind insistence put Kate at ease. "Thank you. After all the strange things that have happened lately, I wasn't looking forward to sleeping in my tent. Plus, I'm still waiting for my replacement credit cards to arrive."

"Honey, it's my pleasure. After all, we're practically neighbors."

"Neighbors?"

"Yes—as Owen's niece, I'm assuming you're his heir."

She sighed from the weighty implications. "That's the biggest surprise of all. I didn't know about his land or fishing lure business before I came here."

"If Owen's lures catch on the way Rick thinks they will, you could become quite an heiress. Don't be surprised if the men start flocking to you once the word gets out. David better get busy and snatch you up while he can."

The prospect of becoming an heiress and all the notoriety and responsibility that came with it didn't exactly thrill Kate, though Grace's mention of David prompted her to think of a couple of projects in need of extra funds. Building the outreach center and restoring the church camp wouldn't come cheap, and from what he'd told her, there hadn't been enough money to get them off the ground.

"David doesn't know yet," she said. Seeing Grace's confused expression, she felt she should explain. "I haven't told him for the same reasons I didn't want to tell you. Someone is targeting me, and I don't want to put anyone else in danger. Plus, David still resents my uncle for taking advantage of his father. Now that Owen is dead, David wants his family's land back more than ever. How will he react when he finds out I'm Owen's niece?"

Grace touched her arm. "That's why you have to tell him before he finds out from someone else. You owe him the truth."

"I don't know how to tell him."

"You have to find a way."

Grace was right, but Kate preferred to think about something else. "Is there any special skill required for collecting eggs, or can a city girl learn how to do it?"

"Come on, I'll show you."

After a quick demonstration from Grace, Kate busied herself gathering the eggs and carefully placing them in her basket. She may have come to Tyler's Glen with hopes of finding family ties, but now that she was here, she would make the best of it. Grace's favorable response to her revelation had been a huge relief and encouragement. As far-fetched as it sounded, the thought of being neighbors with the pleasant woman appealed to her, and living next door to David didn't sound too bad either.

But once he knew of her relationship to Owen, would he want to have anything to do with her?

After harvesting corn into the early afternoon, David took a break and drove to the animal hospital to pick up Buster and bring him to Grace's.

Grace met him in the driveway as he hopped out of his truck. "Hello again, David. What brings you by this time—as if I didn't know?" She gave him a sly wink.

He rolled his eyes at her teasing. "Actually, I have a special delivery." He came around to the passenger door and took out the pet carrier.

"What's in there?" she asked, peering inside.

"Owen's dog, Buster. Didn't Kate tell you we found him in the park?"

"Yes, and also about the knife you found and your narrow escape from the bowhunter."

He stared at her. "I'm surprised she told you all that."

Kate appeared from the henhouse carrying a basket of eggs and strode toward them. She looked fresh and lovely, and perfectly at home on the farm.

He set the carrier on the ground and glimpsed the warmth and pride emanating from Grace's face as she regarded Kate. Returning his focus to the captivating young woman, he greeted her with a smile. "I see that Grace is putting you to work."

"She's been a big help," Grace told him. "And don't let that pretty face and girlish figure fool you—she's as strong as a horse. She's been working nonstop since breakfast."

Bending low, Kate looked inside the dog cage. "Hi, Buster."

David came to his knees and opened the door to the carrier. "The vet says he needs to rest a few more days, but he should be better by next week." The dog lifted his head at Kate, causing David to chuckle. "Now that he's out of the animal clinic, he seems to have perked up."

Kate glanced at David. "As soon as my credit cards arrive, I want to pay his vet bill."

"Don't worry. It's already taken care of."

Grace leaned closer to see the animal. "Nice of you to take him in, David."

He rose to his feet. "Actually, Buster is Kate's dog now." When he saw Grace's brow wrinkle in confusion, he realized Kate hadn't shared that part with her yet. "But I can keep him until he's better."

Grace watched Kate caressing the dog inside the carrier. "Well, I guess he can stay, so long as he's outside. Flash's old doghouse is still in the backyard. He was Wade's hunting dog."

"Oh," Kate replied in a subdued tone. "Couldn't we keep him on the back porch until he's well enough to be outside? He won't be any trouble. I'll take good care of him."

"He's quiet too," David added, wanting to help Kate's case. "I've never heard him bark."

Grace's cool expression warmed a little. "All right, but only until he's better." She took another look at the docile dog. "Not much of a guard or hunting dog, is he? It's a mystery to me why Owen ever took him in."

Kate sat on the layer of leaves and gently lifted him out of the carrier so Grace could get a better look. "How could he have refused that cute little face?"

Buster whined, his brown button eyes gazing adoringly at Kate.

David smiled to himself. The terrier was obviously smitten with her. Well, he might be mangy and malnourished, but at least Buster had good taste in women.

Not wanting to appear as smitten as the dog, David stepped away toward his truck. "Now that Buster is settled with you two, I've got to run. The preliminary rounds for the showmanship competition are this afternoon. Grace, do you want a ride?"

Grace put a hand to her mouth. "Oh, I almost forgot! Thanks for reminding me. I'll drive myself over, but I appreciate the offer." She waved goodbye to him and went inside to get ready.

Kate carefully returned Buster to the carrier and closed the door. "Do you have to leave so soon, David?" she asked as she got up. "I was hoping we could talk."

He needed to be going, but her adorable pout tempted him to stay. "Well, maybe I can stay for a minute. What is it?"

She hesitated, avoiding eye contact with him. "There's

something I've been meaning to tell you—"

His emergency ring tone blared, interrupting them.

Kate frowned at the noise. "What's that?"

David removed his phone from his pocket. "Sorry—it's the dispatcher for the volunteer fire department."

When he answered, the dispatcher on the other end spoke in an urgent voice. "We've got a 911 on 15 Main Street."

Bubba's Diner. "On my way." David ended the call and turned to Kate. "Sorry, I've got to go. What were you about to say?"

She thrust her hands in her jean pockets and rocked on her heels. "It can wait. Thanks again for bringing Buster home from the vet's."

"If you still want to talk, give me a call later. Otherwise, I'll pick you and Grace up Friday at eleven for the festival." He smiled with anticipation before sliding into his truck.

Waving as he backed out of Grace's drive, he regretted that he couldn't stay longer and hear what was on her mind. He didn't like rushing off like that, but under the circumstances, he didn't have much choice.

After parking his truck outside the diner, David rushed in. He spotted Bubba attending to Nadine, who was seated in a chair.

David hurried to them. "What's going on?"

Bubba's voice had an anxious pitch. "It's Nadine. She's dizzy."

"I was a little lightheaded," she clarified in a mildly irritated voice, "but I'm better now. Sorry you had to come all this way for nothing, David. I told Bubba I'd be okay."

"Doc Granger is away from his office today," Bubba

told him, "so I called 911."

"You did the right thing." David addressed Nadine in a calming tone. "Can you stand?"

"Sure, I'm fine." She moved to get up.

David raised his hand. "Take it slow."

She rolled her eyes and came to her feet. "It's only the flu. I've been feeling yucky the last few days."

He felt her forehead for a fever. It felt cool, and her color looked good too. "Okay, why don't you sit down again while I check your pulse?"

"I'm telling you it's nothing," she argued, grudgingly taking a seat. "You and Bubba are a couple of worrywarts."

David ignored her remark as he pressed his two fingers to her wrist, using his watch to determine her heart rate. When he'd finished, he felt somewhat relieved. "Your pulse is strong, but you should take it easy the rest of the day, and see Doc Granger when he gets back."

"I've got to work."

"I'll call Glenda to fill in," Bubba said.

"No, I'm fine. Your wife shouldn't have to take my shift."

He ignored her and looked at David. "Glenda won't mind. She'll take the kids to her mother's."

David turned to Nadine. "Let me take you home."

"No, I can drive myself." She waved him away. "Stop worrying about me, okay? I'm not your problem." Then she tugged on Bubba's sleeve with a rueful look. "Hey, I don't like leaving you short-handed."

"Don't worry. I've got it covered." The big man gave her a reassuring wink. "You take care of yourself and get some rest."

David escorted Nadine to her car outside the diner, staying close in case she felt faint again. "I'll follow you home in my truck to make sure you get there okay."

She abruptly stopped and faced him. "No!"

Her strong refusal took him by surprise.

"I'm sorry," she said, softening her tone. "I appreciate your concern, but I'll be fine. Really."

Seeing he was getting nowhere, he finally capitulated. "Okay, but if you need anything, call me."

"Thanks." She glanced down and leaned against her car. "David . . . I'm sorry about the way I acted yesterday at lunch. I've been under a lot of stress lately, and I guess I lost it."

He felt sorry for her and regretted that he'd added to her angst. "It probably wasn't the best time or place to tell you, but I thought you should know the rumors going around town about Danny. I didn't want you to hear it from someone else."

"I know. Maybe I'm too naïve, but you'd think people wouldn't be so quick to judge a man after he's served his time."

David didn't respond. The less said about his brother, the better.

"You still resent him, don't you?"

"I need to go."

As he turned to leave, Nadine grabbed his arm. "Danny is your brother, David. Please, for both your sakes, give him a second chance. Your father always supported him, even when Danny was convicted and sent away to prison."

"And ultimately it killed him," he shot back.

She gave him a hard look. "Danny didn't kill your father."

"Maybe, but if not for all the trouble he caused, I'm convinced Dad would still be alive. And if you're not careful, my brother will drag you down too."

CHAPTER TEN

HAVING FINISHED HER THURSDAY MORNING RUN, Kate decided to stop by Owen's place on her way back to Grace's. With prowlers roaming the countryside, and her gun and wallet stolen, she wanted to protect his archery equipment. As she ventured toward the barn, keeping an eye out for poachers with rifles, she noticed the yellow crime tape was missing from the burnt rubble of the house. Deputy Travis must have come and removed it.

Cautiously, she entered the barn and looked around. Was she too late? The compound bow and its quiver of arrows weren't where she'd left them. She searched the entire area without finding them. *Then she remembered*—The arrows shot at her in the park had the same red and green fletching as her uncle's. Were his arrows used to target her and David? The thought sent a shudder through her body.

Still troubled by the missing bow hunting equipment, Kate carried the conventional bow and arrows to Grace's. The theft at Owen's barn had put her on guard, so when she noticed the door to the back porch had been left unlocked, she placed an arrow against the bowstring as a precaution before going in.

With her arrow nocked and ready, she slowly entered the porch.

Buster sat up in his crate filled with blankets and tilted his head, giving her a curious look. The smell of bacon frying in the kitchen told Kate that Grace had left the door unlocked for her, instantly erasing her fears, and she removed the arrow from the bow.

She stowed the archery equipment inside the storage

closet off the porch, and stopped to pet Buster. "You're feeling better now, aren't you, boy? Maybe I'll take you with me next time."

After taking her running shoes off and leaving them on the porch, Kate went through the den into the kitchen. "I hope there's enough bacon for me too."

Grace turned around, her face brightening. "There you are. You're just in time for breakfast."

Kate smiled at her. "I appreciate you leaving the porch unlocked, but from now on, you should keep all the doors secured, Grace."

"Oh, I didn't think about that. When you left for your run this morning, I didn't want you to be locked out." She stepped away from the stove, taking off her apron.

"I'll set the table," Kate said, eager to devour the appetizing meal.

"Where did you go on your run?"

"Down the road a bit. I brought some of Owen's archery equipment back with me. The lock on his barn is busted, and I didn't want it to get stolen. Plus, it'll give me a good excuse to brush up on my archery skills." She left off the part about the stolen compound bow and arrows. No use worrying Grace about that, but she should call Harlan and Vicki to inform them of it.

Grace moved closer to Kate, interest gleaming in her eyes. "I didn't know you were an archer."

"It's something I used to do with my foster father, Jim." The pleasant memory cracked her voice a little. "I was the son he never had."

"Are you any good?"

The directness of the woman's question tickled Kate. "I was. I won a few competitions, but that was a long time ago."

Grace went to the stove and grabbed the skillet with the eggs to bring to the table. "You should enter the archery competition at the harvest festival."

Kate shook her head. "It's been too long."

"The grand prize is a $200 gift certificate from Bear Claw Sporting Goods," Grace added as she started to serve them breakfast.

"Really?" It wasn't enough to buy a car, but it would help pay for another gun.

Grace set the skillet back on the stove and put the lid on to keep it warm. "Breakfast can wait. Go see if you can still register online."

Alone in her room upstairs, Kate called Harlan first and told him about the stolen bow hunting equipment. She also informed him of the shooting incident in the park with the arrows that matched Owen's, and that Vicki Bates was investigating it. Harlan told her that Vicki had already contacted him, and they had started working the case together.

That made Kate feel better. With the deputy sheriff and the park ranger teaming up, they had a better shot at finding Owen's killer. She wanted to work the case with them, but it wasn't her jurisdiction and she was supposed to be on vacation. Still, that wasn't going to keep her from finding out what she could on her own.

After ending her call with Harlan, Kate attempted to register for the amateur archery competition online. Since they didn't have a women's division, she called the number on the website and pleaded her case to the man in charge of the event. He made an exception to allow her to compete with the men. That was fine with her, though it would probably be stiffer competition.

During breakfast, Kate asked Grace if she could borrow

her car for her appointment with Lester at ten-thirty. Grace happily obliged and told her to feel free to borrow her car anytime and gave her spare keys to both the house and the car. She also suggested that Kate come and go through the back porch, which was closer to the drive and the garden, and provided easy access to take Buster outside. Kate wished she could repay the generous woman.

Later that morning, Kate drove to town and parked Grace's car on the street in front of Lester Crane's office. As she got out, the hair-raising sensation of someone watching caused her to look around. She saw only an elderly couple walking across the street, but they didn't appear to be paying her any attention.

With the speed that rumors traveled, the whole town would soon know who she was. She had thought about calling David last night and telling him she was Owen's niece, but decided to wait until tomorrow when she'd see him in person. Breaking the news that she was the heir of his nemesis wasn't the kind of thing to do via text or over the phone. She owed him more courtesy than that.

She knocked on Lester's door, and the cordial lawyer ushered her into his office. Noticing the campaign posters had been stacked neatly in the corner of the room, she set her backpack by the vacant chair in front of his desk. She couldn't help comparing his dignified office, outfitted with expensive bookshelves, desk and leather chairs, with Harlan's humble substation. Apparently, being a lawyer in this small town came with more perks than being a deputy sheriff.

Lester waited for her to be seated before he took his place behind his desk. "I hope you've been enjoying your visit here. Fall is the best time to be in the Smokies, in my opinion. Are you staying at the B&B?"

"No. I was camping in the park, but now I'm staying with Grace Holbrook."

He gave her an approving nod. "Excellent. You know her home is a Tennessee historical landmark, built in the late 1800s."

"I didn't know that, but it is very impressive."

"Now, regarding your uncle," he said, switching to the business at hand, "I assume you'll want to be the administrator of his estate."

"I haven't thought much about it, but I guess that makes sense. Do I need to be here in Tyler's Glen to do that?"

"No, you can handle most of it from Nashville, but you will need to come or send a representative for certain things like getting Owen's assets appraised. I'd be happy to assist in any way I can."

Great. She needed all the help she could get. "Thank you. I've been feeling a bit overwhelmed since our last meeting."

"Yes, it's unfortunate that you have to deal with these unpleasant details during your stay here."

Thoughts of the time she'd spent with David also entered her mind. "It hasn't been all bad."

A pleased look came to his face. "I'm very glad to hear that. We want all of our visitors to enjoy themselves."

She glanced at his campaign posters. His concern about the town's image would make a convincing ad for his bid to become mayor.

"As Owen's lawyer," he continued, "I'm very familiar with his estate and can provide whatever help you need to settle it." He picked up a sheet of paper from his desk and handed it to her. "Here is the form to petition the probate office to make you Owen's representative. I'm going there next week. If you fill this out in the next few days, I can deliver it for you if you'd like."

Kate scanned the form. It seemed straightforward enough. "Thanks. I'll take it with me to look it over more in depth, and I'll let you know if I have any questions."

"Certainly. I believe you gave me your number on Monday. I'll be in touch if I think of anything else."

Lester's expression turned more serious. "In case you didn't know, Owen's estate could potentially be worth a small fortune. In addition to his property, he had a fishing lure venture. However, shortly before he died, he received a legal notice that he was being sued for patent infringement."

Blown away, she leaned forward and peered at the lawyer. "By whom?"

"Joe Campbell."

Falling back in her chair, she was no longer surprised. Why hadn't she seen this coming? "Does he have a strong case?"

"That depends."

"On what?" she asked, wondering how Joe could possibly have any claim on Owen's business.

"On your ability to find the original designs for Owen's fishing lures."

Suddenly, she realized her uncle had saddled her with a colossal mess to sort out. "You mean he didn't patent them?"

Lester smiled politely and steepled his fingers together on his desk. "Owen had a strong distrust of lawyers and institutions. He only came to me when he had to."

"Who's been running his business?"

"Rick Travis."

"Rick? But he's an auto mechanic."

"Actually, he's a boy wonder when it comes to business. He developed the website for Owen's fishing lures two years ago. Now a couple of large sporting goods chains are in a bidding war for exclusive rights to feature Owen's products in their stores. It could be very lucrative to whoever owns the rights to those designs."

"And if I can't find a patent or Owen's designs for the lures?"

Lester released a long breath. "I'm afraid you won't be able to settle the estate until Joe's lawsuit is resolved."

After her meeting with Lester, Kate brooded over the new challenge of settling Owen's estate with Joe's lawsuit looming. Wanting to stop by Rick's garage, she decided to take a leisurely stroll there instead of driving.

A sign on Main Street advertising the harvest festival filled Kate with anticipation of going with David tomorrow. Grace had told her last night that he had barely made it in time to the showmanship horse competition yesterday after responding to his emergency call, but both she and David had done well in the preliminary rounds. Kate hoped they both made it to the finals.

As she walked along, she couldn't help noticing the Lester Crane for Mayor signs posted on every corner.

An unwelcome male voice came from behind. "I can't wait until this election is over."

Joe Campbell. Was he stalking her? She quickly crossed the street trying to ignore him, but he stuck with her.

"Hey, little filly, what's your hurry?"

She stopped and turned to look him in the eye. "I'm not a horse, and why are you following me?"

He smirked, raising his palms innocently. "What do you have against people being friendly?"

A pickup covered in red, white, and blue bunting and plastered with Lester's campaign signs passed by them. The loudspeaker in the truck bed blasted a reminder for people to vote in November.

"Good ol' Lester," Joe drawled. "He's pulling out all the stops."

As disgusted as she was with Joe, she was curious about the election. And maybe if she could learn a little more about the man behind the lawsuit against her uncle's estate, she could find a way to convince him to drop it. "You think Lester will win?"

"He'd better. I gave him a hefty contribution, and I don't like betting on a losing horse."

She quickly glanced around and realized she hadn't seen any signs for Lester's opponent. "Who's running against him?"

"No one. He's unopposed. Unless someone attempts a last-minute write-in campaign, he's a shoe-in."

"Then why all the campaign signs?"

"Lester doesn't want to leave anything to chance, and neither do I. Like I said, I only bet on a sure thing. By the way, I saw you leaving Lester's office." His heavy Southern accent twanged with interest. "I hope you're seriously considering my offer to buy Owen's property."

Boy, he was more persistent than a swamp mosquito. "Right now, I'm only thinking about settling his estate."

"Anything I can do to help?"

She stopped and gave him a direct stare. "Actually, there is. You can drop your lawsuit against my uncle's fishing lure business."

He stepped away. "But he stole my designs."

"If that's the case, why didn't you sue him earlier, before the big sporting goods companies got interested?"

He flinched from her pointed question but brushed it off with a sly grin. "I don't like discussing all this legal mumbo-jumbo when I'm in the company of a beautiful woman. What do you say we leave it to our lawyers to sort out while we focus on more pleasant things, like getting to know each other better?"

She rolled her eyes. "If that's the way you want it, then I have nothing more to say."

He stayed with her like a pesky fly as she resumed her walk down Main Street, headed toward Rick's garage. An old, vacant warehouse caught her attention, and she stopped. She realized it must be the same building David had told her about, the one he said would be ideal for the community outreach center.

Joe stepped beside her. "My father owned that building. He used it for a feed warehouse."

She peered at him from the corner of her eye, noting the softening of his tone and demeanor. "Why haven't you sold or developed it?"

A hint of sadness flickered across his face before his cocky façade covered it. "Why, are you interested?"

The wistfulness in his earlier expression caused her to wonder. Had Joe kept the property this long for sentimental reasons? If so, maybe she could convince him to give it away for a good cause. She attempted a more pleasant approach in hopes of persuading him. "Have you thought of donating it to the town? It's in a great location, and you could get a tax write-off."

"That's prime real estate in the heart of Tyler's Glen," he said indignantly. "I could make a small fortune selling it to a developer. Why would I want to give it away?"

"To help a lot of people in need," she replied matter-of-factly.

He eyed her cynically, but then the trace of sadness returned to his face. "My father always wanted it to be used as a medical clinic."

Joe had kept it all this time out of deference to his father? Despite his obnoxious behavior, she felt a pang of sympathy for him. "That sounds like a good use for it. Why haven't you done that?"

"We don't need one anymore. When Doc Granger

wanted to expand his practice, the town donated another building on First for the clinic."

"You could still make good use of your father's warehouse for the community."

His derisive snicker did a poor job of deflecting his personal conflict. "David Jennings must be filling you with his bleeding-heart ideas. Don't let him fool you. He might come off as squeaky clean, but his family has more stink on them than a dead skunk."

She crossed her arms, now incensed by his slurs against David and his family. "I understand you and David used to be friends. How can you say such nasty things?"

"Because it's true. And here's something else you should be aware of—the word on the street is that David's brother, Danny, set the explosion that killed your uncle."

She'd had enough of Joe for one day. "Stop! I don't want to hear any more of your malicious gossip."

He continued to spout off. "His brother is trouble, and that's a fact. I'm telling you for your own good. Unless you want to end up like your uncle, stay away from the whole Jennings clan."

Kate was relieved when Joe finally left to go eat lunch at Bubba's Diner. She tried to dismiss his warning about David and his family, yet a part of her wondered if the rumor about David's brother might be true. After all, Danny Jennings was a convicted felon.

Stepping into Rick's garage, she spotted him finishing up with a customer.

Rick waved when he saw her, and she waited until he was available.

"Hey." Rick said, wiping his hands on a rag as he

approached her. "I haven't seen any mail for you yet, but the replacement windshield and windows for Owen's truck are supposed to come in by Monday, so I should have the truck ready by Tuesday." He fidgeted with the rag, peering at her from under his baseball cap.

"Something on your mind, Rick?"

He finally blurted it out. "I heard you're Owen Bentley's niece."

Uh-oh! Word was starting to spread. Hopefully, not to David yet. "Who told you that?"

"My dad, but he warned me and my mother not to tell anyone else."

"Your mother knows?" She hoped Julianna had more discretion than Harlan.

"I kind of forced the issue when I asked him why you were at Owen's the other day when I towed the pickup. I figured something was up."

She couldn't blame him for being curious, especially since Owen had been his friend and business partner. But was it only curiosity or could there be another reason he was interested in her relationship with Owen? With her uncle gone, it had cleared the way for Rick to run the entire fishing lure business on his own. That is, until she came to town and identified herself as Owen's niece. "Now that you know, I'd appreciate you keeping it between us. I need to tell someone before it becomes common knowledge."

"My lips are sealed." He zipped his mouth with his finger. "Does this mean you'll be taking over Owen's business?"

She needed to find the person who killed her uncle before she could think about taking over his business. "I don't know what it means at this point. I'm still trying to get a handle on how to settle his estate. By the way, I heard you're the brains behind his fishing lure website."

He shrugged modestly. "It wasn't much. Basically, I

manage the website and run the business side of things. My mom does the heavy lifting. She manages the finances for both Owen's business and my car repair business. She's a CPA."

"I look forward to meeting her. I've already met your grandmother. In fact, I've been staying at her house the last couple of nights."

"Mom mentioned that. Grandma called her yesterday and told her. She also said you adopted Owen's dog."

Kate laughed. "Actually, I think he adopted me."

"How is Grandma?" he asked.

"Fine," she replied without giving it too much thought.

"She's feeling okay?" The worry lines on his youthful face had aged him a couple of years.

Kate studied him, wondering what he was driving at. "Sure. Why do you ask?"

He stared at the floor for a moment. "A few months ago, she had a mild heart attack. We've been telling her to slow down, but she never listens."

"Oh." The news surprised and saddened Kate. "I'm glad you told me. I'll make sure she doesn't overdo it."

His lanky shoulders seemed to relax. "I'm glad you're staying with her. I keep meaning to drop by and see her, but work has been crazy lately. I barely have time to eat. If my apartment wasn't over the garage, I probably wouldn't get any sleep either."

"You should get out more and enjoy this amazing place. I met your grandmother at the horse camp near Cades Cove, and got to eat your steak because you were too busy working. I did feel a little guilty though. You probably canceled to fix the damage to Owen's pickup."

"Yeah, that was pretty weird, but Virgil Crane is a kook anyway." He rubbed his nose. "I was thinking, if you managed Owen's business, we'd be working together."

"Would that be a problem?"

"Not for me."

His refreshing openness put her more at ease about his motives and the prospect of her running the business one day. "Good. I think we would make a great team."

"You know, Owen was pretty old-school about things. I wanted him to use social media to market his fishing lures, but he wasn't interested. He pretty much let me handle all that stuff."

"You must be good at it. I hear a couple of big companies are interested in selling the fishing lures in their stores."

His amiable grin reminded Kate of his Uncle Frederick in the picture on Grace's mantle. "It's too bad Owen's not around to enjoy his success."

She nodded in sad agreement. The best thing she could do for her uncle now was to find his killer, and conduct an orderly settlement of his estate—and Joe stood in the way of accomplishing that. "Rick, where do you think my uncle would have kept something important like the designs for his fishing lures?"

"I'm not sure. Why?"

"Joe Campbell claims Owen stole his fishing lure designs."

"No way! Why that no-good, slime—"

She raised her hand to shush him. "We have to find proof that Owen designed the lures so Joe will drop his lawsuit."

"I'll look around, but Owen wasn't much for keeping records. Hey, since you and I are going to be business partners, I think I should take you fishing and give you a demo of our lures."

"I'd like that, but can you spare the time?"

"You tell me—you're the boss." He said it with a slight twinkle in his hazel eyes. "But we'll need to leave early in the morning."

"Okay. Let me know when and where." She waved, turning to leave.

"Wait."

Pausing, she glanced over her shoulder.

"When you see Joe again, tell him he can fix his own Porsche from now on." He scowled. "Never mind. I'll tell him myself."

As David drove the combine through his cornfield, Nadine's words about his brother replayed in his mind. *You still resent Danny, don't you?* How could he not, after the shame his brother had inflicted on his family, and all the grief he'd caused? Now with Danny rumored to be in town, people were already blaming him for Owen's death. Hopefully, his brother had learned from his mistakes and had chosen a new place to start over, far away from Tyler's Glen.

A deputy sheriff's SUV drove up and parked by the road next to David's cornfield. Steering his combine in that direction, David came to the end of the row, killed the engine and climbed down. Harlan exited his vehicle at the same time and they met at the edge of the road.

"How's it going?" the deputy asked in a friendly, casual manner.

"All right. Trying to get as much of the seed corn harvest done before it rains this weekend."

"I heard about you and Kate Phillips finding the knife and becoming target practice for a bowhunter in the national park."

David stuffed his hands in the pockets of his jeans. He had a feeling since Harlan wouldn't look him in the eye that he had come for a different purpose. "What brings you by, Deputy?"

Harlan squinted at the few clouds in the afternoon sky. "I thought you should know— there's been a new development in the investigation into Owen Bentley's death."

From the ominous tone in the deputy's voice, David knew it wasn't good. "And?"

"We've identified a small piece of an explosive device that was found in the rubble."

Arson. "Any suspects?"

"Not yet." He lifted his hat and scratched his head. "What's your brother up to these days?"

David's muscles tightened. "I wouldn't know."

From the way he kept staring, Harlan didn't seem to believe him. "You haven't seen him since he was released from prison?"

Straightening and crossing his arms, David responded in an adamant tone. "No, and I don't expect to. After everything that's happened, he'd be crazy to show his face around here."

Harlan eyed him with a hard look. "I hope you're right."

That afternoon at Grace's house, Kate's cellphone beeped with a text from David, which she eagerly read.

Can't wait to see you tomorrow.

His message delighted her and filled her with excitement at the prospect of going to the festival with him. But as long as she kept the fact that she was Owen's niece a secret, she couldn't fully embrace their day together. She had to find the right moment to tell him at the festival, before he heard it from someone else.

Grace had gone to the fairgrounds for the last preliminary round of the showmanship event in the horse show, so Kate took advantage of having the place to herself by configuring a shooting range in the backyard and practicing her archery skills. She fastened a paper target on the side of the henhouse and lined bottles and cans along Grace's wooden fence. One by one, she shot the items on the fence, her aim becoming more accurate with each shot. Four days after the accident, her shoulder pain was much better, but she still had an occasional twinge.

Buster rested on a blanket on the ground while she took aim. His sudden whining made her curious.

"Bravo!" a female voice exclaimed as the sound of applause came from behind.

Kate spun around. An attractive woman with a dazzling smile and Grace's sparkling eyes was walking toward her.

"You must be Kate. I'm Julianna Travis, Grace's daughter." The lovely woman, with her elegant black wrap jumpsuit and perfectly coordinated jewelry, seemed out of place on a farm.

"I'm afraid Grace is at the fairgrounds with Clementine."

"That's fine," Julianna replied with a slight wave of her hand. "It'll give us a chance to chat a bit. I meant to stop by earlier, but Rick keeps me so busy with all of his business ventures—Say, I hear you're from Nashville. I've always wanted to live there. A small rural town like Tyler's Glen must seem pretty boring to you, coming from a big city with so much to do." The stunning, refined lady's poise, class and lilting Southern accent seemed more typical of a Nashville socialite than the wife of a small-town deputy sheriff.

"Actually, I like it here," Kate said. "At home, I don't get out that much. I'm usually too busy working. It's been a nice change of pace to spend so much time outdoors and in the mountains."

Julianna charmed her with an engaging smile. "I understand you have family roots in Tyler's Glen. Harlan told me you're Owen Bentley's niece."

The woman's directness took Kate by surprise. Though Grace had accepted her wholeheartedly, Kate wondered if Julianna might still harbor some prejudice toward the Bentleys.

"Oh, don't worry. He warned me to keep it under wraps. I won't tell a soul."

That eased Kate's mind a bit.

"What are your plans now?"

If only she had a good answer. "I haven't decided. Things haven't gone exactly as I'd planned."

"Learning of Owen's death must have come as quite a shock."

Kate rubbed the top of her left arm. "Yes. And the last thing I expected was to discover that I'm his sole heir. I'm in the process of petitioning to become the administrator of his estate."

"That is a lot to deal with, and a big responsibility for a young woman. I'll be happy to help. I'm the only CPA in town, and I do have experience with settling estates."

"Thank you. I'll keep that in mind."

Julianna regarded Kate as if assessing her. "My son, Rick, has become quite fond of you."

Feeling a bit uncomfortable, Kate wasn't sure how to interpret her last statement. "He's been very helpful, renting me his pickup after my car accident."

"You know, Rick was very close to Owen."

Kate acknowledged that fact with a nod. "It sounds like your son was one of the few people my uncle warmed up to."

A thoughtful look came to Julianna's face. "Owen Bentley was a complicated man. I went to school with his sister, Mary—your mother."

Kate stared in amazement. "You knew my mother?"

"Why, yes, she was only a couple of years older than me." Julianna's radiance dimmed a little. "I knew your father,

Norm, too."

Kate gazed at the rooster harassing the chickens around the yard. "We weren't close. He left years ago, and I haven't seen him since." When she looked up, it surprised her that the sophisticated woman had become misty-eyed.

Julianna sniffed softly. "That must have been very hard for you at such a young age."

Kate brushed it off as she'd grown accustomed to doing over the years. "It was a long time ago."

An admiring smile brightened the woman's face again. "You look so much like your mother. I was jealous of her because she was the prettiest girl in school."

Picturing her mother's beautiful face, Kate was touched by the compliment.

"You know, when you inherit Owen's estate, we'll be working together. I manage the finances for his fishing lure business. Rick told me about Joe Campbell's ridiculous lawsuit. I want to help you put that sleazy opportunist in his place."

"Finding Owen's fishing lure designs is the key."

"Yes, Rick told me, and we've been searching through our files, but no luck yet. I wonder . . ." Julianna's eyes held a shrewd spark that reminded Kate a little of Grace.

"What?"

"Joe loves to negotiate. Maybe if you offered something else of value to him—like Owen's property, for instance—he might drop the case against the fishing lure business."

Kate couldn't do that to David or to Grace. The fact that Julianna had even suggested it surprised her. But if Joe won the lawsuit, Rick and Julianna's livelihood could be at stake. Either way, it was a no-win situation.

Julianna's phone rang. Kate waited until she finished the call. Then Julianna apologized that she had to leave. Rick needed her help with the billing for one his customers.

After Grace's daughter drove away, Kate went inside and

checked her own phone and discovered a missed call. She hoped it might be David. Though she'd see him tomorrow morning when he picked her up for the festival, she longed to hear his voice.

It wasn't him. Instead, it was the receptionist from the Department of Agriculture returning her call.

Kate played the message, eager to hear if Roy was at work so she could try to contact him again. As she listened, her heart sank with foreboding.

"I'm so sorry to tell you this, Ms. Phillips," the woman said on the recording, "but we got word today that Professor Timmons was found dead in his home, from what appears to be a self-inflicted gunshot wound."

CHAPTER ELEVEN

WHEN KATE ANSWERED GRACE'S FRONT DOOR at eleven Friday morning, the sight of David dressed in his burgundy-blue plaid shirt, crisp jeans, and cowboy boots took her breath away—and lifted her spirits after the disturbing news yesterday about Roy Timmons. Last night, she had searched online for news reports and learned his death was still under investigation, but the authorities had generally concluded it was a freak accident.

"Howdy, ma'am," David said in his best John Wayne drawl, tipping his black cowboy hat in her direction. He looked ready to rope a few steers and steal a few hearts—he'd already captured hers.

She peered toward the driveway. "Where's your truck?"

"I walked over. Yesterday, during the preliminary judging for the horse show, Grace told me she wanted us to go in her car." The blue in his shirt accentuated the color of his eyes as he regarded her clothes. "You look fantastic."

Kate glanced down at her denim skirt and the maroon blouse Grace had loaned her. "This close to Halloween, I was half tempted to wear a mask."

"I'm glad you didn't. It'd be a crying shame to cover that pretty face." He was grinning, but the intensity of his gaze told her he wasn't joking.

She averted her eyes. "You're making me blush."

Grace appeared on the front porch, carrying a large basket. "Okay, I'm ready to go."

Kate's mouth fell open when she saw the horsewoman's fancy western shirt, sparkling with rhinestones. "Love that outfit, Grace."

The older woman mimicked a pirouette with a theatrical air. "I only wear it for horse shows. I figure I might as well go all out."

David stared at his cowboy boots and jeans. "Now I feel underdressed."

Grace huffed as if that was absurd. "You look fine."

More than fine. Kate sniffed his spicy aftershave. He smelled good too.

David clapped his hands enthusiastically. "What do you say, ladies, are you ready to get this show on the road?"

"You two go ahead," Kate said. "I'll meet you at the car."

While David escorted Grace outside, Kate secured the front door and hurried to the back-porch closet to fetch Owen's recurve bow and quiver of arrows. After closing and locking the door behind her, she headed outside to Grace's car.

By the time she'd rejoined them, David had opened the front passenger door for Grace.

"No, I'll ride in back," the woman insisted.

"Are you sure? It is your car."

"I want you and Kate to have the front seat. I'll be fine in the back."

Kate and David shared awkward glances at Grace's obvious intent to seat them together. His eyes shifted to Kate's bow and quiver. "Planning to do a little hunting at the festival?"

She looked down at the equipment and laughed.

"Kate's going to compete in the archery competition," Grace said as she slid into the backseat.

He regarded Kate for a moment, the corner of his mouth rising. "Good. I can't wait to see you show up those bowhunters."

She felt a little silly now, but why not go for it? "I know it's a longshot, but when Grace told me about the contest and grand prize, I figured I didn't have anything to lose."

"We'd better hurry and get there so we have time to eat. The archery competition is right after the horse show."

Once they were all seated and buckled in the car, David backed out of Grace's drive.

"How do you think Samson will do in the showmanship class?" Grace asked.

"If I can keep him calm, he might give Clementine a run for the money. But he was antsy this morning. I think he knows something is up."

Kate laughed. "Maybe you should have brought Delilah along to keep him calm like they do at the horse races."

"Now why didn't I think of that?" he said, sending her an engaging grin.

Fifteen minutes later, the three of them arrived at the enormous field that had been converted to a carnival with large tents, booths, and rides. After parking the car and opening the doors for the ladies, David handed Grace her keys and carried her picnic basket.

When the three came through the festival gate, Kate marveled at the beautiful autumn displays of pumpkins, multi-colored squash and maize decorating the entrance and the walkways. Carnival tents and booths with all sorts of crafts, games, and baked goods lined the main thoroughfare leading to the opposite end of the field, where the Ferris wheel, roller coaster, and other rides were visible in the distance.

Strolling with her companions in the cool mountain air, Kate breathed in the tantalizing scents of caramel apples, corn dogs, and cotton candy. As they passed open grills and slow-cookers emitting scrumptious aromas of baked beans, barbecue and smoked sausage, she wanted to stop at each tent and booth to sample all the food.

"I'm glad Grace warned me not to eat before coming," Kate said to David. "The hard part is having to decide what to eat first."

"Here's a tip—the outreach center tent has the best food at the festival."

"He should know," Grace added. "He was in charge of running it last year."

Kate slanted her head. "But not this year?"

His eyes were smiling as he looked at her. "I told them I was busy."

As they approached the food tent, David purchased tickets for the three of them. Then two members of the community welcomed their party and ushered them inside to the food tables. The volunteers stood nearby like protective hens over their nests, making sure everyone with tickets had at least one helping of everything on the table and at least two helpings of whatever dishes they had supplied.

While Grace set her picnic basket down and began unloading her food contributions, David introduced Kate to a woman and two men who were officers on the outreach committee. Kate listened with interest as they discussed their plans for the center, and then she shared a little of her own experience with the shelter in Nashville. They wanted to know more, so she fielded their questions and gave them ideas about how to help people in need. Touched by their interest and hospitality, Kate attributed it mostly to her association with David, whose standing in the community added considerable weight to Kate's credibility with these people.

When the two of them finally emerged from the food line, Kate balanced their overfilled paper plates in her hands in search of an empty table, and David went to fetch their drinks. She noticed Grace surrounded by the local women. The popular golden-ager acted like a girl, giggling, telling old stories and jokes, and sharing the latest news of the town. Seeing how much Grace was enjoying herself, Kate thought of how nice it must be to have grown up in the small town with lifelong friends, and be so loved and accepted.

Spotting a small table with a couple of empty chairs near the edge of the tent, Kate went to claim it. After setting the plates down, she took a seat and sampled her food.

"How's the barbecue?" David asked as he strode up carrying two large paper cups filled with lemonade.

Kate used her plastic fork to point to her plate. "You were right. It's the best I've ever eaten."

"Told ya."

"All the food here is delicious."

He sat across from her and handed her one of the drinks. It was nice to finally be able to relax and enjoy the food, and it was the first time she'd been alone with David since they'd arrived. This might be the best time to tell him about being Owen's niece.

The sound of men's voices nearby distracted her. A cluster of them were standing around, engrossed in discussions about crop prices and politics. Lester had taken a prominent part in their lively conversation, telling political jokes and drawing laughter from the group.

When he spotted Kate and David, he parted his male audience to come and greet them. "Hello, Kate. David. Good to see you here."

She set her fork down, happy to recognize another familiar face. "You too."

He turned to David, who stood to shake his hand. "How's the campaign going?" David asked in a friendly, casual manner.

The lawyer and acting mayor, wearing a flag pin and campaign button with his picture, appeared to be in full campaign mode. "Fine, just fine. I hope I can count on your vote."

David put a finger to his chin with a tongue-in-cheek look. "I'm still trying to decide. There are so many candidates to choose from."

Lester chuckled at David's coy act. "Then I'll make it easy for you. Check the box and don't write in anyone else's name. After all this campaigning, it would be a shame to be defeated by a write-in candidate." He gestured to a fortyish professional-looking fellow to his right. "Kate, I'd like you to meet Terrence Hastings."

She stood to shake his hand. "Are you part of Lester's campaign team?"

The man stiffened as if mildly offended. "No, I work for Rydeklan Chemicals."

"He's the man in charge there," Lester explained.

The businessman straightened the collar of his white button-down shirt. "He means I'm the V.P. of the division based here in Tyler's Glen."

"Sounds important. If y'all can find a chair, you're welcome to join us." Kate tossed David a casual glance, catching his frosty glare at the man. Apparently, he wasn't too impressed. Now she wished she could rescind her invitation.

Lester responded with an appreciative smile. "Thank you for the offer, but we'll be moseying over to the car exhibit in a few minutes."

Next to Terrance stood a younger man with brown hair and intense dark eyes that seemed to be assessing Kate. She confronted his staring with an arched brow and a cool tone. "Are you a V.P. too?"

Terrance interjected, "This is Claven Ellis, my assistant."

Lester gave Claven a pat on the back. "He's also been helping me out with my campaign."

Kate wondered how much help Lester needed, given he was running unopposed and the town was covered in campaign posters.

Before he left, Lester said goodbye to Kate and David. "Enjoy the festival. And don't forget to stop by my campaign booth later on. We have lots of freebies to give away."

Kate watched as the three men left their table and disappeared into the crowd. When she sat down with David again, she was eager to finish the rest of her barbecue, coleslaw, and baked beans. As she ate, she noticed Harlan entering the tent with Julianna. The intriguing woman looked especially snazzy in her designer jeans and sleek blouse, accessorized with numerous gold bangles on her wrists. The couple spotted Kate and David and headed toward their table.

"Kate," Harlan said, proudly circling his arm around his spouse, "I'd like you to meet my wife, Julianna."

"We've already met, dear," Julianna said.

"Really? When?"

"Yesterday afternoon when I went to visit my mother." She flashed Kate one of her brilliant smiles. "You'll have to come to our house for lunch sometime while you're in town. I want to hear all about Nashville."

"I'd like that," Kate replied, thinking the savvy CPA probably wanted to talk more about Owen's business interests with her too, which reminded her that she should tell Harlan about Roy's death.

The deputy gestured toward his wife as he spoke to Kate in a conspiring tone. "Please promise me you won't fill my pretty wife's head with big city notions or let her buy more expensive jewelry."

"Oh, shush," Julianna cried, brushing him off. Turning to Kate, she shook her head. "Ignore him. He's just an old hillbilly who doesn't appreciate the finer things in life."

"Expensive things, you mean." Harlan had an ironic twinkle in his eye.

Kate enjoyed their good-natured banter, though they did seem to be opposites in many ways. On second thought, this probably wasn't the best time to bring up Roy's death.

Julianna gently nudged her husband. "Why don't we leave this cute couple to themselves, Harlan, and get our dinner before the horse show?"

"Great idea, hon. I can't wait to hit the dessert table." The deputy sent a parting wink to Kate and David. "Have fun, you two."

Once they were gone, Kate wondered why she hadn't corrected their assumption that she was David's date—not that she minded people thinking they were together. The more she got to know him, the more she came to admire his many great qualities. Not only was he a perfect gentleman, he was also fun and interesting.

After finishing her meal, Kate observed the long line at the food tables and realized David had been smart in taking them early, before the crowds. "I didn't realize the festival was so popular."

He finished gnawing on his barbecued rib. "One thing about the people of Tyler's Glen—they never pass up an opportunity to eat." Raising the rib bone in the air like a trophy, he grinned at her.

She sipped her lemonade, amused by him. At that moment, Nadine and Rick emerged from the throng with their food, looking for a place to sit.

"Kate!" Nadine called, hurrying to their table. "May we sit with you?" Her eyes darted to David, and a sly smirk came to her lips. "That is, unless we're interrupting something."

Exchanging reluctant looks with David, Kate reminded herself that Nadine and Rick had been very friendly to her. The least she could do was return the favor. "Nope. We just finished eating. You're welcome to join us."

"Thanks. All the other tables are taken," Nadine replied. The two pulled a couple of unused chairs from the next table and sat opposite each other, with Nadine beside Kate and Rick next to David.

Remembering Nadine sobbing in the bathroom at Bubba's, Kate's curiosity was aroused at seeing her with the mechanic. "I thought you didn't have time to leave your garage, Rick."

"I've been known to make an exception every now and then. By the way, I still haven't gotten any mail for you."

Nadine plunged her fork into her potato salad. "I ran into him at the car exhibit. One of his classic Fords is on display."

"Sweet!" David said. "I'll stop by and check it out."

While the two men chatted about cars, Nadine spoke to Kate. "I'm glad I ran into you." She lowered her voice. "But I'm surprised to see you here with David. When I saw you having lunch with Joe Campbell the other day, I wondered if you two were . . ."

"No way!" The spicy barbecue sauce suddenly left a nasty aftertaste in Kate's mouth.

As if on cue, Kate spotted Joe. Unfortunately, he had seen her too and was swaggering to their table.

"Mercy me. Two of the most beautiful women in Tyler's Glen, seated at the same table. Somebody get me a chair."

David waved his hand to shoo him away. "Get lost, Campbell. This isn't a singles bar. Leave the ladies alone."

Joe scowled at him before refocusing on the women. "Now why would you beauties want to waste your time with these clowns when you could be with me?"

David rose from his chair to go toe-to-toe with Joe.

Harlan rushed over to separate the two men. "All right, boys, break it up! We won't have any fighting tonight. Save your rivalry for the horse show."

David moved away from Joe, but continued to glare at him. "See you in the ring."

Joe grunted. "No contest. Your horse doesn't stand a chance against Thunder."

"That's for the judges to decide."

Later that afternoon, David stood under the partly cloudy sky, holding Samson's lead rope outside the center ring. After two days of preliminary judging, Samson had made it to the final round in the showmanship class. This being his first competition, his horse had done better than expected. The spirited gelding had held his own against the impressive group of horses, even a few purebreds like Thunder.

Grace went first with Clementine, a seasoned showmanship champion over the years. The palomino mare performed all of the maneuvers of the pattern perfectly, thanks to her handler's skillful coaching.

After Grace had finished, Joe paraded Thunder out. The magnificent horse obediently followed as Joe walked him around the ring, weaving around the orange cones, stopping and starting with precision, and pivoting and trotting like a dancer on the stage.

Samson snorted and neighed when Thunder exited the ring with Joe. Passing David, Joe cast him a smug stare, challenging him to beat Thunder's performance.

David ignored him. He was more interested in a certain female in the audience seated with Rick and Nadine in the stands. Kate gave him a big thumbs-up and a cheerful smile, helping him to forget about Joe and focus on winning.

When their turn came, David knew it would be hard for Samson to beat the other nine horses in the top ten, but a portion of the scoring had to do with grooming and appearance. In those categories, his horse could hold his own.

Samson nickered as David guided him by his lead to the center of the ring where the judges kept score with a clipboard. David stopped at the designated location and Samson halted on cue. Though the rules didn't allow him to touch his horse, he used a coaxing tone that calmed Samson a bit. His horse navigated the cones with surprising ease and kept his hind legs stationary when pivoting. When they came to the trot, David thought they might actually have a shot at winning. To his amazement, Samson completed the remaining maneuvers like a champion.

Beaming with pride, David stopped Samson for the final element of the judging—the hardest for Samson to master. Facing his horse, David cued him to square up. The animal adjusted until he stood evenly on all fours. To best Thunder, Samson would need to stay perfectly still, his head upright and ears forward, the whole time the judges walked around him.

David waited expectantly as the judges examined every inch of the gelding, from his head and mane to his feet and tail. His horse exhibited surprising discipline. Only his eyes moved when he blinked.

When the judges came in front of David and Samson to complete their score, the sound of screams from riders on the roller coaster punctured the tense silence. Samson pricked his ears and broke his stance.

David sucked in a breath, knowing that lapse had cost them the win and the satisfaction of beating Joe. He didn't blame Samson though. As his handler, he was ultimately responsible for how his horse did in the competition, and Samson had far exceeded his expectations. "You did good, boy," he said as he walked his horse toward the other contestants to await the announcement of the winners. "We'll get 'em next time."

After the seven remaining contestants took their turn in the ring, the emcee finally came to the center with a microphone. "Ladies and gentlemen, we have the final results. Third place for showmanship goes to David Jennings and Samson."

"Way to go, Samson!" Kate yelled from the stands, drawing a glance and a grin from David as he led Samson to the center of the arena to collect their trophy. *Not bad for Samson's first competition.*

"Second place," the emcee said, "goes to Joe Campbell and Thunder."

As his rival with the disgruntled expression went to get his consolation prize, David took satisfaction that at least Joe hadn't won first.

The emcee addressed the audience for the third time. "And now, it's my pleasure to announce that first place and the grand prize for the showmanship competition goes to . . . Grace Holbrook."

David whistled and cheered enthusiastically as his friend and neighbor in the sparkling cowgirl shirt claimed her winner's trophy. He spotted Kate standing and cheering alongside Rick and Nadine. Her gaze found his, and she sent him a warm smile that almost made up for his bruised pride. He couldn't wait to see her compete against Joe with a bow and arrow. If spunk and determination were any indication, she had an excellent chance of beating him.

Grace and David's excellent placement in the horse show inspired Kate to give it her all in the archery tournament. She checked the time on her cellphone and realized she only had a few minutes to get to the course before the event began, and David and Grace still needed to return Samson and Clementine to their stalls. After congratulating them with hugs, she hurried away, not wanting to be late.

Arriving at the archery course, Kate joined the other contestants near the stands. A few of the men frowned and rebuffed her as she approached them. From her discussion with the tournament organizer, she knew that all of her rivals would be male, many of them seasoned bowhunters who wanted to win as much as she did. But since they'd all be using recurve bows with a forty-pound draw and shooting at shorter distances, it leveled the playing field.

Winning the $200 gift certificate to the sporting goods store would be great, but mostly she looked forward to the challenge. Having gone over the rules online yesterday, she expected the amateur event to be less formal and the rules more relaxed than the tournaments she'd participated in during her high school and college days on scholarship. Still, her competition would be tough.

Joe and Lester appeared in the contestant area with their archery equipment. They did a double-take when they saw her with Owen's bow in her hands, but Lester smiled and waved to her in his usual cordial manner. Joe, on the other hand, like some of the other men who had snubbed her, appeared less receptive to her competing in the men's division.

While she waited on the bench for the event to begin, Joe strode over and sat beside her. "You're actually going to compete with us?"

His incredulous tone fired up her competitive spirit. "Sure. Why not?"

"You should have taken me up on my offer to use my archery range. I could have given you a few pointers."

"With pretend arrows?"

He snorted at her comeback. "I brought real ones today."

Kate thought of the threatening note pinned to the tree in Cades Cove. Had Joe shot those arrows at her and David in the park?

She spotted David and Grace entering the arena. David raised his hand to wave, but his smile faded at Joe sitting beside her.

"He can't stand to see you next to me," Joe said in Kate's ear as if reading her thoughts. "He wants Owen's property all to himself."

She twisted around to look him in the eye. "You're

wrong. His interest in me has nothing to do with Owen's land."

"Are you sure about that?"

The official announced that the preliminary divisions of shooting, known as ends, were about to begin. Kate rose from her bench, welcoming the diversion from Joe's stinging remark about David and his motives.

The official's two-whistle cue prompted her to step behind her line and prepare to shoot at her target forty yards away. She glanced down the line at her thirty male competitors, including Lester and Joe, each with their own target. After she'd placed her arrow against the bowstring, she waited for the official's single whistle to begin shooting.

Twelve ends later, after firing seventy-two arrows, Kate surprised herself by holding her own with the men and making it to the semifinals. The four semifinalists—Lester, Joe, Claven Ellis, and herself—prepared to go head-to-head in pairs, with the winners moving on to the finals.

Lester and Joe competed first. The two men appeared evenly matched as they took turns shooting, aiming for the tiny yellow circle in the center of the target, or the X ring. After they'd shot six arrows each, Joe was announced the winner, though it was close. Now Joe would go on to compete against whoever won her semifinal with Claven.

Claven turned out to be a strong competitor. His first four shots matched Kate's, arrow for arrow, in the X ring. She couldn't let him win, not after she'd come this far. After raising her bow, she fired her fifth shot. It hit just outside of center, giving Claven an opening. He took advantage and struck the X ring again. *You're not out of this yet, Kate.* She released her bowstring and her sixth arrow pierced the bullseye—*yes!* Now it all came down to Claven's final shot. He aimed and fired. When he missed and it hit the outer black ring, Kate felt like dancing.

But it was too early to celebrate. She still had one more

end to go, this time against Joe. And having watched him compete against Lester, she knew he would be hard to beat.

Kate stepped up to the line a few feet away from her final competitor.

He shot first, nailing his arrow in the center.

As she raised the bow to take her turn, a burning sensation seized her left shoulder. The shooting had aggravated her injury.

The crowd murmured and whispered as she aimed again.

She released her fingers and groaned. *Missed.* The arrow hit just outside the inner yellow circle. That would cost her.

"You've got this, Kate!" she heard David yell from the stands. She wanted to look back, but needed to stay focused if she was going to beat Joe.

Joe's next arrow struck the X ring again.

She drew and aimed, powering through the shoulder pain as she launched the arrow. This time it struck dead center.

Three more times she matched Joe as they took turns landing their arrows in the bullseye of their respective targets, even amazing herself. But Joe was still slightly ahead.

The crowd in the stands roared with excitement, anticipating the last crucial shots.

Joe tossed Kate a cocky glance as he nocked his arrow, but she was determined not to let him get to her. He fired at the target, penetrating the blue ring to the right of center.

He missed the bullseye! As Kate carefully drew her bowstring, she glanced up to say a quick prayer. Afterward, she fixed her gaze on the X ring in the distance. *This one's for you, Owen.* When she let go, the arrow soared through the air, striking its target with the precision of a guided missile.

She covered her mouth as the crowd in the stands went wild. The emcee had to quiet the audience to announce the results. Elated and amazed that she had won, Kate spotted David and Grace jumping and cheering in the stands with

Nadine and Rick. After the tournament organizer presented her with the trophy and the $200 gift certificate, she headed in their direction.

David rushed down the stairs to meet her. "You were awesome!" He gave her an exuberant hug, then his lips met hers in a spontaneous kiss. All at once, the clapping of the crowd faded to a distant tapping, like the rain on David's windshield that night in the storm. Everything else was swept away by the overpowering awareness of him and what could be—with no secrets to keep them apart.

The crowd's applause and whistles gradually grew louder, making Kate realize that she and David had become the show. She slowly pulled away from him, heat rising to her face. The warmth of his kiss still radiated from her lips as his spicy scent teased her nose. She longed to escape to their private waterfall at the church camp and pick up where they left off. But the interruptions didn't end.

Joe swaggered up. "Congratulations!"

She groaned to herself, forcing her eyes away from David to acknowledge her competitor. "Thanks."

Beaming mischievously, Joe glanced at David for a second. "Old Owen would have been proud."

David's brows pressed together over his eyes. "What are you talking about?"

Kate tugged at his shirt to pull him away, alarmed by Joe's cunning tone. "David, don't listen to him. Let's get out of here."

"Give me a minute, Kate," he said, glaring at Joe. "What were you saying about Owen?"

Joe's crooked grin widened with devious delight. "You don't know, do you?" He pointed and laughed, making David out to be a fool.

Whirling around, Kate pushed Joe away. "Don't!"

Ignoring her, Joe continued, loud enough for all to hear. "I thought everybody knew. Looks like Kate really pulled one over on you. But then I guess the apple doesn't fall far from the tree, does it? After all, she is a Bentley."

David eyed Joe as if he hadn't heard correctly. "What?"

Joe smirked at him. "You heard right—Kate is Owen's niece."

Kate's heart nosedived off a cliff. Squeezing her eyes shut, she braced for the impact.

Reopening them, she saw David staring at her, expecting her to refute it. *If only she could.* He blinked at her silence, a layer of frost coating his hurt, betrayed face.

Kate's dream of winning the tournament had suddenly become a nightmare. "I meant to tell you sooner, David, but . . ." Her excuses sounded hollow now. She should have trusted him with the truth and let the chips fall where they may. "Please hear me out. Just because I'm related to Owen doesn't mean anything has to change between us."

"That's where you're wrong," he fired back, his voice sounding stark and distant. "It changes everything. If you had nothing to hide, you would have told me before now." He shook his head and snorted. "Well, congratulations. I hope you enjoy your inheritance."

When he brushed past her, Kate started to follow, but Lester blocked her path. "I didn't realize we had an archery pro in town. You should join our bow-hunting club."

She gazed past him to David disappearing into the crowd exiting the arena. "I don't hunt."

"That's okay, Terrance Hastings doesn't either, but he still comes out for target practice." Lester turned to Terrance, standing close by. "Don't you, Terrance?"

"I doubt she wants to hang out with a bunch of men, shooting the bull," the V.P. replied.

Slowly turning her attention to the lawyer and the businessman, Kate glimpsed Joe eyeing her from a distance before he slipped away.

Harlan joined Lester and Terrance. "You sandbagger,

you," the deputy said with a teasing wink at Kate. "Where did you learn to shoot like that?"

"My father taught me."

"Norm?"

She shook her head. "No, my foster father, Jim."

"Hey, maybe she can teach us a thing or two," Harlan said to the two men.

Hunting was the last thing on her mind right now, but the men had shown her respect by inviting her to be in their club, so she put on a good front. "Thanks guys, but I'll be going home to Nashville soon."

"She's a deputy U.S. marshal," Harlan proudly told the others, who in turn nodded with approval.

Seeing Rick coming down from the stands with his grandmother, Kate excused herself from the men and met the two of them at the bottom of the steps.

"I'm so proud of you, Kate!" Grace said excitedly, giving her a warm hug. "Where's David?" she asked, looking around.

"He left. I need to find him."

"He probably went to the pumpkin judging. He's a favorite to win."

"I'll see if he's there and meet up with you later," Kate said, taking her bow and arrows as she headed for the exit.

Vicki, the park ranger who had taken Kate's incident report, stopped her on the way out. "Hey, congratulations. I got here late, but just in time to see you cream that cowboy with your last amazing shot."

Kate almost didn't recognize her out of uniform. "Thanks," she replied rather hastily, wanting to find David. She noticed Vicki was accompanied by David's friend Pete, who had given her a lift to town on Tuesday.

"By the way," Vicki said, "forensics traced the serial number of the arrows that were shot at you. They were purchased by a man from Tyler's Glen named Owen

Bentley."

That got Kate's interest and her attention. "And the blood on the towel and knife?"

Vicki traded disconcerted looks with Pete. "It's a perfect match—to the same man."

CHAPTER TWELVE

VICKI'S NEWS REPLAYED IN KATE'S THOUGHTS as she headed to the agriculture tent to look for David. *Owen's blood was on the knife, and his arrows were used against her and David.* Had someone created the illusion that her uncle's ghost was haunting them, like a sick Halloween joke? Or was it simply a diversion to throw law enforcement off track?

When Kate reached the pumpkin judging area, the emcee announced David's name as the winner. She waited, but he didn't come forward to claim his prize. After searching the entire tent with no success, she left and continued looking for him.

Finally, she came to the horse stables. Roaming up and down the rows of stalls, she recognized Thunder and Clementine. *Samson must be here too.* She continued her quest until she finally found Samson's stall. David was inside it, somberly brushing his horse's mane and coat, as if preparing for a funeral.

She came to the gate, and quietly leaned her bow and quiver against it. Hooking her fingers over the bars, she spoke in the most cheerful voice she could muster. "Congratulations, David. You won the pumpkin competition."

He stopped brushing for a moment but didn't look up.

She tightened her grip on the bars. "I was going to tell you everything when you brought Buster to Grace's, but you were called away on an emergency, remember? Then I wanted to tell you today while we were eating, but I never got the chance."

"There were plenty of other times you could have told

me." His voice sounded distant and hollow.

She stared at the hay on the ground. Despite Samson's clean stall, the place reeked. So did this mess she'd gotten herself into. "I know . . . but your fixation with my uncle's land didn't make it easy." Lifting her gaze, she detected a slight quiver in his jaw.

"What are you going to do with it?" he asked, keeping his eyes on Samson.

There it was again. *The property that kept coming between them.* "I don't know."

"Are you going to sell it to Joe?"

A man and woman with two young boys who were checking out the animals wandered down their row. Kate stopped talking until they'd left the area.

"I told you, I don't know," she replied to David in a loud whisper.

He suddenly looked at her, his blue eyes frostier than a glacier's crevasse. "Whatever he offers you, I'll beat it."

"David, this isn't about the land, and it's not about Joe. It's about *us*. I thought we had gotten off to a pretty good start."

His features tightened in a pained expression. "Maybe that's because you were holding all the cards. Now I don't know who you are."

She released her fingers from the gate and gestured to herself. "I'm still Kate. The same person you rescued from the car accident. The one you took horseback riding and toured Cades Cove with."

He resumed brushing Samson.

She looked down the row to confirm no one was within earshot. "I ran into Vicki Bates before I found you here. They traced the blood on the knife."

His brows pinched together and he put the brush down, giving her his full attention.

"It's Owen's," she told him. "So were the arrows that

were shot at us. Yesterday, I discovered them missing from his barn, along with his compound bow. I think whoever stabbed my uncle set the explosion to cover his tracks, then shot those arrows at us when we found the knife."

David's cool countenance switched to heated outrage as he clenched his fists. "Who would do something like that?"

She lifted her shoulders, inhaling the ripe air and blowing it out. "It has to be someone who has a grudge, or wanted something of his, like his land or his fishing lure business."

His mouth tightened in a thin line. "I didn't kill him for his property, if that's what you're thinking."

She rubbed the side of her face with her hand. "No, that's not what I meant at all. I'm only thinking of motives. You know the people in Tyler's Glen much better than I do. Who would benefit from Owen being dead?"

"Besides Joe, there's only one person I can think of who has the most to gain from Owen's death."

"Who would that be?"

"*You.*"

Her heart lurched from his insinuation, yet she couldn't argue with his logic. "I hardly knew anything about Owen until last Saturday. That's when I received Lester Crane's business card with a note in the mail. It said to let Lester know my mother was Owen's sister. There was also a clipping about the investigation into my uncle's death."

He inclined his head, suddenly appearing intrigued. "That's what led you here?"

She nodded. "That's how I learned that he had been killed."

"Who sent the card?

"I wish I knew. It was sent anonymously."

"Maybe the person who sent it also killed Owen."

His suggestion disturbed her. She wanted to think that whoever had sent it did so for altruistic reasons, but what if it was a trap? The perplexing mystery and the conflict with

David had given her a headache. "I can't think about this anymore. When will you be ready to leave?"

David took a bridle from a hook on the wall and slipped it over Samson's ears. "I'm not going back with you and Grace tonight. Tell her I'll bring Clementine home tomorrow."

She stared at him, her heart clenched in her chest. "Then how will you get home?"

He picked up the saddle blanket hanging over the half-wall of the stable and set it on Samson's back. "How do you think?"

After David took off on Samson, Kate wandered out of the stables with her archery equipment. By now, her head was throbbing.

Grace appeared, carrying the basket she'd brought the food in. "There you are," she said when she saw Kate. "I'm on my way to check on Clementine. Did you find David?"

"He just left on Samson. He said he'll bring your horse back tomorrow."

"Oh, dear." The older woman put a motherly arm around her and gave her a compassionate squeeze. "What do you say we go home? I think we've had enough excitement for one day."

Kate couldn't agree more.

After Grace had seen Clementine, the two women headed toward the exit. They passed Joe and Lester, who were talking in Lester's campaign booth.

"You ladies aren't leaving so soon, are you?" Joe asked in his molasses voice. "It's still early."

"Why don't you mind your own business?" Grace replied, sounding unusually gruff.

Joe ignored her and blocked Kate. "Where's David?"

"He left."

"Already?"

Not wanting to discuss David with Joe, she brushed past him.

"Oh, Kate," Lester called. "I'm still going to the probate office next week. Do you want me to take the form I gave you?"

She stopped to reply to him. "Yes, and thanks for the reminder. I need to fill it out."

As Kate resumed escorting Grace in the direction of the parking lot, Rick called to her. She paused to let him catch up.

"Hey, how about fly fishing with me tomorrow morning at Abrams Creek? We'll use Owen's lures."

"How early?" she asked.

"Nine a.m. That'll allow me to sleep in a little."

It was hard to believe tomorrow would already be Saturday. It had been almost a week since she'd arrived in the area, and she hadn't spent nearly as much time in the park as she'd wanted. This would give her an opportunity to do that—and take her mind off of David. "Why not? But I don't have a pole."

"I can bring an extra rod and reel for you, but you'll need to get a fishing license online."

"I'll take care of it tonight."

By the time she and Grace had reached the car in the parking lot, the wind had begun to pick up as storm clouds gathered in the late afternoon sky.

"Would you mind driving, Kate?" Grace asked, handing her the keys. "I'm not feeling very well all of a sudden."

"Of course." Remembering the woman's heart condition, Kate's focus shifted from Owen's murder and David's rejection to concern for Grace's health. "I hope you're not getting sick."

"No, just tired. I keep forgetting I'm not as young as I used to be."

"Tell that to all the younger people you beat in the horse show."

Grace's wan face brightened a bit. "That's true. I even surprised myself."

Lightning streaked the sky, triggering a flashback to the night of Kate's car accident, and the hooded man crossing the road. "We'd better leave before the storm hits."

The darkened sky cast a shadow over the valley as they traveled the serpentine road toward Grace's farm. Rain began to splatter the windshield, blurring Kate's vision, even with the wipers on high.

"What a storm. Can you see to drive?" A slight quiver reverberated in Grace's voice.

Kate slowed down, opting to err on the side of caution—and keeping Grace calm. "I'm fine."

Large headlights appeared in her side mirror, rapidly approaching.

"Turn off your high beams!" Kate muttered to herself as the throbbing in her head intensified.

Grace stared at her. "Who are you talking to?"

"That truck behind us. His lights are blinding me." She could barely see as the eighteen-wheeler closed the distance between them. "It's tailing us." She glimpsed the worry lines on Grace's face. "A passing lane is coming up. I'll try to lose him."

She gripped the steering wheel to control the car along the narrow, winding road as the truck followed her in tandem. Maintaining her speed through the sharp twists and turns, she managed to stay ahead of him. If she slowed or stopped, the truck would crash into them. With the slippery asphalt, it wouldn't take much to send them skidding into the side of a mountain or off the edge into the river below.

From the corner of her eye, she saw Grace's hand over

her heart. "Sorry, I don't usually drive like this. Are you okay?"

Grace returned a nod of encouragement. "Don't worry about me. You focus on driving and bringing us safely home. Too bad I don't have Wade's rifle with me. I'd like to blow out a few tires behind us."

Kate smiled at the woman's feistiness and prayed they would make it to the passing lane before either vehicle lost control.

As soon as the two lanes widened into three, Kate changed to the right lane. Horn blaring, the truck veered into their lane as it passed, forcing Kate off the road. The sudden move on the slippery pavement sent their car into a tailspin.

The sound of brakes squealing echoed in Kate's mind as she lost control. "Hold on, Grace!" Uttering a quick prayer for God's protection, she braced for the worst.

When he'd left the stables, David hadn't anticipated the sudden storm. He tried to rein in Samson as he galloped through the countryside in the driving rain. The horse needed to work off his excess energy from being cooped up in the stall. David wished the vigorous ride in the rain could fix his own mounting frustrations, but he suspected it would take an act of God, or something close to it.

All this time, the truth had been staring him in the face, and he hadn't seen it. He should have, but he'd been blinded by Kate's charms, like her sparkling, captivating eyes that kept him guessing their true color and her laughter that enchanted him like a seductive song. She had baited him with her feminine wiles and then reeled him in like a fish on a hook, taking advantage of his misplaced trust . . .

No, that wasn't completely true. She had never asked

anything of him that he hadn't been more than willing to give. Still, how could they ever return to the way things were? She would be inheriting his family's land, the land he'd spent the last ten years scrimping and saving to reclaim.

Or worse—she would sell it to Joe, or to a developer who couldn't care less about what happened to his ancestral heritage.

As he approached the road to his house, the sound of a horn and squealing brakes echoed through the dark valley. "Whoa, boy!" After reining in Samson, he turned him toward the noise.

Grace's car had skidded to an abrupt stop. It now faced backwards, precariously close to the ledge of a river canyon. Kate took a deep breath, thankful they had survived in one piece.

"Well, it wasn't as graceful as Clementine's pivot, but at least we lost him." She turned to Grace and was alarmed to see the woman clutching her chest. "Are you okay?"

"I need to take my medicine. Could you please fetch my water bottle from the back?"

Kate reached behind her and then handed the water to Grace.

After taking her pill, Grace's wan complexion improved a bit. "My, that was more thrilling than a roller coaster. I think you have a future as a race car driver."

Glancing out the window, Kate couldn't believe her eyes as David rode up on Samson in the pouring rain, looking like a heroic figure from a bygone era. Maybe she'd hit her head when the car spun out and was dreaming.

After halting the horse and quickly dismounting, he led Samson toward Grace's side of the car.

Grace cracked open her window. "One of those eighteen-wheelers drove us off the road."

"Are you okay?" His voice conveyed concern.

"It's only a little hiccup in my ticker, but I'm better now that I've taken my medicine."

"Let me check your pulse," he said. She lifted her hand to him, and he pressed his fingers against her wrist for a few moments. Then he felt her forehead. "You appear stable, but you should see the doctor in the morning."

Kate released her seatbelt to get out and survey their situation.

Grace gestured over her shoulder. "There's an umbrella in the back."

She grabbed it and popped it open as she cautiously got out, staying close to the car to avoid slipping and falling off the ledge. She hurried around the front of the car to join David on the passenger side.

He frowned as he surveyed the car in the drizzle. "Was it one of those chemical trucks? Did you get a license plate number?"

She shook her head. "It was raining too hard for me to see."

"If it hadn't been for Kate's expert driving," Grace said through the window, "we'd probably be at the bottom of that canyon right now."

David's gaze met Kate's, his frosty demeanor warming a little. "At least the car isn't wrecked this time."

She started to arch her brow at his remark, but let it go. "It could have been much worse."

"Here," he said, handing her Samson's reins. "I'll turn the car around."

"The keys are in the ignition," she told him on his way to the driver's side. Then she led Samson across the road a safe distance away, where she could still keep an eye out for oncoming cars.

David carefully drove the car from the ledge and skillfully maneuvered it in a three-point turn before parking it on the shoulder. When he got out, he left the engine running and strode to Kate.

She handed him Samson's reins. "We have to stop meeting like this," she joked, attempting to lighten the mood between them.

"You mean, before one of us gets killed?"

His dry retort turned her grin into a pout. Catching the faint twinkle in his eye, she forgave him. Disaster did seem to follow her these days.

"You'd better get Grace home," he advised her.

As Kate got into the car, she watched him ride off like some mysterious knight. He'd never let his personal feelings get in the way of duty, but was he noble enough to give her a second chance?

Feeling refreshed from her long, hot shower and the light meal of soup she had prepared for her dinner with Grace earlier, Kate changed into sweats and her fuzzy socks and came downstairs. She found Grace relaxing on the red loveseat by the fireplace, already dressed in her nightgown and robe, as Buster snoozed on the floor at her feet.

When Kate joined her on the loveseat, Grace peered at her over the rim of her mug. "What Joe did today, telling David about you—right there in front of everyone—was inexcusable."

Though her headache had improved, Kate's heart still hadn't recovered from the painful memory. "Maybe I should thank him. I would have preferred telling David myself, but at least now he knows the truth." Soft popping and hissing sounds came from the fireplace. She stared into the flickering flames, recalling the stunned look on David's face right after he'd kissed her.

"He'll get over it," Grace responded as if reading her thoughts.

Kate hoped that was true, but her heart felt like lead. "I don't know. Trust is very important to him."

Grace regarded her with a wise look. "Yes, but don't underestimate the power of love."

Kate nodded, but still had her doubts. "I'd be happy with friendship right now."

Reaching to pet Buster, Grace was seized with a violent cough.

"Are you sure you're all right?"

She patted Kate's hand and cleared her throat. "What's wrong with me is nothing that a good night's sleep won't fix. In fact, I think I'll head upstairs now and turn in."

"Maybe you should sleep down here on the couch in the den tonight and not climb the stairs."

Rising from the loveseat, Grace waved off her suggestion. "No, I'm going to sleep in my own bed."

Given her friend's fragile health, Kate would have felt better if Grace had taken her advice, but she was a guest in the woman's home and couldn't tell her what to do. "Then why don't you sleep in tomorrow morning? You don't need to get up early on my account."

"You know, that's not a bad idea. I think I will. Can you find something to eat on your own?"

"Don't worry about me. I'll be fine. In fact, I'm going fly fishing with Rick at nine."

"That's right. You'll need my waders. They're in the closet on the back porch. Goodnight, hon."

"Goodnight. I'll turn out the lights and lock the doors before I go to bed."

After Grace went upstairs, Kate felt restless and paced around the living room. She came to the mantel and picked up the picture of Grace's son, Frederick. Rick favored him so much, and the sparkle in his eyes resembled Grace's.

She thought of her mother as a teenager, going to school with Julianna and Frederick, and wished she was here with her now. Why hadn't Mom told her more about her family and her brother, Owen? After today, the entire town would know she was his heir. That could make her even more of a target.

Kate went to the back porch to let Buster out before she locked up. The rain had stopped, and she could see a light coming from David's house down the road.

Buster's tags jingled when he'd finished his business and returned to the porch steps. As she bent to pet him, she saw something move in the shadows. The dog whined softly. She put her finger to her lips to shush him, then set him inside the porch, closing the door behind him. When she turned around outside, the figure of a man in a hoody dashed across the yard.

"Hey, you, stop!"

He kept running, so she chased after him. Like a ghost, the man vanished in the darkness.

She stopped at the edge of Grace's yard. Without her gun, it wasn't smart to follow him. Besides, he was long gone by now.

Crossing the lawn on her way to the house, she heard a crackling sound underfoot and stopped. Stooping down to see what it was, she found an empty foil wrapper from a granola bar. *Exactly like the ones stolen from her tent in the campground.*

CHAPTER THIRTEEN

KATE AWOKE AT SEVEN THE NEXT morning, eager to get in a quick run before the fishing trip. She pulled a sweatshirt over her running togs and tiptoed downstairs in her stocking feet to the kitchen, hoping not to disturb Grace, whose door was still closed.

In the kitchen eating a bowl of cereal, Kate thought about the granola bar wrapper she'd found last night. It wasn't a brand you could find in any local grocery. The only place she knew that carried them was a health food store in Nashville, where she'd purchased the ones she'd brought with her.

After finishing her breakfast, she left a note for Grace, letting her know her plans to go running. On her way out, she stopped on the back porch to say good morning to Buster. The dog rose from his bed, his tail wagging and collar jingling. Noticing how much he'd improved from the antibiotics, extra nourishment, and much-needed TLC, she changed her plans.

"Hey, Buster, how about a walk?"

The dog perked up as if he understood.

She slipped on her running shoes and faced the antique trunk on the back wall. Pressing her hands against it for support, she stretched out her legs and calf muscles to warm up. Then she performed a few kickboxing moves, followed by push-ups. Her shoulder was much better, but she still felt a twinge as she finished her reps. On her way out, she locked the back and porch doors and took Buster with her.

Gazing at the sunlight peeking over the Smokies, she breathed in the fresh, clean air. Did she really miss Nashville?

Or was this country life growing on her?

With Buster at her heels, Kate followed the footpath behind Grace's barn until they came to a creek. The dog trotted over to investigate it, sending the floating ducks quacking into the reeds on the opposite bank.

"Buster, come!" Kate called.

He reluctantly obeyed and left the ducks alone.

Soon, they'd wandered into a meadow with tall golden grass that swayed in the wind. Kate traipsed through it, embracing the freedom of this quiet, peaceful place, thinking about her life and her future. With Owen's inheritance, she could do anything she wanted, even move to a new location. She thought about her friends, Chase and Jenny in Washington State. Now she could afford to move there, if she wanted to. The Pacific Northwest was certainly beautiful, but Tennessee had always been her home. And being in Tyler's Glen was the first time she'd felt like she belonged anywhere since Rose passed away.

Buster stopped now and then to investigate a bug or to stick his nose in the air and sniff the breeze. He chased a squirrel and disappeared behind a tree.

She called to him again. "Come, Buster."

The dog returned, wagging his tail, and they romped to a small stand of trees dividing the meadow from a cornfield. She stopped to survey the towering stalks.

Buster's tag jingled in the distance.

She looked around. *Where did he go this time?* She followed the noise into the cornfield to find him.

"Hey, Buster! What are you doing here?" The friendly masculine voice instantly stirred Kate's heart. She turned and saw David bending to pet the dog.

"He's taking me for a walk," she said in a light tone.

David paused to look at her.

The dog wandered away, sniffing the ground.

Tentatively, Kate stepped closer. "I'm glad I ran into

you. I want to thank you again for stopping to help Grace and me yesterday."

He eyed her cautiously, then turned his gaze to the field. "I came to check on Grace's corn after the storm yesterday. I sharecrop her land." He stooped to pick up a stray ear from the ground, then stood tall. His muscular build was pronounced in his T-shirt and faded blue jeans.

"Sharecrop?"

Shucking the ear, David peered at her in disbelief. "You mean, you're about to inherit a farm and you don't know what sharecropping is?"

She folded her arms. "Of course, I do."

He raised a brow, challenging her with a skeptical look. "Well?"

Realizing she may have spoken too soon, she backed off. "All right, maybe I don't know exactly what it means."

"It means I farm Grace's land for her, and we split the profits from the crop."

She casually flicked her wrist to hide her ignorance. "I knew it was something like that."

He tossed the ear of corn to the ground. "Right. I guess it won't matter once you sell Owen's property to the highest bidder. You can cruise around in your little sports car, worry-free."

She thrust her hips to one side and planted her fists on them, angered by his false assumptions about her. "That's not fair! I care about what happens to my uncle's land as much as you, maybe more." Shifting her stance, she crossed her arms again. "I don't know why I'm bothering to tell you this. No matter what I say or do I'll always be Owen's land-grubbing niece to you. But like it or not, we're going to be neighbors, so you might as well get used to the idea."

He regarded her with a doubtful squint. "You're actually going to move next door? What about your job in Nashville?"

She glanced down, annoyed that she didn't have a good answer. "Maybe it could be a vacation home. I already know the kind of house I want. You gave me a tour, remember?"

The memory registered on his face, and his tone softened. "You're serious."

"All I need is someone to build it for me. Do you have any recommendations?"

It took him a moment to respond. "Maybe. I still have the blueprints, if you'd like to see them."

She released the pent-up air in her lungs, sensing they'd crossed a barrier. "Great. How about later today?"

He glanced at the tall stalks that stretched across the field. "Not today. I've got to finish harvesting the corn. Maybe later this week before you leave. I'll give you a call."

As he turned to walk away, she followed him. There was something else on her mind. "David, wait."

After a brief hesitation, he glanced over his shoulder. "Yeah?"

"It's Grace. I'm a little worried about her."

He pivoted around to face her. "What's wrong?"

"She was really tired last night when we got home, and she started coughing. I wouldn't be that concerned except that Rick told me she has a heart condition. Maybe all of the activity yesterday and the reckless truck driver were too much for her."

"If you want, I'll check on her later today when I bring Clementine home from the festival."

"Would you do that?" Kate felt a surge of relief and gratitude.

"Sure." He gazed at her in the sun. "There's something else, isn't there?"

She nodded and stepped closer. "Has the sheriff found the prowler you told me about?"

"No, why?"

"Late last night when I took Buster outside, I caught a

glimpse of someone on Grace's property. I also found a granola bar wrapper on the ground, exactly like the ones stolen from my tent. Maybe it was the prowler people have been reporting."

David frowned. "If he stole your food, that means he probably has your gun too."

"Not necessarily. The person who stole my gun came in the middle of the night while I was sleeping, and passed on the food. I don't think he would have come back for a few granola bars, especially since he took my money and credit cards. I think the person who stole my granola bars was simply hungry and looking for something to eat."

"Interesting point. But then we have two prowlers—the one who stole your food, and the other who stole your gun."

She suddenly realized her dog wasn't around. "Buster!"

"He's headed for Owen's place," David said, pointing to the terrier roaming across the field. "You'd better catch him before he runs away."

She wanted to stay longer, feeling as though she and David had made a small breakthrough, but she didn't want to lose Buster. "Let's discuss this later, okay?"

After parting with David, Kate lost sight of the terrier. She jogged down a row of stalks to the path that led to Owen's property. After running through the woods, she finally reached the ruins of her uncle's house. "Buster!" she called, searching for the dog.

When she turned around, an old man with a long, scraggly beard and a ponytail appeared from between two trees. His eyes narrowed into little slits as he gripped a long rifle with thin knobby fingers.

She placed her hand on her hip, ready to give him the what-for. "Virgil Crane," she said in a loud voice. "You've got a lot of nerve showing your face around here again, especially after what you did to Owen's truck, not to mention almost killing me."

The man stared at her with a confused scowl.

She pulled her badge from her pocket and showed it to him. "See this? You should be arrested for shooting at a marshal."

He turned away, ignoring her, and headed toward the woods.

"Hey!" she shouted, "I'm talking to you. You can't hunt here anymore. Did you hear me?" Furious, she followed him and tapped his shoulder.

The man jumped and gawked at her with wide, frightened eyes.

He really is deaf.

They stared at each other, until the jingling of Buster's tags broke the standoff. The dog loped out of the woods and came right up to Virgil, wagging his tail. The old man's hard expression softened when he saw the dog. With surprising tenderness, he bent to pet him.

When he lifted his cloudy eyes to Kate again, she tried to communicate. "I found Buster in the park." She pointed to herself. "I'm Kate. Owen's niece."

Virgil didn't respond, but watched her lips. Then he stood and headed for the barn. She followed him inside with Buster at her heels. The old man went straight to the workbench and picked up the small digital meter. He shoved it in her direction.

Kate took it from him, confused.

"They killed him," he said in a gruff voice.

"Who?" But he was already striding toward the door. She put the device down, wondering what it had to do with her uncle's death, and followed Virgil outside. "Wait! Who killed him?"

He either didn't hear or completely ignored her. Before she could catch him, he had disappeared into the woods.

Buster trotted up beside her, sat down, and whined. She lifted him in her arms. "You know who killed my uncle, don't you, Buster?" She gazed at the woods. "I have a feeling Virgil does too."

The clear mountain stream known as Abrams Creek snaked through its rock-lined route as multi-colored leaves drifted down from the forest canopy, blanketing the earth and the water like giant confetti. Admiring the tranquil beauty of this place, Kate could appreciate why Rick liked to fish here.

Standing in the stream in Grace's waders, she watched for her strike indicator to move, which would reveal a fish had taken her bait. Rick, who was fishing nearby, had already educated her on the different types of flies and shown her how to use the rod and reel. He'd also given her an ecology lesson about the creek's unpolluted water and neutral pH levels that made it the perfect habitat for rainbow trout.

While she waited for the fish to bite, her thoughts turned to the disturbing encounter with Virgil. What did he mean, *they killed him*? She wished she knew a better way to communicate with him to find out. When she returned from her fishing trip, maybe she should pay Virgil a visit.

Hopefully, Grace was awake and feeling better by now. When Kate had returned from her walk with Buster earlier that morning, Grace's bedroom door was still closed. Not wanting to disturb her hostess, Kate updated her note in the kitchen to say that she went fishing with Rick. At least David would check in on Grace when he dropped off Clementine. She appreciated his offer to do that, as well as to show her his blueprints for the house. She hoped it meant that not all the bridges between them had been burned—and his kiss after the archery tournament had made her want to cross a few new ones.

Eventually, Kate grew restless waiting for the trout to

bite. Keeping her voice down to avoid scaring away the fish, she started a conversation with Rick to pass the time. "Did you enjoy the harvest festival yesterday with Nadine?"

He re-cast his line in the water. "We happened to run into each other there. It's not like we were on a date or anything. I quit asking her out in high school after she went ga-ga over Danny Jennings."

At the mention of Danny's name, Kate became intrigued. "You went to school with David's brother?"

"Yeah. He's a couple of years older than me, but we were friends when we were kids. That is, until he started hanging out with Claven Ellis."

"The guy I beat in the semifinals."

"That's him. He may be rubbing noses with the bigwigs at the chemical plant now, but he's still bad news—hey, your float is bobbing!" He set down his rod on the bank and grabbed his net. "Okay, now reel it in."

Kate cranked the handle on her rod to retract the line until a large trout appeared above the water, flopping in the air. Rick trudged through the stream in his waders and scooped it into the net. "It's a nice one." After he took the fish off the hook, he raised the foot-long trout for her to see. "Next time we fly fish I'll show you how to release them. Owen's signature hooks are super strong, but razor sharp. You have to be careful with them."

The rest of the morning passed quickly as they fished and chatted about the fishing lure business and cars. She enjoyed hearing Rick talk about her uncle. He was one of the few people who had known him well and had good things to say about him.

When the fish had stopped biting, Kate and Rick went to gather their things to leave. Kate stooped to grab her backpack by the oak tree where she'd left it—

Something moved inside it.

"Rick, come here and look at this!"

He rushed over. "What is it?"

"My backpack. It's alive."

They both gaped at the gyrating bag on the ground. Rick pulled out his pocket knife. "I hope you don't mind me ripping it open."

"Nope. It's already been punctured once in the pocket, but why don't you tie that knife to something and do it from a safe distance?" She grabbed a fallen limb and handed it to him. "Here, use this."

"Good idea." He took line from his tackle box and secured his blade to the end of the stick. Then, jabbing with his lance, he pierced a hole through the bottom of the canvas. A rust-colored snake slithered out. Kate jumped away, giving it plenty of room.

"That's a copperhead!" Rick cried. "They usually start hibernating around now, but it's a warm day. You must have left your backpack open and it crawled in."

Revulsion churned Kate's stomach when she thought of how close she had come to being bit by the poisonous snake. "No, I didn't."

Rick's forehead crumpled in confusion. "Then how did it get into your bag?"

"Someone obviously put it there."

He stared at her, still not getting it. "Why would anyone do that? You could have been bitten."

The disturbing thought turned her blood cold. "I think that was the idea."

It was almost noon when Rick drove Kate back to Grace's in his truck. He'd suggested they stop off at the ranger station to report the snake incident, but Kate was more disturbed about Grace right now. After detecting a weak cell signal near Abrams Creek, she had given Grace a call, but no one had answered. She needed to go straight to Tyler's Glen and make sure she was all right. Knowing Rick was already worried about his grandmother's heart condition, she didn't tell him her concerns. Only that she wanted to go home right away.

As soon as they'd left the park and had reliable cell coverage, Kate called Vicki and informed her of the close call with the copperhead at the creek. She also shared her suspicion that the same person who had threatened her with the arrows and the note earlier had probably planted the snake in her backpack. Vicki told her a ranger would check out the area, but Kate and Rick had already searched it and didn't find any footprints with all the leaves on the ground.

Before the call ended, Vicki reported that there were no new leads into finding the person who'd been targeting Kate, and they were still in the process of tracing the knife.

Kate called Harlan next, while Rick kept driving.

"A copperhead?" Harlan said in a surprised voice.

"That's right." She glanced at the deputy's son. "Rick was with me and recognized the species of snake. By the way, I tried to contact Roy Timmons about the letter he wrote to my uncle. I found out Thursday that he died in some sort of freak shooting accident."

There was a brief silence over the phone. "Yeah. I heard about that through the grapevine in town. Terrible."

"Doesn't the timing seem a little suspicious?"

"I'm not following you?"

"Roy was one of the last people to have communicated with Owen, and they both died under suspicious circumstances. If we knew what they had discussed, maybe it would help solve Owen's murder."

"I think you're grasping at straws. According to the news reports, Roy died from a self-inflected gunshot, and Owen was stabbed. Other than the timing and the fact that they had some sort of exchange before they died, it seems coincidental at best. With all due respect, we don't need more theories. What we need is proof."

After they had finished talking, Kate put her phone away. It was discouraging that all of their leads so far had come to nothing. And with Owen and Roy both dead, whatever *matter* they had discussed would probably always remain a mystery.

"I heard you mention Roy Timmons on the phone," Rick said. "What did my dad say when you suggested that his death might be connected to Owen's?"

"He thought it sounded too far-fetched." Maybe it was, but at this point it was the only lead they had. It felt like they were all chasing their tails, not getting any closer to solving Owen's case, or finding the person who'd been targeting her. Meanwhile, a killer was on the loose, getting away with murder.

When Rick dropped her off at the house, Kate carried the small bucket with her fish to the back porch and discovered the door was still locked with no sign of Grace. She didn't want to worry Rick needlessly, so she smiled and waved goodbye to him before he drove off. Then she deposited Grace's muddy waders by the door and quickly let herself in with the fish.

Buster greeted her, wagging his tail.

"Where's Grace, boy?"

The dog tilted his head and whined.

Kate searched the den on her way to the kitchen, but still no sign of her hostess. Growing more alarmed, she set the bucket of fish she'd caught in the sink and hurried upstairs.

The door to Grace's bedroom was still closed. Kate knocked, praying she was all right. "Grace, are you in there?"

After she knocked a second time, a gravelly voice answered from the other side. "Come in."

Kate threw open the door and found Grace sitting up in

bed, still wearing her nightgown. Stepping inside the room, Kate felt relief and concern at the same time. "Are you okay? You didn't answer the phone when I called."

The woman eyed Kate's clothes. "Where have you been?"

Kate glanced at the dried mud on her sweatshirt. "Rick took me fishing this morning. Remember, I told you last night? By the way, thanks for letting me borrow the waders. I left them outside. I still need to hose them off."

Grace leaned forward, her eyes wide with interest. "Sounds like you've had quite a busy day already."

"That's for sure." *Not to mention those early-morning encounters with David, Virgil, and the poisonous snake.*

As Grace swung her feet around to get out of bed, she convulsed in a coughing fit.

"Whoa!" Kate went to pat her friend on the back. Grace's shoulder felt thin, almost fragile. "I think you should stay in bed until you're better. I'll bring you a fresh glass of water and something to eat."

"I don't want you to go to any trouble."

"It's no trouble. I'm hungry too. How about the soup? There's still some left from dinner last night. I'll bring two bowls on a tray and both of us can eat."

Relief flickered across Grace's face. "That sounds wonderful."

Kate grabbed the empty glass on the nightstand and refilled it in the bathroom. She brought it to Grace before she went downstairs to the kitchen to take care of the fish and prepare lunch. A short while later, Kate returned to Grace's room, carrying a tray with the soup, spoons, and two cups of hot tea. She carefully placed the tray over the woman's lap and moved to tuck a couple of pillows behind her.

When Grace had taken a sip of the soup, she smiled. "This tastes even better the second time around . . . Thank you, hon. I didn't feel like cooking today."

Kate sat on the edge of her bed.

"Have you heard anything from David?" Grace asked.

"Actually, I ran into him this morning. He was checking on your corn crop after the storm." Picturing him in the field petting Buster, Kate smiled to herself.

Grace regarded her with a gleam in her eye. "How was he?"

"He's not quite as angry with me as he was last night, but I don't think he'll be inviting me to any festivals for a while."

"He'll come around. Whether he knows it or not, he's smitten with you."

Kate doubted that, especially now that he knew she was a Bentley, but at least he'd been civil to her this morning.

After they'd finished eating, Grace settled into her pillows. "That soup was delicious. Where did you learn to cook?"

"I cared for my mother before she died. She couldn't eat solid food, so I taught myself how to make all kinds of soups."

"I'm sure you were a great comfort to her." Sympathy glistened in Grace's eyes. "Having lost a son and a husband, I know what it's like to lose someone you love. I wish you could have met my Frederick. He was a wonderful young man, and he would have liked you. He had an adventurous side, like us. I guess that's what made him join the Army." She pointed past Kate. "Would you be an angel and look in the chest at the end of my bed? There's a mahogany box inside. Please bring it to me."

Kate removed the tray and set it by the door. She walked over to the antique hope chest and opened the lid. The smell of cedar was strong. Among the collection of quilts and old photo albums she found a folded U.S. flag and a dark wooden box. She took out the box and carried it to Grace's bedside.

The woman lovingly caressed it, then opened it slowly, almost reverently, like a cherished treasure. A layer of black velvet lined the inside, providing a cushion for the assortment of military memorabilia resting there.

"Twenty-nine years ago today, Wade and I learned our son had died fighting overseas. This is all I have left of him."

When Kate saw the small emblems and tokens of his service, tears filled her eyes. Wiping away one that escaped, she spoke in a soft voice. "He must have been very courageous."

"Yes, he was." Grace tenderly touched her hand. "I'm glad you came to Tyler's Glen, Kate. I may not be your flesh and blood, but I care about you very much. This is the first time I've shown these things to anyone except my family. I don't know why, but I wanted you to know something about my boy. He may have gone to be with the Lord, but I don't want his memory to die here."

Kate leaned over and kissed Grace on the cheek. "I will always remember what you've told me about him and shown me today. Always."

That afternoon, Kate went outside with Buster to tend to the farm so Grace could continue resting. After collecting the eggs, she headed for the garden. She was on her knees harvesting greens when she heard a horse's whinny. Coming to her feet, she spotted Joe riding up on Thunder.

He swung out of the saddle and led his horse toward the garden. "Now why on earth would a soon-to-be heiress be slaving away doing farm chores?"

She dusted the soil off her knees as she stood. "I happen to like doing farm chores. It's good, honest work."

Buster came between her and Joe, giving a low, guttural growl.

"What's wrong with the mutt?" Joe raised his foot as if he might kick him.

She quickly scooped Buster into her arms. "You're making him nervous. What do you want, Joe?"

He stuck his thumbs in his belt loops and stuck his chest out. "To make you an offer. I'll drop my lawsuit if you agree to give me Owen's land and half of his business. I'll even throw in the warehouse in town that you're so interested in."

She recoiled at his proposition. "No way!"

"I thought you wanted me to donate the warehouse to a good cause."

"I do, but I'm not giving away Owen's land or half the business for it."

"It's Jennings, isn't it? He's sweet-talked you into selling the land to him."

She balled her fists, tempted to slug him. "For your information, I'm not selling the land to anyone. I want to keep it for myself. And you're wrong about David. He would never take advantage of me."

"Tell that to Nadine."

His remark took her by surprise. "Why? What does she have to do with this?"

A scandalous spark gleamed in his eyes. "You don't know about David and Nadine? The whole town knows."

The sound of another horse's hooves took her attention away.

It was David riding up on Grace's palomino. He reined in the mare as his gaze traveled from Kate to Joe. "I'll go ahead and take Clementine to the barn and unsaddle her," he said briskly.

"Wait, David!" Arms crossed, Kate sent the other man a pointed stare. "Joe was just leaving."

Joe paused just long enough to hurl a derisive sneer at David before he slowly swaggered away to Thunder. After mounting his horse, he tipped his hat to Kate in a mock gesture. "Remember what I told you."

As soon as he was gone, David got down and led Clementine toward Kate. "What did he want?"

"Nothing I can't handle." She ran her hand over Clementine's neck. "He's all bluster anyway."

A trace of a grin crossed David's face. "Sometimes I forget you're a marshal."

"Without my gun, I don't feel as much like one." She turned and walked with him as he led Clementine to the barn.

The horse nickered at the familiar surroundings, breaking the silence between them.

David was the first to speak. "I want to apologize for the way I acted at the festival. I thought Joe was baiting me. When I realized you really were Owen's niece, I guess it threw me for a loop."

"I'm sorry you had to find out like that."

He was silent for a moment. "The way I see it is, if we're going to be neighbors, we have to find a way to get past this."

"I agree. What do you propose?"

"We could start with dinner tonight?"

His invitation surprised and delighted her, but then she remembered Grace. "I'd love to, but I can't. Grace isn't feeling well, and I think I should stay with her."

Kate heard footsteps behind them.

"Clementine!" Grace strode inside the barn. She was dressed in jeans and a light jacket, and Kate thought she looked much better.

David waited for her to catch up. "Kate told me you were feeling under the weather."

She gently rubbed her horse's face, drawing a happy nicker from the mare. "I'm all right. Nothing to worry about. It's only a slight cough."

"Let me take you to see Doc Granger."

Grace addressed him in a stern voice. "Wipe that worried look off your face, David. I'm fine."

To his credit, he didn't seem fazed by her scolding. He obviously knew better than to argue.

Grace pulled a plastic bag with apple slices from her pocket, eliciting an eager snort from her horse. "Thank you for bringing her home." She let the horse take a slice from her palm. "I just got off the phone with my friend Opal. She told me one of her chickens is missing. She thinks the prowler may have taken it last night. I tried to call Harlan, but his phone was busy. Do you know if they have any suspects yet?"

A frown shadowed David's face. "Only one."

Kate and Grace both looked at him. "Who?" they asked in unison.

He blinked hard. "My brother, Danny."

Grace put her hand to her mouth. "No!"

Kate was equally stunned by the news. "He's here?"

Wearing a grim expression, he turned his eyes to the horse. "I haven't seen him myself, but others have." Then he regarded Kate with a serious expression. "You should know, rumors are also flying that he's responsible for Owen's murder."

"That's crazy," Kate said. "Why would Danny kill Owen?"

The frown lines deepened on David's face as he looked down.

A sense of foreboding suddenly came over her. "What is it?"

His tone was terse when he responded. "I need to get back to work." Before he left, he tossed Grace a parting glance. "If you start to feel worse, Grace, don't hesitate to give me a call."

Kate watched him as he strode away, puzzled and disappointed by his abrupt departure. "That's odd. What was it I said that made him leave like that?"

Grace put a comforting arm around her. "Don't worry about it, honey. It's not you. It's the rumors about Danny that has him so upset."

CHAPTER FOURTEEN

THE NEXT MORNING, KATE SAT WITH Grace in the small sanctuary before the Sunday service began. She took it as a good sign that Grace felt well enough to go to church. She'd even cut fresh chrysanthemums from her flower garden to bring to the cemetery after the service. But her nagging cough still worried Kate.

Seated next to the center aisle, Kate glanced around, admiring the simple, but beautiful, stained-glass windows with motifs of the Garden of Eden, Jesus as the Good Shepherd, a poignant rendering of the cross, and a picture of Jesus coming in glory to establish His kingdom on earth. Turning her attention to the people filing in, she recognized a few of them from the harvest festival.

Rick entered the sanctuary with his parents. When the family saw Kate seated with Grace, they warmly greeted her and sat on the same row. While they all waited for the service to begin, Rick recounted his and Kate's fly fishing expedition yesterday to his mother and grandmother, bragging about the size of the fish Kate had caught as if they were small whales. He concluded with the unsettling details of their copperhead encounter, which drew a gasp from Julianna.

Grace turned her head to Kate with an arched brow. "You didn't tell me about the snake."

"I didn't want to worry you," she replied with an innocent shrug.

A woman's quiet sobbing from the center aisle suddenly drew Kate's attention.

It was Nadine, shuffling in with her head down. *And David*—his arm around her—escorting her to her seat. His gaze locked with Kate's briefly, long enough for her to detect his surprise and unease.

Upset and confused, she turned her eyes forward, remembering Joe's gossip about David and Nadine. She didn't want to believe it. *They're only friends,* she told herself, dismissing the ugly rumors, but she couldn't stop the tightness in her chest from seeing the two of them together.

When the minister began his sermon, Kate tried to listen, but her heart and mind kept wandering across the aisle where the sound of weeping created a constant distraction. The sobbing grew louder the more the minister quoted scripture about sin, until David finally escorted Nadine out of the church, drawing curious stares and whispers from the congregation.

Grace must have seen them too, because she gently patted Kate's hand. The trace of doubt in the sympathetic woman's eyes contradicted her reassuring smile, causing Kate to suspect that she too had misgivings about the pair.

The minister's tone grew more passionate as he raised his Bible with conviction. "Friends, the wages of sin is death, but Jesus Christ paid for our sins on the cross and rose from the dead to give us eternal life!" He appealed to the congregation with a searching look. "The question is, do you believe it?"

Kate's heart responded with a resounding yes—her mind, however, continued to wrestle with questions about David and Nadine.

After the service, Kate and Grace walked with Rick and his parents to the parking lot.

"You haven't forgotten about our shopping trip this afternoon, have you Mom?" Julianna asked.

"No, of course not." Grace patted her daughter's arm. "I'll meet you at one o'clock at your house."

Julianna's eyes shifted to Kate with an inviting gleam. "Kate, why don't you come shopping with Mom and me in

Knoxville?"

"Thanks, but I don't want to impose."

"You wouldn't be. We'd love to have you. Wouldn't we, Mom?"

"Of course," Grace responded, "but first I promised Kate I'd give her a tour of the cemetery."

Julianna's bright smile faded a bit. "Oh. Then I'll leave you two. See you later, Mom."

After they'd left, Kate fetched the flowers from Grace's car. Then the two women went to the small country cemetery behind the church. They stopped first at Wade's grave marker, and Grace placed some of the fresh flowers there, and then on the grave of her son, Frederick Williamson Holbrook, as well.

Seeing the empty space reserved for Grace between her husband and son moved Kate almost to tears. The prospect of losing the kindhearted woman depressed Kate. But she took comfort from the pastor's reminder about eternal life.

A couple of rows down, they came to a fresh grave with Owen Bentley's name on the marker. The date of his death hadn't been engraved yet. Kate placed the remaining mums on the dirt. "Did Owen attend church here?" she asked Grace.

"Only recently. Rick invited him to come last Easter. After that, he never missed a service. It's quite remarkable when I think about it."

"You mean, because Owen was a Bentley and Rick, a Holbrook."

"That too, but I was referring to Owen becoming a regular church attender after so many years being away from it. As for their friendship, I think Rick thought of Owen as the uncle he never had because my son Frederick died at such a young age. And since Owen was a loner, he probably enjoyed having someone who shared his interest in restoring old cars."

Kate turned again to Owen's grave. "I can't help being a little sad and disappointed that I'm the last of the Bentley clan, and my family tree ends here with this one grave."

Grace tilted her head, speaking in a grandmotherly tone. "You heard the sermon. Death doesn't have to end here in this cemetery. I think Owen came to believe that before he died. One day you'll see him in eternity."

That truth brought Kate tremendous peace and hope as she imagined a glorious heavenly reunion. But Owen had been murdered, and it wasn't right that his body should be in this grave while the person who killed him ran free. And the only person left who seemed to have any clue about who did it was Virgil Crane.

After they'd returned home and were having lunch in the kitchen, Kate politely declined Grace's offer to go shopping. It sounded like a mother-daughter outing, and she wouldn't be very good company anyway. Seeing David and Nadine together at church, compounded by visiting Owen's grave, had darkened her disposition.

Sitting across the table, Grace's forehead wrinkled as she regarded Kate. "Then I'll stay here with you. I don't think you should be alone right now."

"Please don't change your plans on my account. I'll be fine," Kate assured her. "I'll lock all the doors and keep my cellphone handy. Besides, if anyone dares come around here, I'll use my trusty bow and arrow and sic Buster on him." She cast Grace a humorous look. "But a gun would be handier."

Grace's eyes lit up. "Of course! Why didn't I think of that earlier?"

Kate was intrigued. "What?"

Her hostess sprung to her feet as if her seat was on fire.

"I'm going up to my bedroom. I'll be back in a few minutes."

After clearing away the dishes, Kate met Grace in the hallway when she came down the stairs. She had changed from her church clothes into casual slacks and a blouse, but Kate's eyes gravitated to what she carried with her—a hunting rifle and a box of cartridges.

"I keep Wade's rifle in my bedroom closet, and the bullets in my underwear drawer, but I'd feel better if you had them with you while I'm gone."

Kate had to chuckle at the woman's moxie. "You mean you've been holding out on me all this time?"

Grace smiled as she handed them to Kate. "When you mentioned a gun, I suddenly thought of Wade's rifle."

"Perfect. Now you can go and have a good time with Julianna and not worry about me. If there's one thing I know, it's how to use a gun."

"I just hope you don't have to. Please be safe, hon." Then she gave Kate a parting hug.

After Grace left, Kate turned her thoughts to her encounter with Virgil. Her spirits needed a boost, and she could use some exercise. Now that she had the rifle she felt more comfortable about going out alone. Maybe it was time to pay Virgil a visit.

She thought about taking Buster, but didn't want to wear him out, or risk him getting away from her again, so she left the dog at home on the back porch. After loading Wade's rifle, she slipped some extra cartridges in her pocket just in case.

With the rifle slung by its strap over her shoulder and the safety on, Kate took the long way through Grace's acreage, exploring the creek that meandered through the back of Grace and Owen's land. The beauty of the Smokies, crowned in shades of gold and red, made her realize that selling her uncle's prime piece of property was completely out of the question.

Eventually, she reached the road. Virgil's place was on the other side and up a bit, toward Owen's farm. After crossing, Kate walked along the shoulder until she came to the lot with the shack. She hoped Virgil wouldn't shoot at her this time. Maybe leaving Buster at home was a mistake since the old man seemed to have a soft spot for the dog, and she wanted to be on his good side.

As she approached his ramshackle dwelling, Kate stopped to examine the rickety structure held together by decrepit gray siding devoid of paint. While it didn't look like much, it did provide shelter and protection. She knew for someone who was down-and-out, shelter and protection could mean the world.

Avoiding the rotten planks on the porch, she reached the door and knocked. After knocking again, she listened for any sound of movement inside. Thinking she heard footsteps in the yard, she whirled around and reached for her weapon. Holding the rifle in her hands, an ominous feeling crept over her as she scanned Virgil's wooded, overgrown lot. The property appeared deserted, though it wouldn't be hard for someone to hide behind all the trees and bushes.

"Hello?" she called to anyone who would listen.

No response, no footsteps, no rustling of leaves.

"Is anyone there?" The haunting caw of a raven in the tree above sent a shiver to her bones. Warily, she descended the steps to search around the house. "Virgil, where are you?"

Why did she bother calling him? He couldn't hear her anyway.

With the rifle pointed in front of her, she moved along the side of the house, skirting around a large propane tank as she approached the back. In the distance, she spotted an assortment of old tires, rusted out machinery, and gas cans littering the yard. The ultimate hillbilly man-cave. As she turned the corner, the barrel of her rifle collided with something big, dangling from above.

She gasped and jumped away.

It was the carcass of a wild hog, suspended by its hind legs. The repulsive sight and odor nearly gagged her as she shooed the flies away.

Feeling eyes on her, she cautiously circled around, moving away from the house. *Virgil, is that you?*

She didn't want to stick around, so she headed in the direction of the trail she had taken with David on horseback toward the park.

Having gone about a half mile, she stopped at the fork in the trail and took the route that would lead her back toward Grace's. That's when she sighted a black bear sniffing the air not far away. She grabbed the rifle from over her shoulder and aimed—no, she couldn't kill the animal, especially since he didn't seem to be a threat right now. She could run, but that would trigger him to chase after her. The best option was to mimic David's behavior the day they found the knife in the park. She raised her hand and the rifle in the air and began slowly backing away.

Her foot landed on something soft like a sponge. Suddenly, the ground beneath her crumbled and gave way. Shrieking, she lost her grip on the rifle and plunged straight down. When her feet hit bottom, she rolled, coming to a stop in the dank darkness.

Light shined through the hole at least eight feet above her head. Fortunately, nothing felt broken, though her palms and knees were scraped up, and her shoulder ached.

As soon as her eyes adjusted to her surroundings, she realized she'd dropped the rifle above the cave when she fell in. She focused on the hole in the cave ceiling and attempted to scale the limestone wall to reach it. After slipping several times, she finally gave up. The slick surface made climbing out impossible.

Something white in the shadows on the far side of the

cave caught her eye. After moving closer to inspect it, she drew back in horror.

Bones!

Probably some poor animal trapped in the cave years ago. Would she suffer the same fate? No! She had to do something—but what? Reaching into her pocket, she retrieved her phone. But the display showed no cell service underground. If she still had the rifle, she could at least fire off a shot.

This was a fine mess—alone in a cave, with no way to let others know where she was. "Help!" Her cry echoed through the cavern like a choir of mocking voices.

After shouting again and again with no response, she felt panic rising like flood waters. She couldn't wait around hoping someone would rescue her. She had to find an escape, or die trying. *Lord, show me a way out.*

Using the flashlight app on her cellphone, she searched every nook and cranny. Finally, she found a narrow passage, though she had no way of knowing where it led. As she stumbled through the cavern, the cold, damp air made her shiver. Surrounded by stifling darkness, she followed the beam of her light.

Something flapped overhead, and she ducked.

Bats!

Focus. Stay calm. She continued squeezing through the suffocating abyss for what seemed like an eternity. Finally, a faint glimmer appeared in the distance. Rushing toward the light, she bumped her head and banged her knees in the narrow chamber. At last, she had reached the mouth of the cave and stood in the middle of a large grotto with an outcropping of rock hanging above. She uttered a quick prayer of thanks, overcome with relief.

Taking a minute to recover and revive her lungs in the fresh mountain air, she checked her cellphone. Still no service. She turned it off to conserve the low battery, then looked around. To her right, ten feet away under the rock shelter, was a small tent with a camping lantern. Wisps of smoke swirled from a small pile of burnt wood in the center of a ring of rocks. She examined the lone campsite for a moment. Taking a stick, she poked the smoldering coals until they glowed underneath. The fire was fresh. The footprints in the dirt appeared to be from a man's athletic shoes.

She looked beyond the cave. Judging from the densely wooded, mountainous terrain and her estimate of the distance and direction she'd traveled in the cavern, she must be somewhere in the park. Whoever had been staying there obviously didn't want to be discovered. Otherwise, he'd be staying in the regulation campground. And without a gun, she didn't care to be here when he came back.

Leaving the grotto, she headed for the sound of flowing water until she came to a stream. A trail ran along the bank and she followed it. She hadn't gone far when she heard footsteps from behind. She glanced over her shoulder at the solitary path.

A rustling in the thicket rang alarm bells in her mind. Was it a bear, the rogue camper—or the crazy bowhunter? In any case, she wasn't going to hang around to find out. Jogging away, she heard a man's voice.

"Kate!"

Surprised to hear her name, she stubbed her foot on a rock and nearly fell. Steadying herself, she grabbed a large branch from the ground to use as a weapon and spun around to confront her stalker face-to-face.

A young man about her age, wearing grubby jeans and a worn, navy blue hoody, approached. He had a stubbly beard, but the pink scar on his right cheek and his bandaged hand identified him as the one who'd crossed the road the night of her car accident. "I think it's time we met, don't you?"

His wavy dark-brown hair looked familiar. But the intensity in his blue eyes gave him away.

"Danny." Kate held the branch in front of her. "Why are you following me?"

"Why were you snooping around my camp?"

"Does David know you're here?"

He spat on the ground. "Are you kidding? My brother couldn't care less if I was dead or alive."

"You're wrong, but that's beside the point." If she'd been armed with her Glock instead of a branch, she would have taken him straight to the sheriff's office. For all she knew, he was hiding from the law. What if the rumors were true and he was Owen's killer and had been stalking her all along? "Why are you hiding out in the park?"

"Where do you suggest I go—to the bed and breakfast?" He stepped closer. "I need your help, Kate."

She menaced him with the branch. "Don't come any closer."

He halted and raised his hands. "Take it easy. I'm unarmed."

"How do you know my name?"

"Everyone in Tyler's Glen knows who you are."

Flashing her badge, she warned him in a loud voice. "I'm a U.S. marshal. If you've broken the law, I'll arrest you." Hopefully, her commanding tone was enough to keep him at bay since she didn't have a gun.

"I know."

She stared at him. "You do?"

He nodded, keeping his arms raised. "That's why you're the only one who can help me. You want to know what happened to your uncle as much as I do, and you have the authority and resources to get to the truth."

Masking her surprise that he knew about Owen, she became more wary. "How do you know so much about me?"

"If you let me put my hands down, I'll be happy to tell you."

It wasn't a good idea to stay here talking to him. "Forget

I asked. I'm leaving." Backing away from him, she kept the branch handy in case he tried anything.

He slowly lowered his arms. "I'm being framed for your uncle's murder. I need your help to clear my name."

Her curiosity wanted to hear more, but her instincts told her to keep moving. Finally, she stopped. She couldn't leave until he told her what he knew about Owen's death. "Cut to the chase. I can't stay here all day."

"Claven Ellis is setting me up."

Of course. It's always someone else's fault. "And why would he do that?"

He frowned at her skepticism. "When we were younger, I used to hang out with him. We had a few scrapes with the law, mostly minor stuff. Then Claven came to me with this scheme. There had been a long drought, and the fire danger was higher than normal. He knew these farmers who needed the money from their insurance policies. All I had to do was light the match, and Claven would give me a cut of their payouts. It was more than I could earn in a year. He told me I'd be doing a service in a way, like Robin Hood or something. I'd be helping the farmers out and getting a little something in return. Plus, I could help my father pay the bills.

"So I helped him a couple of times, but then I started having second thoughts. I was supposed to set fire to the Martin property, but when I got there that night, I couldn't go through with it and left. Claven had an agreement with Zeb Martin and went ballistic when I told him I wanted out.

"A few days later, I heard about the propane explosion that killed your grandfather and started the fire that burned Zeb's farm. I knew it was Claven's doing."

She couldn't believe her ears. It was the first time she'd heard how her grandfather had died—in an explosion that was eerily similar to the one at Owen's place. It was all she could do to control her outrage. "You mean to tell me you were involved with my grandfather's death, and now you want me to help you?"

Danny raised his palm. "No—it was Claven." Frustration reddened his face. "You see, Wallace Bentley was renting the house next to the Martin property. Claven had set it all up to make it look like I triggered the explosion for revenge against the Bentleys, because Owen reneged on his deal with my father to sell him back his land. It was all a ruse so Claven could carry out his plan to burn the Martin property and get me back at the same time.

"I know I shouldn't have set those earlier fires. Fortunately, no one died in them, but someone could have, and I have to live with that. There's nothing I wouldn't do to erase the past, but I'm not the same person. I've changed, and I want to set things right. All I need is a second chance."

His remorse for the past was compelling, but Kate couldn't allow herself to be taken in by him. After all, he could be making it all up. "Even if what you're telling me is true, why would Claven kill my uncle?"

Danny stared at the ground as if it might hold the answer. "I don't know. Maybe Owen figured out who started the explosion that killed his father, and Claven decided to kill him before he went to the authorities. Then he framed me for it."

Kate remained skeptical. "How long have you been following me?"

He stared at her anxiously. "If anyone's been following you, it's Claven."

She kept the branch between them. "And I suppose he's also the one responsible for shooting those arrows at your brother and me when we found the knife in the park with Owen's blood on it. We could have been killed."

He gulped hard with a deer-in-the-headlights look.

If he's acting, he's doing a good job.

Danny lifted both hands again, palms out. "You've got

to believe me. I didn't kill your uncle or shoot at you. I doubt Claven expected any Bentleys to show up after Owen's death. If he knows you're a relative, he's probably been spying on you."

She recalled stepping on the wrapper in Grace's yard and glimpsing the hoody and bandages as the prowler ran away. "But you stole my food, didn't you?"

Gazing down with a penitent look, he nodded. "Sorry about that. I'll pay you back, once I get on my feet. I didn't have any money, and I was starving."

Studying the young man, she noted his gaunt features and injuries. His down-and-out appearance reminded her of the young men and women she had known on the street. So lost, so desperate. Suppressing her emotions, she continued her interrogation. "Did you steal my gun out of my tent?"

He lifted his head and stepped back. "No way. I only took a few granola bars. My hunting knife went missing a few weeks ago. Claven probably took them both. He must be plotting another scheme."

It was probably all a lie, yet part of his argument sounded plausible. If he truly wanted to clear his name, it explained why he'd bothered to stay in the area despite the risks. "What happened to your face and hand?"

"They got burned."

"How?" She waited, but he wouldn't look her in the eye. "How, Danny?"

"When I heard the explosion at Owen's, I went to save him, but it was too late."

She glared at him. "You let him burn?"

"No. He was already dead when I got there."

Because he'd been killed by the knife we found.

"I would have called for help if I could, but I don't have a cellphone. Then David arrived with the firefighters—"

"And you conveniently disappeared." Her anger intensified as she remembered the injured, bewildered-looking man in the road right before her accident. "Like the night I wrecked my car to avoid hitting you."

Danny rubbed his scarred face, his eyes dark with fear. "I was going to help, but then I saw David pull over. I knew he'd take good care of you, better than I could."

"Funny, how your brother is always the one left to clean up your messes. Why didn't you just leave town?"

His cheek muscle twitched. "There's someone who has stuck by me through everything. I owe her so much, but until I can prove I didn't kill Owen, we'll never be able to start a new life together." As he spoke, his tough façade shattered. "Look, I'm desperate to clear my name or I wouldn't be here. I know you don't know me from Adam, but if you care about David at all, you'll help me. I've served my time. I can't go back there again."

"The only way I'll help you is if you come with me to see the deputy."

"No!" he cried, his face twisting like David's when Joe told him she was Owen's niece. Backing away, he turned and ran.

"Danny!"

Like a wild buck, he leapt into the woods and vanished.

"It's not here," Kate said to Deputy Travis when they reached the mouth of the cave she'd discovered earlier that day. She pointed to the bare spot on the ground. "That's where I found his tent."

Harlan looked around the cave entrance. "You're sure Danny Jennings has been hiding out here?"

"Yes, but he obviously broke camp after he spoke to me." The only sign that anyone had been there now was a few ashes. All the wood and stones from the fire ring had been removed, and the footprints wiped clean.

"Why do you think he approached *you?*"

"He said he wanted my help. He thinks he's being framed for Owen's murder."

"That's some story." Harlan crossed his arms over his chest. "I hope you didn't fall for it."

His warning annoyed her, even if it was well-intentioned. "I wasn't born yesterday, you know. But he does have an interesting theory. What do you know about Claven Ellis?"

"Claven? He went to high school with my son. One time, Rick came home all beat up because he wouldn't do Claven's homework for him. But what does Claven have to do with any of this?"

"Do you think it's possible he could have framed Danny for Wallace and Owen's murders?"

Harlan rubbed his chin. "Wallace died a long time ago. I wasn't the deputy sheriff then. But even if Claven had something to do with it, why would he kill Owen after all these years? It doesn't add up."

She couldn't disagree, but at the same time, parts of Danny's story filled in the missing pieces, like how he got burned, and who might have stolen her gun. But the bigger question still remained—why would Claven kill Owen and frame Danny?

CHAPTER FIFTEEN

MONDAY MORNING HAD ARRIVED TOO SOON. Kate had stayed awake most of the night mulling over two separate, but disturbing questions—what was going on between David and Nadine, and should she tell David about her encounter with Danny? Closing her eyes again as she lay in bed, she wondered how David would react if she told him his brother had been hiding out in the park all this time—or that he'd asked her to help him.

Now that Deputy Travis knew Danny was in the area, he wouldn't stop until he found him. Given that both Owen and his father's deaths were so similar, Danny was the obvious suspect. That's what bothered her. It was *too* obvious. And Danny was no dummy. He had to know if he killed Owen, he'd be sent straight to prison, this time for life. Why would he take that chance?

Or was he telling her the truth about being framed?

Kate's thoughts shifted to David comforting Nadine at church. She hadn't heard from or seen him since, which caused her to wonder if there might be a grain of truth to Joe's rumors that David's interest in Nadine was more than brotherly concern.

She rolled over and groaned. With her aching shoulder and banged-up knees, it took longer than normal to get up.

As she made her bed, Kate moved the rifle leaning against her nightstand to tuck the sheet under her pillow. After they'd left the cave yesterday, Harlan had driven her to the trail and escorted her to the hole she had fallen through. It was a relief to find Wade's rifle still there on the ground. By the time Grace returned from shopping, Kate was at home, as if nothing had happened. Why tell her about the cave adventure or her encounter with Danny? It would only worry her more, and that was the last thing Grace needed. In fact, last night, when Kate had tried to return the rifle to her, she had urged her to hold onto it out of concern for Kate's safety.

Freshly showered and wearing a pair of jeans and a blue sweater, Kate stepped out into the hallway. Grace's door was still closed, but Kate could hear her coughing so she went and knocked. "Grace, are you up?"

A moment later, Grace opened the door. "Good morning, Kate." She finished buttoning her cardigan as Kate came in.

It was good to see her hostess up and dressed. Kate heard a friendly whine and glanced down at Buster. Had Grace brought him up to her room last night?

"Nine o'clock already," Grace said, looking at the time on her nightstand as she stepped into her slippers. "I can't believe I slept so late. I hope you haven't been waiting on me for breakfast."

"No, I overslept too. I heard you cough before I knocked. How are you feeling?"

"I'm fine." As soon as she'd said it, she started hacking again.

"I think you should see the doctor."

"It's only a cold."

The chime of the doorbell downstairs interrupted them. "I'll answer that—you stay and rest." Kate descended the stairs in a hurry, hoping it might be David. She opened the door wide, then did a double-take. "Nadine?"

The young woman smiled—a major improvement over her mood at church yesterday. "I hope this isn't a bad time."

"No, it's fine." *What does she want?* "Please come in."

Grace came down with Buster and joined them. "Hello, Nadine. What brings you by?"

"I came to see Kate."

"In that case, why don't you two make yourselves comfortable, and I'll bring you some hot tea?" Grace ushered them into the living room and offered Nadine the loveseat before she went to the kitchen. Kate took the chair across from Nadine, not sure what to say.

"I came here to talk to you about David," Nadine began. "I thought you should know the truth."

Kate paused, not sure she wanted to hear it. "Look, you don't owe me an explanation."

"I think I do. You see, I haven't exactly been myself lately."

"I have noticed . . . Are things better now?" Kate couldn't help being concerned about her, despite everything.

"Well, they can't get much worse," Nadine replied with a helpless shrug. "I'm practically broke, and I'm going to have a baby."

Kate's heart stopped. *Whose baby?*

"As if that's not bad enough," Nadine continued, "I don't know how to contact my baby's daddy."

Realizing that ruled David out, Kate's heart sprang with relief. At the same time, she felt a pang of sympathy for Nadine and her predicament, wanting to help her. "You mean he left without telling you how to reach him?"

"It's not like he wanted to leave. He had to. He left to protect me."

Suddenly, Kate put it all together—Rick telling her that Nadine and Danny were high school sweethearts and Danny sticking around to clear his name because of the woman who had stood by him. "Danny Jennings is the father, isn't he?"

Nadine's eyes grew wide at first, then she gave a slow nod.

"What about your family? Do they know?"

"My mother died five years ago, and my father lives in Texas with his third wife and three little kids. He's never wanted anything to do with me, so I'm not about to go crawling to him." She raised her chin in determination. "No, my baby and I will get through this somehow, even if it's on our own."

Kate admired her brave spirit, but it took more than courage to raise a child. She moved to sit beside Nadine on the loveseat and pulled a tissue from the box on the antique credenza behind the couch. "What can I do to help?"

Nadine sniffled and took the tissue Kate handed her. "Well, I've never had many close friends in my life, but I have a feeling I'm sure going to need one now."

Kate gave her a warm hug. "You've got it."

After Nadine had left, Kate went outside with Buster to do the chores so Grace wouldn't have to. While she harvested the herb garden, she prayed for Grace and Nadine. She suspected Nadine would need lots of prayers in the coming months.

The sound of someone pulling into the drive prompted her to get up and see who it was. The sight of David exiting his truck raised her spirits like sunshine after a storm. When she hurried to meet him, she noticed the bouquet in his hand. "Ooh, beautiful flowers! Grace will love them."

"They're not for Grace—they're for you." He presented them to her with a ceremonial flair.

Touched and surprised, she admired the cluster of mini-sunflowers and purple asters, delighting in the vibrant colors. "Thank you, but what's the occasion?"

"Does there have to be a reason? Maybe I'm simply being neighborly."

She laughed. "You're getting used to the idea, after all."

"Sounds like I don't have much choice." The glimmer in

his eye contradicted his ho hum attitude. "But you can't play loud music all night. Some of us have to get up early in the morning."

"I'll be on my best behavior."

He bent down to pet Buster. "How's the little guy doing?"

"He's much better." She crouched low beside him. "Between you and me, I think he's growing on Grace. This morning I found him in her bedroom."

David rolled his eyes. "That dog has never had it so good, with you two fussing over him like he's a baby."

Kate watched him petting the dog and felt ashamed of herself for believing Joe's idle gossip about him and Nadine. "By the way, Nadine came by to see me this morning."

David stood and scratched his forehead. "Really. What did she want?"

"A friendly ear, mostly. She told me about the baby."

The subtle parting of his lips told her that he knew Nadine's secret too. "She did?"

"Yes."

"I'm glad," he said, sounding relieved. "Yesterday morning on my way in to church I saw her crying in the parking lot. That's when she told me she was expecting a baby. I wanted to explain to you why I was with her, but I couldn't break Nadine's confidence."

She smiled in understanding. "And I have a confession to make. I heard an ugly rumor earlier, and then seeing you and Nadine together at church, and at Bubba's last week, I thought . . ."

The corner of his mouth curled into a wry grin. "Why didn't you tell me? I would have set the record straight."

She shrugged, feeling foolish now. "I'm not sure. I wish I had."

"I'd never do anything to hurt you, Kate." His earnest gaze confirmed his words.

"I know that now." Her thoughts returned to Nadine. "I also know that Danny is the father of her baby."

He flinched at the mention of his brother.

She wanted to tell him about her encounter with Danny yesterday, but seeing Grace walking toward them, holding a box in her hands, she decided now was not the best time.

"What pretty flowers," Grace said, admiring the bouquet in Kate's hands. "Sorry for interrupting you two, but I found this on the front porch. It's for you, Kate."

Surprised, Kate took the box from Grace and glanced at David, catching his curious glint. Was he pretending not to know about it? She took the card off the box and read it.

Hoping you'll reconsider my last offer,
Joe

"Well?" David said. "Don't keep us in suspense."

She opened the box and saw an assortment of chocolates inside. "Joe sent me candy. Seems he wants to be neighborly too."

David snorted at that. "Joe never does anything for anyone without wanting something in return."

"I'm afraid I must agree," Grace said.

Kate didn't respond. She focused on the clear morning sky. "It's such a beautiful day. It's hard to believe I've been here a whole week and still haven't been to Gatlinburg."

"Why don't you two go there for lunch this afternoon?" Grace suggested with a not-so-subtle grin.

David slanted his head toward Kate. "You want to go?"

"I'd love to."

The sunny mid-October weather provided the perfect day

for a drive to Gatlinburg. Kate gazed out the window, enjoying her view from the passenger side of David's truck as he drove along the Old State Highway 73 under a brilliant tunnel of foliage. Time passed quickly as he kept her entertained, pointing out interesting sites and sharing amusing stories about the area. He pulled off at several overlooks, including one where they spotted a black bear munching on acorns a safe distance away.

When they'd finally reached the tourist town of Gatlinburg, David parked his truck in a public lot and escorted Kate through the charming village. She enjoyed playing tourist as they strolled along the sidewalk lined with quaint shops and attractions. At one point, they stepped off the curb to cross a busy street, and David protectively took her hand. A thrill tingled through her that he didn't let go while they chatted and enjoyed more sights. She'd never felt so at ease with a man and exhilarated at the same time.

After checking out a few gift stores, they took the tram to Ober Gatlinburg, a ski resort and amusement park at the top of the mountain. Kate and David managed to get a nice table in the restaurant there despite the crowds for Oktoberfest. Seated next to the window with an amazing view of the mountains, Kate found the man directly across from her far more fascinating than the scenery. She couldn't remember when she'd had such a good time.

"How's your chicken schnitzel?" he asked after she'd tasted her food.

"Delicious. You know, I'm glad you took me here for lunch today, even if Grace had to rope you into it."

"She didn't rope me into anything. I had every intention of asking you out this morning. She simply gave me a little push."

"The flowers were to soften me up?"

"Worked like a charm," he replied with a sly wink. "I had to beat Joe to the punch."

"Believe me, there's nothing romantic about those chocolates. He's only trying to butter me up." She cringed after she'd said the last part.

David stopped chewing his steak. "Butter you up for what?"

The thought of Joe always left a bitter taste in her mouth, and she sipped her water to wash it down. "You might as well know. He's made me an offer for Owen's property and his business."

"What did you tell him?"

"That I'm not interested. Frankly, I wouldn't sell to him no matter what. He's suing Owen's estate for rights to his fishing lures. He says the lures are his designs."

David wadded his napkin and tossed it on the table. "The nerve of that guy."

"It's okay," she assured him, wishing she'd never mentioned the subject of Joe. "Rick and Julianna are looking for his designs. When they find them, Joe will have to drop the case."

"And if they don't find them?"

She didn't like to think about that possibility. "I won't be able to settle my uncle's estate until the lawsuit is resolved. By the way, I went to see Virgil yesterday, hoping to find out what he knows about Owen's death, but he wasn't home. I ended up spelunking my way into the park by accident."

She recounted her adventure in the cave to David.

"Good thing you weren't seriously injured," he said after listening to her story in amazement. "I should have warned you about the caves. My brother and I used to explore them when we were kids. We found arrowheads sometimes."

"I didn't find any arrowheads, but there are animal bones down there." She made a disgusted-looking face, drawing a chuckle out of him. "Actually, I discovered something else interesting." She hesitated, hoping this was the right time to mention it, now that he'd finished eating and was casually sipping his iced tea.

"What's that?" he asked.

"A secret campsite."

David took a moment to respond. "Probably a vagrant. Did you find out who it belongs to?"

"Yes. As a matter of fact, I spoke to him." She leaned slightly over the table and whispered. "It's your brother, Danny."

His nostrils flared, and his eyes widened. "What?"

"He looks bad, David. He's injured, and thin as a rail."

"He'll be worse than that if the deputy finds him."

"You want a shocker? It turns out Danny was the zombie I almost hit a week ago, and he claims he's being framed for Owen's murder."

David tapped his knuckles together on the table. "Did you believe him?"

"I don't know what to believe. He says Claven Ellis is responsible for both Owen and Wallace Bentley's deaths. Is it possible he's telling the truth?"

David frowned, releasing a long sigh. "That's what he told my father after he was arrested. It was a tough trial. There wasn't any clear evidence, only motive, and Danny certainly had plenty of that. As for Claven, it was Danny's word against his. The defense couldn't show a compelling motive like the prosecution could with Danny."

"Then he could be telling the truth?"

David looked outside at the view. Suddenly, he was somewhere else, very far away.

"David?"

A couple stopped at their table. "Kate?"

She pried her gaze away from David to look their way. "Buck!" Her ex-boyfriend was standing next to their table with a pretty brunette.

"What a coincidence." Buck turned to the woman. "Marsha, this is Kate Phillips."

The woman gave Kate the once-over and forced a tepid smile. "I've heard a lot about you."

Kate tried to act casual in the awkward situation. She gestured to David and introduced them. "Buck and I work together," she said casually, wondering if David would remember her telling him about their breakup.

His sideways glance at Buck indicated that he had.

"So this is where you went for your vacation," Buck said, peering outside at the magnificent view. "Good choice."

"Actually, I've been staying in Tyler's Glen. We came here for lunch. What brings you to the Smokies?"

The Adam's apple in Buck's throat bobbed as he glanced at Marsha.

"We're here on our honeymoon," she answered for him.

Kate stared at them, speechless.

David came to her rescue and rose to shake Buck's hand. "Congratulations. And you picked the perfect place for a honeymoon."

"Thanks," Buck replied.

"Yes, congratulations," Kate seconded, recovering from the shock.

Buck beamed at his new wife. "I know it may seem kind of sudden, but Marsha and I dated briefly in high school and lost touch when I joined the Army."

"I finally tracked him down on social media," Marsha said, sending him an adoring glance.

Kate eyed her ex. "Buck was always a hard one to keep up with."

He coughed uncomfortably. "Hey, Kate, do you have a moment? There's something I need to discuss with you. It's work-related."

"David, do you mind?" Not that she needed his permission, but she wanted to be polite.

He gestured with his hand. "Go ahead."

Buck smiled at his bride. "Excuse us for a moment,

honey, while we talk shop."

Kate rose and followed Buck to the bar, out of earshot of Marsha and David. "Sorry to interrupt your lunch," he said.

"It's okay. I'm happy for you. I only hope she knows what a car racing fanatic you are. So what's up?"

"Last week, I heard that Ralph Tourreni was released from prison. I thought you should be on your guard."

The news dealt a painful blow to the pit of Kate's stomach. "Thanks for the heads-up."

"That guy you're with—"

"David."

"Yeah. Are you two getting serious?"

His question caused her to smile. "I hope so."

Buck nudged her. "There's no shortage of wedding chapels in this town. Why not join the club?"

She looked over at David who was keeping Marsha company at their table. When he gazed in Kate's direction, he sent her a heart-melting smile. *Definitely husband material. But am I the right wife material for him?* "Can you imagine a city girl like me living on a farm?"

"Ready to retire from the danger zone to a quiet life in the country, huh?" he replied, smirking.

If she told him what she'd been through the past week, he'd never believe her. "Life in the country can be a lot more hazardous than you'd think."

Soon after Buck and Marsha had departed, Kate and David took the tram down the mountain. The packed car made it hard to hold a conversation, so they didn't say much, though Kate had a lot to think about after seeing Buck and learning about Raptor.

As they quietly strolled toward the parking lot, David pointed to the sky lift. "Are you game for another ride before we hit the road?"

She welcomed the suggestion, not wanting to leave yet. "Sure!"

A few minutes later, alone on the two-person bench together, they gazed at the beautiful scenery passing below them. She noticed he hadn't held her hand or put his arm around her since they'd left the restaurant. Was it because of what she'd told him about Joe? Or because of Danny?

David took a break from the view to look at her. "Is everything okay?"

Was she that obvious? "Why do you ask?"

"You've been quiet ever since we ran into Buck and his new bride." The corner of his mouth ticked up. "He's your ex-boyfriend, isn't he?"

She nodded in silence.

"I take it you didn't know about the wedding."

"Not a clue. It's funny . . . one of the reasons I broke up with him was because he never seemed to take our relationship seriously. Now, as soon as we break up, he gets married." She studied David for a moment. "What about you? You must have had other women in your life."

"There's not much to tell."

She nudged him slightly in the ribs. "Come on. What about Vicki Bates? Fess up."

He gave her a reluctant grin. "Okay. There was a girl once. We met at college. But when I left before graduating, and she realized I was going to be a farmer instead of a doctor, that was the end of that."

His admission flooded Kate's heart with compassion. "That must have been devastating."

As if brushing it off, he rubbed his palms against his jeans. "It was for the best. She never would have been happy as a farmer's wife. Not many women would."

"She sounds pretty shallow to me. And what's wrong with being a farmer's wife anyway?"

"Spoken from a woman who's about to inherit a small fortune," he replied with a dry look. "I don't hold it against her that she wanted a better life for herself. The truth is, I wouldn't mind having more money."

"And if you did, what would you do with it? Go back to school?"

"No. I think it was for the best that I returned to Tyler's Glen when I did. This is where I belong." He was staring at the landscape below them again. "What about you? Do you think you could ever live in a place like this—not on vacation, but all year round?"

Kate thought of the anonymous note that had brought her to Tyler's Glen. Though the author still remained a mystery, she knew somehow God's hand had played a part in it too. She came seeking family, and in a way, she'd found one. Not through blood ties as she'd hoped, but through the kindness of people like Grace, Rick, and David.

David was still waiting for an answer.

"Honestly, I don't know what the future holds, but I could see living here one day, under the right circumstances."

"That job running the outreach center is still open," he said in a playful tone.

She laughed. "Thanks, but—"

"But you already have a job. I know. And it's an important one too."

Thinking about leaving brought her down. "It will be strange returning to work after all this, and with Buck married."

David acknowledged her candor with a silent nod. His eyes flickered with a tentative look. "Do you regret breaking up with him?"

"Not at all. In fact, I'm relieved that I never married him. Oh, don't get me wrong, Buck's a great guy. In fact, he saved my life once."

"In the Cascades, right?"

It pleased her that he'd remembered that. "Maybe that's what attracted me to him in the first place, but I realized today when I saw him that I was okay with him being married to someone else. Whatever I felt for him before, it wasn't love."

"How do you know?" David's searching gaze met hers.

She marveled at how his eyes matched the sky. "I don't think I knew what love was before."

"Do you now?" he quietly asked.

The warm intensity in his expression made it impossible to look away. "It's becoming clearer."

Her simple reply registered in his rapt attention. Before her heart could beat again, he wrapped his arm around her and brought his lips to hers. In his embrace, she tingled with warmth and exuberance, feeling completely safe and free to be herself.

Their chairlift came to an abrupt halt, lurching them apart.

"This is your stop," the attendant called. "Everyone out!" He frowned at David and Kate, his eyes narrowing with disapproval. "That means you too, lovebirds."

As they exited their chairlift, David sent Kate a mischievous grin. "Let's go again."

She giggled. "I'd love to, but I don't think the attendant will let us back on."

By the time David delivered Kate to Grace's it was four p.m. He took her hand as he walked her to the back porch. "Next time, I'll take you to Pigeon Forge."

Grace opened the door to greet them. "How was

Gatlinburg?"

"Great!" Kate replied. "Thank you for suggesting it."

"Did you take the tram and the sky lift?"

Kate exchanged grins with David as heat rose to her cheeks. "Yes, it was quite a view."

The wise, perceptive woman gave them both a shrewd look. "And romantic too, I would imagine." Her face suddenly contorted in a violent cough.

Kate rushed to her side. "Are you okay?"

Grace started to say something, but crumpled. David rushed to help Kate catch her before she hit the steps. He picked her up and carried her to his truck. "Grab her purse. We need to get her to the doctor right away."

CHAPTER SIXTEEN

IT WAS PAST SUPPERTIME WHEN KATE rode home with David from the ER, but she wasn't hungry. A country song filled the heavy silence in the truck as Kate struggled to come to terms with Grace being admitted to the hospital for pneumonia. Maybe if she'd insisted on Grace going to the doctor earlier, she wouldn't be in the hospital now. Things seemed to be going from bad to worse.

The sign for the Tyler's Glen exit came into view sooner than Kate expected. She'd been so lost in her thoughts she'd lost track of time. "How serious do you think Grace's condition is?"

Taking the off ramp, David lowered the volume on the radio. "Hard to say. Best case, they may only keep her overnight."

Though his tone sounded relatively upbeat, she suspected he was holding back something important. "Worst case?"

Creases deepened in his brow. "It could turn into congestive heart failure, and she'll need a lot more care."

When David turned onto Maple Creek Road, they saw the deputy sheriff's car approaching from the opposite direction. Harlan slowed and rolled down his window, motioning for David to do the same.

"Julianna called and told me about Grace being admitted to the hospital with pneumonia. Thanks for getting her to the hospital so quickly." Harlan's frown lines deepened. "I hate to pile on bad news, but I was on my way to see you."

"What about?"

The deputy's brows dipped low, shading his eyes.

"Someone says they saw your brother leaving Owen Bentley's place the night he died. I'd like to bring Danny in for questioning."

"Who's the witness?"

"Virgil Crane. I stopped by his place yesterday to ask if he'd seen Danny roaming around after Kate reported that she'd encountered him in the park." Harlan looked past David to Kate. "You did tell him about that, didn't you, Kate?"

David glanced at her. "Yes, she did."

"Well, if you see your brother, tell him it'll be better for him if he comes to see me voluntarily. I only want to ask him some questions."

As Harlan drove away, David turned off his radio.

Kate wanted to cheer him up. "Even if Virgil saw Danny leave Owen's that night, it doesn't mean he killed him. Danny told me he tried to save my uncle from the fire, but he was already dead. His story is plausible."

"Maybe, but it still looks bad, and the deputy doesn't have any other suspects."

Sensing he wasn't in the mood to talk, Kate let him be, while she silently wrestled with her own fears about Grace's health. Maybe it was the woman's warm, grandmotherly manner, or the void left by Rose's passing, but Kate cared deeply about Grace, though she'd only known her for a week. *Please, God, let her get well.*

After David pulled into Grace's drive, Kate got out and he walked her to the door.

When they reached the steps to the back porch, she stopped and looked at him. "Would you like to come in for dinner? I can make something quick."

"Not tonight." He sounded weary and preoccupied. "It's been a long day, and I need to check on Smokey and the horses."

She nodded. "Well, thanks for taking me to Gatlinburg

this afternoon. I'm looking forward to Pigeon Forge."

His serious expression lightened a bit. "Hopefully, Grace will be home by tomorrow night. If you need anything, give me a call."

"Thanks. I'll be fine. It will be a little strange, though, staying in Grace's big house all alone."

David returned home. After he put food and water in Smokey's dishes, he went to work cleaning out Samson's stall, his mind firmly fixed on his brother's dilemma. Harlan's news about Virgil claiming to have seen Danny at Owen's that terrible night sounded pretty incriminating. The thought of reliving the nightmare of Danny's arrest and trial burned a hole in the pit of his stomach as he shoveled the muck and deposited it into a wheelbarrow.

Years ago, when Danny was arrested, his brother had insisted he didn't set off the explosion that killed Wallace Bentley. A couple of witnesses, including Claven Ellis, testified they'd heard Danny threaten revenge against the Bentleys, and another witness said he saw Danny near Wallace's house the night before the explosion. It was no secret that Danny had it in for Owen for the way he'd cheated their father. But if that was enough to convict someone, David was every bit as guilty.

He might have been more supportive of his brother if not for the stress and financial toll it took on their father. Danny should have had more sense than to do something so reckless. But what if he had been telling the truth all along?

Their father never gave up on him. If he were alive today, he wouldn't want his two sons at odds, but the prospect of going through all the scandal and shame of another trial only plunged the knife deeper into the old bitter wound.

Kate took Buster with her for a walk before sunset. Concern for Grace and Nadine occupied her mind as they passed the white barn and traipsed through the meadow. At least Grace had the doctors in the hospital to help her. Danny's situation in some ways seemed more hopeless. She could understand why he took the risk of asking for her help. If she were in his shoes, she'd be looking for anyone who could clear her name too.

She remembered the strange look on Virgil's face as he handed her the small digital sensor in Owen's barn. He knew who killed Owen, and it was somehow connected to that device. If the old man thought Danny had killed her uncle, he would have told Harlan and the deputy would have a warrant for Danny's arrest. Instead, he made it clear that he only wanted to question him.

When she came to the junction in the path that led to Owen's place, she turned. Buster followed at her heels as she strode through the woods. The dog shot out ahead of her, and she hollered for him to stop, but the little rascal ignored her and disappeared. Kate continued to call his name as she emerged from the shadowy forest into Owen's yard. She spotted the barn door ajar and headed there, hoping to find her terrier.

"Buster, where are you?" As she searched the barn, her eyes locked onto the vials and meter resting on the workbench. Virgil's chilling words echoed in her mind. *They killed him.*

A noise startled her.

"Kate."

At the sound of the man's voice, she lunged for the pitchfork leaning against the post and spun around, thrusting it in the direction of her surprise intruder.

Danny raised his hands defensively. "Hey! Take it easy with that thing."

She lowered it slightly, noticing the bandage on his hand was now gone. "I should have known it was you. What on earth are you doing here?"

"Thanks to you, I can't go back to the cave now."

"Well, you can't stay here."

"Why not? It beats a tent on a cold, rainy night."

It bothered her how tired and hungry he looked. "Because you're trespassing, and the deputy sheriff is looking for you. Virgil Crane claims he saw you leaving here the night my uncle was killed, and the deputy wants to question you about it."

"What?" His features twisted in anguish. Like a trapped animal, he began pacing, muttering something unintelligible.

"You know, hiding out like this only makes you look guilty. Come with me to see Deputy Travis. He only wants to ask you some questions."

He continued his agitated gait. "No, not until I can prove my innocence. This town has already convicted me once. Nobody's going to give me a second chance."

"What about David?"

Danny came to an abrupt stop and stared at her as if she were crazy. "Yeah, right. He's the last person I can go to for help. After everything I've put him and my father through, I can't involve him in this. You're the only one who can help me. I figured you of all people would understand what it's like to be desperate enough to do things you might regret later." The pointed edge to his voice caused her to suspect he might be using her checkered past as leverage.

She eyed him warily, keeping the pitchfork in front of her. "What are you talking about?"

He stared at the fork with a strange faraway look. "When you serve time in prison, you meet all kinds of people. There was this one really bad dude from Nashville I got to know pretty well. He told me some of the terrible things he did when he was the leader of a gang, and about the girl who got him arrested."

The chilling revelation gave her goosebumps. "Raptor." She plunged her hand in her pocket to retrieve her cellphone. "*You're* the one who sent the business card with the anonymous note. This has all been a ruse for Raptor's revenge."

He gaped at her and lifted his palm. "No, wait! Please, hear me out. I don't know about any anonymous note, but Ralph did ask me to give you a message."

"I bet he did." She raised her phone and poised her finger. "Now I'm giving you one—I'm calling the deputy and turning you in."

At that moment, an ear-shattering blast rattled the barn and violently shook the ground under Kate's feet.

She pivoted toward the noise. *Virgil's place.* She burst through the barn door and ran toward his house.

At the edge of Owen's property, she halted, horror-stricken at the flames consuming the shack across the road.

Danny ran up, hacking from the smoke.

"We've got to get him out," she cried.

They'd started to cross the road when Buster appeared, darting out in front of them. Kate heard it before she saw it—an eighteen-wheeler barreling around the bend at breakneck speed.

"Buster!" Kate lunged for her dog.

"Watch out!" Danny cried, clutching her arm to restrain her.

The truck honked and swerved at the last minute, sending a rush of air in its wake. Kate's heart stopped as it sped away. She called again, and Buster came trotting across the road, appearing unharmed. Kate closed her eyes and took a deep breath. The smoky air triggered another cough.

"And I'm the one everyone's afraid of," Danny remarked.

She shot him a pointed look as they hurried across the road. "If you want to prove your innocence, help me find Virgil. He may be the only person who can corroborate your story."

When they'd reached the burning house, they searched for a way through the wall of flames.

"You stay here," Danny said. "I'll look around and see if I can get in."

"Be careful, Danny." After he left, she pulled out her cell and called 911 as Buster ran back and forth whimpering.

David drove up in his truck and jumped out. "Kate, what are you doing here?"

"Your brother went to find Virgil!" She pointed to the flaming house.

Danny came running through the side yard, carrying the old man in his arms. "Run!" he yelled, stumbling from his burden. "Gas cans in the backyard are about to explode."

Kate glimpsed David's shocked expression. He quickly changed gears and grabbed her hand. "Let's go!"

"Wait—I need to get Buster." She looked around. The dog had disappeared again. "Buster?"

"We have to go. *Now.*" David put his arm around her and almost dragged her away from the burning house. A powerful blast launched them in the air, sending them crashing to the ground.

When Kate came to, she was lying flat on her stomach, with David's arm protectively draped over her back. "David?" No response. His stillness frightened her. *Please, God, let him be all right.*

Then he groaned and pushed himself up, turning his head in her direction. "What happened?"

"Virgil's house exploded. Don't you remember?"

He blinked hard a couple of times, then nodded. "Danny tried to warn us."

"Right."

"Hey, guys, I need your help." It was his brother calling from a short distance away.

Kate and David got to their feet and hurried to where Danny was tending to Virgil on the ground. The scrawny, wizened man was unconscious and had burns on his leg, but otherwise didn't appear too badly injured.

"I found him behind the house, knocked out from the concussion," Danny said. "Good thing he wasn't inside or he'd be toast."

While David examined him, Kate gently touched the old man's shoulder, hoping to rouse him. "Hang on, Virgil. Help is on the way."

His eyes slowly opened, and he stared at her for a moment. Then he gestured for her to come closer.

She leaned toward his face. He reeked of tobacco and smoke.

"They killed Owen," he told her in a raspy voice.

"*Who?*"

His breathing grew ragged and labored as he stared at her lips. "The chemical—"

"What?"

"We're losing him." David's voice sounded dire as he felt the man's neck for a pulse.

"Stay with us, Virgil!" Kate cried, clutching his shoulder.

His eyes rolled toward her and closed.

"No!" Outrage erupted from her core like a festering volcano. "Tell us who did this to you?"

David began pumping the man's chest to resuscitate him. He glanced at his brother, who had started heading toward the burning house. "Danny, where are you going?"

His brother ignored him and kept on.

"Come back here, Danny! Don't!"

Kate watched, mystified. What was Danny doing? Had he lost all hope? She jumped up and ran after him. "Danny, please stop!" She watched in shocked horror as he disappeared behind the inferno. The fire flared, driving her back.

"Danny!" David cried.

Kate spun around and saw his torn, anguished face in the glow of the flames as he continued trying to revive Virgil. There was no doubt in her mind how much he loved his brother, despite everything, and it brought tears to her eyes.

Seeing David's expression suddenly brighten again, she turned. Danny emerged from around the corner of the house, carrying Buster in his arms. She hurried to them, ecstatic to see them both alive.

"I think his paw may be injured," Danny said. "I found him limping behind the house."

The dog squirmed when he saw her.

She took him from Danny and kissed his ash-coated fur. "Buster, I thought I'd never see you again." The wail of ambulance and firetruck sirens blared in the distance, causing her to look up. Then she scanned the area. But now where was Danny? She turned to David, who was still attempting to resuscitate Virgil. "Where did your brother go?"

Her Good Samaritan continued pumping Virgil's chest. "The sirens must have scared him off."

As soon as the firefighters arrived, the crew jumped off the truck and began to tackle the blaze. David turned over Virgil's resuscitation to the paramedics and threw on his firefighting gear to help the fire crew.

Deputy Travis drove up and Kate gave him her statement about what had happened. When she'd mentioned that Danny had been there with them, Harlan frowned.

"Why didn't you contact me when you found him in the barn?" he asked.

"I was about to, then I heard the explosion. Finding Virgil took priority. Danny pulled him away from the house before the second explosion."

The deputy wasn't buying it. "He probably knew it was

coming because he detonated the first one."

"My brother didn't set that explosion." David was marching toward them. His adamant voice surprised Kate.

Harlan raised his hand, signaling for David to calm down. "I know he's your brother, but he's also a convicted arsonist."

"No, David's right," Kate said. "Danny was with me before it happened. Besides, if he set the explosion, why would he bother rescuing Virgil, especially after I told him that Virgil had seen him leaving Owen's place the night he was killed?"

The deputy didn't have a ready comeback. "Well, I advise you both not to be taken in by him. I got a call from Vicki Bates earlier today. They managed to trace the knife with Owen's blood to the man who purchased it."

Kate exchanged uneasy looks with David.

"That's right," the deputy said. "The knife belonged to Danny."

CHAPTER SEVENTEEN

KATE REMAINED WITH BUSTER AND WATCHED David and the rest of his fire crew finish up after extinguishing the blaze. Harlan and the other members of the sheriff's investigative team had already left.

She thought of Virgil, who had been taken away in the ambulance. She prayed for a miracle, hoping the paramedics might still revive the old man. She may not approve of his trespassing and hunting on her uncle's property, but she had developed a soft spot for him. He was her uncle's friend and neighbor, after all, and he'd been trying to tell her who had killed him. If Virgil died, the truth about what had happened to Owen would probably die with him.

What was it Virgil had told her? Something about chemicals killing Owen. But Owen wasn't poisoned, he was stabbed, then burned from the explosion.

Clearly, the old man wanted her to get the message, but it didn't make any sense. Could it be a riddle of some kind? Was he afraid to tell her in front of Danny?

It was nine p.m. by the time the firemen prepared to leave. David's yellow protective coveralls were coated in soot and ashes when he came to where she sat on a log cuddling Buster in her lap.

"You're still here." He sounded surprised.

"It's pretty dark to walk home on foot."

He grimaced as he removed his firefighting helmet. "I should have given you the keys to my truck, or at least a flashlight. Sorry about that."

"Don't be. I have my cellphone. I could have used my flashlight app to get home. To tell you the truth, after everything that's happened, I didn't want to go back to that big house without Grace."

He coughed from the noxious air. "Well, if you don't mind the smell of smoke, we can go to my place, and I can take a look at Buster's paw."

She spoke to the little dog. "What do you say, Buster?" He whined and wagged his tail. "I think that's a yes."

They got into David's truck and headed down the road to his house. As soon as he opened his garage door, Smokey appeared from inside. He started barking and bounded to Kate as she started to exit the pickup. She cradled Buster protectively in her arms.

"No, Smokey!" David said in a firm voice, silencing the dog, who compliantly followed them into the garage.

Carrying her terrier, Kate entered the unoccupied stall and noticed the utility sink near the door to the house. "Would you mind if I gave Buster a quick bath before we go in? He's covered with ashes and soot, and I don't want to bring him inside like this."

"Good idea." He reached for a bottle on a nearby shelf. "Here's the doggie shampoo." Then David stripped off his soiled firefighting coveralls to his T-shirt and jeans and laid them aside in the garage. "While you're doing that, I think I'll wash up too."

After he went in the house with Smokey, she quickly scrubbed Buster's filthy fur.

David returned a few minutes later with towels, looking fresh and clean after a quick shower and a change of clothes.

When she'd finished drying the dog, he stared at her and grinned.

"What?"

"You could use a good scrubbing yourself." Taking a clean towel, he wet it under the sink and gently wiped the soot off Kate's face.

"Thanks," she said, noticing his curling wet hair and the

fresh scent of soap on his skin. "Can you wipe away the bruises under my eyes too while you're at it?"

"What bruises?" He playfully tossed the towel to her.

She wet it again with a little detergent and wiped the remnant of ashes from her sweater and jeans. "I hope the rest of this soot will come out in the wash."

"It should, but I've got a bottle of stain remover you can use. C'mon. Let's go in and take care of Buster's paw."

Following him through the door, Kate carried the dog into the warm, inviting kitchen. "This is pretty fancy for a man-cave," she said, admiring the custom hardwood cabinets and granite countertops.

"Cave men have to cook too, you know." His eyes were shining at her. "Make yourself at home. I'll be back in a minute."

While he was gone, Kate looked around. The kitchen opened into a spacious central area with a huge stone fireplace. A plush brown sectional and natural hardwood coffee and end tables faced the flat-screen TV mounted on the wall. On the mantel was a picture of an attractive couple with two adorable little boys in scouting uniforms. *David and Danny.*

She heard David's footsteps and turned around. He'd brought a blanket, a couple more towels, and his first aid kit.

"Where's Smokey?" she asked.

"I thought it would be less stressful for Buster if I put him in another room." He set the items in his hands on the couch, then came to the end of the coffee table. She went to the other side, and they moved it to clear a spot in front of the fireplace where he spread the blanket over the carpet. Lifting Buster from Kate's arms, he gently set him down on the covered portion of the rug. Then he took the remote control from the end table and clicked a button. A warm fire flickered to life in the hearth.

Kate sat next to him on the blanket and coaxed the dog

to lie on his side. She scratched the terrier's ears to calm him while David carefully examined his paw.

Lightning flashed through the large window that faced the mountains. A distant rumble of thunder followed.

"Aha! I think I found the problem," David said, holding Buster's paw in his hand. "He's got a couple of pieces of glass stuck between his toes. He must have picked them up after the explosion. I think I can remove them." Taking needle-nose tweezers from his kit, he rose to his feet. "I need to disinfect these first."

He quickly returned with a small tray and went to work on Buster's paw. The dog whimpered a couple of times, but Kate kept him calm by scratching his ears until David finished.

"Poor little guy." David lifted the tray with the fragments of glass and set them on the end table.

"Let's see—volunteer firefighter, first responder, town council member, and now animal surgeon. Is there anything you can't do?"

"Archery."

She laughed, drawing a smile from him as he disinfected the dog's paw over the towel.

"When you live on a farm, you learn to be resourceful. I've had to remove a thorn or two from Smokey's paws, but that's nothing compared to shoeing a horse." He removed gauze and scissors from the kit. "You probably should take Buster to the vet tomorrow to double-check that I got everything out." After he had skillfully bandaged the paw, he went to put away his supplies.

While he was gone, Kate made herself comfortable in front of the fireplace, and carefully lifted Buster into her lap.

When David returned, he joined her on the blanket, using the couch as a backrest and stretching out his legs.

She thought about Grace at the hospital. "I hope Grace's doctors are as proficient as you are, David."

He turned his head and gazed at her, his eyes reflecting empathy and tenderness. "Grace is a strong lady. She'll get through this."

"We've grown so close. I don't want anything bad to happen to her . . ."

"It's okay," he said, scooting closer so he could wrap his arm around her. "She'll be fine."

Kate wanted to believe that, but the emotional fallout from the stressful evening suddenly overwhelmed her and brought tears to her eyes. "I hope Virgil makes it."

David gave her a comforting squeeze and silently nodded.

"I didn't tell you this before, but Virgil shot the tire and the windows out of Rick's truck. I was looking over Owen's property at the time, and I guess he thought I was a trespasser and wanted to scare me off."

"So that's what happened to Rick's classic F-100. What did Virgil say tonight when you asked him who killed Owen?"

She recalled his last words. "Something about chemicals. It doesn't make any sense, but I saw him Saturday morning right after I ran into you in Grace's cornfield. He led me into Owen's barn and thrust this little meter from Owen's workbench at me and said, 'They killed him.' I keep trying to put that together with what he said tonight."

"He might have been delirious from the explosion. Unless . . . he was referring to Rydeklan."

"That crossed my mind too, but Owen didn't have any business dealings with the chemical plant, did he?"

"Not that I know of."

"I wish I could understand what he meant. Virgil may be the only one who knows who killed my uncle. I wonder if that's why he was targeted. Danny doesn't stand much of a chance unless we figure out what really happened."

At the mention of his brother, David released her and

shifted uncomfortably as he focused on the blaze in the hearth. "You heard the deputy. It doesn't sound like my brother has much of a chance anyway." He turned his gaze to her. "You really think Danny is innocent?"

"I don't know about innocent. Before the explosion tonight, he told me he had a message from my former gang boss in prison, which worries me. But, no, I don't think he set those explosions or killed Owen."

Firelight and shadows flickered across David's face. "If Danny didn't kill him, then how did Owen's blood get on his knife?"

"Yesterday in the park, Danny told me his knife was missing. He suspected Claven Ellis was behind it. You know your brother better than anyone—would he lie about something like that?"

David stared into the flames dancing in the fireplace. "The brother I knew was a little immature and brash, but he never lied. However, if he *is* being set up, coming here has only made him more of a target, not to mention putting Nadine at risk." His shoulders stiffened. "I tried to tell her to forget about him, but she's as hardheaded as he is. All those years in prison, she stuck by him, but it's only caused her trouble and heartache. And now they're married and she's expecting his baby."

"They're married?"

He nodded. "They did it right after he was released from prison. She told me at Bubba's the other day. She wanted me to be happy for her, but instead, I told her that Deputy Travis suspected Danny was behind Owen's murder. I thought that maybe she could get the marriage annulled."

"No wonder she was so upset at Bubba's that day."

"That was before I knew about the baby." David gave Kate an adamant look. "One thing I know is that I don't want Danny's problems to come between us. Promise me you'll stay away from him until this all gets sorted out."

She considered his point of view and didn't argue. After all, she was tasked with capturing fugitives, not helping them. "Will you promise to give him a second chance if he's proven innocent?"

He frowned at first and didn't answer right away, but after a moment to think about it, his defensive wall came down. "I guess I can do that."

A flash of lightning caused the lights to flicker. A few seconds later, thunder reverberated off the windows.

Kate glanced outside. "A storm is coming. I'd better leave."

"Wait. With all the strange things happening lately, I don't like the idea of you staying at Grace's alone tonight. You can take my room, and I'll sleep on the couch."

It would be all too easy for her to stay here alone with him in his warm cozy home on the stormy night. That's exactly why it wasn't a good idea. Her strong attraction to him coupled with her emotional vulnerability right now were a volatile combination. "That's sweet of you, David, but I'm a big girl. If Grace can handle living alone in that big house all these years, I think I'll be all right for one night. Besides, before I left the hospital, I promised I'd keep an eye on things for her."

Though reluctant, David went along with her wishes and escorted her to his truck, carrying Buster in his arms.

On the ride to Grace's, Kate held Buster close while she looked out the window. Violent flashes of lightning exposed the charred remains of Virgil's house in the distance and transformed the normally peaceful countryside into a smoky, shadowy wilderness. She'd never been afraid of storms before, but since her car accident, lightning and thunder made her antsy.

"Please pull over here," she said as they came to Owen's place. "I want to check the mailbox. I meant to do it earlier before the explosion."

David slowed to a stop in front of Owen's property.

Setting Buster on the seat, Kate jumped out, hurried around the truck, then crossed the road. She discovered a handful of mail in the box and took it with her.

"Find anything interesting?" David asked when she got back in.

"Only a few letters." She started to peruse them, but it was too dark to read the addresses on the envelopes.

When they arrived at Grace's house, the house was pitch dark. Why hadn't she thought to leave a couple of lights on inside?

David parked so the truck's headlights illuminated the back porch. "I hope the power is still on." He turned on the dome light and reached across Buster and Kate to retrieve a flashlight from the glovebox.

"The storm isn't that bad." Though she spoke with confidence, the thought of walking into a dark, relatively unfamiliar house made her a little uneasy.

"It doesn't take much to knock out the electricity here in the country, and once it's out, it may not come on again for days. You should gather Grace's candles and flashlights to be on the safe side."

"Good idea."

He hopped out and came around to help her with Buster before they headed to the back porch. When they'd reached the steps, Kate tucked Owen's mail under her arm so she could unlock the outer door while David held her dog and the flashlight for her to see. After coming inside, she laid the mail on the antique trunk, and David illuminated the door to the den so Kate could unlock it next. Once she'd entered the house, she felt for the nearest switch and flipped on the lights. "See, the power is on," she said in a cheerful tone. "You can stop worrying about me now."

"Who said I was worried about you? Maybe it's Buster I'm concerned about."

She laughed, taking her dog from his arms and cuddling the small creature. "He smells good after his bath." She carefully laid him in the crate of blankets Grace had moved from the porch to a corner inside the den.

The lights in the house flickered, and she turned to David.

He cast her an uncertain glance. "You still want to stay here tonight? I can take you to the motel or the B&B."

"After everything that's happened today, I think I can handle a little thunderstorm." *But I'd rather be with you.*

David yawned, and Kate noticed his droopy eyes. Though he'd done an admirable job staying alert, the deep creases in his weary brow and his heavy lids were tell-tale signs he desperately needed a good night's sleep.

"It's late," she said, "and you're exhausted." She affectionately patted his chest with her palm. "I think it's time you went home to rest."

He hesitated. "You're sure you'll be all right?"

"Positive." She playfully pushed him toward the door. "Now go before you pass out from exhaustion. I don't want another calamity tonight."

"Don't forget the candles. Here, I'll leave this with you too." He handed her his flashlight. "I have an extra one in my truck." Turning toward the door, he paused. "If you need anything, give me a call. Okay?"

She assured him with a firm nod. "Thanks for everything, David."

"That's what neighbors are for, right?" A half-grin formed on his mouth. "Speaking of being neighborly . . ." He took her hand and led her with him to the back porch, stopping at the outer door to say goodnight.

Slowly, he wrapped his arms around her. A flash of lightning revealed a lively glimmer in his eye that caused Kate to excitedly anticipate his kiss. As their lips came together, his phone rang, interrupting them and spoiling the moment.

"Sorry," he said with an apologetic glance as he checked the caller ID. "On a night like this, I better answer." A moment later, he ended the call and gave her a quick peck on the cheek. "Gotta go."

"What happened?" she asked.

"It's an emergency." He waved goodbye and hurried to his truck. "Stay safe, and I'll see you in the morning."

Gripping his flashlight, Kate felt let down by his sudden departure. It was strange too that his ring tone wasn't the blaring one she remembered for the 911 dispatcher. Was it a personal emergency? After he sped away, the cool, damp air gave her a chill. What she needed was a cup of hot cider. She locked the outside door of the porch and came into the house. On her way to the kitchen, her phone rang in her pocket.

"Grace?" Kate answered expectantly.

"Sorry, it's Rick. I didn't wake you, did I?"

Sleep? What was that? Kate thought of all that had happened that night. If only he knew. "No. How's your grandmother?"

"Better. The antibiotics are kicking in now, and her fever is down."

Kate relaxed with relief. "I'm so glad."

"If she continues to improve, they'll probably release her tomorrow."

She hoped that was the case.

"Is everything okay at the house? You know, a storm is blowing in."

"Yes. The power is still on." She frowned as the lights flickered again.

"Good. It can be kind of spooky in that big house at night, especially if you're not used to it. By the way, my grandmother keeps my grandfather's rifle in her bedroom closet, and the bullets are in her underwear drawer."

"I've already got them handy, but thanks for the tip."

"Stay safe."

After she hung up, Kate finished securing the house. Rick's mention of the rifle made her think that she should fetch it and keep it with her tonight. She also remembered seeing an old kerosene lantern and a trigger-ignited utility lighter in the kitchen.

Once she'd gathered all the items and brought them into the living room, she carried the lighter to the fireplace and pressed the trigger, sparking a blaze under the small stack of wood in the hearth. She watched it grow until it radiated warmth and thawed her inner chill. The flames reminded her of the explosion and subsequent inferno that had consumed Virgil's house. His cryptic last words continued to mystify her. She hoped that somehow he had pulled through, though it didn't seem likely.

As Kate rose to her feet, the photo on the mantel of Frederick drew her attention. She picked it up. What a shame he hadn't survived and returned home to a hero's welcome.

A bright flash with a loud click knocked the lights out completely. Immediately, a deafening clap of thunder shook the house. Unease settled over her when she remembered David's warning about how long a power outage might last. She hoped he was wrong this time.4

No lights were on at Nadine's rundown rental home when David arrived. Rain poured as he jumped out of his truck and ran to the broken-down porch. He pounded on the door. "Danny, it's David."

He heard footsteps.

When the door opened, his brother was holding a flashlight, appearing haggard and troubled. He waved David in and pointed toward the couch. "She's over there."

David brushed past him, carrying his first aid kit. "You shouldn't be here. The deputy sheriff is looking for you." He went to where Nadine was lying on the couch, clutching her abdomen and seizing in pain.

Danny followed him, hovering over his wife. "I know, but I was concerned about Nadine with this storm and power outage. When I got here, I found her like this. That's why I called you. Please help her. I'm afraid she might lose the baby."

"David," Nadine cried when she saw him. "It—hurts so bad."

"I got here as quickly as I could." He knelt beside her to check her pulse and blood pressure. "Danny, why didn't you take her to the hospital?"

"I tried, but her car won't start, and I don't have one."

David took Nadine's hand and spoke in a reassuring voice. "You're going to be fine. I'm taking you to the ER." Then he lifted her in his arms and carried her to his truck.

Danny opened an umbrella and held it over them until they'd reached the pickup. Then he opened the rear door of the cab and tenderly patted her hand before David laid her in the backseat. "It's gonna be all right, babe. Hold on." Then he moved to the front to climb in the passenger seat.

David closed the back and stopped him. "What do you think you're doing?"

"I'm coming with you."

"Why, so you can get arrested at the hospital?"

His brother frowned in the shadows. "I don't care what happens to me. I need to be with her."

"Don't you get it? You're married now, and soon you'll be a father. Whatever happens to you automatically affects your wife and baby. The last thing Nadine needs right now is more stress. If you want to be a hero, quit hiding and running. Man up and go straighten things out with the authorities."

"Danny!" Nadine cried through the open front door.

Looking wounded, he stepped on the running board and spoke to her over the console. "I can't go with you, babe," he gently told her. "David's right. I can't keep hiding."

"What?" she cried as Danny reluctantly got down and closed the door.

David hurried around to the driver's side.

His brother appeared next to him as he hopped in. His expression was disturbingly bleak. "Take good care of my wife and baby. They mean everything to me."

Backing out of Nadine's drive, David caught the lost, woeful look on his brother's face. Had he been too hard on him? He couldn't think about that now. He had to get Nadine to the hospital before it was too late.

CHAPTER EIGHTEEN

A LOUD NOISE DOWNSTAIRS JOLTED KATE from her sleep. Reaching for the alarm clock, she noticed the time wasn't illuminated. The lamp by her bed didn't work either. The power was still out.

She fumbled in the darkness until she found David's flashlight and her cellphone on the nightstand and grabbed them. Getting out of bed, she nearly tripped over her shoes. She headed toward the flicker of lightning coming from the window. Images of Virgil's burning house flashed in her memory as she stared outside at the murky landscape. Was she next?

Illuminating her room with the flashlight, she found her clothes lying over a chair. She quickly changed into them and slipped her phone into her pants pocket. Crossing to her bed, she grabbed the rifle and loaded it with the cartridges from the drawer of her nightstand. With the flashlight in her left hand and the rifle tucked under her right arm, she crept down the stairs.

After checking the hallway, she opened the front door, thrusting the rifle barrel in front of her as she peered outside into the gloom and rain. Satisfied that no one was there, she came inside and locked the door. She moved into the living room and felt a draft. Shining the beam of her flashlight over the furniture and around the perimeter, she stopped at the bay window. The curtains billowed from the howling wind as lightning flashed outside, reflecting off the shards of glass on the floor.

An arm encircled her neck, thrusting a knife to her throat.

Struggling to remain calm, she broke into a cold sweat from the blade pressing against her jugular.

"Put down the rifle," a man's voice growled in her ear.

Keeping her head as still as possible, she lowered the rifle and slowly leaned it against the couch while trying to place the man's voice. Was it familiar?

"Now turn off that flashlight and hand it to me."

After she'd clicked it off, he snatched it from her hand.

"What do you want?"

"Quiet!" The blade grazed her flesh and the arm tightened, restricting her breathing.

She mentally searched the room for anything she could use as a weapon. Her eyes darted to the dim outline of the lantern close by on the table behind the couch. She'd left the lighter there too.

"How are you . . . going to kill me?" she gasped. "Another explosion?"

"I could cut your throat." he said, squeezing tighter.

A spasm wrenched her back, releasing tendrils of torture down her spine. She squeezed her eyelids in agony, afraid she would black out. The slightest move could nick an artery. Hoping to distract him without getting killed, she kept talking. "Maybe—maybe you'd like my gift certificate to Bear Claw Sporting Goods."

"You had no business coming here. You ruined everything."

She heard a jingle, then a bark. *Buster!*

The man swore at the dog growling at his heels.

Kate clutched the man's arm and yanked it down with all her might. Dodging his blade, she snatched the lighter and pressed the trigger toward the intruder's hand.

The man shrieked and dropped the knife to the floor.

Grabbing the rifle, she spun toward him, the end of the barrel pointed in his direction. She clicked off the safety and choked out the words, "U.S. Marshal!"

A flash of lightning filled the room, illuminating the face of the man in the shadows.

Claven Ellis.

"Drop to the floor with your hands over your head!" she shouted, her voice sounding rougher than usual. The rifle butt was pressed firmly against her firing shoulder as she kept her finger on the trigger. "Do it—Now!"

The dim figure of the man did what he was told.

"You should have taken my gift certificate when you had the chance."

An urgent knock came from the front door. Through the shattered window, she heard a man's voice. "Kate, it's David. The power's out. Are you okay?"

His voice was as welcome as a storm shelter in a tornado. "Come in through the window," she shouted. "It's broken."

After carefully climbing over the pieces of glass, David entered the room, illuminating it with his flashlight. He halted, seeing her with a rifle aimed at Claven on the floor.

"Your timing is perfect." She'd dance for joy if she wasn't trying to keep the rifle steady. "Would you mind calling the deputy for me?"

David stood outside with Kate on the front porch, watching the taillights of the deputy's vehicle fade into the darkness. Now that Claven was in the sheriff's custody, they could all breathe a little easier.

The rain had stopped and a few stars were visible in the twilight sky. A rooster crowing in the distance prompted David to look at his watch. "It won't be long before sunrise."

Kate took David's hand and squeezed it. "Want to come in for coffee? I won't be able to sleep after all this anyway."

He couldn't believe how calm she seemed after the harrowing experience. When he'd shown up, Kate clearly had things under control, but that hadn't stopped his insides from burning at the thought of her life being threatened. "By the way, I've got good news."

Her eyes glittered in the beam of his flashlight. "I could use some right now."

"It's Virgil. The paramedics were able to resuscitate him on the way to the hospital. He's there right now."

"You mean, he's going to be all right?" she asked, her eyes brightening with hope.

"That's hard to say. He has second degree burns on his leg, and he's in a coma. He needs our prayers."

She nodded resolutely. "If you hadn't come when you did, he wouldn't have stood a chance."

David went with her through the front door to the hall, shining his flashlight. He stared at the rifle in the corner that Kate had used to turn the tables on Claven. She continued to amaze him.

"Don't worry, I unloaded it right after Harlan arrived and handcuffed Claven," she said, as if reading his thoughts. "Personally, I prefer pistols, but since mine was stolen, I had to make do with that. It belonged to Grace's late husband."

David followed her with the flashlight to the broken window in the living room. A cool, damp breeze from outside whisked Kate's hair as she stared at the gaping hole where the glass had been. Crossing her arms to stay warm, she frowned. "Unfortunately, the window will have to be replaced. That's the last thing Grace needs right now."

David took off his jacket and draped it over Kate's shoulders. "That's nothing compared to what could have happened."

"I guess you're right." She sent him an appreciative glance before she turned to the lantern on the long table. After removing the glass globe top, she handed him the lighter. "Care to do the honors?"

"Sure," he replied, taking it from her.

He lit the wick, and she placed the globe over the small flame, chasing away a portion of the darkness. "I think I'm going to keep one of those trigger lighters with me from now on," she remarked in a light voice. "They're pretty handy."

Eyeing her with a wary look, he spoke in a dry tone. "As long as you keep it away from me."

She faced him and laughed. Her radiant smile lit up the room much better than the lantern.

He pulled his jacket snugly toward her neck. Seeing the faint red line across her throat, he tenderly brushed his finger along it. "Are you sure you're all right? The blade grazed your skin."

"It's only a scratch."

Removing his hand, he made a fist. "When I think about that creep, breaking in, and—"

Her brows pinched together, and she spoke softly to calm him. "Hey, I'm okay, and Claven is in custody."

He nodded in agreement, her comforting words helped to assuage his anger as he silently thanked God for her protection.

"I'd better make that coffee," she said. "How about breakfast? Are you hungry?"

"Maybe later. First, I want to take a look at that window. I have tools and a couple of sheets of plywood in the bed of my truck left over from doing repairs at the church camp. I think I can do a temporary fix by covering the hole."

Kate headed to the kitchen while David quickly went to work boarding up the hole. After he'd finished, he stowed his tools in his truck. When he returned to the living room, he saw Kate carrying a tray with two steaming cups of coffee and a couple of plates with slices of Grace's pumpkin pie. She set it on the coffee table, her eyes darting to him, then to the boarded-up window. "That was quick."

He examined his handiwork, wishing he could do more. "Unfortunately, it's not much to look at. Maybe I can find a replacement window tomorrow before Grace comes home."

"After everything that's happened tonight, I'm happy to have a boarded window."

His thoughts shifted to his friend and neighbor. "Has there been any update on Grace's condition?"

"I forgot to tell you. Rick called and said she's much better. In fact, she may come home later today."

"Really? That's great." The welcome news helped to recharge him after the long night.

Buster's tags jingled at his feet. "Hey, Buster," he said as he bent to pet the dog. "How's that paw doing?"

Kate stepped closer and smiled at the terrier. "I didn't think he could bark, but you should have heard him go after Claven."

When David straightened, he blinked hard a couple of times to focus his blurred vision.

Frowning with concern, Kate took his hand and led him toward the fireplace. "Come, have a seat and relax, David. You look exhausted."

He groaned slightly as he sat on the loveseat and rubbed his bleary eyes. "I hope you made that coffee strong. It's been a long night."

She handed him a cup. "You haven't slept at all, have you?"

He took a sip and set it on the tray. "Only the short nap I took at the hospital before I left. As I drove by on my way home, I saw a faint light coming from this room and figured you were still up. I got to thinking about you being all alone in that storm, especially with a nut-job archer on the loose, making threats, so I turned around in my driveway and came back."

"I'm glad you did," she asserted, her eyes widening emphatically.

"By the way, that emergency call was for Nadine."

"What?"

"I had to take her to the hospital. She needed an emergency appendectomy." He blew out a long breath. "She and the baby made it through okay, but she'll need to stay in the hospital a few days."

Kate lowered herself next to him on the loveseat. "Thank goodness you got her to the hospital in time."

"Danny was at her house. I think maybe I was too hard on him. He wanted to go to the hospital with us, but I talked him out of it." He couldn't help being frustrated when he thought about his brother. "He's in no position to support a wife and child, Kate. Tonight when I showed up, he couldn't even take her to the hospital. Neither one of them has an operable car. Can you imagine the turmoil he would have caused if he'd gone with us and been arrested there?" David rolled his eyes at the thought. "I wish he'd never come home."

"Don't say that. He's your brother, and the only family you have left."

Guilt from her rebuke and from the harsh way he'd spoken to his brother earlier got him to thinking that it was probably time he started to cut Danny some slack. "At least he called for help."

"Don't forget he risked his life to save Virgil. He told me he got those burns on his face and hands trying to rescue Owen too."

Nothing was clear-cut when it came to his brother. "It's hard to know what to believe anymore."

She nodded in agreement. "Especially when things aren't always as black and white as we want them to be. We're all flawed in our own way. We may not be arsonists or murderers, but each one of us has done something that we're not proud of."

He made a shocked face. "You mean I'm not perfect?"

She grinned and shook her head. "Me neither. Not by a long shot. Seriously, David, I don't want to see this friction between you and your brother become a feud like the one between the Bentleys and the Holbrooks."

It had never occurred to him that his rift with Danny might blow up into something on that scale, but he could see how it was possible. "Point taken," he replied, acknowledging her concern. The way the lamplight glittered in her eyes put him in an especially agreeable mood. "But if everyone got along, what would the town have to gossip about?"

"City-slicker heiresses," she replied with a sidelong glance.

He chuckled softly. "And on that note, I think it's time for me to go."

"Aww. Do you have to leave?"

Her winsome pout tempted him to stay. In fact, he suddenly felt very awake, and it wasn't from the coffee. He'd better leave now, before she changed his mind. "I'm afraid so, but I think I still owe you a goodnight kiss."

He took her hand in his, and they strolled together to the front porch. The sound of birds singing filled the air, and the first rays of dawn colored the retreating storm clouds in shades of pink, orange, and yellow. "Looks like it's going to be a nice day."

"Is it still a goodnight kiss if it's morning?" she asked with an impish grin.

Turning to gaze at her, he found her more captivating than the sunrise. "Good point. I guess you'll have to collect my goodnight kiss some other time." He pivoted on his heel as if to leave.

She promptly tapped him on the shoulder to make him about-face. "Oh, no you don't. You're not cheating me out of my kiss again. I'm here to collect."

He glanced at the dawn sky, thinking it over. "In that

case, I guess I better pony up." Playfully, he clasped his hands around her waist and pressed his lips to hers, taking his sweet time and savoring every moment. When he finally released her, it wasn't easy.

"I wish you could stay longer," she said with an alluring look. "I was hoping we could discuss the plans for my vacation home. I want a big hot tub off the master bedroom."

"A hot tub! I better leave now, before you get around to the sauna."

"Don't forget the shooting range and archery course," she said with a wink.

After David drove away, Kate lingered on the porch to enjoy the sunrise. Like daylight chasing away the darkness, her loneliness and sadness had suddenly been vanquished by happy thoughts for her future. One she hoped might include David. And now that Claven had been arrested, things were starting to look up.

Had the young man really killed Owen and framed Danny because of something that had happened over a decade ago? And what about the business card and the clipping? She found it hard to believe that Claven had sent them. As Danny had pointed out, he probably didn't know Owen had any other relatives. But *someone* did, and had summoned her to Tyler's Glen. Until she knew who and why, she couldn't let it go.

CHAPTER NINETEEN

KATE SPENT THE REST OF THE morning cleaning the house and doing outside chores in anticipation of Grace's return. Julianna called around one p.m., shortly after the power had come on, to tell her that Grace had been released from the hospital and would be home soon.

Having finished her work, Kate changed into a turtleneck to hide the knife mark on her throat. When she heard Julianna drive up, she hurried outside to greet her hostess and welcome her home.

"It sure is good to be out of that hospital," Grace exclaimed as she got out of the car. "It nearly drove me crazy."

When the three women headed for the back porch, Grace touched Kate's arm. "How's Clementine?"

"She's fine. I filled her food and water troughs and cleaned her stall this morning."

Grace gently squeezed her hand. "Thank you for taking such good care of things for me."

"It's the least I could do." Kate opened the door for the women.

When they came inside, Buster greeted them with a wagging tail.

"Hello, Buster," Grace said. "Did you miss me?"

The dog whimpered.

Julianna led Grace through the side door off the porch which opened into the hall and staircase.

"Are you sure you want to be upstairs?" Kate asked. "I can arrange things for you in the den if you'd like."

Grace regarded her with an appreciative smile. "Thanks,

dear, but I want to sleep in my own bed. I'm much better now." Her talking evoked a cough.

Julianna took a stern stance with her. "Well, you may feel better, Mom, but you're not out of the woods yet. I want you to stay in bed for the next week and take it easy."

"I can bring you whatever you need," Kate offered.

Grace reluctantly acquiesced. "Oh, all right. But Kate, I don't want you to feel like you need to stay and take care of me. Don't you have to go home to Nashville soon?"

Julianna looked in her direction. "You're leaving?"

"I have to be at work next Monday."

Grace's daughter tilted her head. "Harlan tells me you're a marshal."

"That's right."

"Very impressive. You must be brave."

"It's more about being well-trained and prepared."

"Are you sure you want to spend the rest of your vacation looking after my mother?"

"I don't mind." Actually, Kate wanted to do much more for her. "You know," she said to Grace, "with the hospital bills coming, I'd like to pay you for letting me stay here once I get my new credit and ATM cards."

The woman shook her head in protest. "Absolutely not. You've helped with the chores and looked after the place, and that's more than enough payment."

Kate appealed to Julianna. "Can you please convince your mother to let me contribute something financially?"

Julianna lifted her shoulders. "You know my mother. Once her mind is made up, there's no changing it."

"Are we going upstairs or just standing around here all day?" Despite her grumbling, Grace had a faint, yet discernable twinkle in her eye.

Julianna sighed, but her face showed her warm affection for her mother. "Okay, let's get you upstairs, Mom."

Taking each step slowly, holding onto the rail and

Julianna for support, Grace made it to the second floor as Kate followed. When Grace released her hold on Julianna, her daughter put her hands on her hips. "Mom, please let me help you."

"I'm not an invalid. I can walk to my room on my own steam."

"Fine." But Julianna kept her hand on her mother's back all the way to her bedroom door, exchanging an eye-roll with Kate.

Kate had changed the sheets on Grace's bed and placed freshly cut mums and roses from the flower garden in a vase on her nightstand. She'd also opened the curtains to brighten the room.

"Look at those beautiful flowers," Grace exclaimed as she came into her room. "Now that's better than any medicine." She slowly lowered herself onto the bed, and Kate stooped to remove her shoes. Grace looked at her clock on the nightstand that said ten forty-six p.m. "That can't be right. It's at least two in the afternoon."

"You missed all the excitement last night," Kate replied. "The storm knocked the power out. It didn't come on again until a little while ago. I must have forgotten to reset your clock."

"My goodness, and you had to stay here all alone?"

"I was fine, and David stopped to check on me." She didn't want to burden them with the news about the explosion, the broken window, and Claven's arrest so soon after Grace's release from the hospital. If Harlan hadn't told them yet, it was probably best for her not to say anything right now.

Grace suppressed a grin and exchanged glances with Julianna. "How is David?"

"Fine." Memories of his kiss at dawn filled her with eager expectation, and she wondered when she would see him again. "By the way, he asked about you."

"That was nice of him."

Buster wandered into the bedroom, his tag jingling and tail wagging.

Kate went to pick him up. "You're not supposed to be in here, little guy." She turned to Grace. "Don't worry. I'll take him downstairs."

"No, it's okay. Bring him to me."

Glancing at Julianna, who seemed equally surprised, Kate carried the terrier to Grace's bedside and carefully set him in her lap.

The woman noticed his bandaged paw and frowned. "What happened to him?"

Kate hesitated at first, but decided she should go ahead and tell them. They would find out eventually anyway. "Did you hear about what happened to Virgil?"

"If you mean the explosion and the fire," Julianna replied, "Harlan already told us about it. He said it's a miracle Virgil survived."

Relieved that they already knew, Kate wondered if Harlan had also told them about the break-in and Claven's arrest.

"Poor old Virgil," Grace uttered, cuddling the dog close.

"Thank goodness David was there or he wouldn't have made it," Kate said. "Anyway, Buster got pieces of glass in his paw walking around Virgil's yard after the explosion, and David had to remove them."

Julianna crossed her arms. "Harlan said the sheriff's office has issued a BOLO for Danny Jennings. I hope they catch him soon before he hurts anyone else."

The sternness in Julianna's voice caused Kate to wonder if that was her own opinion, or if Harlan had convinced her that Danny was responsible. Not that Kate was taking his side. After all, he seemed to be friends with Raptor. But everyone was entitled to justice, even Danny.

"Looks like you took excellent care of Buster." Grace

sniffed his fur. "He smells so nice too."

"I gave him a bath."

Grace stroked the little dog. "I know he's a mutt, but I've kind of gotten used to having him around."

"I need to take him to the vet today and make sure his paw is okay."

"Oh, you'll have to wait. We ran into Doc Carter at the hospital. His wife just had a baby. He said he's taking a few days off. Good thing David was able to remove the glass."

"Yes, it was." Sensing that she should let Julianna have some time alone with her mother, Kate excused herself and went downstairs.

A little while later, after unloading the dishes in the dishwasher, Kate went into the living room.

Julianna's voice carried from the hallway. "My mother is crazy about that dog."

Kate turned in her direction as the woman entered the room. "It's mutual. I'm starting to wonder if I should take him home with me to Nashville."

"Why not? He's your dog."

"I'm not so sure about that. I think he's more attached to Grace, plus he can run and play outside here. He wouldn't have much room in my condo."

Julianna's gaze darted to the boarded window. "Is that where Claven broke in?"

So she does know. "Your husband told you?"

She nodded. "I can't believe Claven actually threatened you with a knife. Thank goodness you were able to stop him."

"It was pretty crazy." Kate lightly ran her finger over the collar of her turtleneck.

Julianna shook her head. "I thought when Claven went to work for Rydeklan, he had cleaned up his act. I can't imagine why he would do such a thing."

Unless it had something to do with Uncle Owen's murder. But

Kate kept her suspicions to herself.

Julianna crossed the floor to the fireplace and gazed at the picture of her brother. She lovingly ran her finger over the frame. "I'm glad you're here today, Kate. I've been hoping for an opportunity to speak to you."

"Have you found my uncle's designs for the lures?" she asked, hoping against hope.

"No, I'm afraid not. But Rick and I are not giving up."

The two of them took a seat in the living room, Julianna on the loveseat and Kate in the chair beside it.

"It's bizarre when I think about it," Kate said. "I wouldn't have even known about Owen's death or his estate if I hadn't received an anonymous note telling me to contact Lester Crane. Originally, I thought it was sent by someone with good intentions, but now I'm not so sure . . . Anyway, it's turned out to be a blessing in disguise. Otherwise, I wouldn't have met Grace, or Rick, or . . ."

"David?" Julianna finished with a perceptive look.

Kate smiled and nodded. "When I first came to Tyler's Glen, I was hoping to find family connections. You see, after my foster mother passed away, I was feeling very alone. Although I was disappointed that I don't have any living relatives here, I have made wonderful friends."

Julianna peered at her reflectively. "Kate, what would you do if you found out that you do have family, but not in the way you expected?"

She tilted her head. "What do you mean?"

"Would you want to know the truth about your family, even if it might change everything you thought you knew about yourself?"

Kate squinted in confusion. "I'm not following you."

Julianna leaned in her direction. She seemed to have something serious on her mind. "What if things were different? What if Norm wasn't your father?"

Kate stared at her, wondering if the stress from Grace's

ordeal had gotten to the woman. "What are you talking about?"

Julianna's eyes shifted to the picture of her brother on the mantel. "I told you before that I went to high school with your mother. Well, my brother was quite taken with Mary, but he couldn't date her openly because of the feud between our families. I think her father hated the Holbrooks more than anything. Wallace Bentley was an angry, bitter man, and he blamed my family for most of his problems. Mary was terrified of what he might do if he found out she and Will were seeing each other behind his back."

"Will?" Kate interjected. "I thought your brother's name was Frederick."

"Oh, it is, but his friends and I called him Will. Only my parents called him by his first name. His middle name was my mother's maiden name, Williamson."

Kate remembered seeing the tombstone with his full name, Frederick Williamson Holbrook. "Rick is his namesake, isn't he?"

"Yes," A wistful smile touched Julianna's lips. "After Will graduated high school, he served in the Army. It was while he was overseas that Mary's friend Sally told me she had been a witness at the wedding when Will and your mother eloped in Gatlinburg, right before he was deployed."

"They were married?" Kate felt all the oxygen escape her lungs.

"Yes, but they never told anyone in the family. I was shocked to learn about it, but for Will's sake, I didn't tell anyone. I knew it would create an uproar between our families. Then we got the news. Will had been killed when his convoy was ambushed by the enemy. He was only eighteen." Sadness dimmed Julianna's usual radiance.

"Needless to say, I was surprised to learn that Mary had married Norm and moved to Nashville so soon after Will's death. I couldn't believe she could be that fickle. It seemed obvious to me that she didn't care that much about my brother. Then a couple of years later, right after Harlan and I were married, we went to Nashville for the weekend." She smiled at the memory. "It was the craziest thing. We ran into Mary right there on the street, pushing a stroller. She was clearly unhappy, and we didn't talk long. But when I saw the baby's face, I instantly knew she was Will's daughter . . . You have his eyes."

Kate couldn't believe her ears. Part of her wanted to cry and the other was stunned and confused. All these years she'd had family in Tyler's Glen and didn't even know it.

"I've never told anyone until now," Julianna continued. "But it's always haunted me. I kept tabs on you until I found out that Mary had died. I tried to find you then, but I couldn't. I even hired a private investigator. Eventually he located you, but you were already with your foster parents by then."

"I was living on the streets before they took me in," Kate said in a hollow voice, recalling how alone she'd felt when all the time someone was searching for her. "That's probably why you couldn't find me."

Julianna glanced down at her hands in her lap. "That must have been very difficult. I'm sorry you had to go through it. Once I realized your foster parents were decent, upstanding people, I decided to leave things as they were. After all, Mary's father and Owen were still alive then, and if you'd come here as Will's daughter, you would have been caught in the middle of their feud. And, from what I could tell, you were happy with the Tuckers, so I thought it was best to leave you with them. Were you happy, Kate?"

Kate was still trying to process the mind-blowing information. If this was true, why hadn't her mother told her—or did she try? She recalled her mother's final words to her about the will and her father. She wasn't talking about Norm or a will. Her mother was trying to tell her that Will was her father!

"You should have told me anyway." Hurt and indignation rose inside her. "I had a right to know."

Julianna acknowledged that with a rueful nod. "I'm sorry, Kate. I see now that I was wrong to have kept this from you so long. When Owen died, I realized you were entitled to his estate, and Will would have wanted you to know the truth."

"It was you who sent me the note on Lester Crane's business card."

Tears glistened in Julianna's eyes. "I hope you're not too disappointed."

Kate wasn't sure what she was feeling. There weren't words to express it. "Does Grace know that I'm her granddaughter?"

"No. I'll leave that to you to decide how and when you want to tell her. She'll be thrilled, of course." Julianna hesitated and stared at the shiny gold bracelet on her wrist. "There's something else."

Kate eyed her warily. What could possibly be left to say?

"It's about Norm Phillips, the man you thought was your father. My private detective told me he died in a car accident right about the time you went to live with your foster parents . . . I'm sorry." Julianna's voice broke as she said it.

For the next few moments, an awkward silence filled the room. Julianna glanced at her watch and cleared her throat. "I should get back to work. Rick keeps me so busy these days I can barely keep up. I'll let myself out."

Kate didn't bother to get up or say goodbye. She had too much on her mind. The fact that Julianna had kept the truth from her all these years upset her, and yet it filled in the missing pieces of the puzzle that had perplexed her most of her life.

Grace was her grandmother. Why hadn't she guessed it

before? Her son's picture had intrigued her from the beginning, and while she definitely favored her mother more than him, as Julianna had pointed out, she had his eyes. Grace's eyes too.

Had Grace sensed the connection between them? Why else had she shared her son's cherished military mementos with her? Or maybe that was wishful thinking. Would she welcome her with open arms, or would the shock be too much for her fragile heart to handle?

While Grace took a nap later that afternoon, Kate went outside with Buster to harvest the remaining squash and greens in the garden. Though it kept her busy, it didn't take her mind off of Julianna's revelation.

What does a person do after learning they aren't who they thought they were? Kate sighed. If only her mother was here to help her sort it all out. Now she had to come to terms with her new identity on her own. She wasn't even a Phillips. She was a Bentley and a Holbrook.

Jim and Rose had never told her much about the process of becoming her foster parents, but Owen and her grandfather must have given their consent for them to raise her. Was that because they knew Holbrook blood ran through her veins?

As Kate picked the last of the squash, she realized that soon it would be Halloween, and she would be back in Nashville. The thought of Grace tending the farm and house all by herself bothered her. Hopefully, her grandmother would be well enough to take care of things before Kate had to leave.

Buster, who had been lying close by, jumped up and took off toward the driveway. Kate glanced over her shoulder and saw David petting the dog at the garden's edge. He had changed clothes and showered since he'd left at dawn—before the foundation of her world had been shaken, but seeing him instantly lifted her spirits.

She went to say hello and welcomed his brief kiss. "This is a nice surprise. I thought you'd be busy harvesting corn today."

"I quit early this afternoon so I could stop by the hardware store and order a replacement window for Grace. It should arrive tomorrow." The pleasant look on his face switched to concern. "How is she?"

"Oh, she came home earlier this afternoon. She's much better, though a bit grumpy. Hopefully, she'll be in a better mood after her nap."

"At least someone around here is getting sleep." He held out his hand. "Want to take a break and walk with me to the creek?"

She welcomed the diversion and strolled with him to a log-hewn bench by the creek behind Grace's barn. As they sat together, enjoying the tranquil, scenic spot, David told her about Samson and Delilah's reaction to the new horse that was boarding with them. It seemed his horses were jealous.

A fish leaped in the stream. "Did you see that?" she cried.

"Yeah. This creek used to be chock-full of fish, but not lately."

"How come?" Staring at the clear, babbling waters caused her to think of Rick. *Cousin Rick.*

"I'm not sure. Hopefully, it's temporary and they'll come back."

"Now that I know how to fly fish, you and I should go sometime." She was serious, but for some reason he laughed. "What's so funny?"

"I was thinking how different you are from most of the

other women I know. Guns, archery, and fly fishing wouldn't be high on their list of recreational activities."

"Is that a problem?"

His admiring grin reassured her. "Not at all. In fact, I'd like to personally thank whoever sent you the anonymous note that led you to Tyler's Glen."

Her mood shifted at the mention of the note. "That's not a mystery anymore."

She told him about Julianna's bombshell disclosure earlier that afternoon, and David stared at her in amazement. "Frederick Holbrook is your real father? That's incredible. Does Grace know yet?"

Kate shook her head. "Julianna left it up to me to tell her, but I'm not sure how she'll react to having a Bentley for a granddaughter."

"You need to tell her. I think she'll be happy to know Frederick has a daughter."

She looked around. "Where did Buster go?"

He stood and scanned the area. "I don't know."

Remembering the dog's tendency to wander off, she called his name and began searching for him. David did the same. But Buster didn't return.

"Don't worry," David said in a reassuring voice. "I'm sure he'll show up when he gets hungry."

"I hope you're right." She recalled finding Buster in the park, nearly starved to death, the day they discovered the knife—Danny's knife with Owen's blood. If Danny was right about Claven stealing his knife to frame him, then did Claven also take her Glock? If so, what had he planned to do with it?

CHAPTER TWENTY

KATE CONTINUED TO SEARCH FOR BUSTER after David left. She combed every inch of Grace's barn and henhouse as well as the meadow and yard, but there was still no sign of the dog. David had told her he would stop by Owen's place on his way home and check his barn too.

Realizing there was nothing more she could do but wait and hope Buster returned, Kate finally went inside. Grace had grown so attached to the little dog, it would crush her to learn he was missing. She prayed Buster would return before it came to that point.

While Grace rested upstairs, Kate took her mind off of Buster by searching online for marriage records under her mother's maiden name. Two came up—one to Norm Phillips and the other to Frederick Holbrook. All this time, the truth was out there and she didn't know it.

Kate suddenly felt emotionally drained and decided to take a break with a glass of iced tea on the back-porch swing. After filling her glass in the kitchen, she went through the den to the porch. On her way to the swing, she rediscovered the stack of Owen's mail on top of the antique trunk, where she had left it the night before. She scooped it up before resting on the swing. Sorting through the letters while she rocked, she stopped at the one marked with a University of Tennessee Department of Agriculture return label. She didn't waste any time opening the envelope and removing the folded paper inside to read what it said.

Mr. Bentley,
Professor Roy Timmons referred your water samples to me for

testing. Our lab has identified several contaminants proven to be harmful to the environment. I'd like to speak to you in person concerning the results. Please contact me at your earliest convenience.

Respectfully,

Dr. Milfred Armstone

Kate stared at the words on the page, remembering the testing device in Owen's barn and the letter from Roy Timmons about the mysterious *matter* they had discussed. Is that what he was testing? Water samples? But from where?

Her first thought was to call Harlan. But the last time she told him her suspicions that there might be a connection between Owen and Roy's deaths, he said she was grasping at straws. He wouldn't believe her until she had proof.

There was only one person she could trust who might be able to help her to find the proof she needed—*David*. She called him immediately.

"I was just about to call you," he said when he answered. "I found Buster at my place."

The tightness in her shoulder eased with relief. "What was he doing there?"

"I guess he wanted to visit Smokey. The two of them were playing in the backyard when I found him. He lost his bandage too. I'd like to take a look at his paw and re-bandage it before I bring him home."

"Thanks . . . By the way, there's something else I need your help with." She told him about Owen and Roy Timmons and read the letter to him.

"Interesting," he replied after she'd finished.

She rocked slowly in the swing. "What water samples do you think Owen would have sent them?"

"It could be from the creek that flows through Owen and Grace's property. You know he was an avid fly fisherman. I wonder . . ."

"What?"

"With all the rain we've had this year, it's possible the creek has been contaminated with runoff from Rydeklan's property."

Virgil's words echoed in her mind. *They killed Owen . . .The chemical—* "You think this is connected with the chemical company?"

After a brief silence, David responded with a hint of intrigue in his voice. "What do you say to a little midnight fishing expedition? There's a river near the chemical plant that I'd like to check out. We'll start in the park, and I'll bring jars to collect water samples upstream and downstream of the plant."

The prospect of snooping around the plant with David spurred her pulse to racing. "When?"

"How about tonight?"

Grace came out of the den and saw her sitting on the swing.

Kate greeted her with a smile. "Grace is up," she said to David. "I've got to go." Before ending their call, they arranged for him to pick her up at eleven-thirty and he would bring Buster home then too.

"You shouldn't have let me sleep so long," Grace said when Kate was off the phone.

Kate folded the letter and set it and her phone on the trunk with Owen's other mail. "I thought you needed your rest." She patted the cushion beside her, and Grace joined her on the bench. They sat in silence for a few moments, except for the groaning of the swing as they rocked back and forth.

Grace finally spoke. "You've been such a help to me, Kate. Knowing you were looking after things here while I was in the hospital was a huge relief. But I do feel a bit guilty. You should be enjoying your vacation, not taking care of me."

"I am enjoying it. This is a nice change of pace for me."

"I sure will miss you when you leave. David will too." A note of sadness resonated in her voice.

Kate's eyes misted at the thought of leaving. "You were right about him. He is a great guy. But I don't know how he'll feel about a long-distance relationship."

"If you two truly care about each other, you'll find a way to make it work. It's not a matter of the distance, it's a matter of the heart. And remember, as long as you own the land next door, David won't be able to forget about you even if he wanted to."

Kate laughed, and Grace patted her hand. "I wish you would come and live on that land next door. Nothing would make me happier than having you for a neighbor."

Her grandmother's kind words touched her heart and moved her to broach the subject that had been weighing on her since Julianna left. "I hope you'll still feel that way after what I have to tell you."

Worry lines appeared on Grace's face. "You sound so serious. I hope it's not bad news."

"That depends . . . but regardless, I can't keep something this important from you any longer."

"Does it have something to do with Owen?"

"In a way . . . You already know that my mother was Mary Bentley. Well, today I learned I have other family members here in Tyler's Glen."

Inclining her head, Grace's eyes flickered with interest. "That's wonderful, Kate. Do I know them?"

"As a matter of fact, you do. Your daughter, Julianna, is the one who told me about them."

Grace stared at her. "My Julianna?"

Kate nodded. "She knew my mother when they were young."

The realization registered in Grace's expression. "Yes, of course. They went to school together."

"She also knew my biological father."

"Norm Phillips?"

"No." Kate hesitated, biting her lip. "Before she married him, my mother was briefly married to someone else."

Grace waited expectantly for Kate to continue.

"Your son Frederick married my mother before he was deployed overseas."

Grace's mouth fell open. "What?"

"I went online while you were resting and confirmed that my mother was married to him before I was born. Julianna believes I'm his daughter."

Grace clutched her chest as tears glistened in her eyes.

Kate worried that the revelation was too much for her. Maybe she shouldn't have told her. "I'm sorry you had to hear it from me. The last thing I want is to upset you."

"I'm not upset, honey," Grace said in a tender voice. "These are tears of joy. How could I have been so blind?" She lovingly lifted Kate's chin with one finger. "Why, it's written all over your lovely face. You have his eyes. My own flesh and blood, and I didn't even know it."

Like a surging river, relief and happiness flooded Kate's heart, and she cried like a little girl in her grandmother's arms.

"Oh, dear child. I'm overjoyed."

Kate gazed at her, wiping the tears from her face. "You don't mind that I'm a Bentley?"

Grace firmly held Kate's hand. "Of course not. I'm the one who should be ashamed that my own son thought he had to elope with Mary instead of telling me how he felt. What do you say we continue the truce that Owen and Rick started and declare the feud between the Bentleys and the Holbrooks officially over?"

Kate smiled, happy to keep her end of the bargain. "I'd say it's about time." She hugged her grandmother. "I'm so happy to have finally found you, but how will the town react when they find out who I really am?"

"Never be ashamed of who you are, Kate. You're a gift from God, no matter what anyone says. I couldn't ask for a more wonderful granddaughter." Then a frown dimmed Grace's radiant face. "I can't believe Julianna knew all this time and didn't say anything. I'm going to give that daughter of mine a good talking to."

Kate touched her shoulder. "Please, don't be hard on her. She wanted to tell me, but was afraid it would cause too much trouble after I had been placed with my foster parents. I did love them very much."

"All those years lost," Grace lamented. "What about David? Have you told him yet?"

She nodded. "This afternoon. He encouraged me to tell you right away."

"I'm glad he did." Grace sniffled and composed herself. "Now, you two should go out tonight and make the most of the time you have left before you return to Nashville."

"Are you sure? I don't want to leave you alone until you're better."

Grace gave Kate an adamant look. "Don't use me as an excuse, young lady. I refuse to be the party pooper for the rest of your vacation. They wouldn't have released me from the hospital today if I wasn't better, and after that marathon nap, I'm starting to feel like my old self again. Now call David and tell him to take you out on the town tonight."

"Actually, he invited me to go fishing at midnight in the park." Kate decided not to mention the letter from U.T. She'd tell her later after Grace was stronger and after she and David had checked out the chemical plant.

Grace returned a disappointed frown. "That doesn't sound like much of a date, but at least you'll have the river to yourselves at that hour. The tourists will all be asleep." There was a wry grin on her face. "I've heard the fish do bite after midnight. But if he wanted to spend time alone with you, a sunset hike sounds more romantic."

The sound of a car pulling into the drive caused Kate to peer out from the porch. She spotted a Lexus with a campaign sign for mayor attached to the side window. "It's Lester."

"Oh, good," Grace replied. "I called him before my nap and told him to stop by this afternoon."

Kate rose and greeted the lawyer at the door.

"Good to see you, Kate," he said with a friendly smile. Then his eyes shifted to her grandmother. "Hello, Grace, how are you feeling?"

"Better now. Thank you for coming on such short notice." She turned to Kate. "Lester is here to help me update my will. After seeing the mess Owen left you in by not having one, I decided I should put my affairs in order."

Kate excused herself to leave them alone, taking her mail and her phone with her. She remembered the form Lester had given her and went to fill it out so she could give it to him before he left. Afterward, she went to the kitchen to prepare dinner. The mention of Grace's will evoked a sense of melancholy.

A short while later, Grace joined her in the kitchen. "Mm, what smells so good?"

"I'm baking a chicken. I hope Lester can stay and join us?"

"I'm afraid he's already gone."

"Oh, no," Kate said, disappointed. "I have a form for him. I was hoping to catch him before he left."

"I'm sorry, dear. I didn't know. But he wants me to give you a tip," she said pleasantly. "I mentioned that David was taking you midnight fishing, and he said the best fishing spot is Abrams Creek in the park."

"That's where Rick taught me to fish," Kate replied.

Grace affectionately brushed a lock of Kate's hair away from her face, then rested her hand on her shoulder. "Please do be careful. I wouldn't want my only granddaughter to fall into the river."

Wearing a life jacket around her chest, Kate paddled with David downriver in his canoe. In retrospect, she should have quizzed him more about his plans when he'd picked her up with the canoe strapped to his truck. "When you asked me to go on a fishing expedition, this isn't what I had in mind."

Sitting behind her, David used his paddle as a rudder to steer the craft. "I thought you wanted to check out the river with me."

Traveling through mountain canyons and gorges on the water reminded her of the time she fell into the river in the North Cascades, but that was a distant memory. This tranquility and beauty she could handle. "I did, but I didn't think we'd be in a boat, that's all. Are there any rapids on this river?"

"We put in below the major ones, so it should be fairly smooth. There are some closer to Tyler's Glen, but we'll pull the canoe out before we get to them and hike around."

"I like that idea." She withdrew her paddle to stow the two small water jars that rested near her feet. David had filled them upriver where they had launched the canoe. As she carefully placed them in the compartments of her backpack, she felt inside it, then checked her pants pockets. "Oops, I forgot my cellphone."

"Don't worry, I brought mine. But there isn't any cell coverage in the park anyway, so take it easy and enjoy the ride."

It didn't sound like she had much choice. Looking up, she noticed the sky was clear and littered with stars, and the Hunter's Moon so big and bright it reflected on the water like shimmering gold. As they floated along, the park came alive with numerous pairs of orbs that glowed from the shadowy woods on the bank, while strange, unfamiliar sounds filled the night air. Even the constant croaking of frogs, or the occasional leaping fish, seemed amplified in the nocturnal landscape.

"I'm glad Rick agreed to come over and spend the night at Grace's place tonight. I wouldn't have felt right about leaving her alone." Kate had returned Grace's rifle and cartridges to her before she'd left with David. Now that Claven was in custody, she didn't feel the need to hang on to them anymore.

"Hey, I just realized that Rick is your cousin."

She glanced over her shoulder. "I know. I thought of that earlier. Pretty crazy, huh? Not only am I about to inherit my uncle's estate, but I've discovered a grandmother, a cousin, plus an aunt and uncle."

"I guess you owe Julianna a big thank you."

"I wouldn't go that far. After all, she kept the truth from Grace and me for years. While I understand her reasons, it's still hard for me to get past that. Family relationships can be so complicated, you know?"

"Tell me about it."

She knew he was thinking of his relationship with Danny, and now that she had her own complex family relationships to deal with, she empathized with him more.

David's swift, steady strokes propelled them past a campground. A few tents by the bank were visible in the moonlight, and the residual smoke of campfires brought back happy memories of the s'mores Kate had eaten at the horse camp with her grandmother.

"Did you tell Grace about Frederick being your father?" David asked.

She nodded over her shoulder.

He took a break from paddling, and let the current do the work. "How did she take it?"

"Really well. I can't tell you how relieved I was. By the way, when I told Grace you were taking me fishing at this hour, she said a hike at sunset would be more romantic."

He chuckled at that and gestured toward the sky. "Take a look at that brilliant moon. Now what could be more romantic than a river cruise at midnight, huh?"

She had to admit it was beautiful, and she was having a wonderful time despite her earlier misgivings. Gazing in the distance, she saw faint lights ahead as they crossed the park boundary and continued downriver toward Tyler's Glen.

"Speaking of Grace," she said. "I was happy to report that Buster was with you after she noticed him missing. Thanks for bringing him home when you picked me up."

"Since he's prone to wander, you should keep him on leash from now on, especially in a big city like Nashville."

The thought of going home so soon bothered her. She didn't want to leave until Grace had fully recovered, and the remaining questions about Owen's murder had all been answered. Right now, she still didn't understand why Claven had broken in and threatened her with the knife.

They had reached a wider section of the river. Across the water up ahead, the moonlight exposed two huge holding tanks and an industrial building. As they floated toward it, the distant sound of a man's voice breached the serene atmosphere.

Kate whispered to David. "Did you hear that?"

"It came from the chemical plant." David kept his voice low. "Let's hide under those trees."

They quietly paddled in the shadows until they were past the plant on the opposite bank. Then David held to a branch to keep them from drifting while Kate discreetly filled a jar from the stream.

The figures of two men standing at the water's edge were visible from the canoe. One of them looked like a security guard. He and the other man, who appeared to be a nightshift worker on a smoke break, were chatting.

"Has the cleanup team found the source of the leak yet?"

the security guard asked.

The other man's cigarette glowed in the dark as he inhaled. "No. They're still investigating. It could take a while to isolate it. All we know is that chemicals are leaking into the ground."

"They better figure it out soon. If word gets out, the company will be facing a much bigger problem."

Kate and David exchanged disturbed glances. Then something flew at them from across the river. It struck the side of the canoe.

An arrow!

Kate hastily capped the jar. "Let's get out of here!"

They grabbed their oars and dug them into the river.

Another arrow whizzed past Kate's head.

"Hey, you!" the security guard called.

They didn't stop, but propelled their canoe through the water like an Olympic crew team.

An arrow splashed close to Kate. Adrenaline hammered her heart as she fought to stay in sync with David's paddle strokes. The arrows continued descending like intermittent rain as they traveled into a narrow canyon. When the barrage finally stopped, Kate breathed a huge sigh of relief. "I think we finally lost him."

They continued to descend into the rocky gorge. The roar of rushing water ahead gave her an involuntary shudder. She glanced over her shoulder. "Where's that noise coming from?"

"The rapids."

She shot him an anxious look. "I thought we were going to get out and walk around them."

"That was the plan until we had to outrun those arrows. Now it's too late. We're going too fast."

"Tell me there's another way around."

He shook his head with an apologetic shrug. "Don't worry. We should get through it all right if we stay in the center of the river where there are fewer rocks. We have our life jackets on. We'll be fine."

Easy for you to say. You've obviously never fallen in. Tension gripped Kate at the thought of going through the white water.

As they came to the chop, David called out to her. "Hang on!"

Kate anchored herself as best she could, setting her paddle down and gripping the sides of the canoe. The foamy current bounced and buffeted them like a toy boat in the ocean.

"Pretend you're on a log flume ride at the amusement park," David shouted.

She wished this was only a ride. The moonlit white water and rocky canyon ratcheted her pulse higher than a roller coaster would. As they came to the center of the river, she clenched her fists tighter and took a deep breath. With expert precision David guided the canoe between the rocks, and they descended smoothly through the gap.

Kate closed her eyes, mouthing a silent prayer of thanks. When she reopened them, she spotted a sharp bend looming straight ahead. "David, look out!"

If they didn't turn immediately, they'd collide with a large boulder. He plunged his paddle in the water and dragged it to make a hard turn, but the current was too swift.

Clinging to their vessel like a life raft, Kate's heart stopped as it tipped over. A moment later, she and David fell into the drink, and the rushing water swept them downstream with the canoe. Kate hurtled feet first, water sloshing into her mouth as she gaped at the canyon rocks ahead. Squeezing her eyes shut, she yelled for help.

Something snatched her life jacket from behind and halted her descent. Stunned, she glanced over her shoulder.

It was David, standing in waist-deep water. He pulled her toward the water's edge. Kate found her footing and took his hand, and they trudged toward the bank together.

"Now that was exciting," he exclaimed.

She frowned at him. "I could have done without the rapids."

He gave her an apologetic grin. "Sorry. They're not as intimidating in daylight."

She glanced toward the water and watched his boat bounce downriver. "Looks like you lost your canoe."

"I can get another one. Unfortunately, our backpacks are gone too."

"So are all the water samples," she said as the canoe disappeared from view. The cold river water gave her a chill. "We'd better get out of here before our assailant finds us—or we freeze to death. Do you know the fastest way to Grace's?"

A bright beam clicked on, nearly blinding them.

"Taking a midnight swim?" It was a man holding a flashlight.

Kate squinted until her eyes focused on the lawman with his gun pointed at them. "Deputy Travis—is that you?"

"I got a call about a couple of trespassers in a canoe on the premises of the chemical plant. You mind telling me what you're doing out here at this hour?"

Kate and David exchanged uneasy glances. "I can explain everything," Kate said.

Harlan gave her a skeptical look as he put his gun away. "Good. I can't wait to hear it."

As they rode to Grace's house in the deputy sheriff's SUV, Kate shared her theory with Harlan. She linked the letter from Roy Timmons that she'd found earlier in Owen's barn to Roy's suspicious death, Virgil's cryptic words to her, and the most recent letter from the university that had caused Kate and David to suspect the chemical company was involved. Though Harlan had given her a blanket to warm herself, Kate shivered in her damp clothes as she relayed the conversation they had overheard at the plant before the assault of arrows.

The deputy raised a hand to stop her. "You mean to tell me Rydeklan has been poisoning our waters? Why is this the first I've heard about it?"

"Apparently, there's been a cover-up." She glanced at David, who sat next to her in the backseat.

"That's right," he told Harlan. "If not for Kate's detective work, they might have gotten away with it too."

The deputy drove the SUV into Grace's drive. "Good work, you two. I'll open an investigation into it right away. And since you were canoeing down a public river and not walking on the premises, I'm not going to charge you with trespassing—this time. Meanwhile, stay away from that plant."

As Kate opened the door to leave, David spoke over Harlan's shoulder. "Please wait while I see that she gets in okay."

"Now I'm a limo service," Harlan remarked in a dry tone.

David jumped out and escorted Kate to the back porch. "Sorry about the dip in the river. I hope you'll forgive me after you've had a hot shower."

She tried to restrain her chattering teeth long enough to smile. "There's nothing to forgive. I'm the one who got you involved in all of this. At least we don't have to spend a night in jail. That would have made this the worst date ever."

"I'll make it up to you."

"You'd better," she replied, ribbing him.

Rick burst out from the back porch, interrupting them. "It's Grandma. I think she's having a heart attack."

Kate and David rushed into the house. She let him go ahead of her upstairs to Grace's room, where Buster was pacing and whining in the hallway.

"I called 911," Rick said from behind them.

They found Grace in bed, clutching her chest. She was writhing in agony, her brow damp with moisture.

"Hang on, Grace," David said, in a soft, consoling voice as he checked her pulse. "We're going to take care of you. Rick, we need to carry her downstairs and have Harlan drive us to the hospital. We can't wait for the ambulance."

Rick nodded and stood aside while David lifted Grace in his arms and headed for the stairs. Kate and Rick followed him down. When they reached the back door, Harlan was there waiting.

"Grace needs to go to the hospital, *stat*," David told him.

The deputy sprang into action and hurried ahead of them to his SUV and opened the door to the backseat. David gently laid Grace inside.

Kate waited by the SUV with Rick, who appeared as stricken as she felt.

As much as she wanted to be there for her grandmother, it wouldn't be right depriving Rick of being with her right now, and there wasn't room for both of them in the deputy's SUV. "Rick, you go to the hospital with Harlan and David. I'll meet you there."

With a quick nod, he jumped in the front passenger seat.

Watching the deputy's car speed away with sirens blaring, Kate felt utterly helpless. But she wasn't hopeless. She'd come too far to see her relationship with Grace end like this. And there was something she could do. *Pray.*

CHAPTER TWENTY-ONE

AFTER A QUICK SHOWER AND CHANGE of clothes, Kate arrived at the hospital around three a.m. By then, Grace had already been taken to emergency surgery for a blocked artery. Kate spent the next four hours with Rick and Julianna, awaiting word from the doctor on her grandmother's condition and silently praying for her. David had stayed with them until five. He had more harvesting to do before it rained again, so he left with Harlan, who was going to give him a ride to his truck still parked at the river. Kate had promised to call him if there was a change in Grace's condition.

While Rick fiddled with his cellphone and Julianna paced the floor in the waiting room, Kate's mind wandered back to the ride downriver in the canoe. It seemed like a bad dream now, but the cold, hard facts were real—someone still wanted her dead, and with Claven in custody, that ruled him out as the culprit. This was bigger than a murder cover-up. It smacked of conspiracy and had something to do with the conversation she and David had overheard about the chemical leak. Had Owen's water samples led to his murder?

Rick kept blinking and yawning as he fought the need for sleep.

Her heart went out to him as she shared his concern for their grandmother. She had come to admire her cousin with his strong work ethic and generous spirit. Her biggest hope was that he wasn't somehow involved with Owen's murder and the attack on the river. Unfortunately, the fact that he and her uncle were business partners meant she couldn't completely rule him out as a possible suspect until the archer was caught and the mystery behind Owen's murder solved. "You know, Rick, there's a couch over there. Why don't you get some z's?"

"Nah, I'm okay." After a moment, he peered at her from under his heavy eyelids. "I'm glad you came here, *Cuz.*"

Kate glanced at Julianna, who had stopped pacing and appeared as surprised as she was that Rick knew they were related. He gave them a sleepy, crooked grin. "Grandma told me last night."

Tentative, Kate delved further. "How do you feel about that?"

He returned an easygoing shrug. "It's all right with me. Maybe now that I've given you fly fishing lessons, you can give me a few pointers in archery."

The doctor came into the waiting room, and Kate and Rick immediately joined Julianna to hear his news. "Grace made it through the surgery, but the next twenty-four hours are critical," he told them. "She's in the ICU."

"When can we see her?" Julianna asked.

"It could be several hours before she's awake, so you should all go home and get some rest. We'll contact you if anything changes."

Relieved that her grandmother had made it through surgery, Kate had to believe she would fully recover. Any other outcome she banished from her thoughts.

After the doctor had left, Julianna turned to Kate and Rick. "You're both exhausted. Why don't you go home like the doctor said, and I'll stay here?"

"I'm not leaving," Rick insisted.

"Don't forget you have two businesses to run," Julianna said in a motherly tone. "Go back to your apartment and take a nap. I'll call you if anything changes."

Reluctantly, Rick finally acquiesced and gave his mother a parting peck on the cheek.

As soon as he'd left, Julianna appealed to Kate. "You

need rest too. After the night you've had, I'm surprised you've lasted this long."

How could she rest until she knew that Grace would be all right? "I want to stay."

"I know, but you heard the doctor."

"But . . ."

Julianna put her hands on her hips. "No buts. Go."

Kate didn't want to leave, but Julianna was adamant, and Kate didn't think she should argue with Grace's daughter. "All right, I'll go. You have my cell number if there's any change in her condition."

"Yes. Don't worry, I'll call you." Julianna walked with Kate to the waiting room door. "Oh, Kate—"

She slowly faced her, wondering what new revelation Julianna might have for her now.

"I know you're still recovering from the shock of what I told you yesterday, but I hope eventually you'll come to think of me as your aunt."

Kate wasn't sure how to respond. After the recent loss of her foster mother and her uncle's mysterious death, and now with Grace's life hanging in the balance, Kate felt emotionally drained. It wasn't that she didn't want a relationship with her aunt, but the fact that Julianna had kept the truth from her all this time was something she couldn't easily get over.

"I'm praying about it," she said. "It's the best I can do right now."

Before she left, Kate decided to visit Nadine, who was still in the hospital. When she found her room, she knocked and cracked the door open. "Hi, Nadine. I hope this is a good time."

The young woman peered up from her magazine. "Kate," she said, her glum expression transforming into a pretty smile. "I'm so glad to see you. I've been bored out of my mind. There's nothing to do here but read."

Kate walked in and stood beside her bed. "David told me what happened. How are you feeling?"

"Better, but the doctor wants me to stay in the hospital a couple of weeks until he's sure the baby is out of the woods after my appendectomy. Then I'm supposed to take it easy for the rest of my pregnancy." She gave an ironic laugh. "Like I can take it easy waiting tables at Bubba's, not to mention the ugly rumors flying around about Danny. I just hope I can make it through the next seven months until my baby is born."

"David told me you and Danny are married," Kate said.

A wistful smile crossed Nadine's face as she glanced at the *Brides* magazine in her lap. "Some honeymoon, huh?" She tossed the magazine to the side. "David doesn't believe it, but I know Danny's innocent. He couldn't kill anyone." Deep creases lined her forehead. "And now he's being framed for Owen's murder too." She pinched her lips with her fingers. "I'm sorry. I forgot that Owen was your uncle."

Kate returned a gracious smile. "It's okay."

"Danny said he told you about being framed." Nadine's face grimaced in anguish. "Please, you've got to help him prove he's innocent."

Kate stiffened, remembering that Danny was also friends with Raptor. "There's nothing I can do. If he's innocent, then he won't be convicted."

Nadine had a pleading look in her eyes. "You don't know what it's like to live with your past always dragging you down like a ball and chain. Some people will never be satisfied unless you pay for your sins for the rest of your life."

"Actually, I know more than you think." She was

referring to Raptor and his sworn vengeance against her. Resting her hand on the younger woman's shoulder, she tried to comfort her. Nadine was young and had a lot of living ahead of her, yet she was married to an ex-con who was wanted for questioning in a murder investigation. Now that she was expecting his baby, her future and her baby's were bound to his, for better or worse. But Nadine clearly loved him.

Kate thought of her own mother's predicament after her father had died overseas. She understood now that her mother had married Norm out of fear and desperation, and it had led to a life of unhappiness and regret. Kate didn't want to see Nadine end up the same way.

"So when are you and David going to get married?" Nadine asked, the pitch of her voice rising with interest.

Kate didn't want to encourage Nadine's speculation.. "It's a little premature to start making wedding plans, don't you think?"

"If you two tied the knot, we'd practically be sisters."

"I don't want to disappoint you, but I'll be going home on Sunday."

"Oh, no. You can't leave yet." Nadine's voice cracked.

Her downcast expression tugged at Kate's heart. "On the other hand, I'll still come to visit from time to time to settle Owen's estate. I've even been thinking of building a vacation home here."

Her friend seemed to rally at the prospect. "Really? Where?"

"On my uncle's property."

An ominous look struck Nadine's face. "But it's cursed! When your uncle cheated David and Danny's father out of it, he jinxed it. That's why he was murdered. The curse can't be broken until the land is returned to its rightful owner—the Jennings family."

Surprised by Nadine's superstition, Kate wanted to set

her straight. "It wasn't the property that killed Owen." Her clandestine canoe trip with David and the conversation they'd overheard from the chemical plant replayed in her mind. No, there was nothing wrong with the land, but the water—that was a different story.

After leaving Nadine's room, Kate wished she could see Virgil. She needed to ask him what he knew about the chemicals and her uncle's death, but he was still in a coma in intensive care. However, she could still pray for him. She passed the cafeteria on the main floor and noticed the chapel on her way out of the hospital. Burdened with concern for Grace, Nadine, and Virgil, Kate decided she needed a timeout with God.

Pausing at the door, she suddenly felt she was being watched. Looking around, she saw Julianna standing outside the cafeteria with a cup of coffee, waving at her. But Kate still wasn't sure what to make of the woman responsible for her coming to Tyler's Glen, yet keeping secrets from her for so long.

Inside the small chapel, five empty rows of chairs faced a cross hanging on the wall behind the altar. The sanctuary felt peaceful and safe from all the suffering and turmoil outside its door. After kneeling at the altar, Kate poured out her heart and soul for the next few minutes. She recalled her prayer when she first came to Tyler's Glen—to find any members of her family who might still be alive. With all that had happened since, it seemed like a lifetime ago, and she hadn't given it much thought until now. She suddenly realized God had answered her prayer in amazing and unexpected ways, and a welcome sense of peace and hope filled her heart.

She heard the chapel door open and close. The creak of the floor announced someone had entered. It was time she left anyway.

After thanking God for His faithfulness, she came to her feet. As she turned to leave, she saw David's brother sitting in the last row with his head bowed. "Danny? What are you doing here?"

He looked up, his eyes red and bleary. "I wasn't aware this was a private chapel."

She shot him an impatient glare. "You know what I mean."

"I told you I had a message from Ralph Tourreni."

She pushed up her sleeves and crossed her arms. "You don't give up, do you? Well, his threats don't scare me anymore."

"Will you please hear me out?"

She'd wasted enough time listening to him. Planting her fists on her hips, she fired back. "Why should I?"

"Because Ralph doesn't want to hurt you. He wants your forgiveness."

Her ears must be playing tricks on her—but Danny appeared serious. Tossing him an eye-roll, she pivoted toward the door. "Yeah, right, and I'm the tooth fairy—"

"Please, listen. I met him at a Bible study held at our prison."

Was he pulling her leg? "A Bible study," she repeated with a skeptical look as she faced him again.

He nodded. "I know it sounds crazy, but it's true. After ten years in the slammer, we got to know each other pretty well. When he heard that I would be released before him, he wanted me to contact you in Nashville and ask you to please forgive him for what he did to you."

Recalling her own troubled past and how God's grace and forgiveness had freed and delivered her, some of the coldness in her heart toward Raptor thawed. As a Christian, she was called to forgive, but as a marshal, she couldn't so easily give him a pass. "If what you've said is true—and I sincerely hope it is—it doesn't absolve Ralph from all the terrible things he did."

"He understands that, and he's not trying to excuse himself. All he wants is for you to know he's sorry for what he did to you."

"Then why didn't you come to Nashville and tell me before now?"

"I was planning to, but I had to see Nadine first. When I discovered you were here in Tyler's Glen, I knew I had to give you Ralph's message. But since you're a marshal, I was afraid you'd turn me in."

She recalled her missing Glock and that he had already admitted to taking her granola bars. "So you *did* steal my gun to prevent me from taking you into custody."

"No," he insisted. "It must have been Claven."

An idea occurred to her and she pulled out her cellphone.

He rose to his feet. "Wait, what are you doing?"

"I'm calling the deputy sheriff. I'll ask him if they've searched Claven's belongings yet."

"Please, don't."

She lowered her phone. "Why not?"

"Because I think someone besides Claven is involved. Someone in the department maybe. If you call the deputy, he may tip them off."

Remembering the onslaught of arrows on the river the night before, she realized the bowhunter knew they'd be there. "David and I were attacked again last night. It couldn't have been Claven because he's in jail."

Danny's face constricted. It took a moment for him to respond. "Well, it wasn't me. This is a cover-up, and I'm being made to be the fall guy."

Kate didn't let on that she had come to the same

conclusion, but if the sheriff's office was involved, it was an even bigger conspiracy than she had suspected.

He raised his hand and stepped toward her in earnest. "Before you call the deputy, think of Nadine and the baby. All that time I was in prison, she was the only one who stood by me and believed my story." Sadness shadowed his bleak expression as he pleaded with her. "She doesn't deserve this."

Kate took a chair a couple of seats away from him. "You're right. Nadine deserves a husband who will stand by her and provide for her and the baby, not hide in the shadows like a fugitive from the law."

"How can I do that when I'm a wanted man? Once they lock me up, I'll never be free again."

"All Deputy Travis wants is to question you. He seems like a decent guy. I think he will listen to your side of the story, especially since Claven is in custody now."

"No. The best thing I can do for Nadine and the baby is to leave town."

She leaned toward him. "That's the worst possible thing you can do. They need you now more than ever. Look, I know a defense lawyer in Nashville. He does a lot of pro bono work. He can help you prove your innocence."

A sound at the door interrupted them, and they rose to their feet.

David came in and halted, staring at them with narrowed eyes. He addressed Kate first, his voice cool and distant. "I came to see how Nadine and Grace were doing. Julianna said she saw you come in here." Then he focused on his brother. "You shouldn't be here. It's critical for the baby that Nadine avoids stress until she recovers from the surgery."

Danny eyed Kate and shook his head. "See? My own brother doesn't want me around." He brushed past David as he left the chapel.

Kate followed him to the door. "Danny, wait!" She

looked down the hall, but he'd already disappeared. "You should have gone after him, David. He thinks Owen's murder and the explosion at Virgil's were part of a cover-up, and after last night, so do I. It obviously wasn't Claven shooting arrows at us."

Pain and frustration flared in David's eyes like blue torches. "I've got to go."

She touched his arm before he left. "Please. Can't we go somewhere and talk about this?"

His low-hanging brows cast a shadow over his eyes. "There's nothing left to say."

With a heavy heart, she watched him walk away. Until the mystery behind Owen's death was solved, David and Danny would never be reconciled, and there would be no peace in Tyler's Glen.

David left the hospital without seeing Nadine or Grace. After his encounter with Danny and Kate in the chapel, he wouldn't have been very good company anyway.

He'd received a call that Grace's replacement window had been delivered to the hardware store, so he stopped to get it on his way home. The window was about the only thing he could fix right now.

"What do you hear from Danny these days?"

David spotted Joe standing next to his pickup. He finished loading the truck and closed the tailgate. "Get lost, Campbell."

"I wonder what the penalty is for harboring a fugitive from the law."

Something snapped in David. He spun around and got in Joe's face. "How about I show you the penalty for running your mouth?"

Joe's eyes bulged for a second, and he took a step back. "Is that any way to treat your soon-to-be next-door neighbor?"

David frowned. He wasn't in the mood for Joe's games. "What are you talking about?"

"Kate and I—we've been negotiating the sale of Owen's property. Oh, she's been playing hard to get, but I'm wearing her down. It's only a matter of time before she comes to her senses and sells to me. She'll never get another offer as good as mine. I even threw in my father's old warehouse for the outreach center."

David recalled the chocolates and the note Kate had received from Joe. She'd told him she wasn't interested in Joe's offers, but was that completely true? She hadn't mentioned that Joe had offered her the warehouse. Clearly, she'd been talking to him about the outreach center. Why else would he put it in his offer to buy Owen's property?

"You're bluffing," David finally responded.

"If you don't believe me, ask Kate."

"I don't have to. She already told me the property's not for sale."

Joe scoffed with a sly grin. "Everything's for sale, given the right offer."

Kate burst into Rick's garage and looked around for her cousin. "Rick?"

He popped his head out from under the hood of a nearby car. "Over here."

She strode to where he was working. "I came as soon as I saw your text. You said it was urgent. I hope it's not about Grace."

"No. Mom called earlier —Grandma's stable, but it could

still be several hours before she wakes up."

Kate felt a huge sense of relief that Grace was okay. "Did my credit cards arrive?"

"Not yet."

"Then what's so important?"

After wiping his hands on a rag, he closed the hood. "Come with me." He tossed the rag in the pile against the wall and led her to his small office adjacent to the garage. Stopping at his desk, he unlocked it with a key. "Yesterday, I finished replacing the tire and the windows on Owen's truck. This morning when I opened the glove compartment to update the maintenance log, I found this." He pulled out a small notepad and handed it to Kate.

Excitement rose within her as she flipped through the detailed handwritten drawings with Owen's signatures. "Owen's fishing lure designs!"

"Uh-huh. You think it's enough for Joe to drop his lawsuit?"

"Let's hope so. I'll take this to Lester right away, but first I want to make a copy of all of the drawings."

Rick gestured to his printer. "Use my scanner, and then we'll have an electronic version too."

The happy discovery prompted her to give Rick an enthusiastic hug. "Thank you. I needed good news today."

He grinned, his eyes twinkling like Grace's. "That's not all I found." Reaching into his drawer, he pulled out another piece of paper.

"What this?" Kate asked when he handed it to her.

"It looks like Owen made a will after all."

Apprehensive at first, she glanced at her cousin as she unfolded the sheet. After looking it over, she smiled and pressed it to her chest, happy and relieved. *Thank you, Uncle Owen!*

Rick appeared pleased as well. "Before he died, Owen told me he wanted to make amends for his past mistakes. I didn't know what he was talking about, but I have a feeling you do."

After she'd finished making copies of Owen's will and the fishing lure designs, Kate headed down Main Street toward Lester's office. She spotted David getting into his parked truck outside the hardware store and jogged to catch up with him before he left. She stopped at his passenger door and tapped on the window.

He rolled it down, but there was no welcoming smile.

"David, you'll never guess what happened," she exclaimed, catching her breath as she reached for her backpack to show him the fishing lure designs.

"Nope." His voice was stark and flat.

Her heart sank when she saw his distant gaze. "Are you still upset about Danny?"

Turning away, he stared out the windshield. "Joe Campbell told me you two are in negotiations for Owen's property."

Joe strikes again. I should have known. "He's only trying to egg you on, and it appears from the way you're acting, he's doing a pretty good job of it."

"How should I act when I discover that you're hanging out with my fugitive brother and negotiating with Joe for my family's land?"

The land—it's still all about the land.

"Look, it's not my fault that Danny followed me into the chapel, and as for Joe, I don't know what he told you, but I'm not planning to sell Owen's property to him or anyone else. But if that's the way you feel, maybe it's good that I found out now."

"You mean, before you made a mistake and got involved

with a farmer in this two-bit town."

"Those are your words, not mine."

He shifted his truck into gear and started to drive away, forcing her to step away from the window. "David, wait!"

But instead, he drove off, rubber peeling.

Lester walked up and spoke in his soothing Southern accent. "Is everything okay, Kate?"

"No, it's not." She remembered Owen's designs still in her backpack and did her best to push her raw emotions aside. "Actually, I was on my way to your office. Do you have a minute?"

"Certainly, what can I help you with?"

"It's about Joe's lawsuit against my uncle's business."

A few minutes later, Lester was looking over the fishing lure drawings from behind his desk. "If these are authentic, Joe's attorney will have to drop the case."

"Good." Her argument with David muted what should have been a much more enthusiastic response. "By the way, Rick also found this." She handed him Owen's handwritten will.

The lawyer grinned as he read it. "Well, what you do you know? It's even notarized and witnessed. Old Owen took my advice and got his house in order after all. This will help with the probate process."

She glanced down, wishing she could celebrate with David.

"I know it's none of my business, but I saw the way you and David Jennings parted earlier." Lester's face and tone reflected fatherly concern. "If it makes any difference, I'm sure he's under a lot of stress with the rumors flying about his brother's involvement with Owen's death and the explosion at Virgil's place."

"What if Danny didn't do it?"

He gave her a doubtful look. "I've spoken to Deputy Travis. They've matched Owen's blood on Danny's hunting knife. It's an open and shut case."

"That's the problem. It's too obvious. I think Virgil was targeted because he knows who murdered Owen, and it has something to do with Rydeklan Chemicals leaking toxins into the water."

The lawyer sniffed. "Now that's a fascinating theory, but do you have any proof?"

She started to tell him about the letter from the university confirming the chemicals in the water, but changed her mind. If Danny's conspiracy theory was true, the fewer people who knew about it, the better. Lester had been helpful to her and Grace, but the politician did like to hobnob with the chemical plant executives. She recalled that Grace had told him about her plans to go fishing with David that night on the river. Maybe he had mentioned it to one of his friends at Rydeklan. It was better she not tell him about the letter than for him to slip up and spill the beans.

"Right now," she said, "it's only a theory."

CHAPTER TWENTY-TWO

THAT AFTERNOON KATE ROCKED BACK AND forth in Grace's porch swing, thinking about the possible connection between the chemical plant leak and Owen's death. The letter from the university and Virgil's words to her seemed to link them together. It wasn't proof, but it did provide a motive. The question was, who would kill Owen to keep it under wraps? A chemical plant executive? That seemed pretty far-fetched. She thought of Terrance Hastings, the highfalutin businessman who seemed so out of place in Tyler's Glen. She doubted he'd do it himself, but maybe he'd hired someone else to do his dirty work.

Buster came to her feet and whined for her attention. She picked him up and held him in her lap, noticing with joy that he had put on some weight since she had adopted him. "You miss Grace too, don't you?"

The beep from her cellphone signaled an incoming text. She hoped it was good news about Grace, or David wanting to apologize. Seeing Rick's name as the sender, she quickly read it, wondering if there had been a change in Grace's condition.

Instead, it was an invitation:

Meet me tonight at nine p.m. at the old church camp near the park. I'll be in the barn.

It's about Owen's murder.

Leaning forward in the saddle, David slackened the reins and urged Samson into a gallop as they headed toward the park. The high-strung horse's pinned ears reflected David's own agitation from seeing Kate in town. He didn't want to face her again so soon after their quarrel and had changed his mind about going to Grace's to install the window. Instead, he had driven home, saddled Samson and gone for a long ride.

As his horse sprinted across the countryside, David relished the mountain breeze buffeting his face. The wild and freeing sensation brought welcome relief from the conflicts tormenting him lately—complicated struggles that dug deep into his soul, like Danny's return to Tyler's Glen. And Kate inheriting his family's land.

His father had always believed in Danny's innocence, but defending his son had cost him everything. Now Nadine had staked her entire future and that of her baby on that same belief.

Then there was Kate. Once she inherited Owen's estate with the fishing lure business, she would be a wealthy woman who could live anywhere in the world. Why would she want to settle here, or build a relationship with him?

It was early evening when David rode Samson into the church camp. Parked in the lot was a Lexus with a Lester-for-Mayor sign on the window. After dismounting his horse, David looked around for the owner of the car.

The politician emerged from the woods behind the barn. "Hello, David."

David finished tethering Samson to a sturdy fence rail. "What brings you way out here, Lester?"

"I went for a walk to the falls. I needed a break from all the campaigning." He focused on the gelding. "Beautiful day for a ride. I envy you having such a fine horse. It's a shame you didn't win at the horse show."

"Grace and Clementine deserved the prize. Maybe we'll

do better next year."

"How is Grace? I heard she's in the hospital."

David thought of Kate waiting for word on her grandmother's condition and started to regret their earlier argument. "She came through the heart surgery, but that's all I know right now. She should regain consciousness soon."

"Let's hope for the best." Lester's serious expression lightened a bit. "By the way, I heard your midnight fishing trip with Kate turned into quite an adventure."

David eyed him curiously. "Who told you that?"

"Harlan said that someone was shooting arrows at you two." He shook his head. "Unbelievable. I hope they catch the perp."

"Me too."

Lester casually lifted his leg and rested his foot on the bottom rail of the fence. "I'm glad I ran into you, David. I've been meaning to talk to you about something. When I'm elected mayor, I'd like you to consider serving in my administration. You've done such a good job on the town council I think you'd be a great asset to my team."

David returned an appreciative nod. "Thanks. I'll think about it."

"Well, I'm going to head to town now and grab dinner at Bubba's. Want to join me?"

"Some other time. I need to ride Samson home before dark."

Lester walked to his Lexus and opened his door. "David, remember—the election will be here before you know it. Don't forget to vote."

"How could I forget? Your signs are everywhere."

The candidate chuckled and waved before he got in and drove away.

David gave Samson an affectionate pat. "Wait here for me, boy. I'll be back soon."

Hiking to the falls gave David time to think about his

squabble with Kate. He regretted the way he had acted and decided he should apologize the next time he saw her, which he hoped would be soon. At the overlook, he watched the cascading waters tumbling into the canyon as Kate's words in the chapel echoed in his mind. *It obviously wasn't Claven shooting arrows at us.*

If not Claven, then who was it? Danny wasn't an archer. He was never much of a hunter either. Now, in the solitude of the woods, the question wouldn't leave him alone. As crazy as it sounded, Danny and Kate's conspiracy theory was starting to make sense. Claven worked for the chemical plant. Whoever attacked them last night must be someone who knew both Owen and Virgil, with a vested interest in keeping the chemical leak under wraps. *And wasn't bad with a bow and arrow.* Only one person came to mind who fit all the criteria.

He needed to get to a place with cell reception and make a phone call before it was too late.

It was well after dark when Kate arrived at the church camp for her meeting with Rick. She parked Grace's car in the gravel lot next to Rick's truck and got out.

Cautiously, she headed toward the deserted buildings, guided by her flashlight. Her marshal instincts scolded her for not bringing Grace's rifle as a security precaution. Nothing felt right about this, starting with Rick's mysterious text. She had tried calling him back, but he didn't answer.

When she came to the barn, she noticed the door was cracked open. She went inside and felt for the light switch. "Rick? Are you in here?"

The sound of the door closing from behind, prompted her to spin around. The lights flicked on, but the face she saw wasn't the one she'd expected. "Lester?"

The lawyer grinned in his usual amiable manner, but now his grin appeared twisted. Evil. "Did Rick contact you too?" Then he gestured toward the center of the gym.

Confused, Kate turned to look—and flinched in horror.

Rick was hanging by his wrists, suspended by a rope from the rafters. Hands and feet bound and mouth taped, he wriggled on the line like a fish on a hook, making muffled noises.

Fighting her raging emotions, she confronted Lester. "What's going on?"

He returned a sly look. Thrusting his hand in the pocket of his jacket, he withdrew a gun.

Her Glock.

"That's right. It's yours, but where you're going, you won't need it."

Facing the ominous implications, she closed her eyes. "You killed Owen."

The cultured lawyer leveled her with a terrifying stare. "Your uncle couldn't leave well enough alone. When he came to me with his amateur chemistry project, I told him to leave it alone. The chemical leak would have been fixed soon enough, but he kept sticking his nose where it didn't belong." Lester sneered. "Must be a Bentley trait."

Brushing off his last remark, Kate continued grilling him. "I suppose Roy Timmons's death wasn't an accident either. And what about Virgil? He's your *uncle.*"

He snickered cynically. "I've always thought family was overrated—which reminds me . . ." He glanced at his watch. "In a few minutes, all the killing will be over in a single blast."

She frowned warily at the finality of his words. "What do you mean? Aren't you going to shoot us?"

"That would be too easy. Plus, it's not Danny's M.O. No, I've rigged a little explosive device on the back of the barn that's set to blow in . . . eight minutes, to be precise."

He was looking at his watch again.

Rick's muffled yell coincided with the silent scream in her head.

With a sick grin, Lester waved at the bound young man flailing at the end of the rope. "Sorry, Rick. It's nothing personal. You were a good mechanic. You can thank your cousin here for getting you into this mess." Shifting his eyes to Kate, he winked. "Grace told me about your little family connection when I updated her will. Too bad neither of you will live to get your inheritances."

He backed toward the door.

"Wait!" Kate cried, rushing toward him. "You can't leave us here like this."

He pointed the gun at her. "I'll take care of your cousin right now if you don't back off."

She heeded his warning and halted. Had it been only her, she would have fought back, but she couldn't take chances with Rick's life.

"Tell Owen hello for me," he said as he slipped out the door and closed her in.

"Wait!" She tried the handle, but the door wouldn't budge. She pounded on it and kicked at it, and shoved her shoulder against it, but it didn't move. "Don't leave us, Lester!"

Turning around, her heart plummeted at the sight of her cousin thrashing and moaning from his tether. "Hang on, Rick. I'll get us out of here."

David jogged to the church camp from a trail in the woods. He'd parked his truck down the side road, not wanting to tip Lester off that he'd been followed.

When David had called Harlan earlier to tell him his

suspicions about Lester, the deputy was at the hospital with his wife, visiting Grace. David was blown away to hear that Danny had approached Harlan at the hospital and had volunteered what he knew about Owen's death and the chemical leak conspiracy.

Then the deputy shared more news. Claven, who was hoping for leniency, had been cooperating with the sheriff's office and talking—a lot. He claimed Lester was the ringleader behind the cover-up. In exchange, the chemical company executives would sponsor the new golf resort he planned to develop in Tyler's Glen, once he was elected mayor.

Lester had hired Claven to follow and intimidate Kate to get her to leave town. When that didn't work, Lester pressured him to kidnap her, by threatening to frame him for Owen's murder. The plan was for Claven to deliver Kate to Lester, but make it look like Danny had broken in and was behind her disappearance.

When David reached the barn, he heard a car drive away. In the bright moonlight, he glimpsed the distinctive taillights of Lester's Lexus disappearing down the road.

Harlan arrived on David's heels, breathless from running.

"Lester just drove off." After he'd said it, footsteps approached from the woods. He looked behind him and recognized the man's familiar frame in the shadows. "Danny?"

Harlan spoke up. "He needed a ride back to Nadine's place from the hospital, so I gave him a lift. If we hurry, we can still catch Lester."

"You go ahead. I'm going to stay and look around," David replied.

"What for?"

"I don't know, but this is the second time today Lester's been here. I want to check things out."

"Okay." Harlan turned to Danny. "You coming, Danny?"

He hesitated. "I'd like to stay here with David, if that's all right."

The deputy's brow lifted as he glanced at David.

Seeing his brother's earnest expression, David thought of the pesky kid who used to look up to him and follow him around wherever he went. Then he remembered his promise to Kate that he'd give Danny a second chance. "It's okay. I'll drop him off at Nadine's when we're finished here."

Kate checked the time on her cellphone. She estimated they only had six minutes before the place would blow—and she was out of cell service range.

Oh Lord, show me what to do!

While Rick twisted in the air, trying to free his hands and feet, Kate scoured the area for anything she could use to get him down. She took hold of an old gymnastics mat and tugged it beneath him so he wouldn't fall on the hard ground. *If* she got him down in time.

Given her cousin's dire situation, she needed to find something sharp to cut through the rope. *Like an arrow.*

She flew to the storage locker and grabbed the bow and several sharp-tipped arrows, along with a tackle box and an old worn rope. Rushing back to Rick, she placed the arrow in the recurve bow and aimed high above his head.

"Hold still, Rick."

Rick's eyes stared at her like large saucers, and he stopped moving. She didn't have time to wait until his swaying completely stopped. Focusing on the moving rope and saying another quick prayer, she released the string.

Missed.

She immediately grabbed another arrow and tried again.

Direct hit! The arrow had frayed the rope. Rick kept wiggling, trying to break the rope in two, but it didn't work.

"Keep still, Rick. I've got to shoot at it again." Her cousin obediently froze like an oversized icicle. Beads of perspiration collected on her forehead as her heart drummed a percussion solo. Aiming for the tiny damaged portion of the rope, she knew if she missed, there wouldn't be enough time for both of them to get out.

Closing her eyes, she made one last plea to God. Then she launched the arrow.

Bullseye!

Rick dropped and hit the mat with a thud.

She ran to him with the tackle box and used a knife to cut the twine around his hands and feet. He ripped the tape off his mouth, breathing hard.

"Are you crazy? You could have killed me."

She sighed patiently, while quickly tying the fishing line to an arrow.

"What are you doing?" he asked.

"This is our escape hatch."

"An arrow with fishing line?"

A pounding at the door startled them.

"Kate, are you in there? I saw Grace's car out front."

David's voice!

Joy and horror battled in her heart as she ran to the door. "David, Lester trapped Rick and me in here. In less than four minutes, this barn is going to blow. Please, get away while you can."

"The combination to the lock has been changed," David said.

"Lester made me change it," Rick yelled through the door.

"What is it?"

While Rick called out the code to David, Kate worked at

tying the tail of the fishing line to the end of the old rope she'd found in the storage cabinet. Frayed from wear, it looked as if it could come apart at the slightest tug. But it was all they had.

David's voice boomed on the other side of the barn. "The code isn't working."

Rick hit the wall with his fist in frustration. "Lester must have changed it again."

Cinching the final knot, Kate shouted through the door. "David, I'm going to try to break the upper window on the west side. When the arrow comes through the window, grab the fishing line attached to it and pull. There's a rope at the other end. When you have the rope, tie it off so we can climb out the window."

"Got it," David replied. "I'll handle the rope while Danny finds something soft for you to land on."

Danny?

Rick eyed the arrow and then stared at her as if she were insane.

Maybe she was. "Pray this works."

He nodded, his Adam's apple bobbing in his throat.

She aimed for the window high above and shot the arrow. Streaming the fishing line behind it, the missile sailed to the glass and shattered it. Kate exchanged surprised looks with Rick.

"Sweet!" he exclaimed.

They watched the rope tied to the fishing line quickly snake up and over the window, stopping with the end dangling a foot off the ground.

"The rope is ready," David yelled from outside.

Kate took the end and yanked hard on it, confirming it was secure. Satisfied, she turned to Rick. "Okay, you're up."

"No, you should go first."

"The longer you argue with me the more time we lose. Now climb that rope," she said in her stern marshal's voice.

Rick glanced at her with a nervous look. "What if it doesn't hold?"

"It will," She sounded pretty confident considering she felt like throwing up.

He sucked in a breath, took the rope from her and began to scale the wall.

She anxiously watched him ascend to the window.

After clearing the residual shards of glass, he glanced down and gave her a thumbs-up before he climbed over the sill and disappeared.

Breathing easier now that he'd made it out alive, she glimpsed the time on her cellphone. *Two minutes.*

Gripping the rope, she commenced climbing hand over fist, the toes of her shoes bracing against the wall. As she ascended, the threads from the rope burned deep into her palms. If the cord broke, it was all over.

She couldn't think about that. The window beckoned her like a vertical finish line. By now, her hands were raw, her lungs breathless, and her injured shoulder throbbed as she reached for the last few inches. *Almost there.*

The rope snapped.

Kate plummeted toward the ground. Reaching out by instinct, she grabbed onto a crossbeam with both hands, holding on for dear life. There wasn't time to gather her wits. Fighting fear and pain, she strained her biceps, pressing through her shoulder spasms to pull herself up. Bringing her feet under her, she balanced on the narrow beam, perched like an ape on a branch.

Only a couple of feet away from the window frame.

Resisting the urge to look down, she focused on her target. *She didn't come this far to die now.* Thinking of David and Rick waiting for her outside and her relationship with her grandmother just getting started, she convinced herself she could do this.

Holding her breath, she took a leap of faith and caught

the bottom edge of the windowsill. Glass remnants sliced her burning hands as she gripped the ledge. With sheer determination, she dug her feet into the wall and pushed herself to her forearms, using them as leverage to hoist the rest of her body up and through the window frame.

She slid down the roof and hurtled toward the ground. After landing on a pile of old twin mattresses gathered from the camp barracks, she couldn't believe she was still alive. David immediately gave her a hand and ran with her away from the barn. She could see Rick's vague outline in the dark, and he was shouting for them to run. She glimpsed Danny with him. *What is he doing here?*

Then the earth shook with an ear-splitting blast. She ducked low and covered her head. They had gained enough distance that Kate felt the heat and vibration, but didn't get knocked down this time. She crouched on the ground beneath David's protective arm, her ears ringing.

"Are you okay?" he asked.

"Didn't we just do this a few days ago?" They laughed together and hugged in relief.

Harlan drove up, his lights flashing and sirens blaring. He jumped out of his SUV and ran toward them. "Everybody all right?"

After they'd told him what had happened, he gestured to his backseat where they saw Lester in custody. "I think we'll be needing another candidate for mayor."

EPILOGUE

October, one year later

"THERE!" KATE SAID, AFTER APPLYING THE finishing touches of paint to the wall. She stepped away to admire the color of the newly expanded master bedroom with adjoining screened porch and hot tub. The additions to David's home, after they had married in May, were finally complete.

"What do you think, Smokey?"

The border collie barked his approval, and she rewarded him with a vigorous rub.

When she'd moved in with David, she left Buster with Grace. The two had become practically inseparable, and she didn't have the heart to split them up. Since then, she and Smokey had become buddies, and he eagerly joined her on her runs.

Kate heard David's truck drive up. "Come on, Smokey. Daddy's home." She ran down the hall with the dog, and they hurried into the open garage, side-stepping the leftover paint cans from the house expansion project. The other half of the garage was occupied by Owen's classic Ford truck that Rick had given them for a wedding present.

David parked his pickup outside in the driveway and got out.

Kate greeted her husband with a warm, welcoming kiss. "How was your day, Mayor Jennings?"

"Better now," he replied, his face brightening as he regarded her. "But it's still an adjustment working behind a desk most of the day. I hope the people of Tyler's Glen knew what they were doing when they wrote my name on the ballot and elected me last fall."

"They did," she assured him with a loving gaze. "And without any arsonists, prowlers, or chemical leaks, being mayor should be a piece of cake."

He chuckled as he bent to scratch Smokey behind the ears. "Yep, things have gotten downright boring. Even the town council has stopped bickering. I think I'm gonna kick back and take it easy for a while."

"Not likely," she said with a doubtful grin. "There's still the church camp reconstruction project, plus I need your help with the outreach center now that Joe has finally agreed to donate his father's warehouse."

"So much for taking it easy. At least our master bedroom project is finished." The twinkle in his eyes belied his dry tone.

She snapped her fingers. "That reminds me. Nadine and Danny are moving this weekend. I told her I'd help out. She can't wait to have a nursery for little Davy."

"I'll give them a hand too. It's about time they moved out of Nadine's old rental into a decent house." He moved to open the door to his backseat.

"Yeah. And now that Danny is taking on more responsibility at the garage, Rick can help me expand the fishing lure business."

"You know, if you need a bigger building, the chemical plant is still available." David tossed her a teasing glance before he reached for something in the truck.

Kate rolled her eyes at his comment. "I have to say I don't miss those big trucks barreling down the road since they moved their operations—hey, what have you got in there?"

"A surprise." He whisked out a fall bouquet of mums, roses, and daisies, and handed them to her.

"Oh, they're beautiful." She held them close to her face to sniff their sweet perfume. "But it's not our anniversary."

"Yes, it is. A year ago today we met on that stormy night in the park."

She knew that. The fact that *he'd* remembered surprised and touched her deeply. "How could I forget?"

He reached in his pocket and pulled out a small box. "I got you a little something to celebrate."

"Aww." She shifted the bouquet to her left hand as he gave her the box. Before opening it, she flashed him a look of excitement. Inside, she found a small slip of paper. "It says I O U . . . David, you shouldn't have."

His face lit up in a smile, bringing laughter to her heart. "You once said you wanted an archery course. Now that our home is finished, I'll build you one wherever you want on our property."

She loved hearing him say *our* home and *our* property.

Thunder rumbled in the distance. David glanced at the dark clouds gathering overhead. "Speaking of storms, sounds like one is rolling in. We'd better go inside." He put his arm protectively around her as they headed toward the house.

She stopped suddenly. "I almost forgot. I invited Grace to dinner tonight. Do you mind if I ask Rick, Julianna, and Harlan to come too?" She sent him a winsome smile.

"Again? I was kind of hoping to have you all to myself. With so much family around, we practically have to make an appointment to be alone."

Detecting the glimmer in his eye, she knew he was kidding. "It's not that bad. I'll pencil you in for tomorrow . . ." An idea popped into her mind. "How would you feel about inviting Virgil to dinner tonight?"

"*Virgil?*"

His less-than-thrilled reaction tickled her. Since Lester had been sent away to prison for Owen's murder, Kate had made an extra effort to check in on the old man after he'd been released from the hospital. "He is our neighbor, after all."

Lightning streaked the sky, followed by a loud boom of thunder. Large drops of rain fell, sending Smokey dashing into the garage.

David turned to her with a serious look. "If we don't hurry up and go inside, we might get struck by lightning."

Storms didn't bother her anymore. Neither did bears or rivers—provided she had bear spray and a life jacket handy. Kate threw her head back and held out her hands, embracing the refreshing shower like a parched flower. "Who's afraid of a little rain? Besides, you know what they say about lightning—"

David drew her close, surprising her with an impulsive kiss. "What do they say, Mrs. Jennings?"

She laughed, basking in the warmth of his love. "Who cares? Kiss me again."

Now, a Sneak Peek at Book Three
WILDFIRE

Releasing Late Spring of 2018

CHAPTER ONE

PROFESSOR RACHAEL WOODSTON LEANED AGAINST HER Subaru Outback as she studied the data displayed on the small screen of her handheld computer. An ominous chill crept up her spine from the implications. Below the dirt road where her car and the fire engine were parked, the crew fought to contain the ground fire. Yet the blaze seemed to gain momentum.

This was the second wildfire in Rocky Mountain National Park in two weeks, and it was only June. She was still trying to come to terms with the loss of her former graduate student, Lucas Sheffield, who had died in the first fire while camping. The cause of that fire still remained a mystery. If she could find out what had happened, it might advance her research and save others from the same fate.

She turned toward the cloud of smoke emanating from the firefighters' location. They needed to know about the escalating danger.

Dylan Veracruz inspected the trench his ten-member initial attack crew had been digging to starve the flames. Their yellow fire-resistant shirts and hardhats were now covered in soot and ash as they plowed the earth with the grub hoe of their Pulaski axes. The fire had first been reported at three-thirty that Wednesday morning, and after four hours of backbreaking work, the blaze would not let up.

A whistle sounded in the distance behind Dylan. He glanced over his shoulder but couldn't see anyone through the billowing cloud of smoke. When he refocused on the fire, a machine no higher than the top of his boots emerged from the flames in front of him. It rolled across the scorched terrain on tracks, like a miniature Army tank.

Dylan stared in amazement as it advanced in his direction. Then it stopped and went around him as if detecting his presence. He watched the contraption travel toward the embankment that led to the road, forty feet away. Through the haze, he managed to see the roving tank halt at the boots of someone suited-up as a firefighter, whose face was shrouded by the smoke.

Holding a handheld device, the person knelt in front of the tank, then turned and shouted in Dylan's direction. "Are you the Engine Boss?"

A woman's voice. Dylan faced her and straightened his back. "Yes. Who are you?"

She rose to her feet and stepped a little closer, but the smoke still obscured her face. "I'm Professor Rachael Woodston with Alpendale University. You and your crew need to clear out. This fire is about to crown."

He glanced over his shoulder at his team digging the firebreak a few feet away. The fire was contained. Why would she think it was about to spread at treetop level, beyond their control? He recalled her name on the application for a research permit he'd recently approved. It wasn't unusual for college professors to request to do wildfire research in the park—but he was the Engine Captain here, and a research permit didn't authorize her to give him orders.

She slanted her head. "You don't have much time."

Professor or not, his patience was wearing thin. "Look, Professor, we've got a job to do, and you shouldn't be this close to the fire."

A gust of hot air brushed against him from behind. *The wind had shifted.*

His friend and Assistant Engine Captain, Rod Clement, appeared from the woods, breathless from running. "The fire is jumping the line up ahead."

Dylan's gaze darted to the woman. He didn't want to retreat before they'd extinguished the fire.

The woman turned to leave. From under her hardhat, her long red ponytail flared in his direction. Then she shouted over her shoulder. "If I were you, I'd evacuate. That is, unless you want to be barbecued." With that, she scooped up her toy tank and headed toward the road.

Rod's voice echoed her warning. "Whoever that was, she's right. We better get to the safety zone."

At the same moment, Dylan spotted a branch burning in the tree above. "Watch out!"

Rod glanced up as the fiery limb fell and crashed into his shoulder, knocking him to the ground.

Before Dylan could reach him, two sharp whistles pierced the air. The miniature tank reappeared and sped to Rod. It halted, then spat some watery agent that immediately extinguished the flames.

The professor who controlled the roving machine was standing on the hillside in the gray mist. She whistled once again, then turned and scrambled up the hill toward the road. Her mechanical pet obediently followed her.

By now, Dylan could feel the escalating temperature. The burning branch was a sure sign the fire was crowning. He quickly helped Rod to his feet and called to the others on the line. "Get back to the rig!"

At the fire station in the park, Dylan stood across from Rod, who was pulling his T-shirt on after being treated for his shoulder burn. Trudy Reed, Rod's blonde, park ranger girlfriend, returned her medical supplies to her first aid kit. In addition to being a park medic, Trudy was also a trained firefighter and sometimes joined their crew when they fought bigger fires in the park.

Rod peered at Dylan, his blue eyes bloodshot from the smoke and his white T-shirt oddly contrasting with his ash-coated reddish-brown hair and smudged face. "What was that thing that sprayed me?"

The professor and her mechanical sidekick had stayed fresh in Dylan's mind. "A remote-controlled robot, I think." It was strange how the woman had mysteriously showed up and then disappeared. By the time Dylan and his crew had reached the top of the hill after hauling their seventy pounds of firefighting gear on their backs, she was nowhere to be found. Still, she did warn him and his crew to evacuate. In retrospect, he probably should have listened.

Trudy eyed Dylan with a curious look. "A robot?"

"It was the weirdest thing, Tru," Rod interjected. "This woman at the fire line where we were working had this freaky toy Army tank. It sprayed a fluid on me that put out the fire, but made my Nomex shirt so stiff I could barely move." He turned to Dylan. "Why was she there in the first place?"

"She's a professor at Alpendale U. I approved her application to do research on wildfires in the park this summer." He wished he'd gotten a better look at her face, so he could recognize her next time.

"How did she know that fire was going to crown? Is she

a fire whisperer or something?"

Dylan recalled the toy Army tank that responded to her whistles. "Her robot must have told her."

Rod's eyes narrowed. "Or maybe she set the blaze."

Trudy responded, sounding intrigued. "They say an arsonist always returns to the scene of the crime."

The word arsonist plagued Dylan's thoughts. He'd never understand it, but some seriously-disturbed people actually enjoyed setting fires and watching them burn, destroying not only the fragile forest ecosystem, but endangering the lives of people and animals as well.

Dylan, on the other hand, had been fighting fires since he was eighteen. Before joining his first engine crew in Washington State, he'd had a few scrapes with the law, and his youth leader at church, Jenny Matthews, and her husband Chase had mentored him and helped him get a fresh start. He soon discovered that firefighting gave him the sense of purpose and discipline he needed, but had lacked growing up. A couple of years later, he and his mother moved to Colorado, where his older brother Mark had been working as a wildland firefighter too.

The twelve years Dylan had spent fighting fires made him pretty good at predicting wildfire behavior. But this one was different. It had resisted his crew's efforts to extinguish it and accelerated without the usual signs. It took two additional engine crews to contain and extinguish the blaze after it had crowned.

As Trudy closed her first aid kit, Rod playfully slipped his hands around her waist. "Hey, babe, how about I come over to your place tonight?"

She pushed him away, a pained expression creasing her freckled face. "Stop it, Rod."

He released an audible sigh. "How long are you gonna stay mad at me?"

"You know the answer to that. We're not getting any

younger, and after five years of dating, it's time for us to seriously think about getting married."

As she turned to leave, she tossed Dylan a parting glance. "I'm finished with him, Dylan. He's *all yours*."

Dylan caught the frustration in her tone. He couldn't blame her for being angry. Trudy was a nice girl. Maybe too nice for Rod.

After she had left the room, Dylan shifted to his friend. "So why don't you marry her?"

Rod raised his hand in a defensive gesture. "I will . . . as soon as I get enough money saved up. I've had a run of bad luck lately that has set me back a little."

Dylan gave him a wary look. "You're not gambling again, are you?"

Guilt further sullied Rod's face as he glanced away.

"You told me you'd quit."

Rod grimaced uncomfortably. "I did—for a while. But now I need to recoup the money I lost. I'm flat broke." With a hopeful grin, he appealed to Dylan. "What do you say? How about helping out your old buddy in his time of need, just until I get my next paycheck?"

Dylan hesitated, then groaned as he reached in his pocket for his wallet. "Don't make me regret this, Rod."

Wildfires Threaten Rockies this Summer. The headline on the front page of the Saturday morning paper immediately caught Rachael's attention. Sipping her mocha cappuccino at the Tanglewood Coffee Shop, she scanned the aerial picture of the latest blaze and the featured story. Fortunately, there were no fatalities this time, but the long-standing drought and higher than normal temperatures meant more wildfires were inevitable.

After she'd finished reading, Rachael folded the paper and set it aside on her table. The sweet aroma of fudge, pastries, and desserts behind the counter teased her taste buds. Why hadn't she ordered fudge with her coffee? Now the line of customers stretched outside to the busy sidewalk.

She gazed through the window next to her table at the tourists shopping for souvenirs, clothes, and tempting treats in the alpine village she called home. The tourist season in Tanglewood Pines, Colorado had officially begun. From now until Labor Day, both the town and the national park would be bustling with people. Not that she minded tourists enjoying nature, but the constant tension between providing so many people access to the park and keeping them safe, along with the park's wildlife and natural habitat, could be challenging. Lightning storms, bear and moose attacks, not to mention wildfires were only a few of the hazards that could quickly turn a happy vacation into a nightmare.

The sun streaming through her window heated her arms under her long-sleeved shirt. She ran a hand over her sleeve, tempted to push it up. It was June, after all, and most people were already wearing T-shirts and tank tops. But she had grown used to keeping her arms covered, regardless of the weather. After all these years, exposing them now would feel strange and uncomfortable.

Her nose took her mind off the heat and back to the sweets counter again. A tall man with thick dark hair, wearing blue jeans and a purple Colorado Rockies T-shirt, caught her eye. She'd seen him at the coffee shop before, and around town. Something about him had piqued her interested. He had a book tucked under his arm, and a coffee and small plate in his hands as he looked around for a place to sit in the crowded café. When he turned in her direction, she moved to get up. "You can sit here. I'm finished."

A relieved smile spread across his face when he came over and placed the items he was carrying on the table.

"Thanks, but I hope you're not leaving on my account."

His large, chocolate-brown eyes and amiable tone changed her mind, and she settled back in her chair to enjoy the last few sips of her coffee. Gesturing to the book, she glanced at him. "What are you reading?"

He pulled out the chair across from her and sat down. "A commentary on the book of Daniel."

Surprised by his answer, she hid her curiosity behind a casual facade. "Sounds pretty dry."

"Are you familiar with the book of Daniel?"

A small grin escaped her lips, blowing her cover. "Since I'm a P.K., it was required reading when I grew up."

He tilted his head. "P.K.?"

"Preacher's kid."

"Ah." A humorous glimmer flickered in his eye. "Then I'm glad I ran into you. I don't find many people familiar with the Bible these days."

She lifted her shoulders. "It's been years since I've read it. The main thing I remember about Daniel is when his friends are cast into the fiery furnace." The thick slab of fudge on the man's plate triggered a craving in her stomach.

"Want some?" he asked. "It's too much for one person."

She shrugged. "Well, if you can't eat it all . . ."

"Here." He took his napkin, broke the fudge in two, then handed her half.

After breaking off a smaller piece, she nibbled it, relishing the sweet taste as it melted in her mouth.

He pointed to the newspaper with the picture of the wildfire on the front page. "That was some fire."

"You already read the article?"

"No, I'm a firefighter. My crew and I were there earlier this week."

She suddenly recognized the man's voice. "Wait a minute, you're the engine boss from the fire line—the one who ignored my warning about the fire crowning."

His eyebrows lifted. "You're the professor with the robot?"

She set the fudge on her napkin. "Well, thank you for the treat. Like I said, I was just leaving." She started to get up.

"Wait. I'd like to talk to you . . . about that fire."

His earnest tone stopped her, or was it the appealing look on his face? She dropped into her seat again and broke off another piece of fudge. "What about it?"

"How did you know it was going to crown like that? Are you some sort of fire behaviorist?"

"I teach courses in Wildfire Science at the university. I also do research and consulting on wildfires."

He leaned back and grinned. "So you *are* a fire whisperer."

She shrugged off the term. "It's not like I have any special powers or insight. I only know what the data tells me."

"So what's with your robot?"

"I'm developing new technology to help fight the fires."

"Good. We need all the help we can get. By the way, my name is Dylan Veracruz." He reached to shake her hand.

His firm grip enveloped hers with warmth. Her gaze lighted on his bulging tanned biceps, then discreetly shifted to his sculpted face.

After releasing her hand, he sipped his coffee. "Did your robot tell you the fire would crown that fast?"

"My computer model did. The robot's sensors had detected a slight shift in the wind ahead of the fire line. That, combined with the high temperatures and low humidity we've been having, plus the fact that the ground fire was against a hill—and *voilà*—you have a recipe for disaster. I have to admit though, it happened more rapidly than I anticipated. There was something odd about that fire."

The muscles in his face tightened with an ominous look.

"That's for sure. I checked and there were no storms in the area when it was first reported. And it was a small Type 5 fire—we should have been able to extinguish it before it crowned like that. I don't claim to be a fire whisperer, but in my line of work, you develop a good sense for how a wildfire will behave, and that one was suspicious."

After glancing around the café, Rachael leaned toward him and spoke in a quieter voice. "There's something else that's strange. I received a text about the fire from an unknown number. That's how I found out about it. I'd like to go back there and collect data for my research."

His eyes sparked with interest. "Okay . . . Let's go together and check it out."

The decadent dessert had put her in an especially agreeable mood. She usually preferred to work alone, but he did authorize her access to the wildfires for her research, and she needed his support. She quickly polished off the last bite of her fudge, then pointed at the piece still on his plate. "Aren't you going to finish that? I'd hate to see it go to waste—*Or* you could give it to me."

He returned a sly look. "No, way. I'm guarding this with my life." He popped a morsel in his mouth and chewed, closing his eyes blissfully. "Mm. Delicious."

While he enjoyed teasing her, she realized that his crew had probably responded to the fire that had killed Lucas. Maybe he could help fill in some missing pieces of the puzzle. "Speaking of wildfires, what do you know about the one that happened last week?"

Her question seemed to have burst his bubble and dropped him back to earth as his brows pinched together over his serious expression. Having watched his happy mood disappear, she almost wished she hadn't brought it up.

He stopped chewing, then took a long sip from his cup and swallowed. "Unfortunately, it was in the backcountry. By the time we got there, a young man had already died. The fire investigator says it looks like the man started the blaze while he was camping."

The news struck a raw nerve in Rachael. "No, that's impossible. I knew him. Lucas was a former graduate student of mine. He'd never violate the park's fire ban, especially out in the backcountry."

Dylan stared at her for a moment, then spoke in a quiet, measured tone. "It's likely he was under the influence. The autopsy report came back showing he had drugs in his system."

Drugs. She bristled at the word. She recalled the work-related parties where Lucas had shunned all drinks except purified water. "That can't be. Lucas never touched alcohol or even sodas. He was an avid hiker and fitness fanatic." Until she had answers that made sense, she wouldn't be satisfied. "Can you take me to his campsite after we check out the other fire?"

A hint of reluctance crossed his face. "Yes, but we can't drive there. We'll have to go part of the way on foot."

"I'd climb Longs Peak if I thought it would help explain what happened to Lucas."

His dark eyes flickered when she'd mentioned climbing the highest mountain in the park. "It won't be quite that strenuous." He wrapped the rest of the fudge in his napkin. "I'll save this for later."

Gathering her trash to throw away, she glanced in his direction. "If you don't mind, I'd like to take my car. I have extra food and water in the back. Plus, I want to bring FIDO to sniff around."

He paused getting up from the table. "Dogs aren't permitted on the backcountry trails in the park."

She waved off his concern. "Oh, FIDO's not a dog. That's the name of my robot."

Author Note

When I think of the Great Smoky Mountains, images of beautiful misty mountains, adventurous hikes, and scenic waterfalls and overlooks come to mind. Having grown up in Tennessee, I've always been drawn to the Smokies and felt a special connection to them, so it was the natural choice for the setting of *Dangerous Ground*.

Less than a week before I planned to visit there to do research for this book, I was horrified to learn that wildfires threatened this peaceful mountain community. On November 28, 2016, the town of Gatlinburg, a charming Bavarian village in the heart of the Smokies, had to be evacuated. By the next day, the fires had killed 14 people and injured 134. The place where I had planned to stay was completely destroyed, along with hundreds of other businesses and homes.

While it is a profoundly sad, unexpected ending to this chapter of the Smoky Mountains, I take great comfort in knowing it is not the end of the story. Having seen other devastated natural areas eventually restored to their original state, I know God's creation is amazingly resilient and constantly renewing itself. So I hope as you read *Dangerous Ground*, this special place will touch your heart and remind you of God's regenerative power to bring beauty from ashes.

In time, the Great Smoky Mountains will be renewed. Until then, I'll cherish the memory of its previous splendor, which I'm privileged to share with you through this book.

Book Club Questions

1. Tyler's Glen may seem like a nice town with warm, friendly people, yet the residents are plagued with fear, gossip, and mistrust. How is that like or unlike your community or family? Can you think of any ways you might help that to change?

2. The feud between the Bentleys and Holbrooks has been going on so long no one seems to know how it started. Why do you think some feuds start and persist, given the toll on everyone involved? In what ways can we be peacemakers in our family and community?

3. Like the Good Samaritan in Luke 10: 25-37, David wants to help those in need. However, when he can't bring himself to forgive his brother for his past mistakes, David is more like the older brother in the parable of the Prodigal Son from Luke 15: 11-32. Why is it sometimes easier to help strangers than someone close who has hurt us? Which of the sons in this parable do you most relate to and why?

4. Kate is stunned to discover family secrets that cause her to re-examine her own identity. On what do you base your identity: heritage, circumstances, accomplishments, your personality, finances, or something else? How might the way you see yourself and your life change if your personal identity was based solely on the fact that you are a child of God?

5. The nearest neighbors to Kate's uncle's property are David, Grace, Virgil and Joe. Think of your nearest neighbors and the relationship you have—or don't

have—with them. What do you think Jesus meant when he commanded us to "Love your neighbor as yourself"?

6. Kate is amazed to discover some very unlikely people have been radically transformed by God's grace. How has God's grace impacted your own life?

7. At the beginning of the book, Kate prays to find her family. By the end of the story, her prayer is answered in unexpected ways. How have you been surprised by God's answer to your prayers?

8. Kate believes in the promise of eternal life. Do you have this hope? Why or why not? What would change in your life if you did or if you didn't?

68634637R00187

Made in the USA
Lexington, KY
16 October 2017